Jeffery and Dunn are the funniest new writing team to have emerged for years. The comic thriller Perfect Murders marks their first venture into the world of crime with hilarious consequences.

Paul Dunn is a priest in the Church of England, and is the author of articles, columns and booklets.

Colin Jeffery is a professional writer and poet.

The writing partnership of Colin Jeffery and Paul Dunn has resulted in the world-wide syndication of their humorous work.

PERFECT
MURDERS

Colin Jeffery & Paul Dunn

Perfect Murders

Vanguard Press

A CIP catalogue record for this title is
available from the British Library
ISBN 1 843860 67 8

Vanguard Press is an imprint of
Pegasus Elliot MacKenzie Publishers Ltd.
www.pegasuspublishers.com

First Published in 2003

Vanguard Press
Sheraton House Castle Park
Cambridge England

Printed & Bound in Great Britain

Dedication

For
Frank "Gab" Jeffery

Chapter One

Ronald Perkins was a professional killer, who advertised for clients in the personal columns of up-market women's magazines. The adverts read: "QUICK AND EASY. Discreet removals. Fast reliable service. Reply to Box No. 3951." The majority of people replying to the adverts thought it was for a furniture removal firm, and tried to book Ronald Perkins to transport their household goods. To them, he would say he was fully booked, or the van had irreparably broken down. But there were a few, one or two a year, which read between the lines and understood the darkly sinister business on offer. "I aim to please," was Ronald Perkins's proud boast, "and never miss a likely target." Needless to say he was an expert pistol and rifle shot, having been trained in the army, serving two years National Service as a second-lieutenant with the Third Parachute Regiment. But he preferred less blatant methods than shooting, creating a masterpiece of sudden death, a demise not obvious as foul play. Proud of his murderous achievements, he even guaranteed clients a full refund if the killing was not quick and comparatively clean in its execution. He found that a messy murder mostly upset clients, and could even ruin the reputation of a flourishing business.

There was nothing about Ronald Perkins to mark him out in a crowd. Small of stature, five foot six in elevated shoes, blond, middle-aged, slightly over-weight, clean-shaven, single, well spoken with a BBC announcer's plum-in-the-mouth accent, he lived with his unmarried mother Hetty Rose Perkins. She conceived him under the West Pier in Brighton, during a May Day Bank Holiday day trip in 1936, when she was nineteen. The father, who spoke in a broad Glasgow accent, offered to share his fish and chips in a newspaper, and ended up giving her a baby when the tide was out. He never gave his name, but said he was a Glasgow Rangers supporter, and worked nights as a hotel porter. He was the first and last man to ever know Hetty Rose Perkins in the biblical sense.

Ronald Perkins was a quiet, thoughtful man, whose hobbies were chess, the Times crossword, stamp collecting, oil painting and amateur dramatics. He was an active member of his village amateur dramatic society "The Bumstead Players", organised and run by the aggressive humped-back vicar Howard Peel, who loved to swing on the church bell-ropes bellowing "It's the bells, the bells". Ronald Perkins used the theatrical costumes of the amateur dramatic society, stored in big oak chests under the stage in the village hall, to disguise himself when carrying out a murder. He would wear male or female disguises depending on the assignment. But, he preferred when meeting a client discreetly in a dimly-lit pub to discuss a killing, to wear his favourite disguise – that of a plump spinster lady in green tweeds and matching hat. She had ginger hair, and was an upper class member of the horsy set, with huge breasts, and he played her magnificently. He knew a pillow tucked up a skirt to give him prominent buttocks, and a couple of melons in an extra large bra, did wonders to conceal his identity and true sex. And whenever he killed, he wore a new pair of cotton gloves, which were burnt immediately the crime was committed: fingerprints had been the downfall of many a murderer and he was not going to make that mistake. And if things did go wrong, and police questioned a client, they could only get a description of a robust woman with big buttocks, dressed in green tweeds with ginger hair. The ginger wig was a lucky talisman for Ronald Perkins, exactly the same as a rabbit's foot was for other superstitious people. The wig was used annually by the Bumstead Players for their pantomime dame, and Ronald Perkins had worn it once on stage playing the part of Widow Twanky in "Aladdin". It had been the happiest experience in his life, prancing about uproariously in drag with hoots of laughter ringing in his ears. He was a brilliant actor, and could have achieved stardom and world acclaim if he had taken it up professionally. But he enjoyed too much the intellectual stimulation of planning and executing perfect murders.

Ronald Perkins had committed his first murder in March

1949, when he was twelve and at public school. He pushed an unpopular master, unpopular for him that is, from the top of a 150-foot cliff in Dorset. Cyril Cooper-Davies, rotund history master at the Modern School for Boys, was nicknamed "Curly" by pupils, because his head was as bald as an egg. The body was found three days later washed up on a beach half-covered with seaweed. Police believed the master committed suicide over a broken love affair while his mind was deranged. It seemed that although a bachelor in his late forties, Cyril Cooper-Davies had met a woman of equal age, rotundity, intellect and status, Miss Peggy Murry-Royston, biology teacher at a girls' public school in Kent, through a South London dating agency. The agency's motto was "It's never too late to get a mate," and they catered solely for the more desperate marriage-seeking clientele: those of a dire physical appearance, well beyond their sell-by date who could not afford to be choosy, and would take anything still upright and breathing.

There had been talk of marriage between the couple. But she finally went off with a door-to-door vacuum-cleaner salesman, who offered her a cottage in Surrey with roses around the door, and three holidays a year in sunny Spain. The best Cyril Cooper-Davies could offer was for her to be the wife of an assistant housemaster with persistent piles and no career prospects, stodgy school dinners, and the back seat of his tandem bicycle for one week's holiday annually in the Lake District.

The murder of the history master taught young Ronald Perkins two important things: first that murder was easy to commit, and second it could be rewarding. He had crept up behind the master as he stood at the cliff edge enjoying the view out to sea. It was a bright sunny day and the seagulls swooped high overhead making piercing cries. One quick push with both hands, and the rotund history master was airborne. Ronald Perkins would never forget the look of utter astonishment on Curly's face, as he glanced back over his shoulder, and saw who had pushed him to his death. And as he descended at an ever-increasing speed down towards the wave-dashed rocks below, he called out in a shrill voice "It's now a double detention for you, Perkins."

The death of Cyril Cooper-Davies meant the young Ronald

Perkins would not have to write out the punishment essay, given by the master the previous day for talking in class. It was to have been on Charles the First, and how not to lose your head in a crisis. Nor would he have to attend detention class every afternoon for a whole week, for not getting his extra history work done on time. Murder could be beneficial, and the boy, although he did not know it at the time, was learning his trade.

Ronald Perkins committed his next murder while doing National Service in Cyprus in 1958. British troops were fighting EOKA: an underground movement dedicated to the expulsion of the British from Cyprus. Ronald Perkins was twenty-one years old, and had spent most of his time on the island leaping in and out of aeroplanes. He spent the last two months of his army career in Cyprus, flat on his back in a military hospital bed in Famagusta, with both legs in plaster up on pulleys towards the ceiling. He had made thirty-five parachute jumps without damage to himself – but had tripped on a banana skin when stepping out of a jeep outside the officer's mess in Larnarca, breaking both legs and a collar bone. Second-lieutenant Ronald Perkins was put in a side room in the military hospital, where he was at the tender mercy of sadistic man-hating ward sister Brenda O'Leary, who held the rank of Major. She was a big tough Irish woman from Dublin, with muscles and hair in places where no woman should have muscles and hair, and with huge hands like shovels, with a dark hint of a moustache on her upper lip. She kept bedpans and urine bottles for male patients in the icebox in a fridge, and would hand them out cold as ice, with a sweet innocent smile on her thin lipped face. And having a bed bath from her, which she insisted on performing daily on male patients, was a disturbing and frightening experience, with manly dangling bits and pieces being pulled and yanked aside, and a stiff scrubbing brush applied to delicate areas. Three days after Ronald Perkins was discharged from hospital, Brenda O'Leary fell mysteriously under a train. The only other person on the railway platform, and witness to the tragedy was Second-lieutenant Ronald Perkins.

He was called to give evidence by an army enquiry board, and told how the Irish nurse had spotted a chicken on the line. She had gone too close to the edge and slipped, falling to her death under the wheels of a slow moving passenger train. The enquiry, chaired by Brigadier-General Sir John Gooseblaster concluded the death was "misadventure", and because of the involvement of a chicken was a "fowl deed". Ronald Perkins had successfully committed murder for the second time.

Ronald Perkins left the army with a medal for active service in Cyprus plus a fear of bed-baths and ice-cold bedpans, in October 1958. He entered civilian life, and went to Oxford University, where he read English literature for a Master's degree. He was, at that stage in his young life, giving serious thought to a future in the higher realms of the teaching profession, thinking he might climb even to the dizzy heights and become a university don with his own chair.

Ronald Perkins entered the hallowed cloisters of Oxford University as a student in January 1959, and wanted to be a university don by the time he was forty. But that was still nineteen years away, and life is often fickle and soul-breaking, especially for a hard up young English literature student with a taste for wine, women and song. The best laid plans of mice and men so often end in tears and the loud snap of a mousetrap breaking the mouse's neck.

Ronald Perkins found life at Oxford idyllic, enjoying student life, with pubs, girls, booze, parties and even more pubs. It was during his second year at Christ's College, when he suddenly had the idea as he sat in the bath trying to wriggle his left toe free from the cold water tap, that murder could be a profitable business. He worked out how much he could earn in the teaching profession over a thirty-five year career, then how much he could earn doing discreet murders over the same period at £4,000 a murder, working on an average of one killing per calendar year. The amount of money he would make as a serial murderer was staggering. He decided right there in his bath that murder would be his life's winning ticket. Plotting perfect murders would be a tantalising intellectual stimulation and challenge which he could not refuse. Surely there were people in the world ready and willing to pay a considerable sum of money to have somebody killed for them. Hate was basic to human nature, and the need to hit back at those people who hurt or ridiculed you was fundamental. Revenge was a burning human

15

passion, which for some, especially those with plenty of money, could not be denied.

Ronald Perkins saw the prospect of becoming a professional murderer as a special calling, almost like being called to the priesthood. "Many are called but few are chosen," an elderly Bishop told him when he was thirteen, after a confirmation service when the boys gathered for tea in the chaplain's study. Ronald Perkins, crafty as ever, tried to impress the old cleric, by asking him how he could enter the priesthood when he was old enough. This was something he would never do, because he considered God to be a spoil-sport with his strict Ten Commandments, imposed with the purpose of ruining everyone's fun and games. Ronald Perkins had received advice from the Bishop about passing exams and applying for a selection board when he was eighteen, followed by a gentle pat on his blond head from the Bishop's podgy hand, and a thick slice of Victoria sponge cake from the school chaplain. The other boys, waiting in line to meet the Bishop and kiss his ring, who did not enquire about entering the priesthood, received only a weak smile and a thin slice of Victoria sponge cake. Ronald Perkins learnt from his experience that it always paid to tell people what they wanted to hear. It was the conman in the making.

It was the annual Oxford and Cambridge Boat Race on the River Thames, which caught second-year student Ronald Perkins attention as being ideal for his first money-making murderous venture. He was thumbing through a boating magazine "Rowlocks For All" in a Barbers shop, and read an article on the history of the Boat Race. Ronald Perkins knew hundreds of bets would be placed by fellow students in local betting shops, and that a small percentage out of sheer devilment would bet on one of the boats sinking. This, according to the article, had occurred five times up to 1959. Cambridge sank in 1859 and Oxford in 1925. On 31st march 1912, both boats sank and there was no winner that year. And on 24th March 1951 Oxford sank. Bookies considered a sinking in the spring of 1959, with the new extra-buoyant lightweight boats, to be almost impossible, and gave a "sinking" as thousand-to-one odds.

The idea to use the Boat Race to make his fortune entered

Ronald Perkins's mind as he sat in Fred's Barbershop in Oxford High Street. He decided to bet on the Oxford boat sinking. Now this was, to his mind, a most sporting and generous act on his part, to sink his own university boat. But at that time in his life he still possessed a modicum of fair play and gentlemanly conduct, learnt on the playing fields of his public school. This attitude would change with the passing of the years, when he would believe with a dreadful certainty that he was right in whatever he did. Ronald Perkins planned to make his fortune from the Boat Race by placing £30 bets in six cities throughout Britain. For this purpose he had selected Glasgow, Liverpool, Cardiff, Manchester, London and Belfast. Then, at amazing thousand-to-one-odds, he would win £180,000, which would set him up in the killing business and provide his mother with a three-bedroom detached house and a lifestyle of luxury. He relaxed in the barber's chair, thinking how to raise the money needed for the bets, and for travelling expenses to the cities and his bed and board. But where would he get the money? Then it came to him in a flash of inspiration – the money would come from the sudden demise of a family member. Somebody, who would leave lots of money in a last will and testament – and the demise of that family member would, of course, be a perfect murder. "I always bet a few pounds on the home crew," lisped Fred Bryant the barber, a skinny flamboyant man with a neat waxed moustache, as he interrupted Ronald Perkins's thought process. "You'll be doing the same I expect, sir, being an Oxford gentleman yourself?"

"I'm not a betting man," replied Ronald Perkins, "but I think that on this occasion I'll make an exception."

Fred Bryant smiled warmly, and walked over to the wall cabinet where he kept packets of rubber contraceptives and bottles of hair lotion.

"Would sir like something for the weekend?" he asked quietly in almost a whisper, winking his eye knowingly. He knew young rampant students and their insatiable sexual appetites and did remarkably well financially selling them contraceptives on Fridays in readiness for their forthcoming weekend's bed wrestling bouts.

"Weekend? Now what do I need for the weekend?"

"Something for the old fella," replied Fred Bryant with a chuckle. "We surely don't want our young lady to be in the pudding club by Monday morning, now do we sir?"

Ronald Perkins laughed heartily. "I quite agree, Fred," he grinned, "but I'm going to be too busy to be bothered with that nonsense. I've other more important plans for the weekend, which don't involve the fair sex, I'm afraid."

"Nonsense, you say sir?" responded Fred Bryant with a surprised look. He frowned, thinking of his demanding wife and her over-active libido. Oh, if only my Sybil thought it was nonsense – she ruins my Sunday afternoons pleading for it."

With less than three months to the Boat Race, Ronald Perkins knew he must formulate the first part of his plan: to mastermind the sudden demise of a family member with lots of money, whom he had convinced to name his mother as sole beneficiary in a last will and testament. There was one family member other than his mother, her father George Perkins, a retired tram conductor, who lived in Dorking. But he had never forgiven his daughter Hetty Rose Perkins for being an unmarried mother, which in 1937 was considered to be a great social affront. He made her pack her bags and leave the moment her bump started to show. George Perkins was a mean-minded stubborn man, who vowed never to speak to his daughter again. She lived on social benefits, raising her son Ronald in a seedy tower-block council flat on a run-down housing estate in south Croydon. Ronald Perkins was a bright boy, and won a scholarship to public school when he was twelve, where he had committed his first murder, pushing the history master off the top of a cliff. Which was, one might say, the master's instantaneous fall from grace.

Ronald Perkins tried, for his mother's sake, when he was eighteen, before being posted overseas with his parachute regiment to Cyprus, to visit his grandfather and make peace with him. He got the old man's home address from a letter, written eighteen years earlier, found in a drawer in his mother's bedroom. The letter was a plea for help for her newborn babe, young Ronald, and begged for money to buy him food, clothes and toys, but had never been posted. Hetty Rose Perkins lacked the courage, knowing how hard-hearted her father was, and that it was impossible to get blood from a stone.

Ronald Perkins, looking impeccably smart in a grey suit, white shirt, blue tie, trilby hat and polished black shoes, knocked twice very hard on the red front door of his grandfather's house. He was nervous about meeting his grandfather for the first time, unsure of the old man's reaction. The door opened, and there stood George Perkins, shabbily dressed in a faded green cardigan, grey crumpled trousers, and worn green carpet slippers. He was a tall bony mean-faced man with a square jutting jaw, wearing thick spectacles, and was in need of a shave, and was smoking a foul-smelling pipe. The old man, who hardly ever went out of the house except to do some shopping or to collect his pension, had let personal hygiene fall drastically with the passing years. Old age meant to him the freedom to dress, wash and shave as he pleased. "Yes," he snapped angrily glaring at the young man on his doorstep. "What do you want?" George Perkins disliked callers, mostly because they turned out to be over-bearing social workers, wanting to poke their noses into his private business. The old man was in his seventy-fifth year, and was a horse race betting fanatic, the bookie's best friend, who never won a bet in his life. He had been listening to the Epsom races on the radio and was furious at having to leave halfway through a race to answer the door.

"You have a daughter, sir," declared Ronald Perkins, studying the old man's face to see his reaction.

"I've no daughter," retorted George Perkins hotly with a scowl.

"But that's not true. You've a daughter and her name is Hetty Rose Perkins."

"And I say I've no daughter – now sod off."

"But I'm Hetty's son – your grandson, Ronald."

The door slammed shut missing Ronald Perkins's nose by less than an inch. He found himself standing alone on the doorstep trembling with rage. He had met his grandfather and had taken an overwhelming dislike to him. On the train back to his mother in south Croydon, he fantasised about the sudden demise, of his grandfather. "Slamming the door in my face when I told him I was his grandson, the old bastard," he thought bitterly as he walked from the railway station. "Someday, I'll give that old blighter such a surprise that it'll kill him for sure.

Four years later, at the beginning of the spring term 1961, second-year Oxford University student Ronald Perkins disguised as a priest in black suit and Roman collar, wearing a false black goatee beard and horn rimmed spectacles, clipboard in hand, rapped thrice upon his grandfather's front door. He had come to formulate the first part of his plan to sink the Oxford boat, and his grandfather's imminent death and legacy was a vital part of the plan. Ronald Perkins was counting on the old man's greed and gullibility to convince him he had been left a bequest of a great deal of money. He waited a few minutes but the old man did not answer the door. He rapped again and called through the letter box in a high-pitched singsong voice which the clergy use when saying church services, "Halloo Mr George Perkins, I know you're there. I won't go away until you see me. I've got good news for you. I know you'll be delighted when you hear it." He heard the old man, muttering angrily under his breath, come shuffling down the hallway to answer the door. George Perkins had not changed much in four years, except that now he was a little more frail, and walked with the aid of a walking stick. He was dressed in a grubby blue pullover, crumpled grey trousers and very worn red slippers. The old man smelt powerfully of tobacco. He glared at his caller, sniffed loudly to show his contempt for a clerical collar, and held the door half open ready in an instant to slam it shut. Bible-punchers were high on the old man's hate list.

"Well," he demanded gruffly, "what the hell do you want?"

"I'm Jonathon Needham, your new vicar," replied Ronald Perkins brightly holding out his hand.

The old man stared at the extended hand with a sour look, and made no effort to grasp it. "So what?" he exclaimed fiercely. "Now sod off to where you've come from – I don't give to the Church."

"I'm not collecting."

"Well, that's a first then – a vicar on my doorstep who's not after money."

"Please Mr Perkins – you misjudge the Church, I can assure you. We give as well as we receive. Didn't Jesus say it's far better to give than to receive?"

"That doesn't help me."

"Oh, but it does I can assure you – I've money to hand out to the poor and needy... a considerable sum of money in fact."

The old man, his interest and greed aroused, opened the door a few more inches. He forced himself to smile, a sickly grin showing tobacco-stained teeth.

"Well, I'm poor and needy, Vicar."

"So you are, and that's why I'm here," replied Ronald Perkins glancing down at the clipboard as if studying it. He glanced up at his grandfather. "You're George Perkins, retired transport worker and living alone, isn't that so?"

The old man nodded. "Money to give away, you say?"

"Only to an elderly gentleman of this parish who can qualify for a special bequest. But perhaps you're not interested? There are others on my list to visit you know."

"Call me George, Vicar."

"Ah yes, George."

"Come in Vicar. I'll put the kettle on. We'll have a cup of tea and chat about this money you've got to give away. I think there's a few biscuits left in the tin."

The tea was weak; two cups made from one teabag which had already been used once before. George Perkins was a frugal man who did not like waste or spending money.

"Well Vicar," he said as he relaxed back into his favourite armchair next to the gas-fire, "now tell me of this considerable sum of money. I'm all ears."

Ronald Perkins sipped his tea, which tasted more like water than tea. "Lord Kelly of Wexford Castle, in the Republic of Ireland you know, has left a bequest to this parish..."

"How much? The bequest, Vicar, how much?"

"Twenty thousand pounds."

"Blimey," gasped the old man, almost dropping his cup of tea with shock. Smiling warmly, he held out a round tin of shortbread biscuits, "Have a biscuit, Vicar," he said in a friendly voice. George Perkins never shared his biscuits, being too mean and greedy, not even with his wife when he badly wanted sex, and she had been dead for over thirty-five years. But this was a unique occasion, and he wanted to impress the young vicar with

21

his open-hearted generosity. Vicars, he knew, liked charitable folk who shared their worldly goods, and it was important this vicar liked him if he were to be in the running for the bequest money.

"Thank you, George," said Ronald Perkins taking a biscuit. "It's most kind of you." He bit into the biscuit, then wished he had not. The biscuit was soggy, showing it had been in the tin for a considerable time, and was well past its eating date. Forcing himself to swallow, he grimaced, and put the remaining biscuit onto his saucer.

"Now what were you saying about the bequest, Vicar?"

"Oh, yes, the bequest, George. Well, it seems Lord Kelly of Wexford Castle, who died three months ago, was involved in a most tragic accident while out foxhunting. His horse refused to leap a farmyard gate. But Lord Kelly still continued over the gate... and dived head first into a working combine harvester. The farm labourers working nearby did not see him or hear his muffled screams. The body was mangled inside the machine, and put into a bale of straw, which was tied and stacked in a field."

"Not a nice way to go, Vicar."

"No, George – Lord Kelly wasn't found for five days."

"Five days, but that's awful."

The old man felt queasy at the thought of Lord Kelly's remains being neatly stacked and baled, and decided to change the subject. "You were saying about the bequest, Vicar, and how I might qualify for it."

"So I was, George, so I was. Well, it seems that Lord Kelly when he was a young man was full of beans and hot-blooded, and seduced a pretty young English chambermaid called Irene Penny. She came from this very parish originally, and went over to Ireland to work at Wexford Castle when she was seventeen. It was the usual thing I'm afraid, a baby conceived on the wrong side of the blanket. If only they kept the blanket between them there wouldn't have been any trouble. But alas, that's life isn't it? Well, when Irene Penny found she was pregnant, and knowing she would then never receive a good reference as an under-maid who had been under Lord Kelly thrice weekly, she fled back to her parents in England. But Lord Kelly, who loved her passionately, pursued her. He wooed and wed her, marrying her in our own little Saxon church, St Bernard the Much Surprised. They returned to Wexford Castle after the birth of their daughter Colleen. But Lord Kelly never forgot the debt he felt he owed to our parish for his happiness, the birthplace of his wife and daughter. He made a special bequest in his last will and testament, for the sum of £20,000 to be paid to the most deserving elderly person in our parish. The candidate must be a man, retired, have worked in transport, be living alone, have a good character and..."

"But that's me without a doubt," interrupted the old man eagerly. "I'm a man, retired, live alone and have worked in transport, and have a good character."

"That's true, George, but there's still something else required before you can qualify for the bequest."

"And what's that, Vicar?"

"The recipient must have offspring... fruit of his loins, you'll understand, George, to prove his manhood was in good working condition and he once fired on all cylinders. Lord Kelly was a stickler for a happy sex life in marriage. And most importantly, the offspring must be female – this is because Lord Kelly himself had an only daughter, and so favours in his bequest the recipient with an only daughter himself. Now I've heard you have a daughter. Is that true?"

There was a long silence while the old man thought deeply, wondering if he should admit to having a daughter whom he had not seen for over twenty-five years, and did not ever want to see again. She had shamed him with her pregnancy outside marriage, and made him a laughing stock down the tram garage and in the pub. Finally, he asked quietly with his voice trembling. "Does the money come tax-free, Vicar?"

"Most certainly it does, George – paid by cheque from the late Lord Kelly's estate into the recipient's bank or post office account."

"All right then, I've got a daughter."

"Congratulations, George. And what's her name?"

"Hetty Rose Perkins."

"Perkins? Then she's not married?"

"No, Vicar, not as far as I know. But it wouldn't surprise me if she had tied the knot by now. She was a flirty young madam at the best of times."

"I'm rather shocked to hear you say that."

The old man sadly shook his head. "Haven't seen her in years, Vicar. She left home after falling pregnant, and I haven't seen hide nor hair of her since."

"Oh, dear, but how very sad."

"I hope that not seeing her for years won't affect my chance to qualify for the bequest, Vicar?"

"Well, according to the bequest you're supposed to love your daughter, George, and be able to prove it."

"But I do, Vicar – absence has made my heart grow fonder."

"You'll have to provide me with some proof that you still love your daughter. The legal proof of a loving bond between father and daughter is, I'm afraid, a vital condition for the bequest."

"Legal proof? What sort of legal proof, Vicar?"

"Well, some legally binding document signed by yourself and witnessed by two people of good character and social standing, which I can show to Lord Kelly's solicitors. I would suggest to you that a last will and testament be made out with your only daughter Hetty Rose Perkins as sole beneficiary would be ideal."

"Then I'd get the twenty thousand pounds?"

"Absolutely, George; every single penny of it."

"Give me a week, Vicar, to see my solicitors, Skinner, Hardy, and Pickerstaff, then I'll have the very document you require here waiting for you, all signed and sealed."

The cunning old man was well pleased with himself. He planned to make a will out in his daughter's favour, claim the late Lord Kelly's bequest money, then revoke the will the moment the money was paid into his bank account. Nobody would know what he had done. It would be like taking candy from a baby. George Perkins gleefully thought of how he would spend the money, on placing bets on horses that he hoped would actually finish the race they had started.

"I'll have a cheque made out in your name for twenty thousand pounds, George."

"You mean I qualify for the bequest, Vicar?"

Ronald Perkins nodded and smiled weakly at his grandfather. He was surprised how gullible and greedy the old man was, a really nasty character without any redeeming qualities, and his greed would cost him his life.

The old man grinned happily, and feeling generous, held out the round tin of shortbread biscuits. "Have another biscuit, Vicar?"

Chapter Two

One week later, on the Friday afternoon, Ronald Perkins, disguised as the Vicar Jonathan Needham, with false goatee beard, horn-rimmed spectacles, and carrying a battered old suitcase, arrived at the main gatehouse of a convent. There was a large sign on the wall: SISTERS OF MERCY. TRESPASSERS WILL BE PROSECUTED. The convent was surrounded with a twelve-foot high wall, topped with broken glass, and was three miles as the crow flies from his grandfather's house. The convent would make an ideal base, from where he would conclude his murderous business with the old man. First he had to see the last will and testament to verify it was signed and legal, then he would commit a perfect murder and gain the inheritance for his mother. He had chosen the convent because nobody would think a vicar staying there on a religious retreat was a serial killer. The Sisters of Mercy were an enclosed order, and no man, with the exception of the frail old priest father Gilbert Harper, the eighty-six-year-old nun's father confessor, who visited fortnightly from a nearby nursing home where he was a resident, was allowed to enter the main convent building. The Order began in 1901, when Glenda Pritchard, an energetic kitchen maid with the physical grace of a rhino, slipped on a cake of soap which she had inadvertently dropped, hitting her head on the side of the cooking stove. She had a sudden and most startling vision of stars. And, convinced there was more to life than being a mere kitchen maid, and with money received from suing her employer, she purchased an old country house, and started her own religious order.

Ronald Perkins tugged on the bell rope dangling outside the gatehouse. The mighty booming clang of the thundering bell made him clutch at his ears until the sound died away. There was a small hatchway in the heavy oak door which slid slowly open

26

and a pair of beady eyes peered out.

"Who's there," called an old woman's tremulous voice. "Is it the dustman again?"

"Not the dustman," replied Ronald Perkins in his vicar's singsong voice, "But Jonathan Needham."

"Jonathan who?"

"Jonathan Needham – I'm the Vicar who's come on a visit."

"Vicar? Has someone died? I haven't been told."

"No, no one's died as far as I know. I'm here for a weekend's religious retreat... to recharge my spiritual batteries for doing my parish duties. Mother Superior is expecting me."

"We don't give retreats for men – it's women only here."

"I know that – but Mother Superior booked me for a retreat. She said the convent hasn't had any bookings from women for over a year."

"Oh, so that's why it's been so quiet in the guesthouse of late. I've not been told about you, Vicar, and I deal with the gatehouse keys, and see the dustbins are regularly emptied. The dustmen around here are a lazy bunch, I can tell you. The trouble we've had because we didn't leave them a tip last Christmas."

"I can imagine, er Sister..."

"Tulip – all the sisters are named after a flower."

"May I please come in, Sister Tulip; it's cold standing out here."

There was the sound of bolts being drawn and locks turned. Slowly the heavy oak door was pushed open. Sister Tulip, in her seventy-third year, wrinkled like a prune, thin as a rake, red-faced and puffing and blowing with the effort of pushing open the heavy door, stood on the threshold. Before entering the convent to become a career virgin and penguin look-a-like, she had been a waitress at a Lyons tea shop in Sheffield, where she had been daily hopeful of some man sweeping her off her feet and making indecent proposals. Sister Tulip held out a bony right hand.

"I'm the Guest Mistress here," she declared stoically, shaking Ronald Perkins's hand. "I'm in charge of visitors' hospitality. I should have been told you were coming so I could have aired the sheets. But it's just like Mother Superior, doing things without telling me."

"Bit forgetful, is she?" asked Ronald Perkins, as he struggled to free his hand from the nun's vice-like grip. Sister Tulip did not want to let go. It had been a long time since she had gripped a man so tightly, and she was enjoying the experience.

"Oooh, Vicar, you're so young and strong," she cooed huskily, eyeing him up and down with a radiant look on her wrinkled face. Sister Tulip was delighted with what she saw, a young vigorous man in the prime of life with a nice pert bottom. She liked young men, especially those with nice pert bottoms. And it had been many years since any man other than old Father Gilbert Harper, the convent's father confessor, had entered the convent grounds. "I expect you work out in a gym with weights – wear tight shorts, with your body glistening with sweat and..."

"I never go to a gym," interrupted Ronald Perkins, alarmed by the sparkle in the old nun's eyes, and her growing interest in his body. "I do jog for a few miles every morning, but that's all."

"Surely you do press-ups as well, Vicar, don't you?"

"Never – not even as a schoolboy at public school."

"I suppose you're not a vicargram are you? I haven't seen a naked man for fifty-one years, five months and nineteen days. Sadly, my memory isn't what it was, and now I find it difficult to remember the hard reality of seeing a naked man."

"Sister Tulip," called a woman's angry voice with an Irish accent, "I hope you're not having another relapse. Remember what happened the last time in September 1931? When you cornered the milkman and the diary stopped deliveries for a whole year?"

Ronald Perkins turned in the direction of the voice, and saw a small round butterball of a nun, black habit flapping in the wind; rosy-cheeked, in her late forties, striding purposely towards them.

"You must be Jonathan Needham," she said brightly, shaking his hand warmly. "I'm Sister Rosebud, Mother Superior of this..."

"Please Reverend Mother can I..." interrupted Sister Tulip as she reached out tentatively with a claw-like hand towards Ronald Perkin's right knee.

"No, you may not, Sister Tulip," retorted the Mother

28

Superior glaring fiercely at the old nun, as she pushed her hand aside. "That's another sin for you to tell Father Harper when he comes to take confession tomorrow."

The dinner that night in the convent dining room, because it was Friday and a non meat eating day, was thick green pea soup, a crusty bread roll, cod and chips, followed by spotted dick and custard. There were eighty-seven nuns in the Order of the Sisters of Mercy. They sat silently on hard benches at three long wooden tables, looking like nesting penguins, and although there was no rule of silence at mealtimes, they said not a word, but stared between mouthfuls at the hapless Ronald Perkins. He felt a growing unease at their rapt attention, and regretted his decision to come on religious retreat to the convent. He sat next to the Mother Superior on the top table, who kept making angry clucking noises with her tongue, showing her displeasure at the other nuns for staring at their male guest.

"Will you say grace, Vicar?" asked the Mother Superior when the pea soup was served.

Ronald Perkins, whose thoughts were elsewhere, busy planning the perfect murder of his grandfather, did not understand what the Mother Superior had said to him.

"Pardon?" he asked, quickly collecting his thoughts.

"Grace," beamed the Mother Superior sweetly. "Grace."

"Grace who? Have I met her? Point her out to me. What shall I say to her?"

"No, no, Vicar, will you say grace?"

Ronald Perkins, even more confused than before, nodded his head in agreement. "Well, if you want me to, Mother Superior, then of course I'll say it for you. But I don't understand why you want me to say it." He stood up and coughed to clear his throat, then called out in a loud voice, "GRACE."

The Mother Superior, shocked and flustered, looked at him as if he had lost his senses. "Grace, Vicar," she exclaimed hotly, "a short prayer said before a meal to thank God for providing it."

Ronald Perkins was embarrassed. The penny had finally dropped.

"Oh, that grace," he muttered despondently, "I knew it was that grace you meant, Mother Superior. I was only having a little joke with you." He nervously said grace, making it short and to the point. "Thank you, God, for this meal, amen." He then sat down with his face crimson and burning. It had not occurred to him before, but while he was impersonating a vicar, some people, especially nuns, would expect him to respond as a real vicar would, by saying prayers and taking church services. This could be a disaster for a man whose only knowledge of the Book of Common of Prayer was that it was indeed a book. He desperately hoped the Mother Superior would not ask him to take a church service over the weekend. He had managed to say grace, but only because the prayer was said by staff and pupils throughout his schooldays. But taking a church service was totally beyond him, and would surely expose him as a fraud.

Sister Tulip, helping out in the kitchen as the Guest Mistress, served him a plate of a dozen tinned oysters which had been saved for the Bishop's next visit. But Sister Tulip had other ideas, hearing that oysters were a stimulant for a man's libido. The nuns knew the Bishop liked shellfish, and especially collecting his own crabs. This they knew for certain, because the Mother Superior had once overheard him telling the Archdeacon how he had caught crabs in Soho's red light district. Sister Tulip saucily winked an eye at Ronald Perkins as she put the oysters down in front of him. "Something to perk you up, Vicar," she said smiling broadly, "And to stir cold cinders into flame."

Ronald Perkins gazed down in horror at the oysters.

"Take them away, Sister Tulip," cried the Mother Superior angrily, thumping the table with her fist. "He'll have cod and chips the same as the rest of us."

Scowling, and muttering bitterly under her breath, Sister Tulip took the oysters and shuffled back to the kitchen. She sat quietly in a corner unseen by the kitchen staff, sprinkled the oysters with lemon juice and ate them with a spoon. She remained seated for a long time waiting for her libido to be stimulated. But her libido was too old and beyond any stimulation.

After Sister Tulip had left the table with the oysters, the Mother Superior leant over with a worried look, and whispered in Ronald Perkins's right ear, "I think you'd better lock your door tonight, Vicar. It looks as if the bromide drops I've put in Sister

Tulip's tea aren't working."

Ronald Perkins retired to bed the moment he saw the nuns filing
into the chapel for evening prayers. He excused himself to the
Mother Superior, saying he was sorry to miss evening prayers,
but was not feeling well, and thought the thick pea soup had
disagreed with him. This was not true of course, but he was
desperate to miss having to endure the nuns' awful off-key
singing.

"Sorry you don't feel well, Vicar, but don't worry, I'll get
you a purgative from the medicine cupboard," she replied
sympathetically. "It'll blow out the system, and stop you from
being bunged up all night long."

Ronald Perkins agreed, thinking a purgative followed by a
nice warm bed was more acceptable than a prayer service in a
freezing chapel, listening once more to the dreadful singing.
Shivers ran up and down his spine from just thinking of the nuns'
screechy singing, which reminded him of fingernails being
scraped down a blackboard. He had attended the afternoon
prayer service after arriving at the convent, and thought for a
few terrifying minutes when the nuns ceased singing that both
eardrums had been irrevocably damaged. In one quick swallow,
Ronald Perkins downed the half glass of foul-tasting brown
liquid, which the Mother Superior poured from a large green
bottle labelled "Purgative – to loosen stubborn stools. Not for
children or the fainthearted". The Mother Superior was most
attentive, worried that he, being the only man staying at the
convent, might attract the unwanted attention of some of the
more worldly nuns. She insisted on accompanying him, armed
with a torch and a hefty stick, to his bedroom door in the
guesthouse.

"I must leave the convent tomorrow afternoon," he told her
bluntly, "Just for a few hours. It's on church business, you'll
understand. I have to make funeral arrangements for an old
gentleman who is dying. The family doesn't want him to know
his end is near. They want his passing to be quiet without fuss or
bother."

"Death is so tragic, isn't it, Vicar?"

"Yes, especially for the person who's dying."

"Has the old gentleman a terminal illness?"

"Yes, very terminal I'm afraid, Mother Superior."

"Oh, dear. I'll pray for his passing to be quick and painless."

"It'll be quick, very quick indeed, I can assure you, Mother Superior."

"I've just had a thought, Vicar, about you leaving the convent tomorrow afternoon – if you're not here, then you'll miss an important bible study session with Sister Primrose. The session is a vital for your religious retreat. Sister Primrose gives a lively portrayal of the trial and crucifixion of Jesus with her splendid reading. She does all the voices you know."

"Well, in that case, Mother Superior, I'll do my best to conclude my business and return here as quickly as possible."

"Goodnight, Vicar – don't let the bed-bugs bite."

"What? Good heavens, don't say my bed is infested with bugs?"

"Oh, no, of course not, Vicar, it's just my little joke," chuckled the Mother Superior merrily. "My mother, God bless her, used to say it to me before I hopped into bed when I was a little girl. Ah, but what a sweet memory it is, to be sure."

"Goodnight, Mother Superior."

Ronald Perkins entered his bedroom and switched on the light. He gasped in horror. There was something on the bed, which turned his blood to ice... a solitary tulip lying on the pillow. With trembling hands, he hurriedly locked and bolted the bedroom door. It was after midnight, before he managed to calm the turmoil of his deeply troubled mind, caused by the sight of the tulip on the pillow, and he finally fell into a fitful sleep. He was woken in the early hours of the morning by the rasping sound of the doorknob being vigorously twisted back and forth. He lay in the inky darkness petrified with fear.

"Cooey," called a familiar voice through the keyhole, "are you awake, Vicar?"

Ronald Perkins pulled up the bedclothes to cover his head.

"Cooey!" called Sister Tulip. "It's only me."

Ronald Perkins closed his eyes pretending to be asleep. He began to snore loudly, hoping the old nun would hear and go away. And after about five minutes he was relieved to hear her footsteps shuffling away from his door. The Mother Superior was right, the bromide drops were definitely not working.

In the morning, at six o'clock while it was still dark, Ronald Perkins was woken by the ringing of a hand bell outside his bedroom door, rung by Sister Lily, a strange looking broad-shouldered six-foot nun with a big dark secret, who shaved twice daily (not her legs), and possessed a male husky voice. It was Sister Lily, who resembled a big tough rugby scrum forward, who was responsible for getting the nuns and their guests out of bed in the mornings.

"I'm still waiting for my operation," confided Sister Lily gruffly, as she led Ronald Perkins to the dining room.

"I'm sorry to hear that," replied Ronald Perkins, who was wondering what operation the burly nun was talking about. "I hope you don't have to wait long."

"Plastic surgeons can do wonders you know," continued Sister Lily. "I've heard there are some people who haven't got a thing they started out with – it's all been removed, replaced or improved."

When Ronald Perkins entered the dinning room, he found the nuns already seated and eating breakfast. They were noisily chatting among themselves like a flock of starlings crowded on a tree, but fell silent the moment they saw him. Nervously he took his place sitting next to the Mother Superior.

"Did you sleep well, Vicar?" she asked kindly, as she poured him a cup of tea.

"Like a log, thank you."

"And the purgative, did it work for you?"

"Just like a dam bursting."

"Oh dear, I hope it didn't take you by surprise?"

"No, I'm fast on my feet and got out of bed in time."

Sister Tulip, who was once more helping in the kitchen, came shuffling over to Ronald Perkins carrying a plate of hot buttered toast. "It's eggs this morning, Vicar," she declared brightly. "I hope you like eggs."

"Yes, I do, Sister Tulip, thank you."

"And how would you like them?"

"Like them?"

"Scrambled, boiled or fried?"

"Scrambled if you don't mind."

"Well, I'd prefer my eggs fertilised, Vicar," she replied saucily.

"Sister Tulip," cried the Mother Superior hotly, her face black as thunder. "Go to your room this instant. Remain there until it's time for your confession with Father Harper this afternoon. I'll send your breakfast up to you. And, being a nun, you'll have unfertilised eggs like the rest of us."

Ronald Perkins borrowed the convent bicycle after lunch, and rode five miles down leafy lanes to his grandfather's house. The old man, smoking a pipe, showed him his last will and testament. The three-page document was a properly signed legal document, and would be accepted as such in any court in the land. The sole beneficiary was Hetty Rose Perkins.

"Can I have the cheque now, Vicar?" asked the old man greedily holding out his hand.

Ronald Perkins smiled weakly and nodded his head in agreement. "But of course you can, George." He took a long brown envelope from his inside jacket pocket and gave it to the old man. "It's a lot of money. Wouldn't you like help from church financial advisers on how best to invest it? Perhaps you might even consider making a small donation to my own little church, St Bernard the Much Surprised? The bell-tower's a bit wobbly these days and could do with restoration to the stonework."

The old man scowled and shook his head. "No, I'll spend the money in my own way, Vicar," he said gruffly, as he took the envelope and tore it open. He went over to the french windows, held the cheque up to the light and studied it with a look of triumph on his face. The cheque was an extremely poor forgery, done by Ronald Perkins with a home printing set, but it easily fooled the old man whose eyesight even with spectacles was very poor.

"I'll have to take your last will and testament away with me," declared Ronald Perkins as he slipped the document into his pocket. "To show Lord Kelly's legal representatives. They'll need to be certain that you've qualified for the bequest."

"What? Does that mean I can't pay the cheque into my

bank? I wanted to pay it into my bank account first thing on Monday morning."

"You can still do that, George. I only need to borrow the document for a few days."

The old man was most reluctant to part with such a legal and binding document, planning to destroy it the moment the money was paid into his bank account. The last thing he wanted was for his daughter Hetty Rose to benefit in anyway whatsoever from his estate. But he finally agreed, because he had possession of the cheque from the late Lord Kelly's estate administrator. "How long do you want to keep the document, Vicar?" he asked.

"Only a day or two, three at the most, George."

The old man puffed gloomily on his pipe. "All right, Vicar," he agreed with a grim look. "But no longer. My solicitors are expecting it back in their office safe on Monday morning."

"Wednesday afternoon at the latest, George, I promise you."

"Would you like a cup of tea and a biscuit, Vicar?"

When Ronald Perkins cycled back to the convent an hour later, his mind was sharply focused on murdering his grandfather. The deed, he knew, must take place before Monday morning, when the old man was planning to visit the bank. If he tried to pay the forged cheque into his bank account, it would be quickly spotted by a cashier, and the police summoned. The murder must look like an accident, and had to take place within the next thirty-six hours. By the time Ronald Perkins reached the convent gatehouse, he had formulated the perfect murder plan for his grandfather... and the old man's pipe would be his executioner.

It was shortly after midnight on the Sunday morning, when Ronald Perkins, dressed entirely in black with woolly balaclava, gloves and wellington boots, face smeared with boot polish, moved stealthily across a ploughed field at the back of his grandfather's house. There was a full moon half-hidden by cloud and nearby an owl hooted eerily. He had used a torch to see where he was going so he would not trip, stumble or fall into a ditch, while walking the three miles' trek cross-country from the convent of the Sisters of Mercy. But now, within a few hundred yards of the rear of his grandfather's house, he switched off the torch, and slipped it away into his jacket pocket. Coming to a barbed wire fence at the edge of the field, he held the top strand of wire firmly pressed down with both hands, and nervously stepped astride it. But in the darkness he misjudged the distance, and the barbed wire sprang up between his legs, catching his scrotum. The acute pain caused him to leap upwards, and a gaping hole was ripped in his trousers. He came down astride the wire, which instantaneously sprang up again like a trampoline, catching his scrotum once more. This happened four times, and each time he managed to suppress an urgent need to scream. Finally, he was able to dive sideways onto the lane behind his grandfather's house and away from the offending barbed wire. In a wild panic, he knelt in the soft mud beside the fence as if in prayer, and gingerly felt between his legs, fearful the episode on the bouncing wire had cost him that which he held most dear... his precious manhood. But he sighed with relief, finding that everything was safely in place without any apparent lasting damage, except of course to his trousers.

Ronald Perkins entered his grandfather's house using a small rubber sucker from a child's arrow, which he positioned on a pane of glass in the french windows. He cut a small circle in the glass around the rubber sucker, large enough for his hand to go through, with a glass cutter on his Swiss army knife. Then he reached inside and opened the french windows. Once inside the living room, he took out the torch and switched it on. The door leading to the hallway was half-open. He closed it firmly, took a long strip of cotton wool from his pocket, wedged it firmly under the door to seal the crack. Next he went over to the gas fire and knelt beside it, and used an adjustable spanner to loosen a connection at the back. Gas, hissing softly, slowly leaked into the room. Satisfied with his handiwork, he crept from the house, sealed the fist-sized hole in the pane of glass with a piece of cardboard held in place with sticky tape, and then returned to the convent.

George Perkins arose from his bed at his usual time, woken by the cockerel crowing from the farmyard down the road. He went to the toilet for a prolonged sit down visit to get his bowels open and moving. Then, dressed in candy-striped pyjamas, faded red dressing gown, and worn carpet slippers, he went downstairs to prepare breakfast. He put a dab of lard in the frying pan, placed it on the electric cooker, switched on, and fried an egg with two slices of bacon and a tomato. He ate standing over the kitchen sink from out of the frying pan with a fork, to save washing up afterwards. Carefully he wiped the frying pan clean with a piece of bread, which he ate with great relish. When he finished eating, he took out his pipe, filled the bowel with tobacco, and strolled leisurely over to the living room door, with the idea of going in to listen to the BBC news on the radio. It crossed his mind for a fleeting moment when he saw the closed door, that when he retired to bed the night before, he had left it open to keep the room well aired. He opened the door, paused on the threshold in choking disgust. There was a most pungent smell coming from the room.

"What's the hell's going on here," he thought, "it smells worse than a roomful of fat blokes' farts after they've been eating a curry." He took out a box of matches from his dressing gown pocket, while he pondered on what the awful smell might be, then struck a match to light his pipe. There was an instantaneous explosion, heard at the convent of the Sisters of Mercy three miles away. The house disintegrated in a split second into millions of bits and pieces, showering a circumference five hundred yards wide where the house had stood with bricks, dust and household remains. The largest item found on the grim site by emergency services, was George Perkins's pipe. It was solemnly buried in the coffin with the rest of him, in one of the three dozen plastic bags which contained his remains.

Chapter Three

It came as a tremendous shock when Ronald Perkins learnt his grandfather's house was not owned by the old man, but was a council house rented with money from his social benefits. And, almost as bad, the old man's life savings amounted to a paltry £91. George Perkins had lived in poverty and died in poverty. The shortage of funds from the legacy drastically affected Ronald Perkins's plans. But he was still determined to go through with sinking the Oxford boat no matter what. He needed the money from his winning bets to set himself up in business as a professional killer, a gentleman murderer with style, which only the wealthy upper classes would hire, complete with his own office, typewriter, waste-paper bin, and of course ex-directory telephone number. Clients would make their initial contact through an up-market woman's magazine box number, then communications would either be face to face in a dimly-lit pub, or by telephone with calls being made by Ronald Perkins to the client from GPO red call boxes. Ronald Perkins also wanted money to provide his mother with a lifestyle of luxury, without her having to worry again about where the next penny was coming from. She made great sacrifices for him when he was growing up, taking in washing and cleaning other people's houses. Now it was his turn to do something for her. When his grandfather's solicitors handed the £91 over to his mother, Ronald Perkins asked her for the money as a loan, saying he wanted to buy an open top sports car to buzz around Oxford and impress the girls. He planned to buy a car, but not until after he collected the winnings from the six bets placed for sinking the Oxford boat. His mother agreed to the loan, thinking he was a young man with lusty urges who needed girlfriends to satisfy them, and she was hopeful he might settle down and make her a grandmother. But she insisted the loan should be for one year at ten per cent interest. Hard times had taught her to be a hard businesswoman. With his mother's small legacy in his wallet, Ronald Perkins had only enough money to place £10 bets, instead of the £30 bets originally planned. This would leave him with just £31 to cover travelling expenses and bed and board, when visiting the six cities to place the bets.

With less than three weeks to the Boat Race, Ronald Perkins still had not finalised his plan to sink the Oxford boat. He had placed the six bets at odds of 1,000-to-one, but was baffled on what to do to sink the boat. The four-mile Boat Race course, he knew, would be packed with crowds of people cheering on the riverbanks, and swarming like bees over the bridges. There would be millions watching from home on TV, with BBC television cameras following the race. The plan to sink the Oxford boat had to be beyond reproach – apparently an accident pure and simple, or, as the insurance companies liked to say "an act of God". Ronald Perkins had been visiting London at weekends to reconnoitre, travelling down from Oxford by coach. He walked the length of the Boat Race course three times, starting at Putney Bridge and finishing at Chiswick Bridge, and noticed during these riverside walks there was one bridge which did not allow the general public access – Barnes Railway Bridge.

Barnes Railway Bridge was less than half a mile from the finish of the race, and was an ideal spot for the mishap to occur to the Oxford boat. Ronald Perkins took a train from Barnes station on the south side of the river, and crossed Barnes Bridge to Chiswick station on the north side of the river. He wanted to reconnoitre the layout of the bridge. The bridge was deserted except for two railway workers, one tall the other short, dressed in black donkey jackets, yellow hard hats, and brown boots, checking the spikes on the sleepers on the down track from Chiswick station. It was these two men, who blended almost unnoticed in to the background of the bridge, who gave Ronald Perkins the answer he needed on how to move freely on the bridge. Who would think twice about a railway worker checking the tracks? Nobody would think he was up to no good.

Next morning at first light, dressed in grubby donkey jacket, blue faded denim jeans, brown boots and yellow hard hat,

Ronald Perkins cautiously stepped onto Barnes Railway Bridge, unshaven, sporting a false ginger Hitler-style moustache, with padding tucked up under his jacket to give the appearance of a pot belly. He had clambered over a six-foot high wire-netting fence to gain access to the bridge. Slowly he walked the length of the bridge carrying a small two-headed hammer, stopping every few yards to gently tap on a railway track as if testing for metal fatigue. He was on the bridge for forty minutes, checking for ideal places where he could stand above the arches as the Oxford boat passed beneath. The method for sinking the boat came to him, as he was walking across the bridge for the third time. It was simple and deadly. He would drop a heavy stone; identical to the grey stones used to build the arches under the bridge. The stone would smash through the boat's frail hull sinking it, and the police would think a piece of stonework had come loose and fallen from the bridge, an accident pure and simple. The Oxford boat crew were good swimmers, so there should be no loss of life, unless one of the crew was inadvertently sitting on the exact spot where the stone smashed onto the boat.

There was a good clear view upriver to Chiswick Steps over a mile away, and through binoculars on the day of the race, Ronald Perkins would see the Oxford and Cambridge boats come sweeping round the bend. This should give him between six to eight minutes to prepare, depending on weather and tides, to determine which archway the Oxford boat would pass beneath. After making sketches of the bridge and river approaches from all angles, and with copious notes scrawled on his notepad, Ronald Perkins felt well satisfied with his reconnoitre of Barnes Railway Bridge. He returned to Braddock Towers, the small hotel where he was staying near Victoria Coach Station. He stopped to change out of his railway worker's clothes in a public toilet's cubicle, putting on a blue tracksuit and white running shoes. Then he went to a nearby barber's shop for a shave before continuing to the hotel. He carried his railway worker's disguise in a holdall, which had been previously hidden behind a cistern in the public toilet. Ronald Perkins wanted the hotel staff to think he was returning from an early morning run before breakfast. When he entered the hotel lobby, he nodded amicably to Allan Hawes, the gangly desk clerk. Allan Hawes, intelligent and brooding, was a tall thin dark-haired man in his late twenties, with a long beak of a nose and protruding eyes. Skin almost as white as chalk with bushy eyebrows meeting in the centre of his forehead, he sat gloomily behind the lobby desk reading a Sunday tabloid newspaper, with a disinterested expression on his thin pinched face. Allan Hawes, whose big flat feet had stopped him from becoming a policeman in his late teens, because Metropolitan police accept men and women with big feet which are not flat, still dreamed nightly of pounding the streets of London in pointed helmet, truncheon in hand, wearing size ten boots. His life so far had been a failure, failing the eleven plus, a police medical and to lose his virginity. Fed up with being a mere hotel desk clerk, he badly wanted excitement and challenge in his flat-footed life, and recently had taken out a year's subscription for "Private Detective Monthly" magazine. Allan Hawes, an avid fan of Sherlock Holmes, had read every story written by Conan Doyle of the adventures of the famous fictitious detective. The desk clerk saw for himself a most brilliant future as a private detective, modelled on Sherlock Holmes, solving major crimes which baffled Scotland Yard's brightest detectives. He was saving £5 weekly to set himself up within two years in the private detective business, and had plans to take a set of rooms in Bakery Street, with a fat housekeeper, an assistant with a medical title, a typewriter, phone, second-hand violin (with strings), pipe rack and the all-important deerstalker hat. Allan Hawes glanced with a bemused look at Ronald Perkins over the top of his newspaper as he entered the hotel lobby. It did not surprise him to see him dressed in tracksuit and running shoes. Indeed, several of the younger American male hotel guests went jogging in the early mornings, all running desperately in a vain hope of living forever.

"Got any mail for me this morning, buddy?" called out Ronald Perkins in a well-practised Texan draw, learnt from watching cowboy films. He was pretending, as his cover story for hotel staff, to be an American tourist from Houston, Texas, with wealthy parents, travelling throughout Europe for one year, before beginning a career in his father's advertising business.

"No, sorry Mister Shepherd, sir," replied Allan Hawes. He

liked Americans, and was an avid film fan, especially of the big Hollywood epics, where the hero saves the world and gets to know biblically everything in a skirt. "There isn't any mail for you again, I'm afraid."

Ronald Perkins strolled over to the desk. "I was wondering," he began with a smile, offering the desk clerk a crisp one pound note, "Whether you might direct me after breakfast to somewhere in London, where I can catch a glimpse of a member of the Royal Family. The Queen will do nicely for my purpose."

"That's what Prince Philip thought on their wedding night," muttered Allan Hawes under his breath, as he took the banknote and put it in his pocket.

"What? What did you say?"

"I said, would Prince Philip do?"

Ronald Perkins nodded his head in agreement. "Yeah, sure thing Buddy, any top member of royalty will do," he said brightly. He was now getting carried away with his portrayal as American tourist Roger Shepherd, and his obvious success in speaking the Texan drawl was making him over-confident and far too bold with his acting abilities. He now thought he could fool anybody with his superb acting, and wanted to see how far he could go with the desk clerk. "But I'd sure like to tell folks back home how I saw the Queen in the flesh."

For a fleeting moment, Allan Hawes felt a cold shudder of trepidation go up and down his spine, as the image of Her Majesty the Queen in the flesh sprang vividly into his mind. She was totally naked except for her royal coronation crown, and a sparkling diamond necklace, and was dripping from head to toe with water after stepping out of a bath. With a gasp of panic, he speedily focused his thoughts away from the birthday-suited monarch with her jewels so openly on display. How cruel and remorseless an over-active imagination could be if not kept under strict control. Allan Hawes could never understand why Americans had such an enthusiastic desire for seeing the British Royal Family. He knew the top British royals were out of London on holiday. Indeed, they were nearly always away on holiday.

"You'll not see the Queen or the Duke of Edinburgh in

London this week or next, sir," he responded emphatically. "They're away chasing sunshine on the Isle of Wight. They've got a nice house there."

"Gee, what a pity," replied Ronald Perkins despondently in his mock Texan drawl, "Then I'll have to make do with an Egyptian mummy at the British Museum."

"The only difference you'll find, sir," responded the desk clerk dryly, "between the British royals and old Egyptian mummies is a swathe of bandages. In Britain we only bandage our royals when they need medical attention."

"Can I have the key to my room? I'd like to change before breakfast."

Allan Hawes handed over the key. It was only after Ronald Perkins had gone up to his room, that a suspicious thought crossed the desk clerk's inquisitive mind – the young American had been out jogging and should be drenched in sweat... and yet, there was not a single bead of sweat glistening on his face. Strangely, he was looking as fresh as a daisy. The desk clerk decided that from now on he would take more than a passing interest in the American Roger Shepherd.

Three weeks later, and with less than twenty minutes to the start of the Oxford and Cambridge Boat Race, Ronald Perkins, disguised again as a railway worker, complete with false theatrical ginger Adolf Hitler-style moustache, clambered over a six-foot high wire-netting fence close to Barnes Railway Bridge. He advanced at a steady pace walking beside the northbound railway track leading towards the bridge, carrying a heavy holdall with both hands. Confident his plan would succeed, he was somewhat surprised that he was not suffering from his usual stage fright, which previously had plagued him before a performance. Actors, he knew, performed their best work if they had stage fright before the curtain went up, and the worse the stage fright the better the performance. Indeed, he felt physically sick to his stomach before performing his brilliant portrayal of the Vicar Jonathan Needham at the convent of the Sisters of Mercy. But at this precise moment, as he walked steadily towards Barnes Railway Bridge, he felt no fear whatsoever, and his mind was sharp and crystal clear, and his resolve and determination unbreakable. The plan to sink the Oxford boat was now firmly set within his mind, with every detail clearly worked out. He chuckled quietly to himself, believing that by nightfall he would be a very rich man indeed. Trains clattered noisily across the bridge, rattling and rolling in both directions. There was a train crossing the bridge on average every seven minutes. The drivers peering ahead from round cabin windows, eyes focused on the tracks winding away in front of them, ever watchful for red signals warning them of danger.

Ronald Perkins stopped halfway across the bridge and put down the holdall. Inside the holdall was a heavy grey stone the size of a man's head, and he had gone to a great deal of trouble finding a matching stone, identical to the stonework of the arches under Barnes Railway Bridge. He had found a small quarry in Sussex which he visited at dead of night to steal the stone. Police would think the stone had come loose, and fallen from an archway sinking the Oxford boat accidentally. Some of the crew would see the stone as it hit the boat, and give police statements accordingly. The six bookies with whom he had placed the £10 bets, would pay up without protest because it was an "act of God" which had sadly sunk the Oxford boat.

Ronald Perkins glanced at his pocket watch. Three minutes to the start of the Boat Race. With a loud clitter-clatter a passenger train came towards him on the down line. Stepping to the track side, he gave the driver the thumbs up, but the driver, a young man with bushy hair and staring eyes, was too busy concentrating on the signals ahead of him, and did not notice the workman standing beside the track with thumb raised. There was only one weakness in Ronald Perkins's plan – he would not know until the last few minutes under which archway under Barnes Railway Bridge the Oxford boat would pass. And it was crucial for him to be standing over that archway with stone ready to drop if his plan was to succeed. Ronald Perkins studied the river through binoculars up to Chiswick Steps. The riverbanks were crowded with people.

"Hi, there," called a man's deep baritone voice coming from behind him. Startled, he spun round to face the owner of the voice. Standing a few feet away was a middle-aged broad-shouldered black man, dressed in donkey jacket and yellow hard hat. He held a gigantic spanner in his left hand.

"I didn't know there was anyone else on the bridge," replied Ronald Perkins, greatly alarmed. He spoke in a heavy Cornwall accent, sounding like Robert Newton doing Long John Silver. His mind spun with confusion and shock. What should he do now? He could not drop the stone on the Oxford boat while this black man was here. Somehow he must be made to leave the bridge.

"I'm Barry Coles," said the black man, eyeing Ronald Perkins suspiciously. He noticed the white man's hands were smooth and soft, not rough and covered with calluses like any real railway worker's hands should be.

"Richard King," replied Ronald Perkins forcing a weak smile.

"I'm here to tighten nuts."

"That'll bring tears to the eyes."

"What will?"

"Having one's nuts tightened," replied Ronald Perkins, hoping the black man would see the humour of his comment and warm to him, "You know – with such a big spanner as yours?"

Barry Coles, a serious individual with no sense of humour, was a regular churchgoer and did not appreciate dirty jokes, especially those about himself.

"That's not funny," he snapped angrily with a fierce look.

"No, you're quite right," agreed Ronald Perkins. "I apologise. It was a rude and thoughtless of me."

"What are you doing here?" demanded Barry Coles.

"Working like you."

Barry Coles knew this could not be true, because only track workers based at Chiswick and Barnes railway stations were allowed on Barnes Railway Bridge, and he knew every single worker by sight and name. This white man was a complete stranger to him, and there was something not right about him, which for the moment he could not put his finger on. He had not yet noticed there was no British Rail logo inscribed in big white letters on the back of Ronald Perkins's donkey jacket, which was the official logo displayed on all legitimate British Rail track workers' donkey jackets. Barry Coles found the tiny ginger Adolf Hitler-style moustache irritatingly familiar, and it rang

45

bells of recognition in his head, but he did not know why, except that it reminded him of someone very famous. But who among the ranks of the most famous would dare to wear such a silly little moustache? He dismissed the thought knowing the answer would come to him eventually. White folk, he had found since coming to England, with their narrow noses and wafer-thin lips, looked exactly the same facially, often reminding him of sheep with white bland faces.

Barry Coles had come to England from Kingston, Jamaica, in September 1949, and joined British Rail as a track maintenance worker. Over the following years he was promoted three times to gang foreman, and was in charge of a five-man work crew. Keen on politics, he voted Labour, and went on the knocker for the party at election time. Barry Coles was working alone on Barnes Railway Bridge because his work crew had time off to watch the Boat Race. They were somewhere up by Chiswick Steps with family and friends. The black man had walked from Chiswick railway station with the purpose of tightening any loose nuts he found on the railway tracks on Barnes Railway Bridge. Barry Coles was married with a son in his final year at medical college, a daughter who was a primary school teacher, and a cuddly roly-poly wife called Connie, who had an enthusiastic appetite for adventurous sex. She once had him perform on her doggy fashion over a freezer... which got them both banned for life from their local corner shop. He was paying off an oppressive thirty-year mortgage on a semi-detached three-bedroom suburban house, disliked gardening and sport, except cricket which he loved, and thought England's climate was too wet and cold. He planned, when he retired at sixty-five, to return to the sunshine of Jamaica, where he would drink rum and grow bananas. "Who gave you permission to come on the bridge?" he demanded, with as much authority as he could muster.

"The Barnes station master," replied Ronald Perkins flatly. "He wants me to do an urgent check on the up-line tracks – it seems several drivers have reported the line as being bumpy and a possible derailment hazard."

"What's his name?"

"Who?"

"The Barnes station master."

"I don't know – I only know him as Sir – I'm new on the work crew at Barnes station and haven't been told his name yet."

"Then you've met him?"

"Well, not face-to-face – but I've seen him sitting in his office drinking tea."

"All right, describe him then?"

Ronald Perkins was in a panic. Beads of sweat glistened on his forehead. He gave no reply, but glanced nervously at his pocket watch. The Boat Race had started and there were now less than eight minutes before the two boats would pass under Barnes Bridge. Things were going horribly wrong with his plan to sink the Oxford boat. Picking up the heavy holdall with both hands he stumbled back across the bridge the way he had come. He had decided there would be no sinking now... only his escape back to his hotel.

It was then, just as Ronald Perkins turned away and exposed the back of his donkey jacket without a British Rail logo on it, that Barry Coles knew for certain he was not a railway worker. But what was he doing on the bridge? Was he a member of a terrorist organisation come to blow up the bridge? Was there a bomb in the holdall?

"Stop," he bellowed, taking a firm grip of his huge spanner, "I'm making a citizen's arrest."

Chapter Four

Police Constable Edgar Briggs had been in the River Thames Division for ten weeks, and was finding it, as a dedicated non-swimmer with an overwhelming fear of water, a most arduous occupation. He did not like boats at all, and was prone at certain tides to suffer from chronic seasickness. Tall, mousy-haired with piercing blue eyes, a wide mouth with jutting teeth, the twenty-three-year old was eminently ambitious, with his mind fixed firmly upon eventually rising to the exalted rank of Chief Constable of the Metropolitan Police. He had begun his police career on horses a year earlier, but found to his embarrassment that he had no empathy with animals whatsoever, finding he could not control a horse from breaking into a wild uncontrollable gallop, when it should have been standing perfectly still or walking extremely slowly in a crowded area. The young policeman had no control over a fast moving horse, which in turn caused the utmost panic to members of the public, and a job dilemma for his superiors. The horse on which he sat, and he had sat upon all the horses kept in the police stables, would suddenly in heavy rush-hour traffic, set off on an alarming wild gallop with its mane and tail flying in the breeze, with a young terrified policeman clinging frantically to its neck for dear life. Horse riding was an absolute disaster for the ambitious Briggs, not to mention a multitude of irate car owners whose vehicles had been badly damaged by flying hooves, or the Lloyds Insurance Company which insured the Metropolitan Police against breakages, who because of Officer Briggs had been going steadily broke because of his hapless horsemanship. There had finally been an "incident" which resulted in his immediate transfer to the Police Dog Division, when a large horse bolted and raced into Buckingham Palace, scattering royals, courtiers and guests attending a garden party like ninepins. The horse, an old nag called Jenny, finally bucked Briggs off into an ornate fountain, soaking the Queen, who was out walking her corgi dogs with Prince Philip. Needless to say, Her Majesty was not amused, nor was Prince Philip, who for a fleeting moment thought a corgi had deliberately misbehaved itself to wee down his trouser leg.

Edgar Briggs was a determined young officer, who was always trying to impress his superiors with an array of bright ideas, hoping they would mark him out as being of command potential. It had been his idea for police horses to wear special nappies, in an effort to stop horse dung from being scattered like little brown apples all over the streets of London. But his superiors in their wisdom had turned down the idea on the grounds that London police stations had nowhere to store great heaps of A steaming horse dung gathered by the nappies. Constable Edgar Briggs did suggest, as an answer to the steaming heaps of dung, that roses, both red and white, could be grown at the police stations in little pots or large window boxes. It was a known gardening fact he had insisted, that roses always grew exceptionally well when bedded down in lots of horse dung. But this plea was also vetoed. Senior police officers did not want steaming piles of horse dung at their police stations, insisting that members of the general public might mistake them for being horse toilets. Edgar Briggs, police officer No. 69, had a very short stay with the Police Dog Division, being transferred under a black cloud to the River Thames Division because all the dogs kept trying to mate with his right leg. This had proved embarrassing enough during training sessions, but highly impractical when he was out walking with a dog in public. It was simply too perverse for the general public to see a young policeman trying to walk down a crowded London street with a huge Alsatian dog wrapped around his right leg excitedly humping it. Chief Inspector Owen Mackey, the senior officer in charge of the Metropolitan Police Dog Division, had tried every dog in his command, including his wife's little Pekinese Wey Lin, with the ill-fated young policeman, but they all made straight for Edgar Briggs's right leg. There was something about his right leg which attracted them, and got their hormones racing madly about with a desperate need to mate.

Edgar Briggs stood at the back of the police launch, face a sickly green, legs unsteady, swaying slightly as if hopelessly drunk. He was wearing a peaked hat with the chin strap down to stop it from being blown away by the wind, and his eyes were tightly closed as he tried desperately not to be seasick. The other policeman on the launch, sitting at the controls with the wheel grasped firmly with both hands, was a big thick-set Scotsman, Robert McDougal, a dark-haired bearded ex-mariner, who had sailed the seven seas for nine years before joining the Thames River Police. It was said of him that salt water flowed through his veins and not blood. He was, every single inch of him, a jolly jack tar with a saucy tattoo of a naked mermaid with big breasts on each arm. Robert McDougal was thirty-three years old, and had given up the merchant navy and the sea, after falling in love and marrying one Elsie Sagbucket, an ex-Woolworth toiletries counter assistant from London's East End.

The police launch was less than fifty yards behind the Oxford University boat, which was racing towards Barnes Railway Bridge. The Cambridge boat was less than two boat lengths ahead of the Oxford boat. There was a police launch following each University boat, to rescue any crew member should there be a mishap, and to keep the following launches full of journalists from getting too close. There was a great cheer from the crowds thronging the riverbanks, as the University boats jockeyed for position to pass beneath the bridge. "Avast there, me hearty. Avast there I say," shouted Constable Robert McDougal gleefully in a salty seafaring manner, as he swung the launch hard over to follow in the wake of the Oxford boat. He had shouted out a warning to Edgar Briggs that they were about to pass under the bridge.

Edgar Briggs opened his eyes in a wild panic, knees knocking like castanets.

"What's the hell is he talking about?" he wondered, his mind reeling with both shock and alarm as the launch pitched and rolled. "And a vast what, for goodness sake?" What was McDougal trying to say? Was there something huge and vast out there in front of the launch? Could it be something overwhelmingly gigantic like the iceberg which sank the Titanic? But where was it, for God's sake? It was then that he saw Barnes Railway Bridge looming up alarmingly fast. And, thinking the bridge was the imminent danger for them, he struggled to pull on his yellow life jacket, remembering as he did so his one golden rule on how to survive a boat disaster, which he had learnt the hard way as a passenger on board the Mersey ferry. The ferryboat had run aground on a sandbank three years earlier, and he had been forced to wrestle a hugely fat woman to the deck before taking her place in a crowded lifeboat. The golden rule was: "Edgar Briggs comes first – women and children second." Frantically, fingers trembling with fear, he began to inflate the life jacket, blowing hard into a plastic tube, his face red and flustered with the effort.

"Here we go, me hearty," cried McDougal excitedly, "Now watch out for the swell from our bow wave bouncing back off the bridge."

"Oh, dear God, please save me," implored Edgar Briggs in a frantic whisper, as he dropped reverently to his knees, hands clasped prayerfully in supplication, face chalky-white with terror. Oh, but how he now wished he had taken the trouble to learn how to swim when he had the chance as a boy at public school, when the swimming master, James Topper, who hated boys who could not swim, regularly threw him and other non-swimmers into the deep end of the swimming pool, only to hook them out a few minutes later, half-dead and gasping for air. The headmaster, after numerous complaints from worried parents, reluctantly agreed to issue water wings to the non-swimmers, and make a new school rule that boys should not be drowned by a master during school time. "Oh, but I'm far too young to die like this," groaned the miserable young policeman. "I haven't even used my truncheon in anger yet."

"IN OUT, IN OUT, IN OUT," bellowed the Oxford University boat's coxswain, Joseph Flint-Edwards, a small bony third-year medical student with a nose much too large for his small hatchet-like face, as he pushed the rudder hard over to port. He had decided to take the boat under the bridge by passing beneath the second archway from the riverbank to his right. The boat's crew, grim pain-racked faces glistening with sweat, arms and leg muscles aching dreadfully, pulled strenuously upon the oars, each one determined to win the Boat Race for his

University's honour, and hopefully have a celebration leg over with a Boat Race groupie.

Meanwhile, high up on Barnes Railway Bridge, Barry Coles stood with his huge gleaming silver spanner gripped tightly in both hands standing determinedly in a most threatening manner. He was facing the astonished Ronald Perkins as he tried to make a citizen's arrest.

"You're under arrest, sir," he declared fiercely with a resolute look on his face. "Come quietly or else."

Ronald Perkins, holding with both hands, his heavy holdall, which contained the head-sized stone for sinking the Oxford University boat, stared incredulously at Barry Coles, his mind racing over the possibilities for escape. "Are you open to a bribe by any chance?" he asked hopefully. "I could write you out a cheque here and now if you like."

Barry Coles solemnly shook his head. He could see there was no danger coming from the man he was trying to arrest, and thought that by making the arrest he would surely gain promotion with British Rail, with a substantial reward in the bargain. He might even be hailed a national hero by the media, with his picture displayed on the front of the tabloid newspapers. Surely catching a terrorist with a bomb was a most heroic deed? Barry Coles felt a great surge of pleasure rise up in his breast at the very thought of such a brave act. He could even imagine the pride of his dear old mum back in Jamaica when she saw the press clipping which he would most certainly send her.

"But surely there's got to be something I can offer you to let me go?" asked Ronald Perkins hopefully. "How about a great deal of money and a football season ticket for any first division club of your own choice?"

Barry Coles solemnly shook his head. "No, sir, there's nothing you can offer to make me change my mind – you're coming with me directly to Chiswick railway station under citizen's arrest. I'm going to hand you over to the transport police to be duly processed by the full force of the law."

"And what if I refuse to come with you?"

"Then you'll wake up in a hospital bed with a nasty headache, sir."

"All right, I'll come quietly, but first lower the spanner."

Barry Coles slowly lowered his spanner, relaxing his threatening stance. He had mistakenly thought that he had achieved his purpose and had made a successful citizen's arrest.

"Let's have no funny business now," he declared with a grim look, "I won't hesitate to bash you over the head with my spanner if you try to run away."

Ronald Perkins nodded gloomily, turned away as if to walk towards Chiswick railway station, but then suddenly swung back swinging the heavy holdall, catching the unwary Barry Coles a most violent blow to the chest. With a wheezing gasp of surprise, Coles, badly winded, dropped his spanner and crumpled to the ground on his knees. Ronald Perkins, still holding the holdall, turned away to try and make a run for it. But Barry Coles, regaining his breath, picked up his spanner and hurled it at the back of Ronald Perkins's head, knocking his yellow hard hat flying. With a startled cry, Ronald Perkins toppled forward like a felled tree, blood flowing profusely from a three-inch gash where the spanner had struck him behind the left ear. Knowing he must keep moving if he were not to end up in a prison cell, Ronald Perkins staggered like a drunken man to his feet, and, with head spinning and battling against a black tidal wave of unconsciousness, managed to shuffle painfully away down the track towards Barnes railway station. Barry Coles, determined to stop him, crawled after him on hands and knees. The two men moved slowly down the railway tracks one following the other. Taking a deep breath to gather his failing strength, Barry Coles dived forward in a rugby tackle, knocking Ronald Perkins off his feet and slamming him hard down across a wooden railway sleeper. The holdall flew from his hands and disappeared over the side of the bridge.

The police launch driven by Constable Robert McDougal was passing under the bridge following the Oxford University boat, when the holdall dropped from above, killing him instantly. Edgar Briggs watched in horror as McDougal's head burst open like a hen's egg dropped from a great height onto concrete, then fainted dead away. The police launch, with a dead man's hands clasped on the helm, with the body slumped over the throttles open at full speed, raced away, narrowly missing the Oxford University boat. Half a mile down river, the launch ran aground at a bend near Mortlake, embedding the bow several inches into the soft mud of the riverbank. The police would later recover the blood-stained holdall with the head-sized stone inside it. The Metropolitan Police forensic laboratory team found sets of fingerprints on both the stone and handles of the holdall. This prompted Scotland Yard to launch the biggest murder investigation in history since the hunting of Jack the Ripper. They were determined to track down the murderer of a London River Thames policeman who had died so courageously at the helm of his police launch. The case file of a murdered policeman would never be closed, not until the murderer responsible was safely under lock and key.

On Barnes Railway Bridge, Ronald Perkins watched in wide-eyed trepidation as his holdall disappeared over the side of the bridge. He thought it would splash harmlessly into the river and sink, never to be seen again, not knowing a police launch driven by Constable Robert McDougal was passing beneath the bridge at that precise moment. Ronald Perkins was frantic to flee from the bridge and escape from London. He lay face down with legs held in a tight rugby-tackle by Barry Coles. With a cry of frustrated rage, he twisted round and beat wildly at the railwayman with both fists. Barry Coles, thinking only of his possible promotion and reward from British Rail for the arrest of a terrorist, fought valiantly. The men rolled backwards and forwards between the tracks, missing the live rail by inches, as they punched, bit, kicked, gouged and scratched wildly at each other, one desperate to escape and the other desperate to make a citizen's arrest. The fight lasted but a few agonising minutes, before Ronald Perkins, who was the younger and fitter of the two, struggled to his feet and tried to step away. But Barry Coles refused to let him go, grabbing him in a vice-like grip around the legs. Ronald Perkins reached for the spanner lying nearby, and bought it down on Barry Cole's head with a glancing blow aimed to stun him. The railwayman collapsed without a sound into a crumpled heap in the foetus position, and lay unconscious. But gripped tightly within the fist of his right hand was a false theatrical ginger Adolf Hitler-style moustache, which he had ripped off Ronald Perkins's face as they struggled together. Barry Coles's head injury was not life-threatening. He opened his eyes, sat up and saw the distant fleeing figure of Ronald Perkins scurrying away across the bridge. Staggering to his feet to give chase, Barry Coles tripped on his gleaming spanner, and fell, hitting his head a cracking blow on a railway track. He was killed instantly. Later, the police would misjudge the evidence of Barry Coles's accidental death as being cold-blooded murder, and also that of Police Constable Robert McDougal. Scotland Yard would seek a double killer.

Ronald Perkins, sore-headed, feeling dizzy and with a buzzing like a swarm of angry bees in his ears, and not thinking clearly, escaped from the bridge. His plan for making his fortune by sinking the Oxford University boat was in ruins. There was only one priority left for him, to flee London and a long prison sentence. But he did not then know of the police officer's death, or that of Barry Coles who had fallen and died. He thought, if arrested, he would be charged with trespass on private railway property, and for causing grievous bodily harm to a railway employee by striking him with a holdall. Desperate to escape from London and to return to the safety of Oxford University and continue his life as second-year student Ronald Perkins, he foolishly did not stop and change out of his railway worker's disguise in the public toilet as originally planned. But continued, without thinking of the consequences because he was concussed and not thinking rationally, and still dressed in the filthy dishevelled railwayman's clothing to his three-star hotel, Braddock Towers, holding a handkerchief to the egg-sized lump behind his left ear.

Desk clerk Allan Hawes was on duty in the lobby reading the latest edition of "Detective Monthly" magazine. He glanced up as Ronald Perkins came tottering through the revolving doors. The desk clerk was shocked to see the dishevelled state of the supposedly wealthy young American known to hotel staff as Roger Shepherd. But why was he dressed in railway worker's clothing? Surely this was the same young American tourist who had professed a desire to see British royalty in the flesh, and was not the sort of person to parade around London dressed in such filthy clothing? Ronald Perkins, aching from the blow to the head, still feeling dizzy and unsteady on his feet, moved quietly on tiptoe across the lobby towards the open lift doors. He was hoping the desk clerk would be too engrossed with his reading, a usual practice for Allan Hawes while on duty when the manager was not around, for him to be spotted sneaking over to the lift. Ronald Perkins wanted to slip unseen up to his room, hastily pack his suitcases, then do a runner down the back fire escape.

"Mister Shepherd, sir," called Allan Hawes as he stepped out from behind the reception desk to hurry after Ronald Perkins. "What's happened, sir? You look as if you've been in a road accident. Would you like me to call a Doctor?" The desk clerk's curiosity was aroused, and his detective's premonition told him that something was very wrong indeed. He had just been reading an article in the "Detective Monthly" on conmen, and it told how they pretended to be somebody else carrying out their crimes. Could this be why Roger Shepherd was dressed in filthy workman's clothing? Was he pretending to be somebody else? Why was he trying to creep unnoticed across the lobby to the lift?

Ronald Perkins paused as he was about to enter the lift, and with sinking heart turned to face the desk clerk. "Good afternoon," he responded with a forced smile, forgetting in the heat of the moment to speak with the Texan drawl he had been using when speaking to members of the hotel staff. He spoke in his real posh English plum-in-the-mouth BBC announcer's voice, which he had learnt at public school while fagging in the third form before becoming a full sized cigar in the upper sixth. His precise crisp English accent made the desk clerk raise his eyebrows in bewilderment.

"I beg your pardon, sir?" gasped Allan Hawes, thinking he must have misheard the upper class English accent suddenly coming from the lips of the young American hotel guest from Texas. What had happened to his Texan drawl?

"I was wondering if there might be some mail in for me today," responded Ronald Perkins quickly, but still talking in his normal public school English accent.

Allan Hawes eyed Ronald Perkins curiously, his mind now keenly focused and the little grey cells of his brain working in overdrive. There was something most strange and bizarre happening here, and he wanted to know what it was. The desk clerk, with his detective brain in full gallop, felt like he was a lean mean ferret who had just come across a scent trail of a juicy rabbit, and he was determined to relentlessly track it down to its burrow. "What's happened to your American accent, Mister Shepherd?" he asked suspiciously. "You're sounding more like a member of the British aristocracy than an American from Texas."

Ronald Perkins flushed a bright red. "Oh, yeah, is that so, buddy," he replied quickly reverting to a Texan drawl. "It must be because I've been around you English people too long. I guess the accent has just rubbed off on me."

"Really, Mister Shepherd," replied the desk clerk with a faint smile, who had not believed a word he was hearing. Con men, according to an article in his detective magazine, were brilliant liars, who could easily convince most people that black was really white.

"Sorry, but I really must go up to my room and get changed," insisted Ronald Perkins as he began to close the sliding lift door. "I need a shower and some fresh clothes, as you can see."

The desk clerk moved swiftly and jammed his right foot down to stop the lift door from sliding closed. "Can I have a few more moments of your time, Mister Shepherd, to clarify a few points."

"Not right now, if you don't mind. I'm tired and need a shower. Please remove your foot so I can continue to my room."

"Could I please see your passport, Mister Shepherd?"

"My passport? But why? I don't understand?"

"It's only a formality, Mister Shepherd, just to confirm your identity for the hotel records."

Ronald Perkins stared at the desk clerk in open-mouthed astonishment. "My identity? But I've stayed here three times in the last four months and nobody ever asked to see my passport before."

"It must have been overlooked, Mister Shepherd. Passports from overseas guests should be handed over to the hotel for safe keeping. It's Home Office regulations I'm afraid."

"Well, in that case I'll hand my passport over. But it's up in my room so I'll go and get it."

"Thank you, Mister Shepherd," responded the desk clerk as he removed his foot from blocking the lift door, "That's most helpful of you."

Ronald Perkins, panicking, quickly closed the lift door, pressed the button for his floor, the fifth, and the lift shot rapidly upwards. He was now more desperate than ever to get away from the hotel, and to escape down a rear fire escape and leave London far behind. He felt like a rat caught in a trap. Things had gone badly wrong, the fight on the railway bridge, and now this stupid business over a passport. And all his well-laid plans had fallen apart, and he was in terror of his eminent arrest.

Allan Hawes, quietly satisfied with his questioning of Roger Shepherd, thinking it was all good practice for when he later became a private detective, strode back to the reception desk to await the passport. Roger Shepherd was a con man and he was going to prove it. Sitting down at the desk, he made a few rough notes of his conversation with Roger Shepherd, on hotel headed notepaper. People only conceal their true identity for criminal purposes. And budding private detective Allan Hawes knew from reading his detective magazines just how important it was for police to have a detailed statement of a conversation or interview with a criminal suspect. Allan Hawes wrote it all down while it was still fresh in his mind. The desk clerk wanted to be certain of his facts, and have them all clearly down on paper in black and white before calling the police. There was of course, the remote possibility that Roger Shepherd was innocent of committing a crime, and had a valid reason for faking his identity. When he finished writing his two-page statement, Allan Hawes glanced at the wall clock. "He's taking his time," he thought, but then remembered that Mister Shepherd, or whoever he was, had badly wanted a shower and change of clothes, and that would surely account for his delay in coming down to the desk. "I'll give him five minutes more, then I'll go up to his room."

Allan Hawes switched on the radio to listen to the news while he was waiting, and was dumfounded to hear that the Oxford and Cambridge Boat Race had been abandoned. The radio announcer in crisp tones told how there had been a double murder – a policeman from the river boat division, and a black railway worker. The police were now seeking a man seen dressed in railway worker's clothes, clambering over a six-foot high wire fence several yards from Barnes Railway Bridge. Allan Hawes, face flushed with excitement, switched off the radio. His hands shook and the adrenaline raced through his veins. Could Roger Shepherd be the man the police were seeking? He was dressed in railway worker's clothes. And surely, he pondered, in the world of detection that was too much of a coincidence. The desk clerk, with his little brain cells now thrashing madly about, had a hunch Roger Shepherd was the man. Now everything was slipping into place like pieces of a jigsaw. Picking up the reception desk telephone, Allan Hawes hastily dialled 999 and when a woman operator asked which emergency service he required, he replied in a loud voice, "Police, get me the police."

Meanwhile Ronald Perkins was up in his hotel room, and still had no idea whatsoever about the two murders of which he had accidentally been the cause. He changed quickly out of the railway worker's clothes, scattering items of clothing all over the place in his haste. And ten minutes later, dressed in white shirt, grey tie, navy blue three-piece suit, black polished shoes, and carrying two bulky suitcases; he clambered out of a rear bedroom window and scurried down the fire escape. He flagged down a passing taxi just as a police car, with siren blaring, pulled up in front of the hotel, and twenty-five minutes later was sitting on a coach leaving Victoria Coach Station for Oxford.

Three days later, Chief Superintendent Sidney Masher of Scotland Yard sat at his desk reading from a thick file with a red cardboard cover. The Chief Superintendent was an enormously fat man who bulged out in all directions. Because of his size and weight, he had all the chairs at home and at work specially widened and reinforced to take his great bulk. This was done because he once had been wedged in a chair at a police annual Christmas dinner for two hours, before a carpenter arrived with a saw to cut him free. The incident resulted in him being cruelly called "Lardy Arse" behind his back by colleagues. Sometimes a policeman's lot is not a happy one.

Sidney Masher was married with three grown-up children, a boy and girl, and a "Hello sailor." He had been a policeman for over thirty-two years, and was within three years of retirement. He wore a surgical support next to his groin on the right side, to hold a misbehaving hernia in place. The fat man had suffered with the hernia for six years, but refused to have it surgically treated, being terrified of having an operation and giving himself up to unconsciousness, when he would no longer be in control of himself or the situation. He wore thick pebble glasses, which greatly magnified his little piggy eyes, giving him a strange appearance, with two big eyes staring out from a tiny oval double-chinned face. Facially he resembled a gasping goldfish but in temperament he was a great white shark. There was a timid knock on the door.

"Enter," he called out in a surprisingly squeaky voice.

The door opened and Police Constable Edgar Briggs entered the room. He stood smartly to attention in front of the Chief Superintendent's desk.

"You sent for me, sir," he said as he removed his helmet which he then held in the crook of his right arm.

The Chief Superintendent, sighed, closed the file, adjusted his glasses and closely studied the young policeman standing before him. He had just read Edgar Briggs's police service record file. It was the only one with a red cardboard cover, and he was not impressed with it. Briggs was the most inept policeman ever to serve in the Metropolitan Police Force. He was a jinx, causing chaos in whatever division he served. There were stories of horses galloping wildly out of control damaging cars, soaking Her Majesty the Queen, dogs doing indecent things to his right leg in public places, and finally a colleague murdered and a valuable police launch run aground.

"Do you know why you're here, Constable?" asked the Chief Superintendent, who was hoping to convince Edgar Briggs to resign or take early retirement.

Edgar Briggs nodded and grinned. "Promotion, sir," he replied brightly puffing his chest out proudly.

"Promotion?" gasped the Chief Superintendent, hardly able

to believe his ears.

"Thank you, sir, I won't let you down."

"What are you thanking me for?"

"My promotion, sir."

"Blithering idiot – I haven't promoted you. God knows what would happen if you were ever made a Sergeant. We can't have the inmates running the asylum."

The smile faded from Edgar Briggs's face as the insult sunk in.

"I wanted to see you, Constable," continued the Chief Superintendent briskly, "to discuss your future in the police."

"My future, sir?"

"Perhaps you're feeling that you're in the wrong job – you know, a round peg in a square hole. I'd like to explore with you the possibilities of a new career. How about the fire brigade? Wouldn't you like to be a fireman? Don't you like fires?"

"Yes, sir, I like fires well enough. When I was in the Boy Scouts I made fires. I was the best scout in the whole troop for making fires."

"Well, there you are, Briggs, there's something you're really good at."

"Yes, sir, but the scout master didn't think so – I kept setting fire to the scout hut."

"How long were you in the Boy Scouts?"

"Five weeks, sir."

"How many times did you set the fire to the scout hut?"

"Five times, sir, at every troop meeting."

"And that's why you left the Scouts?"

"Yes, sir, the scout master said he couldn't hold troop meetings any more."

"And why not?"

"Because I'd burnt the scout hut to the ground, sir."

"And how did you feel about that?"

"Oh, really bad, sir. The scout master refused to give me a fire lighting badge."

Chief Superintendent Sidney Masher took out a handkerchief and mopped his sweating brow. "Do you like being a policeman?" he asked.

Edgar Briggs nodded his head in agreement. "It's the only

career for me, sir. I want to pull my truncheon out in public and show people I'm ready for action."

"I see from your service file you've been transferred three times in the last year, and yet haven't made a single arrest. Now why is that?"

"People and animals don't like me, sir"

"Dogs like you, don't they?"

"Only my right leg, sir."

"What all this about never making an arrest? Aren't you ashamed to be the only constable in your class at Hendon who's never made an arrest?"

"I came close this morning, sir, to making an arrest. I put handcuffs on a violent motorist who parked illegally right outside Scotland Yard's front doors."

"That was the Chief Constable. He was wearing a raincoat over his uniform. And it was his own parking bay."

"Yes, sir, I know that now, but at the time I thought he was illegally parked. He refused to come quietly and so I had to restrain him. It wasn't until I bashed him over the head a few times with my truncheon, that I realised my mistake... when the raincoat fell open and I saw the uniform."

"Did the hospital say when they're discharging him?"

"The casualty Doctor wants him to stay in overnight, sir. She said he might be concussed. But he seemed quite lively to me. He kept trying to leap off the hospital trolley shouting he wanted to throttle me."

"Are you sure you really want to remain in the police force?"

"Yes, sir, it's the only place for me."

"Well, I can think of other places. Can't I say anything to change your mind? What about becoming a milkman or perhaps a Vicar with nice church bells to ring?"

"No, sir, I'm quite happy as I am."

"Very well, Briggs, then you leave me no choice. I'm going to transfer you from the River Police Division to CID, in the hope that when you're in plain clothes the general public won't think you're a copper."

"Thank you, sir."

62

Chapter Five

Twenty-three years and twenty-seven murders later, Ronald Perkins, now an experienced and successful serial killer, was living in an eight-bedroom country mansion in the rolling Kent countryside, the bountiful garden of England, near the little village of Bumstead on the Wold. He lived with his mistress Angela Cobblers, and his mother Hetty Rose Perkins, passing himself off to the locals as a retired stockbroker, living in style and posing as a wealthy country gentleman. There was a household staff of nine including a French gourmet chef, butler, footmen, maids, chauffeur, and two gardeners with green fingers and brown thumbs. In the stables were eight thoroughbred horses, mares and stallions, and he regularly rode with the local foxhunt, the Bumstead Hunt. The Master of Fox Hounds was Colonel Ivor Biggan, late of the Suffolk Fifth Artillery, a regiment who performed gallantly with their artillery pieces during the North African desert campaign during the Second World War, when they both frightened the Germans and delighted the Arab women with the size of the barrels. Ronald Perkins was captain of the local golf club, and made a point of keeping his balls immaculately scrubbed and monogrammed with tiny letters of gold. He was the only golfer with his balls inscribed in gold.

Over the passing years, since the fiasco of the Oxford and Cambridge Boat Race, with the untimely demise of the riverboat police officer and railway worker, Ronald Perkins had developed a keen expertise for creating the perfect murder. He had learnt from his mistakes to leave nothing to chance when planning one of his murderous escapades. And indeed, everything was most carefully planned right down to the minute detail, with a fool-proof back-up plan with two escape routes should things go badly wrong. Of course, he regretted the unfortunate deaths of

Police Constable Robert McDougal and railway worker Barry Coles. But only because their deaths did not provide him with a nice fat financial reward. Death was such a waste without a cash incentive, he had always thought. Ronald Perkins was the only man in the whole world who knew that both deaths were accidental. The Metropolitan Police, ever quick to have a conviction to bring their unsolved crimes figures down, declared the two men had been murdered, and opened an investigation which was still on going some twenty-three years later.

Edgar Briggs, now a Chief Inspector in CID, with a passion for jam doughnuts and doing crosswords, which he never completed, was determined to track down the elusive killer, and kept the "Barnes Railway Bridge Murders" file on his desk in readiness for instant action. There had been a few clues – like the man dressed as a railway worker, seen clambering over a six foot high wire fence several yards from the bridge. And the small Hitler-style ginger moustache found tightly clasped within Barry Coles's dead fist. There were samples of blood collected from a wooden railway sleeper – which did not match Barry Coles's blood, which was Rhesus Positive. The blood from the sleeper was Rhesus Negative. And finally, there was the statement giving the best eyewitness description of the suspect, which was provided by hotel desk clerk Allan Hawes. He told in his statement of a mysterious hotel guest at Braddock Towers, who claimed he was an American called Roger Shepherd, from Dallas, Texas. Roger Shepherd was last seen dressed in a railway worker's clothes, going up in the lift to his hotel room. Scotland Yard sought the help of Interpol, who contacted the CIA in America, who confirmed, with the help of Edgar Hoover's FBI, that no passport had ever been issued to an American citizen called Roger Shepherd from Dallas, Texas. Indeed, there was no paperwork found anywhere in the whole of the United States on a person named Roger Shepherd from Texas. Fingerprints found in the bogus Roger Shepherd's hotel room in London matched those found on the holdall and grey stone, which had dropped on Police Constable Robert MacDougal, killing him instantly.

The mysterious American tourist Roger Shepherd was never

64

traced. He simply vanished from the face of the earth. But Scotland Yard believed the man they were hunting was really an Englishman with a public school background, because he had made the mistake of speaking briefly with a posh upper class English accent, during his last conversation with hotel desk clerk Allan Hawes, before reverting back quickly to a Texan drawl. Edgar Briggs was still pursuing the notorious "Barnes Railway Bridge Murderer" with a resolute determination, which became stronger with each passing year. He had vowed at his colleague Robert McDougal's graveside that only death or his retirement from the police force would prevent him from hunting down the elusive killer.

Sir Rupert Slattery, knight of the British theatre, thespian of world renown, founder member of the Watford Shakespearean Players advanced slowly towards the glaring footlights. Resplendent and alone on stage, a theatre legend held within a bright spotlight, he cut a magnificent figure in black tights with jewel-encrusted codpiece. The codpiece was twice the normal size to invite the curiosity of female members of the audience and to tickle their fancy. The bold knight was playing the lead role in Shakespeare's "Richard the Third". And on his back was a huge artificial hump, strapped beneath his ermine-trimmed red jacket. Limping skilfully, as if one leg was much shorter than the other, he shuffled forward to make his opening speech. The audience waited spellbound with bated breath for the great thespian to begin to speak. Sir Rupert was at the peak of his acting career, the darling of the London and Broadway critics. He had recently been offered a part in a Roy Rogers western film as the trusty old sidekick Gabby Winkler in "Tex Does It Again". Sir Rupert was fifty-seven years old, married to fellow thespian Lady Doris Slattery, with four grown-up children; all girls who had followed their parents into the theatre, and were now seated in the front row with their spouses. In the pitch-darkness beneath the stage, Ronald Perkins crept forward, guided by a slender beam of light from a small pocket torch. Above him he heard the shuffling steps of the great actor as he advanced towards the footlights. "Now is the winter of our discontent," boomed the theatrical knight in his clear clarion baritone voice, as he waved his Shakespearean character's withered right hand in the air, bringing gasps of surprise from the audience.

"Now is the time for you to go," muttered Ronald Perkins as he slid back the bolts holding the stage trap door in place, "either straight to heaven or straight to hell."

"Made glorious summer by this son of York..." continued Sir Rupert as he took a fateful step forward onto the trap door — which suddenly gave way beneath his weight. With a shrill scream Sir Rupert Slattery vanished feet first down into the gaping black hole. The audience, expecting to witness Sir Rupert's own brilliant and personalised interpretation of the role of Richard the Third, thought he had cleverly devised his disappearance as part of the production. What an opening to the play it was for them, to see the bold knight in his well-padded codpiece disappearing from sight down through the trapdoor. It had never been done before, not even on Broadway in a musical with comedian Danny Kaye. Slattery was a genius, of that the audience had no doubt. They rose up from their seats like one person and wildly applauded the vanished thespian. Meanwhile, the old theatre knight lay in a crumpled heap under the stage in pitch darkness. He was not seriously hurt, having twisted his right ankle and bruised both buttocks when landing and bouncing on them across the room. He looked up and saw the shadowy figure of Ronald Perkins, dressed entirely in black, advancing towards him from out of the darkness, and thought he was a stagehand coming to his aid. "Oh, listen, young stagehand," he cried, "Can't you hear the bumptious applause from above? Oh, hearken to how my beloved audience are calling for me." He wiped away teardrops from both cheeks with the index finger of his right hand. "It is for their sake that the show must go on. How could I ever let my dear audience down? Help me to my feet, my dear boy. I'm going to play Richard on stage from a wheelchair. It'll be a first in the history of the theatre, never done before. Oh, but how the critics will praise my bold performance, with me racked with pain performing Richard the Third from a wheelchair. It'll give the play so much more depth and meaning. Oh, but the heart-rending pathos of it all. I'm filling up. Yes, I'm coming over all unnecessary."

Ronald Perkins shone his torch beam onto the old knight's flushed face. The actor smiled, enjoying the spotlight, and turned his head slightly to the left so his best side was in the small pool of light. "There won't be any wheelchair for you tonight, Sir Rupert," said the serial killer grimly.

"No? But why ever not?" asked the bewildered knight of the theatre.

"Because you'll be dead and won't need it."

"Dead? But I don't understand What about my final curtain? I can't leave my audience without doing a final curtain call!"

"This is your final curtain, Sir Rupert," cried Ronald Perkins hotly as he swung a small claw hammer to shatter the knight's head with a single killing blow. When Sir Rupert was found moments later, crumpled up alone on the floor by shocked stage hands, with his head shattered, it was thought he had fallen through the trap door onto his head. Which was just the perfect murder Ronald Perkins had planned.

Sir Winston Royston, knight of the British theatre, well-known thespian and TV talk show bore, sat at a small table in the corner of a dimly-lit Dorset pub. The public house, sixteenth century with low oak beams, was called the "The Queen's Headache," named after Queen Elizabeth the First of England and her legendary headaches. She would, according to the history books, proclaim herself to have a bad headache whenever a suitor such as the Earl of Essex suggested a swift leg over – hence her dying in extreme old age as the famous wrinkled virgin queen. Sir Winston Royston, thin and bony, of average height, with a balding head too large for his skeletal looking body, a large droopy grey moustache waxed at the ends, with the worse bow legs ever seen on man or beast. Indeed, he walked as if he had just done a poo in his pants, and looked absolutely awful in tights, resembling a freshly-plucked oven ready chicken. Sitting opposite him was a plump ginger-haired spinster lady dressed in green tweeds with matching hat. Sir Royston had come to pay the final half of the money he owed for the demise of his arch rival of the theatre, Sir Rupert Slattery. The two great thespians, rivals both in the theatre and in love, with Sir Rupert marrying the woman of Sir Royston's dreams, cherished childhood

67

sweetheart Nelly Updyke. The knights of the theatre were born in the same year, in the same month, on the same day, under the sign of the rutting Ram. They had met when they both started their theatrical careers as twelve-year-old boys at the Betty Boo Stage School in Catford. Sir Rupert was the star pupil, taking to acting and tap-dancing like a duck to water. But Sir Royston, who suffered dreadfully with stage fright and wearing tights, took to acting and tap-dancing like an ostrich to flying. But he persevered, because he had been born into a famous British theatrical family, going back a generation to his late father Sir John Royston, who threatened to disown his only son should he fail to achieve an acting diploma from the Betty Boo Stage School. Rupert Slattery was a natural born actor, with poise and a great delivery (once working as a postman while resting between roles), and after leaving stage school at the age of eighteen with three diplomas and passion for tights, he was soon playing major Shakespearean roles

Meanwhile, Sir Royston, racked with jealousy against his arch rival, was playing minor roles such as the third spear carrier on the left in Royal Shakespearean productions performed on the end of Brighton pier. Sir Royston did not get a major role until he played Bottom in "A Midnight Summer Night's Dream" at a run-down theatre in Lower Watford, next door to Fred's Pie and Eel stall, when he was thirty years old. He implored and bribed family, friends and neighbours, to come and see his fabulous Bottom, declaring proudly, "It's got to be seen to be believed," and adding "Courtney Howler, theatre critic of the Sunday Times' had said in his weekly column that it was a truly magnificent Bottom, the best he has ever seen on the British stage." However, Sir Royston's Doctor, Gordon Spence, who had gone into medicine to see naked women, totally disagreed with the theatre critic. He had seen the bottom in question many times in his surgery over the years, and whenever it was exposed to view, which was a most startling experience, he would insist upon a second medical opinion from a colleague.

Sir Royston nervously eyed the plump spinster woman. There was something weird and unfeminine about her, like the sturdy legs and deep rather manly voice, which sent shivers up and down his spine. Sir Royston took a quick gulp of a whisky on the rocks to steady his nerves.

"I read with the greatest delight of Sir Rupert Slattery's obituary in yesterday's Daily Bugle, Miss Pringle," he said quietly in almost a whisper, keeping his voice low so he would not be overheard by people sitting at nearby tables. From his inside jacket pocket he took out a fat brown envelope which he handed to the woman. "It's all in hundred pound notes as requested. I'm pleased with your expertise with the demise of that would-be thespian. How he had the nerve to call himself a Royal Shakespearean actor I'll never know. The man couldn't even act his way out of a paper bag with a hole at both ends."

Ronald Perkins in his tweedy disguise as the ginger-haired Miss Marion Pringle, dowager of a wealthy countryside horsy set, nodded his head in agreement, and replied in a posh upper class accent which only faintly resembled a woman's voice, "I was privileged to help Sir Rupert with his last performance." He took the brown envelope and slipped it away into a large black handbag on the table in front of him.

"Was it any good?"

"Good? I'm sorry but I don't understand, Sir Royston."

"Was his last performance any good?"

"No – I'm afraid he corpsed at the end."

They both laughed.

Doctor Albert Windrush was visiting his best friend and fellow criminologist, super-sleuth Allan Hawes, who resided at 42B Bakery Street. The Doctor was a part-time semi-retired consultant, employed twice weekly at St Thomas's Hospital for Sick People, where he dealt with flatulent disorders, persistent piles and floppy penises. He was a tall jolly man with long grey sideburns and long spindly legs. When working at the hospital he wore a plain glass monocle over his right eye to impress patients into thinking he was an intellectual. Doctor Windrush, being a gentleman of clean habits and intentions, insisted each morning on putting on freshly-laundered underpants, washed and ironed by his mother, a widow without means who resided with him in a red-bricked detached house in Chelsea. Doctor Windrush was immensely proud of his regular bowel movements and liked, whenever possible, to bring the subject of bowel movements into a conversation. He was a martyr to gout, which mostly affected his big toes, and to the constant nagging of his mother, who thought that at the age of forty-one her only child should be married with grandchildren for her to spoil.

Doctor Albert Windrush was immaculately dressed in a charcoal-black suit with a white and blue spotted tie, and a pink carnation in his buttonhole. There was a stethoscope dangling from his left jacket hip pocket ready for any emergency. He sat at Allan Hawes's breakfast table spreading butter over a slice of toasted bread, which he then carefully cut into six equal lengths to dip into the runny yolk of his boiled egg. At the far end of the room, poised before an open window with the morning breeze gently fluttering the floral curtains, stood the tall, gangly, imposing figure of the great detective. Allan Hawes was dressed in his favourite purple silk smoking jacket with gold piping, black trousers with razor-sharp creases. On his head he wore an old tattered deerstalker hat, sold to him from out of a battered suitcase in a crowded street market by a fast talking cockney, who claimed it had once belonged to Sherlock Holmes himself. Allan Hawes wore the deerstalker all the time, even in bed, but not as a personal tribute to his famous role model, but to hide his progressive baldness. Allan Hawes, eyes tightly closed, a look of sheer rapture on his narrow rat-like face, was playing lovingly on an old violin. The instrument was an original copy of a Fred Steinberg. The room was filled with beautiful soul-stirring music, Chopin's Fourth and Three Quarters To The Finish Violin Concerto, which wafted sweetly, bringing tears to the eyes of both men. Allan Hawes rapidly moved the violin bow back and forth across the taut strings of his instrument as the music reached a towering crescendo. It was then, with a gasp of shock and pain, that he caught his index finger in the strings. Distracted by the pain and sucking his index finger, Allan Hawes put the violin and bow down on the table – but the violin music continued playing. The detective strode over to a portable record player on the sideboard and switched it off. The music ceased playing.

"My dear chap," cried the Doctor, leaping to his feet with a look of concern. "Are you in need of my medical services?"

Allan Hawes shook his head. "No, Windrush, it's only a

finger," he said quietly with the resigned air of a man of supreme courage and fortitude. "I've another eight fingers you know."

The Doctor nodded. "I've experienced a most excellent bowel movement this morning before setting out from home to come here."

"Why are you telling me this, Windrush?"

"Well, to try and take your mind off your finger, old chap. It must be dreadfully painful. I just thought the news of my bowel movement might cheer you up."

"Please, Windrush, I don't want to hear any more about your bowel movements. Please keep them to yourself, for God's sake."

"Sorry, Hawes."

"All right – but let's hear no more about it, if you please."

There was a knocking on the door. "There's a visitor here to see you, Mister Hawes," called an old woman's rasping voice from the other side of the door. "Don't worry, it's a lady – I sent the debt collector away like you said, but I don't think he believed me when I said you'd gone away on holiday to Australia for a year."

"Please bring her in, Mrs Howard," called the super-sleuth as he stepped quickly over to stand in front of the fireplace. He knew that first impressions counted in the private detective business, and liked, whenever possible, to pose himself before the fireplace for visitors to 42B Bakery Street. He glanced in the mirror hanging over the mantelpiece and adjusted his deerstalker. He wanted, as a successful crime-buster, to look his best for a client. Positioning himself in a prominent position on the tiger skin rug, he stood with left elbow resting on the corner of the mantelpiece. He stuck an empty pipe in his mouth. The pipe made him look wise and thoughtful. He turned his head slightly so it was in profile to the door. Allan Hawes always looked his best in profile... or so he thought.

The door opened, and a small robust woman in her early sixties, with rosy-red apple cheeks, face wrinkled like a dried-up prune, wearing a white apron with matching frilly cap, hands covered with flour (she had been doing her weekly baking), stepped briskly into the room. Mrs Brenda Howard had been a widow for over twenty years. Her late husband Chester, an alcoholic and Crystal Palace football supporter, came home drunk as usual from the pub one dark rain-swept night, and with a friend, equally drunk, had lifted up a manhole cover in the middle of the Edgware Road, and, declaring he was going in for a midnight swim, had leapt down into the flooded sewer below, never to be seen again. Mrs Howard had hobbies to keep herself occupied in her widowhood, like the baking of bread and cakes, knitting endless football scarves for a long-dead husband, and collecting Victorian glassware. She was the epitome of the cheery cockney landlady, born within the sound of London's Bow Bells, which she contended made her more of a cockney than Michael Caine, which not many people knew. And like all cheery cockneys, she possessed the irritating characteristics of forever smiling in adversity, and making inane jokes and bright breezy quips when all around her were utterly miserable and wanted nothing more but for her to shut up. Close on her heels there followed a petite woman in her early forties, with a face that had been lifted more times than Tower Bridge. She had a contemptuous expression and piercing green eyes. The woman was expensively dressed in the very epitome of bad taste, which clearly marked her out as an aristocrat with either a very rich husband or well-heeled lover. She wore a low-cut blue silk dress, with a white mink stole draped over her slim alabaster shoulders. There was a single rope of real South Sea pearls the size of small pigeon eggs dangling around her swan-like neck. She advanced confidently into the room, head held high in a haughty manner. On each finger of her black velvet gloved hands were sparkling gold rings, each set with a precious stone. She wore a monstrous floppy white straw hat (she was on her way to the Ascot races), with an ostrich feather stuck in the blue headband. Her huge nose, which overwhelmed the rest of her small oval face, was held deliberately high as if there was a nasty smell in the air, like a naughty puppy had done a mess on the carpet. And indeed there was a nasty smell as far she was concerned, the smell of ordinary common people with hardly a penny to their name. In her pampered world, only the very rich were important, and being important never ever had to mention money. This was because having so much money herself, she thought it the height of vulgarity to talk about it. Money to her was a chequebook and an array of credit cards carried by a butler for her acquisition when out shopping in up-market stores.

The whole persona of the woman screamed out wealth and position. She was somebody who believed without question that she was the most important person at any aristocratic gathering, with the exception of royalty of course.

"Mrs Mabel Frogmorton, sir," called out Mrs Howard brightly as she introduced the woman to Allan Hawes, bowing her head slightly in homage as the lady in question swept past her like a Spanish galleon in full sail. Mabel Frogmorton was the third ugly daughter of an impoverished Earl, who had gambled away his estate and fortune. She had married for money – in the hope it would buy her a title, and had set her heart on becoming a duchess. She married multi-millionaire Sidney Frogmorton, a fifty-six-year-old man with poor eyesight, who was old enough to be her father. He had started work at the age of fourteen selling fruit and vegetables from a street-market barrow, and ended up owning an empire of fish and chip shops.

Doctor Albert Windrush, on seeing the haughty-faced woman enter the room, gallantly sprang to his feet with a half-eaten slice of toast and marmalade in his hand. He had instantly recognised Mabel Frogmorton. Only three months earlier he had treated her husband at his clinic in St Thomas's hospital for sick people, for persistent piles and a floppy penis.

"Mrs Frogmorton," exclaimed the Doctor as he stepped out from behind the table to offer the lady his hand, "It's very good to see you again." But unfortunately he offered the hand holding the toast and marmalade, and without looking down Mrs Mabel Frogmorton clasped it firmly, her fingers squelching on the marmalade. She looked disdainfully down to see orange marmalade oozing from between the fingers of her black velvet glove.

"I'm so sorry," spluttered the Doctor in a wild panic as he swiftly withdrew his hand with the offending mangled slice of toast. His face turned red with embarrassment, and he began to laugh uncontrollably sounding like the braying of a donkey. Allan Hawes quickly strode over to him and delivered a hard slap with his open hand across the face. The laughing immediately stopped. The Doctor sat down on a chair. "Thank you, Hawes," he gasped, "I needed that. I was out of control for a moment."

"Have a nice hot cup of tea, Doctor, with plenty of sugar in it," said Mrs Howard brightly. "I know what'll cheer you up – have you heard the one about the flasher who was going to retire? He decided to stick it out for one more year?"

"Please Mrs Howard," cried Allan Hawes, "There's a time and place for your bawdy cockney humour, but it's definitely never here in front of a visitor."

Meanwhile Mrs Frogmorton had removed her marmalade-covered glove, and had slipped it away inside her crocodile-skin handbag. She took a deep breath to steady herself, and wished she had bought her smelling salts along with her.

"Mrs Frogmorton," called the Doctor. "Don't you remember me? I'm the consultant at St Thomas's Hospital for sick people. It was I who treated your husband for his penile problem. Surely you remember me? Doctor Albert Windrush?"

Mrs Frogmorton looked steadily at the Doctor with a look of disgust. Doctors were, in her book, the same as jobbing plumbers or other such manual tradesmen who made their living doing crude things with their hands, and such people had to use the back door when visiting her palatial home. She shook her head disdainfully.

"Sorry, but I don't recall you, Doctor," she replied coldly. "You look like any other tradesman to me."

Doctor Windrush was aghast. He prided himself upon his close relationships with his wealthier clientele, and had thought they in return took an equal pride in knowing him, as a respected top consultant in his field. How could she have forgotten him?

"But surely, Mrs Frogmorton," he continued hopefully, "You must remember me? I corrected with surgery and a small battery power pack, your husband's failure to arise and remain upstanding for those special occasions."

"Special occasions? What special occasions?" demanded Mrs Frogmorton.

"Those special and very private occasions when you and your husband express your love for each other, Mrs Frogmorton."

"What are you talking about, Doctor? Have you lost your

74

wits? My husband expresses his love for me by buying expensive jewellery and clothes."

"I meant making love, Mrs Frogmorton – that's why your husband had a penile corrector surgically inserted. He wants a son and heir does he not?"

"Oh, yes, I do place you now, Doctor Windrush," responded Mrs Mabel Frogmorton her face a mask of fury, "Both you and your totally inadequate handiwork on my unhappy husband's plumbing."

"Inadequate? But I don't understand, Mrs Frogmorton. The patented penile corrector, which I personally implanted during a two-hour operation, was working perfectly when I tried it out in the operating theatre. We had it going up and down like a yo-yo for several minutes to amuse the theatre nurses."

"The penile corrector was an utter menace, Doctor," retorted Mrs Frogmorton angrily, "operating when it should have remained dormant."

"But I don't understand, Mrs Frogmorton."

"Whenever I pressed the electric bell in my drawing room to call for a servant to attend me... my husband's trousers would extend by a few inches."

"But, Mrs Frogmorton that's..."

"And my unhappy housemaid Hilda," interrupted Mrs Frogmorton who was getting into her stride; "who had been with me for over ten years gave in her notice on the spot and left my service scarred for life. She entered the drawing room to answer my bell-press summons, I wanted tea and cucumber sandwiches, to find my husband with his trousers fully extended. He promptly thrust his hands down inside his trousers to adjust the corrector, and in doing so, suffered an electric shock to his private parts when the battery pack supplied with the device exploded. The resulting fire caused him a total loss of pubic hair."

"Oh, but what a dreadful story," said Mrs Howard sympathetically. "I used to worry a great deal before my wedding night, when I was young and innocent, about men and their extended trousers."

"That'll do, Mrs Howard," exclaimed Allan Hawes, "You may return to your duties now. I'm sure you've lots to do in the kitchen."

"I've had some saucy encounters in my time, mostly on buses, with men's extended trousers, I can tell you," continued Mrs Howard, looking directly at Mrs Frogmorton. "There was this young fella on a number nine bus who…"

"Mrs Howard, please, that will do," interrupted Allan Hawes as he pointed towards the open door. "Mrs Frogmorton does not want to hear of your experience on a number nine bus. Return this instant to your kitchen."

Mrs Howard, muttering under her breath, went out the door and slammed it behind her.

"Well, there goes spotted dick and custard for pudding tonight," sighed Doctor Windrush wistfully. "She won't bother with it now. It'll be something awful stewed from a tin I expect."

"Please be seated, Mrs Frogmorton," said the detective. "I must apologise for my housekeeper Mrs Howard. But you just can't find the staff these days, can you?"

Mrs Frogmorton sat down on the sofa, her face as white as chalk. "Thank you, Mister Hawes, you are most kind. But I do feel rather faint."

"Would you like a glass of water?" asked Doctor Windrush.

"No, thank you, Doctor," responded Mrs Frogmorton fanning herself with her handbag. "I'll be all right in a moment."

"Would you like me to loosen your clothing?"

"I beg your pardon, Doctor? I'm not that sort of a woman."

"I wasn't suggesting that you were, Mrs Frogmorton," replied the Doctor hastily. "I'm a medical man and I've seen it all before."

"Well, you haven't seen mine, Doctor, and you're not going to."

"Go and finish your breakfast, Doctor," said Allan Hawes, "Mrs Frogmorton isn't in need of your expert medical attention."

Doctor Windrush returned to the table, sat down and began to butter a slice of toast. "Just as you say, Hawes," he said quietly. Women were a complete mystery to him, and indeed the more he learnt about the fair sex, the more he was convinced they were minefields of explosive emotions ready to go off at the very least little thing.

"Now, Mrs Frogmorton," said the detective, taking up his

regal pose in front of the fireplace, turning his profile towards the lady in question, right elbow resting on the mantelpiece and empty pipe clenched in his mouth. "How might I be of service to you?"

"You are the renowned private detective Allan Hawes?" she asked, "The man who retrieved the Duchess of Ditchwater's stolen diamond necklace?"

"I am that man, Mrs Frogmorton."

"There are so many Allan Hawes to be found in the phone book that I had to be sure I was talking to the right one."

"What can I do for you?"

"I want to employ you, Mister Hawes. I will double your usual fee."

"Not so fast Mrs Frogmorton. I'm not sure yet that I want to take on your case."

"But I thought..."

"Sorry, Mrs Frogmorton," interrupted the detective, "But I don't take on just any case. I'm very selective about my clients."

"But if it's a question of money, Mister Hawes, then I'll pay whatever you ask. This is a matter of life and death, family honour and dishonour."

"I only take on cases which stretch my intellect and further my knowledge of the criminal mind. I will not accept an easy case that could be solved by Scotland Yard's CID. I like to pit my wits and superior intellect up against the greatest criminal minds, and engage them in a turbulent game of mind chess, out-thinking them at every turn and bringing their evil twisted careers to checkmate in some prison cell."

"I'm sure my case will stimulate your intellect, Mister Hawes."

"Really Mrs Frogmorton – then please tell me more... as you can see I'm all ears."

"So it's the ears again is it, Hawes," exclaimed Doctor Windrush. "Haven't I told you countless times they can be reduced drastically by plastic surgery?"

Allan Hawes glared angrily at the Doctor. "What I told you about my ears was strictly in confidence, Windrush, between a patient and his Doctor and not to be blurted out in my sitting room in front of a visitor."

"I'm sorry, Hawes, it won't happen again."

"All right, then, please be quiet, Windrush, I'm trying to have a serious conversation with Mrs Frogmorton, if you don't mind."

"But of course, Hawes, I won't say another word."

Allan Hawes turned to Mrs Frogmorton. "Please continue, Mrs Frogmorton," he said with a smile. "We won't be interrupted again."

"Would murder be stimulating enough for you, Mister Hawes?" asked Mrs Frogmorton.

The detective's jaw dropped in astonishment and his pipe fell to the floor. Allan Hawes had never had a murder case before.

"Murder," he gasped.

"Yes, murder, Mister Hawes, a murder most wicked."

"My God, a real murder at last – but are you sure?"

"As sure as I'm sitting here talking to you, Mister Hawes."

"Who was murdered?"

"Pardon?"

"Who is the murder victim?"

"Ah well, now there's a slight problem about that, Mister Hawes."

"What sort of problem, Mrs Frogmorton?"

"Well, the victim isn't dead yet!"

"What? Isn't dead yet? But how can it be a murder without the victim being murdered, Mrs Frogmorton?"

"There's going to be a murder, Mister Hawes, I can assure you of that."

"But I don't understand, Mrs Frogmorton – please explain yourself."

"Well, I overheard my husband speaking on the telephone yesterday afternoon. He was in his study with the door locked. I know it was locked because I tried to look through the keyhole and saw the key was still in it. I just happened to pick up the extension phone in the bedroom and heard him talking to a woman..."

"So he's got a mistress," interrupted the detective.

"No, not with his penile problem – sex is the last thing on his mind. I can assure you of that."

"Then who is the woman?"

78

"He called her Marion Pringle – it seems she's a professional serial killer and my husband has hired her to commit murder."

"Murder who?"

"The one person whom he hates the most in all the world, Mister Hawes."

"You mean," gasped Doctor Windrush, looking deeply shocked, "that he's going to pay to have you murdered, Mrs Frogmorton?"

Mrs Frogmorton glared at the Doctor. "No, Doctor, it isn't me he wants murdered."

"Not you?" exclaimed the Doctor, looking disappointed, "well, I'm surprised."

"No, he wants the man whom he holds responsible for leaving his name off the Queen's honours list – the same man whom he blames for not rewarding him with a knighthood, even though he runs the biggest fish and chip empire in the whole of the British Isles!"

"You don't mean?"

"Yes, Mister Hawes, the British Prime Minister, Sir Antony Dingle, is to be murdered."

"Mrs Frogmorton, I'll take the case."

Chapter Six

Peter Catchpole was the new curate at the little sixteenth century church of St Freda the Ever Ready, in the village of Bumstead on the Wold. He was being sent by the Vicar, the aggressive humped-back Howard Peel, who insisted on lending him his wife's sturdy black lady's bike with a basket on the front, to visit the Perkins residence. It was to be the curate's first solo parish visit without clerical back-up since his arrival in the parish six weeks earlier.

"This is a big day for you, Peter," the Vicar told him before he set off on the bike. "But I know you won't let the Bishop or me down. Try not to mention God too much to the villagers, there's a good fellow, they're simple country folk and religion tends to make them nervous and think priests have an imaginary friend. Now I've chosen Ronald Perkins as your first solo visit because he's a jolly good chap at heart, keen as mustard on amateur dramatics with pretensions to play this year's pantomime dame. I don't mind telling you that I shall of course be playing the dame. But I'll let him play Buttons as consolation."

"That's nice of you, Vicar," replied the curate who was feeling very nervous indeed about his impending visit to the Perkins residence. He thought his missionary zeal was being tested by his superiors to judge the strength of his character in an operational scenario, and was determined to make a success of the visit.

"And do remember, Peter, that Ronald Perkins isn't a churchgoer."

"He isn't – then should I be visiting him?"

The Vicar nodded and smiled happily. "But of course, it's all good practice for you, Peter, putting your parochial skills to the test and seeing how much you've learnt in theological college on the care of wayward souls. Ronald Perkins might not be a churchgoer, but he does have one very important redeeming feature as far as the Bishop is concerned – Ronald Perkins has pots of money. Now off you go, there's a good fellow, and see if you can get a donation for the church bell tower."

It was a hot sticky summer's afternoon with clouds of midges buzzing around, biting any exposed area of human skin they could find. The curate was dripping with sweat before he had cycled more than a hundred yards. He was not a countryside loving person, seeing no poetical romance in birds chirping noisily among the hedgerows, herds of mucky cows and flocks of sheep munching idly away in field or meadow as he cycled along. The countryside was for him a rather disgusting earthy place with wide open spaces, trees scattered about here and there, and clouds of nasty insects buzzing biting or stinging, piles of manure, mostly rounded cow pats, found wherever the unwary stepped away from road or lane into an innocent looking field or through a farmyard gate. The curate knew that nothing was as it appeared in the countryside, and that it was much safer to stay indoors whenever possible. He was not dressed for cycling in such hot weather, wearing a long thick cassock and tight dog collar. This was because he felt as a priest that he should proclaim and advertise his godly vocation, revealing by his dress code and quiet serious disposition to the parish the sort of man he really was, a dedicated pious Christian with clean habits and cookery books. But what he did not know, as he rode along down leafy country lanes, was that most of the villagers, especially those who gathered nightly in the public bar of the Pig's Head, who had already made up their minds to what sort of man he really was. They had judged him, in the few weeks they had known him, to "a right wanker". This was the agreed assessment by all the regulars including the landlord William Styles, a churchgoer at Easter and Christmas, who generally respected clergymen who had a strong liking for beer. Peter Catchpole did not like beer, nor did he like any other alcoholic brew. A nice cup of tea was his favourite beverage. Only a wimp disliked beer, contended the landlord, and there was something badly wrong with a non-drinking clergyman who washed his own socks. William Styles had known some really boozy clergy in his time, like the Reverend Brian Price, who had to be carted home in a wheelbarrow by his wife from the Pig's Head on a Friday night. "If it looks like a duck, walks like a duck, and quacks like a duck," the landlord told his laughing regulars before casting his vote, "then you can be sure it is a duck."

Peter Catchpole was coming up to his twenty-seventh birthday, and had the sort of body often seen displayed in bodybuilding magazines, the one shown before doing the exercises. He was a shy, godly man, who came from a sheltered childhood brought up by two elderly maiden aunts, who had reluctantly taken him in after his parents had run away together after seeing him for the first time in the maternity hospital. The elderly aunts, twin sisters Mavis and Doris Fundy, were career virgins with a dread of sex and ping-pong balls. They raised their nephew to have the same fears. Indeed sex was never discussed in their household, and ping-pong was strictly banned. Peter Catchpole was a deeply modest man, so modest in fact that he even sat down on the toilet seat to pass water, so he would not have to handle himself more than was necessary. Before entering theological college, he had been an assistant housemaster at a prep school in East Sussex. There had been a really bad case of bedwetting – but he convinced the headmaster to see a renal specialist and the teacher was cured. Sex was never part of Peter Catchpole's lifestyle, and he became a committed celibate from the moment he learnt how babies were made. He was twenty-one at the time, and overheard women talking at a bus stop. They were factory workers and had been both graphic and boisterously humorous in describing the mechanics of the entanglements of the physical act, stressing with gales of girlish giggles the importance of a man's size and his stamina to finish what he had started, and for the woman to have an orgasm before he finished doing what he had started. To Peter Catchpole, who had not even experienced a wet dream, it all sounded very messy and extremely rude. And from that moment on, sex was to be totally banned from his life, in thought, word and deed. But a man's penis has a way of its own, as all men know, becoming upstanding and demanding attention without regard to its owner's plight, wanting to be petted and fussed over when it should be well-behaved and flaccid. And this was to prove both a nuisance and an acute embarrassment for the curate.

One day, when Peter Catchpole was up in London looking for a religious bookshop to buy some books before entering theology college, he had got himself hopelessly lost among the maze of streets surrounding Soho Square. He had paused on a street corner under a lamp post, confused about what he should do and where he should go, when a tall, shapely, blonde scantily-dressed in a tight green mini-skirt sauntered up to him. She wore bright red lipstick and mascara and had long legs which went right up to her well-rounded buttocks. Her breasts were huge, like two matching beach balls blown up to near bursting. She smiled sweetly and asked him in a sultry voice, "Are you looking for business, mister?"

He nodded, thinking she was a London tour guide offering her services to show him the sights. She would surely know the way to the bookshop. "Yes, I'm looking for a..."

"I know what you're looking for, dearie," interrupted the woman with a saucy wink of an eye.

"You do? But that's amazing. I haven't even told you where it is."

"Oh, I know where it is, dearie."

"You do?"

The woman smiled and nodded her head. "Where's it's always been, dearie," she said softly. "Now you come along with me and I'll show it to you." She took him firmly by the elbow and led him briskly away down a nearby alleyway. They walked for several minutes until they came to a dark secluded area with dustbins and a brick wall. "Well, what do you fancy – hand, French, or screw?"

Peter Catchople in his naiveté had no idea what she talking about, and thought she was asking if he could speak French.

"Well, I speak French fluently if that's any help," he replied with a puzzled look.

Without a word the woman dropped to her knees, deftly opened his trousers, pulled out his penis and popped it into her mouth. It was the biggest and most traumatic experience of his life. And for one terrifying moment he thought she was going to eat it. With a shrill scream of panic he jerked himself away,

83

turned and fled back up the alleyway hotly pursued by the woman who shouted at the top of her voice, "Come back, you rotten bastard. Where's my money for sucking your dick?"

Peter Catchpole rode slowly up the gravel driveway towards the Perkins residence. The large red-bricked house impressed him, and he knew the White Fathers had once owned it, an order of missionary monks, known for their clean habits, which were washed twice weekly. There were acres of garden with rolling immaculately-trimmed lawns, flowerbeds bursting with multitudes of colour, and orchards of apple, pear and cherry. On the front lawn a peacock displayed its arch of tail feathers. The curate put the bike up against a tree, walked up the steps to the front door and rang the bell. He was startled to hear, instead of the expected harmonious bell chimes, a thunderous cascade of classical music, which he recognised as coming from the Pomp and Circumstance March. A stocky grey-haired man wearing black tails and a bow tie, who was obviously the butler, opened the door. He peered at the curate over the top of his spectacles with a faint look of disdain on his face. "May I help you, sir?" he asked in a broad Irish accent with monotonous tones. Butlers spoke in monotonous tones to sound humble and servile.

"I've come for a visit," replied the curate brightly.

"Are you expected, sir?"

The curate shook his head.

"Whom shall I say is calling, sir?"

"The Reverend Peter Catchpole."

"Very good, sir, if you would please follow me."

Peter Catchpole followed the butler through the house and kitchen and out into the back garden. There was a large swimming pool in which a young woman dressed in a skimpy red bikini was floating lazily on her back in the deep end. The sun shimmered on the water like a thousand tiny lights.

"The Reverend Peter Catchpole to see you, madam," called the butler from the side of the pool. The woman, who was about twenty-five years old and was looking as lovely as a Hollywood film star, with long black hair and pouting lips, glanced at the curate then swam over to him. She climbed slowly up a ladder from the pool, water dripping from her luscious young body with

84

its pert breasts and hourglass hips. Peter Catchpole, who had never seen such a beautiful woman, felt a strange stirring beneath his cassock. "Angela," she said holding out her hand and smiling sweetly, "Cobblers."

"Pardon," gasped the shocked curate.

"Angela Cobblers," repeated the woman.

"Oh, Cobblers, it's your name – and there was me thinking I'd upset you in some way."

The woman laughed gaily and they shook hands. "Please call me Angie, all my friends do."

"Thank you, Angie, I'd like that."

The butler suddenly appeared at the woman's side holding a towel. Angela Cobblers took the towel and began to dry her long black hair. Peter Catchpole gazed at her with wondrous fascination, his heart beating faster, a warm glow spreading throughout his body, the tips of his ears turning crimson, a sure sign of racing hormonal activity, as his misbehaving penis boldly swelled beneath his cassock. The curate did not know it then, being as unfamiliar with this new bodily response as he was to the dark side of the moon, that he had fallen hopelessly in love with the gorgeous creature standing before him. She was the epitome of all feminine loveliness with her full luscious lips and sparkling eyes.

"Would you like a cool drink?" asked Angela Cobblers. "A lemonade?"

"Thank you," muttered the curate, "I am feeling rather hot." He took a handkerchief out of his cassock pocket and mopped his bow. He was finding it increasingly difficult to keep his eyes away from Angela Cobbler's breasts. There was something wondrously appealing about them, something which made his toes curl, and he felt strangely warm throughout his body and bizarrely elated for the first time in his life.

Angela Cobblers turned to the butler. "Get the father a lemonade, Flynn, with lots of ice please."

"Yes, madam," replied the butler stoically. He turned and walked away into the house to fetch the lemonade.

"But I'm not a father," muttered the curate weakly, still staring at her breasts.

"You're not? But I thought all priests were fathers."

"Not in the Church of England – unless they get married first."

Angela Cobblers laughed, showing her sparkling teeth, every tooth expensively whitened by a Harley Street dentist. "I must have been thinking of Catholic priests then," she said, "They're called father aren't they, Peter?"

The curate nodded. "Are you a Catholic, Angie?"

"No, but I was once a member of the Liberal Party, and I voted for the Green Party at the last election."

"Why? Are you worried about world pollution?"

"Oh, no, I just like the colour green."

The butler returned carrying a silver tray on which stood a single glass of lemonade with two ice cubes floating on the top. He walked up to the curate, bowed his head slightly and offered the tray.

"Your lemonade, sir," he said quietly.

The curate took the glass. It felt nice and cool in his fingers.

"Thank you, Flynn," he smiled gratefully and took a sip of the refreshing drink.

"I'd better go and change out of my wet costume," exclaimed Angela Cobblers. "You finish your drink, Peter – Flynn will show you to the lounge. I'll join you there in five minutes for a cup of tea."

Peter Catchpole sat on a sofa in the lounge of the Perkins's residence waiting for Angela Cobblers to make her appearance. He had already been waiting impatiently for almost an hour, having no understanding of the female need to take three times as long as a man to get ready for anything. There was a large silver-framed photograph on a nearby table, showing a smiling middle-aged balding man with his arm around Angela Cobblers's waist. Both were sun-tanned and smiling, and obviously very happy to be in each other's company. The curate supposed the man was her father Ronald Perkins, and that Cobblers was Angela's married name. But where was her father? And where was her husband? The butler Flynn had come and gone several times, bringing first a pot of tea and iced cakes, then returning three times to replenish the teapot with fresh hot water.

"Madam doesn't like cold tea," he had explained blandly.

"The gentleman in the photograph," asked the curate, pointing towards the silver frame, "I was wondering if he might be Ronald Perkins?"

"Yes, sir, that is the master."

"It's a nice picture with his daughter, isn't it?"

The door opened and Angela Cobblers came gliding in. She was wearing tight black leather trousers, a low-cut white blouse, and red high heel shoes. Her black hair the colour of raven wings was hanging down to her shoulders. Peter Catchpole gasped with pleasure at the young woman's magnetism and animal sexuality as she moved towards him. She moved with the grace of a young gazelle on the great African plains, her supple body language proclaiming her eagerness to find a rampant mate.

"Sorry I took so long, Peter," she said apologetically as she sat down on the sofa next to him, "But I just couldn't decide what to wear. I've such a huge collection of clothes to choose from up in my wardrobe, and I wanted to look my best. It's not every day that a nice young Vicar comes to call."

"I'm not a Vicar, Angie, I'm a curate."

She picked up the teapot and looked the clergyman steadily in the eyes. "Shall I be mother?"

"Oh, God, yes," he gasped, his penis twitching uncontrollably. "Please do be a mother."

She poured the tea.

"Will that be all, Madam?" asked the butler.

"Yes, thank you, Flynn, you may go."

The butler left the room and quietly closed the door behind him.

"I was wondering about your father, Angie," began Peter Catchpole. "I'd very much like to meet him if possible."

"My father?"

"Yes, perhaps you'll introduce us, Angie."

"Well, That might prove rather difficult, Peter."

"Surely not. Can you tell him I'm the new curate at Bumstead on the Wold, and my vicar wants me to meet the most prominent people in the village? I'm sure your father won't mind meeting me."

"Sorry, but I can't do that, Peter."

"But why not?"

87

"Because I never knew my father."

The curate looked stunned. "Never knew your father? But I don't understand."

Angela Cobblers nodded her head sadly. "Mummy was a dedicated lesbian and Daddy a sperm donor – he was introduced to mummy's ovaries from a test tube. On my birth certificate where it should have a father's name and occupation, the gynaecologist who delivered me wrote... 'Masturbation'.

The curate did not speak for a moment, being too shocked. Then, after regaining his composure; he pointed to the silver-framed photograph. "Then who is the man with you in the photograph? He looks old enough to be your grandfather."

"That's Ronald Perkins – my lover and benefactor."

"But aren't you a Cobblers and not a Perkins?"

"Yes that's right, I'm a Cobblers... we're not married."

"Then you're his..."

"Mistress," interrupted Angela Cobblers with a giggle. "But of course I am, and we have an ideal relationship – he gives me lots of money and I spend it."

"That's nice," gasped the curate whose face was red as a beetroot. He was so embarrassed that he wished the floor would open up and swallow him.

"What's nice?" asked Angela Cobblers with a mischievous glint in her eyes, "Being his mistress... or spending his money?"

"Eh, both... I suppose," muttered the curate unhappily. Angela Cobblers was living in sin, and he was now finding it difficult to continue the conversation with her. There were strict church rules about living in sin and having a sugar daddy.

"Another cup of tea, Peter?"

"No, thank you, Angie."

"Cake?"

The curate glumly shook his head. Wayward souls were his stock-in-trade, and returning lost sheep to the fold was a clergyman's number one priority. He must do whatever he could to save the wanton souls of Ronald Perkins and his mistress, the lovely curvaceous Angela Cobblers.

"Where is your... Oh, dear... I mean Mister Ronald Perkins? I'd like to meet him. I'm sure we'd have a great deal to discuss."

"My darling Ronnie is up in London with his mother for a few days. It's her birthday treat. They'll be back at the weekend."

"Oh, I see, never mind, I'll call back next week."

Angela Cobblers put her hand on his knee and squeezed it gently. "I'll look forward to your visit," she said, then took her hand away.

The effect of her hand on his knee was electric and overwhelming, and was the most exciting thing that had ever happened to the young clergyman. For almost a full minute he could not speak as he tried without success to use mind over matter, strength of thought to control and reduce his rock hard erection. But the wayward organ would not be controlled. Peter Catchpole crossed his legs to conceal his predicament, hoping he would not have to stand up during the next five minutes.

"I haven't seen you in church, Angie," he finally blurted out in a squeaky voice showing his distress.

"That's because I never go. It's not my scene, Peter. Church is far too boring I'm afraid."

"Well, there's plenty of empty pews should you change your mind," replied the curate with a smile as he forced his thighs closer together. Thank God he was wearing a cassock, which hid his rampant embarrassment. "The church doors are never closed you know, Angie. We're always looking and praying for new parishioners."

"That's nice, but it's not for me."

"We do really nice weddings at a most competitive price compared to the Catholics, which includes an organist and the church choir with Mister Derek Howie ringing the church bells. But we don't allow confetti in the churchyard... just rice for the birds. Confetti makes such a mess."

"It's a nice thought, Peter, getting married, but I don't think so, thanks all the same. My Ronnie isn't the sort of man to tie the wedding knot – he prefers to be single with all the benefits of married life."

"How long have you been together?"

"Four years – we met in a plane flying to Gatwick Airport from Israel. We sat together in business class seats. It was lust and greed at first sight. He lusted for me and I was greedy for his money."

"How does he earn his money? He must be very rich to own a big house like this with servants and a swimming pool."

"Ronnie was in the stock market before he retired from the city. That was before he met me. Now he works part-time as a removal consultant. He does specialist work once or twice a year, and travels all over the work."

"Removals?"

"Antique furniture I believe, but he never talks about it, saying it would break customer confidentiality if he did so. Sometimes he comes home with suitcases full of money."

The train pulled slowly out of London Bridge railway station. It was early evening and darkness was falling. Seated in a first class carriage were Ronald Perkins and his mother Hetty Rose Perkins. They were returning home to Bumstead on the Wold after spending eight days staying at the five-star Ritz Hotel. Hetty had thought their visit to London was a birthday treat for herself from her son, so she could see a production of "The Mousetrap," a play which she had longed to see for many years, and to do some shopping, such as buying an emerald necklace and a ruby brooch. Ronald Perkins had used the trip as his cover for committing a murder, and while his mother was sitting in the third row at the theatre watching the play, he was a few miles away putting the end to a man's life. The man he murdered was Giovanni Congui, a young handsome Italian diplomat working at the Italian Embassy in London. Congui, a lustful young man with an eye for the ladies, had made the mistake of having an affair with the beautiful young wife of a French cabinet minister when he was stationed in Paris. The minister, suspecting something was wrong when his wife kept pleading a headache whenever he wanted to be frisky, had searched through her handbag and found some letters from the diplomat to his wife, making it clear they were regularly meeting secretively for a sexual liaison. The cabinet minister complained in private to the Italian Ambassador in Paris, a close friend who was always open to a bribe, and Giovanni Congui was transferred within twenty-four hours to exile in London, away from the woman who adored him. But that was not enough for the jealous, humiliated, cuckolded cabinet minister. It was for him a matter of family honour which had to be revenged in full, and that meant the killing of the young Italian diplomat. The services of Marion Pringle were employed.

Giovanni Congui was an addicted gambler at cards and dice, and made regular nightly visits to a casino in North London, and would travel there by tube train on the Circle Line. He was followed three times to establish his travelling timetable; then on the fourth occasion, as he waited on a Circle Line station, he was pushed under a train. He was quite cut up about it. Ronald Perkins, disguised in green tweeds as Miss Marion Pringle, the elderly spinster lady with a horsy background, stepped back into the crowd milling about in a wild panic on the platform.

"Blimey, he's been cut up like a bleeding tomato," gasped a cockney train guard as he peered under the wheels of the train at the mangled remains of the young Italian diplomat. "We're going to need a bucket and spade to move him, poor blighter." Within forty-three minutes, and changed out of his Marion Pringle disguise, Ronald Perkins was in the theatre in black dinner jacket and bow tie, seated in the third row with his mother watching a scene from "The Mousetrap", just before the curtain came down for the half-time interval.

The train gathered speed as it pitched and rolled across London Bridge, clattering down the tracks, and Hetty Rose Perkins, who sat opposite her son, was deeply engrossed in reading a newspaper, "The Evening Trumpet," holding it open with both hands as she read an item on the woman's page. Across the front page was the shocking banner headline: "ITALIAN DIPLOMAT COMMITS SUICIDE." Ronald Perkins read the headline from where he sat with a satisfied smirk on his face – it was yet another perfect murder to add to his impressive list. And he estimated he had made enough money from killing Giovanni Congiu to buy a sixty-foot motorboat. He had dreamed for years of owning such a sea-going boat, which could sleep up to six people, with toilet, shower, and galley. It would be moored in the harbour of Cape Croisette in the South of France, a sunny holiday paradise, where he would also buy a little holiday villa on the hillside overlooking the sea. But the purchase of the motorboat would have to wait until after the New Year, because three days before he and his mother had left for their trip to London, contact had been made to the box number of the up-market woman's magazine in which he was advertising his specialist "Removal business", in the personal columns section on the back pages. The initial contact was a letter from the client sent to the box number at the magazine's offices. The letter contained the client's phone number. Communication between killer and client would be telephone calls to the client's number. Face to face meetings would occur only for the client to hand over money, half the agreed sum before the deed was committed, and the second half on completion. The meetings would take place in a pub of Ronald Perkins's choice. The murder contract had been too tempting for him to refuse.

Ronald Perkins had already murdered twice in less than six months. There was the old thespian knight of the British theatre Sir Rupert Slattery, bashed over the head with a claw hammer to make it look as if he had fallen on his head through the stage trap door. And less than eighteen hours earlier, the lusty young Italian diplomat Giovanni Congui was pushed in front of a tube train without a return ticket. Ronald Perkins did not like to do three murders in one year, believing that for him the number three was unlucky. But he had agreed to take on the contract because the person to be murdered was definitely going to be the biggest challenge of his serial-killing career. The murder victim was to be the British Prime Minister, who was surrounded night and day by hand-picked security men recruited from the SAS, MI5 and MI6. To murder the Prime Minister would surely take all his brilliance and super intellect. It was a challenge he just could not refuse.

"I've got to go away for a week on business next month, mother," he said in a matter-of-fact voice as he lit up a large Havana cigar with a gold cigarette lighter.

Hetty Rose Perkins frowned, and glanced at her son over the top of her newspaper. The years had not been kind to her, and she had turned into a dried-up, mean, selfish, embittered old lady whose life focused on her son. He was the sun and the moon of her universe.

"You're not leaving me alone with Angela again are you? Whenever you go off on one of your jaunts, Ronnie, I have to stay behind and put up with her silly endless chatter. That girl could talk for England and bore the hind legs off a donkey without even trying."

Ronald took a puff of the cigar and blew out a cloud of smoke. He nodded his head, chuckled quietly and said, "Angie's all right, mother, it's just that you don't understand her."

"Oh, but I do understand the little gold-digging madam. She's money mad. Money is all she thinks about. She'll take you for every penny, just you mark my words."

"Angie has her good points, mother."

"Well, I've never seen them – she can't cook, sew, or do housework. I just don't understand what you see in her. What is she good for?"

Ronald Perkins smiled knowingly. Angela Cobblers was a genius in bed, which made her worth every penny he gave her. She was also very decorative and highly desirable, making other men envious when they saw her on his arm. With her as his live-in girlfriend he felt like the cat with the cream.

Hetty Rose Perkins scowled. "I don't like the girl – always walking around the house in skimpy clothes showing off her bits and pieces."

"Well, she likes you, mother. "I really wish the two of you would get on together."

"And pigs can fly."

The carriage door slid open and a fat red-faced man with a bristling grey handlebar moustache stood at the threshold looking in. He was wearing a smart navy blue blazer with glittering brass buttons. There was a Royal Air Force Association badge on the breast pocket. He wore a trilby hat and white trousers with creases that could cut bread. Wing Commander Hughie Lampton retired, widower, pompous, self-opinionated, was on his way back home after spending the day at the Oval cricket ground, watching England take a sound beating from Australia. The Ashes had been lost, and the Wing Commander was not in a good mood; in fact he was in a foul mood. He carefully studied the two occupants of the carriage unsure whether to enter or not. There were such ill-bred loutish people on the loose in England these days. When he was a boy people could leave their houses unlocked when they went out.

But not now; thieves would take anything not nailed down. The couple in the first-class compartment were a rum-looking pair, and to his surprise he noticed the man, who was well dressed in a pale blue three-piece suit, was wearing elevated black shoes. The extra inches of the high heels were a dead give-away. This was a small man ashamed of his real height. Could he have other personality disorders? Was he the sort of man who wrote filthy graffiti on walls? What was England coming too? In recent years it had gone to the dogs. What was needed was a firm hand, and to hang people for all criminal offences except illegal parking, which he regularly committed himself. There was a red no-smoking sign on the window of the sliding door.

With a snort of anger, his jowls wobbling like jelly, the Wing Commander spotted the Havana cigar. How he hated smoking. Such a filthy and disgusting habit. Anti-smoking was his pet campaign – his ideal to stop all smokers from ruining other people's travelling or leisure experiences with their foul self-abuse. Who but somebody of very limited intelligence, would put leaves rolled up in a piece of paper between their lips, then light it, and inhale the smoke? And why did he always find a smoker sitting near him in a restaurant, theatre, or on a bus or train? And like now, in this small, enclosed area of a railway compartment? What a ghastly lot smokers were inflicting their filthy habit on others. But the Wing Commander had purchased a first class ticket, and this was the only first class compartment on the corridor train with empty seats. It was either stand for the rest of his journey in the cold corridor, or take one of the vacant seats in this compartment. And so, with an angry scowl, the ill-tempered Wing Commander entered the compartment and sat down next to Hetty Rose Perkins. Being a gentleman, he politely raised his hat.

"Madam," he said softly. Good manners make the gentleman he always thought. He turned to Ronald Perkins and gave him the filthiest look he could muster. "Sir, do you mind?" he asked loudly.

"Pardon?"

"The cigar, sir."

Ronald Perkins took out his silver cigar case with his initials embossed in gold on the side, opened it with a flourish, and offered a cigar to the Wing Commander.

"Would you like one?" he asked. "They're Havana. Best money can buy."

"No, sir, I most definitely would not like one, and I do not like you having one. This is a non-smoking compartment. Can't you read the notice on the door?"

Ronald Perkins shrugged his shoulders and made no reply. He had not noticed the no-smoking sign, but it would have made no difference if he had, for nothing was going to make him give up the pleasure of his one daily cigar after he had lit up. He had been looking forward to the cigar all day. His Doctor at his last medical check-up, after listening to his wheezing chest, had strongly advised that he should in future only smoke one cigar a day and not his usual six.

The Wing Commander glared fiercely at him, then coughed as if the cigar smoke was affecting him.

Ronald Perkins took no notice and continued to puff contentedly away on his cigar. A good cigar was like a good woman, to be enjoyed at one's leisure, making it last as long as possible.

The Wing Commander coughed again.

There was still no response from Ronald Perkins, who blew a small billowing cloud of blue smoke slowly above his head.

The Wing Commander coughed again – this time a long spluttering gasping cough so there could be no mistaking his repulsion to the cigar smoke.

"Someone needs cough syrup," chuckled Ronald Perkins winking at his mother, who not wanting to get herself involved was pretending to read her newspaper.

The Wing Commander's face turned purple with rage. He coughed a third time, a huge racking cough that echoed around the small confinement of the railway apartment.

"What do your stars say today, mother?" asked Ronald Perkins, deliberately taking no notice of the coughing Wing Commander. "Will you meet a tall dark stranger who will sweep you off your feet?"

"Sir, I find your cigar most offensive."

"And I find your tone most offensive."

"Are you going to put out your cigar, sir?"

"Not until I've finished it."

"I'm Wing Commander Hughie Lampton, sir. Will you do me the courtesy and good manners of informing me to whom I am speaking?"

"I'm the man who's smoking a cigar and enjoying it."

"Give me your name, blast you. I demand to know your name, you impertinent fellow."

"Just call me Smokey Cigar."

The Wing Commander leapt furiously to his feet. His eyes almost popping out of his head with rage. "I flew Spitfires against the Hun during the war, Sir," he thundered, the veins sticking out on his forehead. "And I'll have you know that you're dealing with the type of man who's not afraid to stand up and be counted when his country needs him."

"Sit down you're making a fool of yourself."

"How dare you."

"Sit down, you old windbag."

"You're nothing but a rude-mannered, cigar-smoking lout. And you wouldn't have lasted two minutes flying Spitfires. They needed real men to be pilots in those days, not ill-mannered cigar smoking midgets in elevated shoes."

Ronald Perkins had never been so angry. Leaping to his feet he thrust his face within inches of the Wing Commander's crimson face, inhaled deeply on his cigar, and blew a cloud of smoke slowly into the Wing Commander's face.

"How dare you, sir," spluttered the Wing Commander, coughing this time for real. "What boorish loutish behaviour. If you had been under my command in the RAF you'd have known it. I'd have had you in the guardhouse in double-quick time. Your feet would not have touched the ground."

"Oh, shut up, you silly old fool."

"Silly old fool is it – well, let me tell you I know karate."

"Oh, really, and where do they live... next door?"

"You're asking for a lesson in fisticuffs, sir."

"Don't tell me you've been a boxer?"

"I was champion three years running at Winchester."

"Really – and what did you box, oranges or lemons?"

The Wing Commander glared, his moustache bristled and his top lip trembled with rage. "Lout," he declared furiously, his eyes sticking out like organ stops. "You ought to be locked up and the key thrown away."

"All right, let's take this out in the corridor."

The Wing Commander's face suddenly turned as white as chalk. He realised his bluff had been called. People mostly backed down when he bullied them. "Would you hit an old man who was wearing spectacles?" he asked nervously.

Ronald Perkins shook his head. "Of course not."

The Wing Commander promptly took out a pair of horn-rimmed spectacles from his blazer breast pocket and put them on. "If I wasn't wearing glasses," he declared hotly, "Then I'd give you a thrashing you'd never forget."

"Come on then – try it."

"I'll accept an apology."

"Sit down and shut up."

"I'll report you to the guard."

"Oh, for God's sake, it's only a cigar!"

"That was Hitler's attitude before he invaded Poland."

"Sit down, you pompous old fool."

The Wing Commander quivered with fury. "I'm going to report you," he exclaimed as he slid open the compartment door and stepped out into the corridor. "We'll see what the guard has to say about people who smoke in a non-smoking compartment. You'll end up in court without a doubt." He walked quickly away down the corridor towards the guard's van at the rear of the train.

"Oh, Ronnie," cried Hetty Rose Perkins, "what have you done now?"

"It's all right, mother, I'll sort it out." Ronald Perkins moved swiftly after the Wing Commander following him down the corridor of the pitching rolling train. The last thing he wanted was for his name and address to be taken by the guard. And what if the guard was not satisfied with his explanation and called the police, and they found the suitcase full of money on the luggage rack? How could he explain it? Then the police might want to visit his house to search it, and they might find his secret notebooks detailing the plans for the murders that he had committed over the years. Seething with fury, and not thinking clearly in his anger, he quickened his pace to catch the Wing

97

Commander before he reached the guard's van. Clenching his cigar tightly in his teeth, he grabbed for the startled Wing Commander from behind in a stranglehold.

"Aaaaaaah," screamed the terrified Wing Commander. The pressure on his windpipe quickly muffled the scream, and choking and struggling for breath, he was manhandled to the nearest door.

"Out with you, bloody old windbag," hissed Ronald Perkins as he flung open the door. "It's goodbye for you."

"What are you doing?" cried the terrified Wing Commander. "Are you trying to kill me?"

"Not trying – I really have killed you," retorted Ronald Perkins as he pushed the Wing Commander out the door. "Sorry but you've got to go."

"Noooooooo," screamed the Wing Commander as he made a desperate grab to catch hold of Ronald Perkins to save himself from falling, but caught hold of the cigar instead. And with the cigar stub clutched tightly in his hand, he fell away into the darkness, bounced head first down a steep railway embankment and halfway across a ploughed field. Ronald Perkins closed the door. He was sweating and breathing heavily. He had murdered in white-hot fury. It was a big mistake. Now in the calm after the frenzy of the killing storm, he regretted the murder. He had murdered the Wing Commander because he had not controlled the great surge of anger which had swept over him like a tidal wave, engulfing his reason and intellect. He waited a few minutes to regain his composure, then walked back to rejoin his mother. He felt ashamed of his lack of control, and vowed that he would never again commit murder in a white-hot fury, but only in cold blood, calm and patient, with every detail carefully planned beforehand.

"What's happened to the Wing Commander?" asked his mother as he entered the compartment and sat down. "Has he reported you?"

"No, mother, we came to an amicable agreement. I apologised to him. He even ended up having one of my Havana cigars."

"You apologised, Ronnie, oh, but I'm so pleased. Will the Wing Commander be coming back here to join us?"

Ronald Perkins shook his head and smiled faintly. "No, Mother, he's found another compartment further up the train."

"And he's quite happy there?"

"But of course, mother, I even opened the door for him. I think he was really sorry when I said goodbye to him."

Chapter Seven

The body of Wing Commander Hughie Lampton was found early next morning by farm worker Clive Mitchell, who mistook it for a scarecrow. The body, in rigor mortis, was stiff as a board, clothes and face smothered with mud, a light frost covering it from head to toe. Mitchell, already late for milking, propped the late Wing Commander into a standing position, then set off across the field to the cowsheds. It was not until two days later that farmer John Dale saw the scarecrow, and called the police. John Dale had gone to the field on his tractor to finish some ploughing, and was astonished to see a scarecrow standing in the field. He had not put a scarecrow in that particular field. "Bugger me silly, but if it isn't the ugliest scarecrow I've ever seen in all me life," he thought as he climbed down from the tractor. It was then, as he stood gazing upon the late Wing Commander and with a sudden wind change, that he caught the repulsive overwhelming smell, which reminded him of badly rotting meat. He took a step towards the scarecrow and prodded it gingerly with his right index finger. The head fell slightly forward exposing the dead staring eyes of the late Wing Commander.

"Oh, my God," gasped the farmer feeling sick with horror, "It's a body."

Detective Chief Inspector Edgar Briggs of the Metropolitan CID walked from his police car across a ploughed field. His new Sergeant, Jenny Hopper, accompanied him. They were both wearing light grey mackintoshes and wellington boots. Jenny Hopper was a high flier in the police force, marked for rapid promotion to the highest possible command. She was Welsh with no love of leeks, slim, blonde, and extremely beautiful, so beautiful indeed that she could easily have got a job as a top fashion model or been a Hollywood starlet. Twenty-four years

100

old, a university graduate, with three first class degrees in World History, Psychology and English Literature, she was the brightest rising star in the Metropolitan police. Jenny Hopper, keen as mustard and sharp as a needle, was top of her class at Hendon Police Training College, passing out with the highest honours, and a box of chocolates and an indecent suggestion from an instructor. And in less than six months service in the traffic division, she had been promoted to the rank of Sergeant.

Jenny Hopper kept her hair close-cropped like a man, wanting to look as much like a man as possible in a man's world, feeling it would benefit her police career and open doors for rapid promotion. However, she still looked incredibly feminine and amazingly desirable, and the only difference the close-cropped hairstyle made was to attract butch, hairy-faced lesbians as well as rampant men like moths to a flame. She was a honeypot of sexual desire, other people's desire. Jenny Hopper was not interested in sex, although she fancied men. Her career came before any boyfriend, husband and children.

"There's time for all that sort of thing when I'm a senior officer," she would tell her parents when they asked her to bring a boyfriend home to tea. She was transferred to CID for work experience. Her new boss was Detective Chief Inspector Edgar Briggs, who had been promoted only because of typing errors. He believed himself to be a great detective with a focused mind, like a laser beam for solving crime, although in reality he was an incredibly stupid person with a major talent for making cock-ups. The success rate of his department over the years was due to a brilliant team of junior officers who listened to him and then did the opposite of what he told them.

"Now, Sergeant," he told Jenny Hopper, as they walked across the ploughed field towards a small group of people standing around a green tarpaulin spread out on the ground, "you've been sent to me to be trained up in the art of detection. So I want you to think of yourself, from now on, as a pliable piece of plasticine, any colour you want, but warm and ready for me to shape and mould. Do you understand?"

Jenny Hopper glanced at her superior officer with a faintly bemused look. She had heard stories of how stupid and grossly incompetent he was before joining CID, but had not wanted to believe them, wanting to form her own opinions of the man in action.

"I've a wise old head on my shoulders," continued the Chief Inspector, "and although I shouldn't say it myself, I'm the best detective in the force. So just you listen and learn from me, and you won't go far wrong. Now tell me, Sergeant, what do you need to be a police officer?"

"Flat feet, sir?"

"No, Sergeant, it's a nose."

"What? Like my Uncle Stanley, sir?"

"Your Uncle Stanley?"

"Yes, sir, his nose is so big it enters a room two seconds before the rest of him."

"No, Sergeant, not like your Uncle Stanley's nose. I was thinking of an experienced copper's nose, a reliable nose for crime busting, and a police officer's best tool for sniffing out clues and tracking down criminals. I'm an old fashioned cop with such a nose myself. And I want you to have a nose just like mine before you leave us. Now what do you say to that?"

Jenny Hopper smiled sweetly, thinking the stories about the Chief Inspector were obviously true. He was indeed a very stupid man.

"Thank you, sir," she said stifling a giggle by pretending to blow her nose in her handkerchief. "It's very good of you to take the trouble."

"It's no trouble to teach a keen young police officer how to have a good nose, Sergeant. You'll thank me for it one day."

"Yes, sir."

Police pathologist Professor Arthur Dean, forty-three years old, divorced with two grown-up daughters, dressed in a white plastic zip-up jump suit used for examining bodies at the scene of death, sighed audibly when he saw Chief Inspector Edgar Briggs approaching across the ploughed field.

"Oh, God, it would have to be him," he thought miserably. "The bloody man's a menace like a bull set loose in a china shop." Nearby, under a green tarpaulin lay the mortal remains of Commander Hughie Lampton. Professor Dean had just finished carrying out a quick preliminary examination to determine a cause of death.

"Morning, Professor," called the Chief Inspector jovially. "Nice day isn't it."

"I thought it was, Chief Inspector," replied the Professor sourly.

"Well, what have we got?"

The Professor nodded towards the tarpaulin. "There's a man over there," he replied as he removed his rubber surgical gloves. "I see you've got your wellington boots on the wrong feet again, Chief Inspector!"

"Sergeant," called the Chief Inspector going red with embarrassment, "Let me lean against you while I change my boots around."

"Yes, sir."

After changing his boots to the correct feet, Chief Inspector Edgar Briggs walked slowly over to the corpse, bent down and pulled aside the tarpaulin. There was a long thoughtful pause before he looked up at Professor Dean and asked, "Dead?"

"But of course he's dead, Chief Inspector," snapped Professor Dean impatiently. "Why else would he be lying out here in the middle of a field, stiff as a plank of wood, cold as ice with his flesh in a state of decay?"

"Yes, I had noticed the awful repellent smell. Reminds me of the mother-in-law on a hot day. Have you examined the body, Professor?"

"Yes, but I'll still need to give it a full post-mortem examination back at the mortuary. I can tell you the deceased is male, white and about sixty years of age. He is a member of the Royal Air Force Association, drives a Bentley, is a non-smoker, and likes to watch cricket."

"My God but that's amazing. How do you know all this, Professor?"

"Because I found a wallet in his pocket containing a driving licence, his car insurance certificate, ticket for the Oval cricket ground, a lifetime membership card for The British Anti-Smoking League, and he's wearing a blazer with a Royal Air Force Association badge on the breast pocket."

"Cause of death? Was it a natural death?"

"Natural death? I very much doubt it, Chief Inspector. He

obviously fell from a train and bounced down the railway embankment. There are indents in the soft mud where he bounced along to reach here. Death, I would say at this point, was caused by head injuries and a broken neck."

"It couldn't have been a heart attack?"

"Didn't you see the extent of the head injuries when you saw the body just now, Chief Inspector? The man must have bounced here striking his head."

"I did – but I must look at every possibility, Professor, that's my job. If a serious crime has been committed here then the person responsible must be caught and punished for it. But are you sure it wasn't a road accident?"

"What? Out here in the middle of a field?"

"Might it be suicide then?"

"It's possible – if he jumped deliberately from a train."

"So what are the facts so far?" said the Chief Inspector thoughtfully, hoping to impress his beautiful young Sergeant. "We have a dead man. And we know he came off a train, and that he drove a Bentley and likes cricket."

"And doesn't like smokers," added the Sergeant.

"What makes you say that, Sergeant?"

"The membership card for the British Anti-Smokers League found in the dead man's wallet, sir."

"Quite so, Sergeant, I was about to mention that myself."

"Yes, sir."

"I suggest we don't inform the deceased's family, Sergeant," said the Chief Inspector in a whisper, so he could not be overheard by the other police officers standing around the body, "that he was a scarecrow in a field for two days after his death. It would only distress them. What do you think?"

"What an idiot," muttered Professor Dean under his breath.

"May I look at the deceased, sir?" asked the Sergeant.

"Yes, Sergeant, but I suggest you stand upwind."

Jenny Hopper went over to the corpse, pulled away the tarpaulin uncovering the Wing Commander from the waist up. After a few minutes, she bent down and began to force open the rigor mortised fingers of the Wing Commander's right hand, which were clenched tightly in a fist.

"Stop hand wrestling the deceased, for God's sake, woman,"

shouted the Chief Inspector, rushing over and pulling the Sergeant away from the corpse.

"This isn't happening," muttered the Professor looking deeply shocked.

"What would the deceased's family say if they saw you, Sergeant?" asked the Chief Inspector stepping between the corpse and Jenny Hopper to prevent her from grappling with it again. "They'd sue both you and the police for sure. And anyway it's cheating if your opponent's dead and can't wrestle you back."

"But I wasn't wrestling the deceased, sir," replied the Sergeant. She triumphantly held up a two-inch-long Havana cigar butt. "I found this clenched in the dead man's hand, sir. It's a vital clue."

"What does it mean, Sergeant?"

"That a man who's a non-smoker doesn't commit suicide with a cigar butt clenched in his hand, sir."

"And that means..."

"Yes, sir," interrupted the Sergeant excitedly, "This man was murdered."

"Murder?" gasped the Chief Inspector.

"It's when a life is taken away forcibly by a second party," explained the Professor impatiently.

"I know what murder is, Professor," retorted the Chief Inspector indignantly. "I'm a Chief Inspector in the CID, aren't I? Murder and catching murderers is my daily bread and butter. I wasn't asking what murder is... I was merely agreeing with my Sergeant's assessment of the facts regarding the cigar butt. But I still must ask myself, is this really murder?"

"Definitely this is murder, Chief Inspector."

"Sergeant, give me the cigar butt," said the Chief Inspector holding out his hand to the Sergeant.

Jenny Hopper put the cigar butt in the Chief Inspector's hand.

He put it to his nose and sniffed it. "Now, Sergeant, remember what I told you about an experienced copper's nose?"

Jenny Hopper nodded.

"Well, I can tell you that this is a Havana cigar..."

"It says so on the cigar band," interrupted the Professor with a scowl.

"And it was rolled in Cuba on a woman's naked thighs..."

"Everybody knows that about Havana cigars," snapped the Professor impatiently. "Tell us something we don't know!"

"Well, it's the best cigar money can buy, Professor," replied the Chief Inspector as he put the cigar butt into his coat pocket. "I'll smoke it later."

"But you can't do that, sir," cried the Sergeant.

"It's all right, Sergeant, I don't mind smoking someone else's thrown-away cigar butt, especially if it's a Havana."

"But it's evidence in a murder case, Chief Inspector," declared the Professor stoically, "and mustn't be smoked by anyone."

"Forensics must examine it, sir," said the Sergeant. "There might be DNA on it. The last person who smoked it might be the person responsible for this man's death."

The Chief Inspector reluctantly took the cigar butt from his pocket and handed it back to the Sergeant. "Pop it in an evidence bag, Sergeant."

"Yes, sir."

Early the next morning, Sergeant Jenny Hopper sat in her boss's office at Scotland Yard, awaiting his arrival at work. She had arrived while it was still dark outside without having her usual breakfast of cornflakes and cold milk. She believed cornflakes kept her bowels regular. The Sergeant wanted to impress the Chief Inspector with her eager-beaver style of police work, and so had come to work extra early to show she was keen as mustard to work with CID. After waiting for over an hour twiddling her thumbs and counting flowers on the floral pattern wallpaper, she found herself becoming increasingly bored. After reading the wanted notices pinned to the notice board on the wall, she decided to try and relieve the boredom by reading a file laying on the Chief Inspector's desk. On the cover of the red file was printed "The Barnes Railway Bridge Murders." It made riveting reading for the young policewoman. The murder of black railway employee Barry Coles and white River Thames policeman Robert McDougal, was clearly a black and white case. The murders had occurred over twenty years earlier, and they intrigued and challenged her. There was one very similar aspect to the Barnes Railway Bridge Murders, and CID's most recent case, the man found in a ploughed field with a cigar butt in his hand. Railway employee Barry Coles was found with a fake theatrical Adolf Hitler style ginger moustache, clenched tightly in his right hand. Could it be too much of a coincidence? Both men clutching a vital murder clue in their dead right hand? Was there a link between the murders? The cigar butt had already been sent to Forensics for exhaustive tests. But what about the fake theatrical Adolf-Hitler style moustache? Perhaps laboratory tests would reveal DNA evidence taken from the spirit gum used to attach it to the face that had last worn it. There must be human skin cells still attached to the dried spirit gum on the moustache. Jenny Hopper picked up the phone, a determined look on her face.

"Give me the department where evidence is stored," she told the female police switchboard operator.

"Stored? Do you mean the canteen stores?" asked the operator. "Is there another out-break of food poisoning? I thought the shepherd's pie yesterday was a bit duff."

"No, there's nothing wrong with the shepherd's pie."

"Well, I am surprised."

"I want the department in Scotland Yard where criminal evidence of on-going investigations is stored."

"Putting you through."

All the evidence collected at the time of the Barnes Railway Bridge Murders, including the holdall, grey head-sized stone, blood samples, fingerprints and fake theatrical Adolf Hitler-style ginger moustache, were still safely stored away in the vaults of Scotland Yard, kept in a large cardboard box. Jenny Hopper asked for the blood samples and fake theatrical Adolf Hitler-style ginger moustache to be sent immediately to Forensics for DNA testing. She had just put the phone down when it rang. Picking it up she said brightly, "CID, Sergeant Jenny Hopper speaking."

"Professor Dean here, Sergeant, I'm at the mortuary doing a post mortem."

"Yes, Professor. How can I help you?"

"Well, I'm calling about your Chief Inspector."

An icy shiver of apprehension ran up and down the Sergeant's spine. Could this explain why he was late for work this morning?

"Oh, not the Chief Inspector," she gasped, horror-stricken. "Don't say you're doing a post mortem on him." She thought her boss must have been killed somehow, possibly on his way to Scotland Yard, and was now laying stretched out like a piece of cod fillet on Professor Dean's mortuary table. "I was wondering why he was so late coming in this morning."

"The Chief Inspector's isn't dead."

"He isn't?"

"No, Sergeant, he's only fainted. That's why I'm calling you… to ask if you'll come over right away and collect him."

"He fainted?"

"Yes, he came to the mortuary to observe my post mortem on the body found yesterday morning."

"Body?"

"With the cigar butt in his hand."

"Oh, yes. And the gory sight was too much for the Chief Inspector?"

"No, Sergeant, it wasn't that – a mouse ran across the changing room floor and he went out like a light."

"I'll be right over, Professor."

"Sergeant Hopper, may I ask you something off the record?"

"But of course, Professor."

"Well, I'm a man and you're a woman, isn't that so?"

"Yes, I had noticed, Professor."

"Well, I was wondering if you would have dinner with me sometime?"

"I never mix work with pleasure, Professor."

"We could talk about pathology in police work if you like. It could be a learning experience for you. I could book a candlelight dinner for two at my favourite Italian restaurant. What do you say?"

"I'll think about it."

"Please call me Arthur."

"Arthur."

"Jenny."

"We might have an identity for the body on your mortuary slab, Arthur. There's a missing person report that came in this morning from Crawley Police, which seems to match him exactly. But we'll need a member of his family to make an identification to be absolutely certain."

Nine days later, the Master of Foxhounds at Bumstead on the Wold, Colonel Ivor Biggan, was out in the late afternoon on a Friday, exercising his stallion Big Boy, riding along the edge of Grime-Dyke woods. The Colonel had just galloped Big Boy for half a mile, and was now walking him before setting off back home at the trot. Something caught the Colonel's eye, a movement among the grass some fifty yards away under a spreading oak tree. It was too far away and too low on the ground to been seen clearly, but it looked remarkably like a man lying flat on his stomach with his bottom raised slightly in the air.

"Wehey, there boy," called the Colonel, reining in the horse. "Now what have we here? Could it be some damn poacher setting a trap for rabbits? Well, if it is then he's in for a big surprise." He dismounted, and moved quietly forward leading the horse by the reins. When he was within twenty-five yards he recognised the bottom, which to his astonishment was naked, as belonging to the new curate, Peter Catchpole. The curate in the missionary position was furiously engaged in strenuous sexual intercourse with cassock drawn up above the waist, trousers and underpants around the ankles, and his naked white buttocks rising and falling like a steam hammer... between the open thighs of Angela Cobblers. The steamy couple, lost in the wild ecstasy of the moment, were making loud gasps and cries of mutual rapture, and were totally lost to anything else happening around them. For them both, there was only the sweet joy and increasing pleasure spreading throughout their heaving sweating bodies from their interacting genitals, as they thrust and bucked in perfect harmony together. Nothing else existed in the world for them at that wondrous thrilling moment but the need to experience orgasm. The Colonel watched for a few moments, envious and feeling his age, then he turned and led Big Boy away.

"My God," he thought gleefully, "This is going to put the cat among the pigeons and no mistake." He mounted the horse and rode quickly home to tell his wife Gloria what he had seen. "You should have seen the new curate," he told her excitedly, "There he was firmly in Angela Cobblers's saddle... riding her for all he was worth."

"But are you quite sure it was the curate, dear?"

"Must have been, old thing. Who else could it have been? He was wearing a cassock and dog collar – and the buttocks were too skinny to have been the overweight vicar's."

"All right then, as long as you're quite sure. I don't want to name the wrong clergyman when I write my anonymous letter to the Bishop."

"And what about Ronald Perkins, dear? Shouldn't he have a letter too? It's about time he was bought down a peg or two, lording it over the golf club with all his money, treating everyone to drinks in the bar. It should have been me who was elected golf club captain and not him, the pretentious bastard."

"But of course I won't forget him, dear. Ronald Perkins has a right to know what his partner Angela Cobblers has been getting up to."

"Or who has been getting up her... what, what, old thing?"

They both laughed heartily.

The late Wing Commander Hughie Lampton's body was identified by his elder sister, Mrs Annie Quemby, who travelled down from Edinburgh with her husband Jock, a haggis wholesaler. After viewing the body laid out in the mortuary's chapel of rest, in the presence of Professor Arthur Dean and Sergeant Jean Hopper, Mrs Quemby had quietly observed with some pride.

"He looks better dead than he did when he was alive. Do you think we could have a photograph of him laid out like this for the family album?"

"I'll ask the undertaker Mister Beesley," replied Professor Dean sympathetically. "I'm sure he won't mind taking a snap for you before the coffin is screwed down."

"Oh, thank you, that's most kind," muttered tearful Mrs Quemby dabbing her eyes with a handkerchief. "My poor unfortunate brother was always unlucky. He was once told by a gypsy woman fortune teller at a fair, that he was soon going to die... and now, fifty-three years later, it has come startlingly true."

"Spooky isn't it?" muttered her husband with a fearful look. He believed in ghosts and the supernatural, and did not want to remain in the presence of a dead body longer than was necessary. He had never liked his brother-in-law and his brother-in-law had never liked him, and he was now ready to believe that the late Wing Commander would do something really unpleasant from the other world to upset him.

"Death comes knocking for us all at some time or another," said Mrs Quemby sadly, "coming like a sly thief to steal us away forever. It'll soon be my time to pack up my bags for the last great journey into the unknown. Oh, and that reminds me, Jock, when I do go, don't you go having me cremated. I've an awful fear of the all-consuming fire which leaves nothing but ashes."

"Are you drunk?" demanded her husband, eyeing her suspiciously.

"Only with grief," responded Mrs Quemby, dabbing her eyes.

"Grief my eye, woman, you've been at the bottle again," declared her husband. "Didn't the Doctor warn you about your drinking? Your liver must look like a brewery."

"Well, at least I don't have to be carried home on Saturday nights from the pub," retorted Mrs Quemby glaring fiercely at her husband.

"There you go, woman, embroidering the truth again," replied her husband.

"Has you memory gone with the booze? It's you they carry home, not me."

"FLUUUMPH!" Suddenly there was the sound of a loud raspberry-like fart, a clarion-call of a fart. Mrs Quemby, startled, going ashen and fearful she would be blamed, turned on her husband and cried, "Go outside and shake yourself, Jock. Whatever will Professor Dean and the Sergeant think?"

"But it wasn't me, woman," declared her husband defiantly. "I only fart when I've had a curry."

Mister and Mrs Quemby stared suspiciously at Professor

Dean, who turned bright red and shook his head.

"Oh, no," he insisted taking a faltering step backwards, "It most certainly wasn't me."

"FLUUUMPH!" The rip-snorting sound of a second fart boomed forth. All eyes promptly turned to Sergeant Jenny Hopper.

"I didn't do it," she cried. "Don't all look at me as if I'm the guilty one. It wasn't me trumpeting. I eat plenty of cornflakes for breakfast to keep myself regular, so I won't embarrass myself in public."

The others looked at the Sergeant as if they did not believe her.

"FLUUUMPH!" There came a third rattling fart.

"Don't panic," cried Professor Dean pointing at the late Wing Commander Hughie Lampton. "It's coming from the corpse."

"What? A dead man farting!" exclaimed Jock Quemby with a look of sheer terror on his face. He was now convinced his dead brother-in-law was making ghostly farts from the spirit world, and was doing it especially to upset him personally.

"Dead bodies often expel wind from their bowels after death," explained the Professor in a calm voice. "The undertaker must have forgotten to insert a cork stopper."

"My brother certainly can fart can't he?" smiled Mrs Quemby proudly. She was greatly relieved that the culprit had been found and she was no longer a suspect. "Hughie, even as a boy," she said, "could produce a real rip-snorter. He suffered badly with flatulence most of his life."

"Must have been hell for other pilots flying with him during the war," retorted her husband coldly. "Isn't that why he was transferred from Wellington bombers to single-seater Spitfires? So he wouldn't have to share the cockpit?"

"Oh, for goodness sake, Jock, do try and show some respect for Hughie now he's dead," snapped Mrs Quemby angrily.

"Well, what I'd like to know is how much money he's left us," said her husband, eyeing the body with a disdainful look. "He's probably left it all to a cat's home, the tight old sod."

"Please, Jock, not in front of the body," replied Mrs Quemby quietly. "Let's have some dignity if you don't mind."

"Well, I'm off to the nearest pub for a few pints," cried Jock Quemby making a run for the chapel door. "There's still five hours left before closing."

"Wait I'll come with you Jock," cried his wife running after him.

Chapter Eight

The Metropolitan Police launched a nation-wide murder investigation to hunt down the murderer of Wing Commander Hughie Lampton. The investigation was given the name "The Cigar Butt Murder", and Chief Inspector Edgar Briggs was put in charge. It took ten days for Forensics to complete the DNA tests carried out on the various items of evidence, sent to the laboratory by Sergeant Jenny Hopper. Chief Inspector Edgar Briggs sat at his desk drinking coffee as he studied the Forensic report, which had been handed to him by Sergeant Jenny Hopper.

"As you can see, sir, there's a definite link," she said confidently, pleased her hunch about DNA had been right. "Between the Barnes Railway Bridge Murders and the Cigar Butt Murder. Forensics report that DNA found on the false theatrical Adolf Hitler-style ginger moustache match exactly with DNA found on the cigar butt. This means the moustache was worn, and the cigar smoked, by the same man. And although there was a twenty-year interval between the Barnes Bridge murders and the ploughed field murder, the DNA evidence has established the same killer committed both murders."

"Brilliant police work, Sergeant, well done."

"Thank you, sir."

The Right Reverend Christopher Ashley, Bishop of the diocese of Wentworth, sat at his desk reading again the letter which had been sent to him anonymously, denouncing one of his priests as a sexual pervert. The Church of England Bishop was a leading theologian, an intellectual, and a dedicated member of the Conservative Party, selected by the Conservative Prime Minister to be a Bishop because of his strong interest in politics, and his active support in the media of Conservatism. Like a dancing bear on a chain, he danced to the tune being played by 10 Downing Street, knowing which side of his bread was buttered. He had been promised the archbishopric of Canterbury when it became vacant. The bishop was tall and lean with a grey face. He mostly always smiled, even in bed, which worried his wife, a false sickly smile, used to conceal what he was really thinking. He ran his diocese with the ruthlessness of a newspaper empire magnate. There was a timid knock on the door.

"Enter," called the Bishop brightly.

The door opened and curate Peter Catchpole entered, bleary eyed, face pale and drawn, dressed in a black suit and clerical collar. The suit was dusty and dishevelled and looked as if he had been sleeping in it.

The Bishop stood up. "Ah, Peter, so you're here at last," he said with a sickly smile, shaking the curate's hand warmly.

"Sorry, Bishop, but I didn't know the train was a non stop sleeper to Glasgow until it was too late and I was on board."

"Never mind, Peter, better late than never, I say. Although in your case it's now two days later."

"I shouldn't have tried to hitch-hike back, Bishop."

"But didn't you think that trying to thumb a lift the wrong way down a one way-street wouldn't work, Peter?"

"I did eventually, Bishop, when nothing was going my way."

"Still you're here now, Peter, and that's what counts. Come and sit down and rest yourself, you must be feeling weary after your travels." The Bishop led the way over to two brown leather armchairs in front of a roaring log fire. The Bishop sat down in the larger chair, and gestured to the smaller one with his right hand. Peter Catchpole nervously sat down. The chairs had been so arranged in both size and position that the Bishop was now some eighteen inches higher on his seat than the curate, and could look down upon him to dominate the interview. The curate had no idea why the Bishop had summoned him except that it was for something serious. Howard Peel, his vicar back at Bumstead on the Wold, had taken him aside and had advised him with a smirk, before he set off to the Bishop's palace "I'd glue up my flies if I were you, Peter; the Bishop might accept that as a demonstration of your future good conduct." But what did the vicar mean? And what had his flies to do with the Bishop? It was all a great mystery to him. He had racked his brain to think of what he could have possibly done to warrant the Bishop's most urgent summons, but could come up with nothing at all.

"Well, here you are, Peter," beamed the Bishop, giving the curate a strange inquiring look. "Now is there anything you'd like to tell me?"

"No, Bishop, I can't think of anything."

"Something you want to get off your chest?"

"No, Bishop, nothing."

"Confession is good for the soul, Peter. Are you sure there isn't anything you'd like to tell me? Something which could affect your vocation?"

The curate shook his head. "Not that I can think of, Bishop."

"This isn't easy for me, Peter, but I've got to take the bull by the horns and come straight out with it. I've had a letter." The Bishop bent forward and looked the curate straight in the eyes. "A letter, Peter," he repeated slowly. "What do you say about that?"

"The postman did a good job, Bishop!"

The Bishop sat back in his chair with a look of exasperation on his face. This interview was proving to be far harder than he had imagined. He could not decide if the curate was being very clever or just being very stupid.

"The letter was written anonymously, Peter. Surely you've some thoughts on that?"

The curate thought for a moment then nodded. "The letter writer suffers with a loss of memory, Bishop, and forgot to put a name."

"No, no, Peter, the letter writer knows who he or she is. The letter writer wants to remain anonymous so nobody else will know who he or she is. The envelope had a Bumstead on the Wold postmark, so it's probably somebody in your parish, possibly a member of the congregation. The letter contained a very serious allegation."

"Allegation, Bishop?"

"Of a sexual nature, Peter, concerning yourself and a young lady."

"Oh, dear."

"Does the name Angela Cobblers mean anything to you?"

"She wrote the letter, Bishop?"

"No, didn't I say it was anonymous – now have you anything to tell me? I'm trying to give you the chance to speak up and confess, Peter."

"But I still don't understand, Bishop. Tell you what?"

"About the letter, Peter."

"But I haven't read the letter, Bishop, it was addressed to you."

"I know that – I'm talking about the serious allegations made about you."

"What allegations, Bishop? I don't understand what's going on here."

"So you don't understand, Peter, just like the time you didn't understand in the cathedral vestry after your ordination. When I was disrobing out of my vestments and the Archdeacon told you kiss my Bishop's ring before leaving. He meant the ring on my finger."

"I apologised afterwards, Bishop. I got carried away in the excitement of the moment. It was just as embarrassing for me as it was for you."

"I don't think so, Peter, not in front of all the other ordinands. They were shocked and frightened. But anyway it's over and done with now, and I don't want to rake over old coals. I don't hold a grudge against you, and accept it was a most unfortunate experience for both of us. I've only recounted the story to illustrate how you have a tendency to do foolish things without thinking."

"I do try my best, Bishop."

"I know, Peter. Now what's all this about you and Angela Cobblers? I'm very worried about your relationship with her. Tell me, have you known her in the biblical sense?"

"Biblical sense, Bishop?"

"Doing what Adam and Eve did to have Cain and Abel."

"Eating an apple, Bishop?"

The Bishop sighed and shook his head. "All right, Peter, I

117

can see there's no easy way for me but to come right out with it... so I'm going to ask you man to man. Have you and Angela Cobblers been intimate?"

"Pardon?"

"Have you had intercourse with her?"

"Talking to her you mean?"

"No – sexual intercourse."

Peter Catchpole's jaw dropped. He was astonished the Bishop knew of his affair with Angela Cobblers. But who had written the letter? Who was "Anonymous of Bumstead on the Wold?" Was the poison-pen writer a member of his congregation at St Freda the Ever Ready? And how did he or she know that he and the lovely Angela were lovers? He thought it was a secret, and that nobody else but he and the lusty Angela knew. She was terrified of her partner Ronald Perkins finding out, and of what he might do. "He's got a wicked unbridled temper," she had told him fearfully as they lay naked and exhausted under a tree, "and I dread what he'll do if he ever finds out that we're lovers." The affair had started only a month earlier, when she had invited him round for tea and crumpet. He ended the visit by drinking hardly any tea but having lots of crumpet.

"Well," said the Bishop impatiently, "and what have you got to say for yourself, Peter?"

The curate nodded his head. "It's true, Bishop, Angela Cobblers and I are lovers."

The Bishop was aghast. "I was afraid it would be true, Peter. You do understand how serious this is? You can be unfrocked."

"Not in public, Bishop?"

"No, by myself, and a specially formed Church court. Your licence to preach and administer the sacraments will be revoked, and you will have to hand in your clerical collar."

"Oh, dear, not the clerical collar."

"The lawyers tell me that the Church can be sued by Angela Cobblers's husband. Because you are a priest, Peter, and took advantage of his wife, when you should have been the good shepherd guiding a lost sheep safely back to the fold."

"But she's not married, Bishop."

"Not married – but that's marvellous news, Peter. If she's

not married then adultery has not been committed, you won't have to be unfrocked, and Ronald Perkins can't sue the Church."

"That's good to hear, Bishop, but what about Angela Cobblers?"

"Are you in love with her or in lust?"

"Well, I'm not really sure, Bishop. I'd never been with a woman before Angela Cobblers – and I'm not really sure what my feelings are at this precise moment, except that I think of her most of the time, and especially of the things we did together in private."

"So you were a virgin before you met Angela Cobblers?"

The curate nodded shamefully.

"And would you like to marry her?"

"Only if she'd have me, Bishop."

"And will she have you, Peter?"

"Well, not unless I can make as much money as her partner Ronald Perkins. She enjoys the luxuries of life and spending lots of money."

"Can you give her up, Peter?"

"I don't know, Bishop."

"What about the priesthood – can you give that up?"

"I hope not, Bishop."

"Well, I've thought a lot about this since reading the letter, which made riveting reading I might add. And I've decided that I do not want you to return to your old parish, Peter. I think it best for you to make a clean break with St Freda the Ever Ready. Take time away from Miss Cobblers to think out your future."

"But where will I go and what shall I do, Bishop?"

"I think you need time to reflect quietly and prayerfully on your future, Peter, To consider what you want from life, the importance of your priestly vocation. I suggest you go on retreat for a month to the convent of the Sisters of Mercy. They're an enclosed religious order. I know the Mother Superior, Sister Rosebud; she's an old dear friend of mine. I'm sure the good sisters will help to sort you out."

"Thank you, Bishop."

"And if, at the end of the retreat, you decide you still have a vocation in the priesthood, then I'll arrange for a new parish for you, well away from St Freda the Ever Ready in Bumstead on the Wold. It'll be a fresh start with exciting challenges. Now what do you say? Shall I arrange the retreat with Sister Rosebud?"

"Yes, thank you, Bishop."

Ronald Perkins opened his anonymous letter as he sat at the breakfast table with his partner Angela Cobblers. He was dressed in white silk pyjamas, red dressing gown and matching slippers. She sat opposite him, noisily sucking orange juice from a glass through a straw. Angela was on a diet to get a few inches off her thighs and buttocks. She wanted to look nice and sexy for the curate. Her dressing gown was open to the waist so she could expose her breasts. She did not want Ronald Perkins to think she was losing interest in him sexually. It was the curate she saw in her mind's eye, naked and rampant beneath the elms, thrusting boldly away. The curate always put Angela's pleasure before his own. And to her astonishment, she found herself falling in love with him. And the more they made love the more she wanted. She was insatiable.

Ronald Perkins began to read the letter. And as he read, his face turned a deathly pale. The letter was far more descriptive and sexually explicit than the one, which had been sent to the Bishop. It was as if a small bomb had exploded inside his head, leaving behind a red angry mist. His knees shook under the table.

"Are you all right?" asked Angela Cobblers with a look of alarm on her lovely face. "I've never seen you looking so ill before, Ronald. Has something disagreed with you?"

"Just a little something I've swallowed, dear," he said, giving a little cough to illustrate the point. "It went down the wrong way I'm afraid." He folded the letter and slipped it away into his dressing gown pocket. He needed time to think. Was his Angela having an affair with the curate as the poison pen letter writer claimed she was? A seething red fury of volcanic hatred towards the curate swelled up within Ronald Perkins, and it was with the greatest difficulty that he managed to remain outwardly calm and collected. If young Peter Catchpole had been getting his leg over with Angela, then the curate must pay the ultimate price for it. Angela Cobblers was his partner, she belonged to him body and soul and had been bought and sold more than a dozen times over with gifts and money. Peter Catchpole would be a marked man without any hope of mercy. Ronald Perkins would arrange the sudden untimely demise of Peter Catchpole. But first he wanted irrefutable proof that the curate had cuckolded him. There was nothing worse than killing the wrong person, especially if there was no financial reward involved. He forced himself to smile at Angela Cobblers.

"That's better, Ronald," she said flashing her breasts at him with a beaming smile. It always brightened him up whenever she flashed her breasts. He enjoyed seeing them, and called them Pinky and Perky.

"I was thinking of attending church on Sunday morning," he said in a matter-of-fact voice. "I'd like to hear the new curate in the pulpit. I've heard he gives a really good belting sermon just like the old Victorian hell-fire preachers."

"Peter does give thrilling sermons," agreed Angela, then quickly adding "or so I've heard." She did not want to show her own interest in the young curate of Bumstead on the Wold.

"You've met him, I believe?"

"He came here on a visit. We had tea and crumpets together."

"That was when I was up in London with my mother for her birthday treat? We had gone to see 'The Mousetrap'?"

"Yes, that's right, Ronnie."

"What a pity I missed him – but I'll make sure I won't miss him the next time... I promise you that."

Howard Peel the hunch-backed vicar of St Freda the Ever Ready swung up and down on the bell rope like a yo-yo, shouting excitedly, "It's the bells, it's the bells." He was calling the faithful of Bumstead on the Wold to Sunday morning family communion service. Jake Turner, verger and gravedigger, a sturdy middle-aged muscular man with protruding eyes, stood ready to launch himself at the vicar's command.

"Now," roared the Vicar.

"Here I comes, Vicar," cried Jake Turner diving forward like a rugby centre to grab the vicar's legs below his knees. Up rose the vicar with the verger firmly clasped to his legs. The two men rose some fifteen feet into the air carried by the bell rope. They rapidly came down towards the stone slab floor. The verger's knees buckled as his feet touched the floor.

"I've landed, Vicar."

The vicar promptly released his hold on the bell rope and fell on top of the verger. The two men sprawled across the floor. The vicar always landed on the verger whenever he rang the church bells, treating him like some old mattress to break his fall.

"Good man, Jake," smiled the Vicar as he dusted himself down." We never let the bell rope beat us do we?"

"No, Vicar," replied the verger, "we're used to its swinging ways."

"Oh, that reminds me, I've been meaning to tell you, Jake, about that funeral on Thursday morning. Can you ask the undertaker for the size of the coffin before you dig the grave? It was three inches too short, and there you were jumping up and down on the coffin lid, shouting 'Get down there, you bugger'. Needless to say the deceased's family were very distressed by your antics. And as for myself, well, I didn't know where to look in my embarrassment.

"Sorry, Vicar, it won't happen again."

"I should think not – you ask for the coffin size before you dig a grave."

"But he was a giant wasn't he, Vicar?"

Howard Peel nodded and laughed. "I want you to be my server this morning during the service. Can you light the altar candles then slip into one of my old surplices?"

"Will the curate be assisting you with communion, Vicar?"

"No, he's left the parish, Jake."

"Left the parish, Vicar? But why? I thought he was settling in nicely. He asked me for some fresh vegetables from my allotment on Friday. I've got a basket in the vestry for him, with a nice big marrow, lettuce, tomatoes, a few King Edwards and some spring onions."

"Pity to waste them, Jake, I'll take them home to the wife."

"Why has the curate gone, Vicar?"

"The Bishop thought it expedient for him to go."

"Oh, so there's a woman involved is there?"

"My lips are sealed – it's all highly confidential."

"Who is she, Vicar? Did the Bishop tell you?"

"I couldn't possibly say, Jake."

Ronald Perkins sat with Angela Cobblers on a front pew. The vicar, who was in full flow, gave his usual long fatuous sermon, taking as his theme "Let he who is without sin cast the first stone". He kept taking furtive glances throughout the sermon at the married women seated before him, hoping to catch one guilty face, so he would know the woman who was involved clandestinely with the curate, but spotted no one to arouse even the smallest glimmer of his suspicions. Ronald Perkins was disappointed at not seeing the curate, having hoped to be introduced to him. When the service was over the vicar stood at the church doors to shake hands as people left to go home. The last couple to leave the church were Ronald Perkins and Angela Cobblers.

"Nice to see some new faces among the congregation this morning," he beamed as he shook Ronald Perkins's hand. "It made my heart rejoice to see you both."

"I was hoping to meet the curate," said Ronald Perkins. "He came to visit me the other week, but I was out up in London with my mother. To see 'The Mousetrap' you know."

"He's gone I'm afraid," said the Vicar sadly.

"Not dead?" gasped Angela Cobblers, a look of great alarm on her face.

"Dead?" responded the Vicar surprised to hear her say that.

With a groan Angela Cobblers collapsed into the arms of Ronald Perkins, who, by her reaction, was almost convinced that the curate had been getting his leg over with Angela. But he still needed proof before he would wreak vengeance on Peter Catchpole.

"But the curate's not dead," cried the Vicar, fanning Angela with his prayer book. "He's just gone away on retreat – to the convent of the Sisters of Mercy."

"Sisters of Mercy," repeated Ronald Perkins slowly. The name was familiar to him. But where had he heard it before? Then he remembered his visit to the convent of the Sisters of Mercy some twenty years earlier, disguised as Vicar Jonathan

Needham. It seems that the Reverend Jonathan Needham might again be visiting the convent... only this time, if he had the irrefutable proof, with a cold murderous intent for a certain young curate on retreat.

.

Chapter Nine

Mrs Brenda Howard, the housekeeper of Allan Hawes at 42B Bakery Street, opened the front door to be confronted by a tall man with a grey goatee beard, black top hat, and long opera cloak and white gaiters. Ronald Perkins in disguise raised his top hat respectfully.

"Good day, madam, is Mister Allan Hawes at home? I've come to seek his help as a private detective."

"He is at home, sir, but I believe he's far too busy working on another case at the moment. You see, he's dealing with a case of major importance – a case of national crisis one might say. I don't know what it but it is all very hush-hush, if you know what I mean."

"But my case would not take Mister Hawes more than a day at the most, madam, and I would pay him well."

"Then follow me, sir. He likes money, does Mister Hawes," said Mrs Howard as she led him down the hallway towards the stairs. She thought it was time to say one of her bright cockney quips. "Do you know what an Ig is, sir?"

"No," replied Ronald Perkins," What's an Ig?"

"It's an Igloo without a loo of course," chuckled Mrs Howard, who enjoyed the joke the more she told it. The sound of a violin being beautifully played wafted down the stairs. Mrs Howard paused, listened for a moment with a look of rapture on her face, then turned to Ronald Perkins who was a few steps behind her, and said in an awed tone, "Doesn't Mister Hawes play lovely. It brings tears to my eyes every time I hear it." "She then proceeded up the stairs. There was a half-open door, and the resplendent lanky figure of the detective Allan Hawes, wearing deerstalker hat, purple smoking jacket and blue carpet slippers, could be seen playing a violin. Mrs Howard knocked on the door. "There's a gentleman to see you Mister Hawes," she said.

125

Allan Hawes stopped playing the violin, the bow poised above the strings. The music continued playing.

"What gentleman?" he asked.

"Says he wants to employ your services," replied Mrs Howard.

"But I'm engaged on a case already."

"I've told him, but he said he'll pay you well."

"With money?"

Mrs Howard nodded.

"Show the gentleman in, Mrs Howard."

Doctor Albert Windrush sat on the sofa with a notebook on his lap in which he was busily writing. He glanced up as Ronald Perkins entered the room. He liked to think he was a good judge of character, and judged by the man's top hat and opera cloak that he was an opera lover with a liking for top hats. Doctor Windrush stood up to be introduced. Meanwhile Allan Hawes had switched off the record player and the violin music stopped playing. He put the violin and bow down on the table and then stepped forward to shake Ronald Perkins by the hand.

"Allan Hawes," he said, introducing himself.

"No," replied Ronald Perkins taking the hand and shaking it, "I'm Robert Basilweight."

"No, you misunderstand me, sir. I was introducing myself as Allan Hawes."

"But I already know that..."

With a puzzled look Allan Hawes turned to Mrs Howard.

"Ah, Mrs Howard," he said brightly, "What about a nice cup of tea for our visitor?"

"But of course, Mister Hawes. Shall I take the gentleman's top hat and cloak?"

"As long as you give them back," joked the detective with a wry smile.

"What a wit," chuckled Doctor Windrush as he advanced to be introduced.

Ronald Perkins removed his hat and cloak and handed them to Mrs Howard.

"What did the mummy biscuit say when her little boy biscuit was run over by a four-ton truck?" It was another of her quips. "CRUMBS!"

There was silence as the three men all looked at each other without a flicker of a smile on their faces. Doctor Windrush looked bewildered and confused.

"Thank you, Mrs Howard," said the detective finally, "Please return to the kitchen. I'm sure there must be a pudding, some delicacy like a steak and kidney pudding, waiting for your expert touch to finish preparing it for our dinner."

"But how did you know that?" gasped Mrs Howard in amazement. "It's true, sir, I've have been preparing a steak and kidney pudding for your supper."

"Brilliant, my dear Hawes, utterly brilliant," cried Doctor Windrush, who never ceased to be amazed by the detective's logic and assumptions.

Allan Hawes smiled a self-knowing smile. He did not reveal that only five minutes earlier he had slipped down to the kitchen for a glass of milk, and had seen the half-prepared steak and kidney pudding on the kitchen table. Mrs Howard turned to go.

"Don't forget the tea for our visitor, Mrs Howard," he called after her. "Wonderful housekeeper," he said quietly to the other men, "But hopeless with her quips."

Doctor Windrush shook Ronald Perkins's hand.

"Windrush," he said.

"Robert Basilweight," responded Ronald Perkins.

Allan Hawes looked at his visitor as he shook hands with Doctor Windrush, and closely studied him. There was something very familiar about the face. But what was it? He had a strong feeling that he had seen it before. But where and when was it? He was very good with names and faces. And he had definitely seen Robert Basilweight's face before. But he had not yet placed the face as being the same he had seen over twenty years earlier on the hotel guest at Braddock Towers, who claimed to be an American tourist, when he was working there as a desk clerk; the same mystery man the police had been hunting in connection to the Barnes Railway Bridge Murders.

"Please be seated, Mister Basilweight," said Allan Hawes, gesturing towards an armchair.

Ronald Perkins sat down. He felt uneasy with the

inquisitive look with which the detective held him. He wondered if his flies were open. But a quick glance down into his lap quickly confirmed that all was safely buttoned in.

"Now, to business," said Allan Hawes, sitting on the sofa where he was joined by Doctor Windrush. "What can I do for you, Mister Basilweight?"

"I need your expert help," replied Ronald Perkins, "to sort out a very delicate matter involving the Church."

"Good God," gasped Doctor Windrush, "not the archbishop of Canterbury again?"

Allan Hawes sighed. "Please let Mister Basilweight continue, Windrush. But why you seem to think that anything criminal involving the Church must involve the archbishop of Canterbury beats me."

"Well, he's the top fella isn't he? The buck always stops with the top fella, don't you know."

"Please continue, Mister Basilweight."

"I'm not married…"

"Nor are we," interrupted Doctor Windrush.

There was a long silence.

Then Doctor Windrush mumbled, "We are just good friends."

Allan Hawes turned to Ronald Perkins. "My relationship with Doctor Windrush is strictly a working one. We're friends, but no more than that."

"You don't have to explain yourself to me, Mister Hawes. It takes all sorts to make the world go round."

"Please continue, Mister Basilweight," said the detective.

"My partner Miss Angela Cobblers. I believe she is being unfaithful with a Church of England clergyman…"

"The Archbishop of Canterbury," exclaimed Doctor Windrush excitedly.

"No, it's not the archbishop," replied Ronald Perkins grimly, "but a young curate called Peter Catchpole. I need irrefutable proof of the affair before I confront my partner."

"And what makes you think there's been an affair?"

"I received an anonymous letter – and at church the other morning my partner fainted when she heard the curate had gone."

"Dead?"

"Not, just gone away. He's been sent away on retreat to the Convent of the Sisters of Mercy by the bishop."

"But if the curate's gone away, then how can I gather evidence of his possible affair with your partner?"

"I want you to follow the curate on retreat and talk to him there. He might confess to you if you ask him the right way."

"And you'll pay good money for this?"

"Just name your fee, Mister Hawes."

"Very well, I'll do it. It so happens that I do have a few days free before following up on a case which I'm presently engaged upon. It's a case of national importance you'll understand. I can tell you no more on the matter without breaking confidences."

"Thank you, Mister Hawes, I'm most grateful."

"Doctor Windrush, get out the Yellow Pages," cried Allan Hawes, "and book a retreat for two with the Sisters of Mercy."

One week later, Sister Rosebud the Mother Superior of the Sisters of Mercy, was walking from the convent gatehouse with two men. She had aged well over the last twenty years, and her sweet Irish accent was as melodious as ever. But her hair had turned to white and she walked with a slower step. Surprisingly, the convent gatekeeper and guest mistress Sister Tulip, now ninety years old, was still performing her role at the convent. But it took three times longer for her to unbolt the front gate as it did when she was a mere slip of a thing in her seventies. She was in no hurry, taking things slow and then even slower. The grave which had been dug for her when she suffered a serious bout of bronchitis in her eighty-eighth year was still waiting for a coffin, because, as Sister Rosebud said at the time, "You never know when it might come in handy for dear Sister Tulip. And it'll save paying a gravedigger to dig a new grave when her time does come." The Mother Superior had just collected from Sister Tulip at the gatehouse two men who had booked into the convent for a weekend retreat a week earlier. One of the men wore a deerstalker hat; the other had a stethoscope dangling from his right jacket pocket. The men were each carrying a suitcase.

"Are you Church of England?" Sister Rosebud asked as they walked up a gravel path toward the main convent building.

"It doesn't matter really but we do take our bible readings from the King James Bible, which might make things a bit confusing if you're a Roman Catholic."

"We're Church of England," replied Allan Hawes.

"We don't have men here," continued Sister Rosebud.

"Well, you wouldn't expect to see men in a convent," said Doctor Windrush with a giggle.

"Sadly the number of nuns in our order is in serious decline. We only have a quarter of the sisters we had ten years ago. And only have three novices today. Ten years ago it would have been twelve novices at least. Women are just not entering the religious life these days. They'd rather be home with a husband and children, than getting up in the dark on cold mornings for a one-hour prayer session on their knees in the chapel. I can't understand why!"

"Have you others here on retreat, Reverend Mother?"

"Yes, like another man, sister?" asked Doctor Windrush, who was thinking of the curate Peter Catchpole.

"Yes, we do have another man on retreat here," replied Sister Rosebud. "He's a young curate, Peter Catchpole. But you won't be seeing much of him. He spends most of his time in the chapel contemplating."

"Contemplating what?" asked Doctor Windrush.

"I don't really know," replied the nun, "His troubled life I suppose."

"It's not woman trouble?" asked Allan Hawes.

"Woman's trouble? Good heavens no. Men don't have that. It's a monthly event which happens only to women. And it's no trouble but a blessing from God."

"I meant an affair of the heart, Reverend Mother," said Allan Hawes.

"Oh, you mean has he been doing that which he should not have being doing in the first place?" asked the nun.

"Pardon?" asked Doctor Windrush confused by the nun's answer.

"Getting a leg over," smiled the nun sweetly.

"Precisely," replied Allan Hawes.

"Well, I couldn't possibly say," replied the nun. "It's all very confidential here. The reasons why a person comes here on retreat are never discussed outside the confessional."

"Oh, what a pity," said Doctor Windrush, "It would have made the discussion groups so much more interesting, don't you think?"

Later that evening, curate Peter Catchpole stepped out of the chapel after a long session on his knees. He had been reflecting, and praying about his vocation and feelings for Angela Cobblers. There was a tall man wearing a deerstalker hat who stepped forward from the shadows.

"Peter Catchpole," he said holding out his hand, "I've been looking forward to meeting you."

The curate shook Allan Hawes hand. "Do I know you?" he asked.

"No, but I'm sure we have a common interest."

"What common interest is that?"

"Miss Angela Cobblers."

"Did she send you?"

"Well, not exactly – but I've come from someone who has your best interests at heart."

"My mother?"

"No, let's say a good friend of Angela Cobblers who's concerned about the two of you. There is... two of you isn't there?"

"There was... but sadly no more."

"What happened?"

"Somebody wrote an anonymous letter to the Bishop spilling the beans. I'm here trying to sort my life out. It's hell, I can tell you, trying to decide if I want Angela Cobblers or to remain in the priesthood."

"Then your relationship with Angela Cobblers was an intimate one?"

"Pardon?"

"You were lovers?"

"Who is this friend of Angela's who sent you to see me?"

"A close friend of Angela Cobblers, I can assure you."

"Yes, you've said that, but who is it?"

Allan Hawes glanced at his wristwatch. "Oh, dear," he said walking rapidly away down the corridor, "Is that really the time?

I must go or I'll be late for supper."

"Who are you?" called the curate after him.

"Just a good friend," called back Allan Hawes.

Early next morning, Allan Hawes rang Robert Basilweight (Ronald Perkins), and told him of his conversation with the curate Peter Catchpole. "It seems the anonymous letter to the Bishop was correct," he said, "And Angela Cobblers has been playing away."

"There's no doubt of it?"

"None whatsoever. The curate mentioned the letter and said it had spilled the beans to the Bishop."

"Thank you, Mister Hawes. The cheque will be in the post."

"Guineas, I hope, and not pounds."

"But of course."

The next day at eleven o'clock precisely in the morning, the Reverend Jonathan Needham, wearing false grey goatee beard and horn-rimmed spectacles, arrived at the convent gatehouse. Ronald Perkins in his brilliant disguise as clergyman Jonathan Needham had decided to promote himself to the esteemed rank of Archdeacon. He considered that over a twenty-year period Jonathan Needham would have most certainly risen in the clergy ranks from being an ordinary vicar. He had come on a mission of murder. Sister Tulip slid back the grill on the heavy oak door of the gatehouse, and peered through it. Only her eyes could be seen.

"Who's there?" she asked in her old trembly voice. "Is that the pizza delivery boy?"

"No, sister, it's the Archdeacon come on retreat."

"Speak up, I'm a bit hard of hearing. Is the pizza ham and pineapple as I ordered?"

"IT'S THE ARCHDEACON!" shouted Ronald Perkins.

"What? The pizza's an Archdeacon. What sort is that then? It's not vegetarian is it? I can't stand a pizza without meat. I like to get my false teeth into something I can really chew not a wet limp piece of lettuce and half a tomato."

"I'M HERE ON RETREAT!" shouted Ronald Perkins.

"What's wrong with your feet?"

"CAN I COME IN?"

"What's that about the bin? Oh, I know you want the dustbin. You're a dustman and you want to empty the dustbins. Well, why didn't you say so in the first place instead of going on about your feet."

Ronald Perkins decided not to try and argue the point. "LET ME IN."

Sister Tulip opened the bolts on the door. "Don't keep going on about the dustbin. You'll have to push the door from your side; I'm too old and feeble to manage it by myself these days."

Ronald Perkins pushed open the heavy oak door. "THANK YOU," he shouted as he stepped inside the gatehouse

"You want the loo?" asked Sister Tulip, eyeing Ronald Perkins suspiciously. "You don't look like a dustman. You look more like a Vicar to me."

"ON RETREAT," shouted Ronald Perkins who was fast losing patience.

"I'm fed up hearing about your feet."

"Daft old biddy," he muttered under his breath as he smiled sweetly at her.

"I heard that – daft old biddy yourself."

Ronald Perkins was given a bedroom next door to Peter Catchpole's bedroom. It was ideal for his planned murderous visit during the night. He was surprised to find at dinner that night he was sitting on the high table opposite to Allan Hawes and Doctor Windrush. He thought they would have left the convent the moment their business had been concluded the previous day. But the pair had decided to stay on with the Sisters of Mercy, to have a few more days' break away from London. They saw it as a nice short holiday with expenses paid by Robert Basilweight. The meal was toad-in-the-hole with mashed potatoes and sliced beans, followed by a milky rice pudding. The toad-in-the-hole was mostly batter with hardly any toad, a beef sausage, to be found. Peter Catchpole sat at the head of the table opposite the Mother Superior, Sister Rosebud. He kept looking at Allan Hawes, who was still wearing his deerstalker hat having told the nuns it was standard religious headgear back in London's East End, and when he caught his eye would form with his lips the words, "Who are you?"

"I remember you well, Archdeacon," smiled Sister Rosebud. "You came to see us some twenty years ago, and you had to lock your bedroom door against Sister Tulip. We've been putting Bromide in her tea ever since to slow her down."

"I've a strange feeling," said Allan Hawes, staring fixedly at Ronald Perkins, "that I've seen you before. But I can't place where or when."

"We've never met," said Ronald Perkins nervously. "I would have remembered. I've got a good memory for faces."

"It's your facial bone structure, Archdeacon," said Allan Hawes, "and the boldness of the nose which dwarfs the rest of the face."

"I wouldn't say my nose was that big."

"Have you ever stayed at Braddock Towers Hotel in London when you were a young man, Archdeacon?"

"No, I haven't."

"There's something so familiar about you, Archdeacon. I just know we've met before. And I won't sleep a wink tonight trying to remember."

The convent tower clock had just struck midnight when Jonathan Needham (Ronald Perkins), disguised in goatee beard, quietly opened his bedroom door and stepped out bare-footed wearing red and white striped pyjamas, and a yellow dressing gown. In his right hand he carried an empty plastic syringe. It was all he would need to arrange for the early demise of Peter Catchpole. He walked down the corridor on tiptoe, and reached out and slowly turned the door handle. The door was unlocked. The curate had obviously not been warned about the night time wanderings of Sister Tulip. But perhaps the bromide the Mother Superior had put in her tea had finally slowed down the elderly nun, and the Mother Superior felt there was no need to warn male guests. Ronald Perkins entered the room. From the light in the corridor he could see the curate stretched out on his back, mouth open and snoring quietly. Advancing towards the bed Ronald Perkins pulled up the syringe plunger a little way, allowing air to go through the hollow needle and into the syringe. Holding the syringe between two forefingers with his

134

thumb steady on the plunger, Ronald Perkins advanced towards the sleeping curate. Air injected into a vein and carried quickly to the heart would result in a heart attack, without anything being found in the post mortem but a tiny needle mark on the forearm. This would make the pathologist doing the post mortem think something had been administered. And a blood check to find drugs or poison would find nothing whatsoever. Air leaves no trace but is deadly when a small bubble arrives within the heart.

Ronald Perkins bent over the sleeping curate and prodded him with the index finger of his right hand. There was no response; Peter Catchpole was a heavy sleeper. Gently Ronald Perkins eased aside the bedclothes to uncover the curate's left arm. He kept pausing, to see if his movements had woken the curate. But he snored happily on, blissfully unaware of what was happening to him. Ronald Perkins looked for a vein in the crook of the arm. The light coming in through the doorway from the corridor was not bright enough. He reached over and switched on a bedside lamp. Peter Catchpole lay dreaming of Angela Cobblers. Within a minute the syringe needle had been inserted. The sharp pain of the needle going into his arm woke the curate. Opening his eyes he was astonished to see the Archdeacon bending over him.

"What's happening?" he asked still half asleep.

"Go back to sleep," whispered Ronald Perkins as he pushed with his thumb on the syringe plunger, "You've having a nightmare that's all." The small lethal bubble of air entered the curate's arm.

"Ooooh," gasped the curate as he felt a sudden violent stabbing pain in his heart. He reached out with his right hand and grabbed a few hairs from out of Ronald Perkins's false goatee beard, as he went into a convulsion. The heart attack was mercifully short and in less than twenty-five seconds after the air bubble had been injected the curate was dead.

Ronald Perkins switched off the bedside table lamp, and crept back to his bedroom. He put the syringe in his suitcase between two shirts, then got into bed and went to sleep.

The next morning, when Peter Catchpole failed to come down for breakfast, a nun was sent to find him. Sister Daisy, tall and willowy, who had been in the religious order for thirty-five years and was Novice Mistress, knocked on the curate's door. When there was no response she knocked again, and called out, "Reverend Catchpole." Again no response. Thinking the curate had overslept she opened the door and entered the room. She stood horrified and frozen to the spot. Peter Catchpole lay in a twisted convulsed position, hands clutching at his chest, with an expression of sheer agony on his face. Sister Daisy could see he was dead. It took a full minute for the nun to regain her composure, and then with a piercing scream she turned and fled from the room of death. The Mother Superior summoned a Doctor, who declared after examining the deceased that he had suffered a massive heart attack while asleep in his bed. The body was collected by ambulance and taken off to a hospital mortuary. Ronald Perkins watched the body being loaded into the ambulance with a sense of a job well done. The few hairs snatched from the false goatee beard were still clutched tightly in the dead fingers of the curate's right hand.

The pathologist at the mortuary found the needle mark in the curate's arm, and reported it to the police as being a "suspicious death". The post mortem was inconclusive. The curate had died from a massive heart attack, but according to his medical records, he had been given a thorough medical check-up by his own GP only a week before his death. And his heart was in good normal shape. The hairs from the false goatee beard were taken away by police for forensic tests. When the results of the test came back a week later, the police launched a murder enquiry. The DNA on the hairs matched exactly with DNA found on the small ginger Adolf Hitler-style moustache from the Barnes Railway Bridge Murders, and with the cigar butt found in the hand of Wing Commander Hughie Lampton. Chief Inspector Edward Briggs was put in charge of the Peter Catchpole case, which was titled "The Curate's Murder".

"The same killer," he told his Sergeant Jenny Hopper, "is responsible for the murder of five men."

"That we know of, sir."

"What? There might be more?"

"We could be dealing with a serial killer, sir."

"But a serial killer who makes mistakes and the net is

closing in, Sergeant. Once we can match the DNA with somebody we've got our killer."

"But we must find that somebody, first, sir, to match it."

"Precisely, Sergeant."

"The killer is very clever, sir. We wouldn't have known the curate's death was murder if it hadn't been for the hairs, and only then because they matched the forensic tests on two items from other murder cases."

"Well, at least we know our man..."

"Or woman," interrupted the Sergeant.

Chief Inspector Edgar Briggs nodded. "Yes, the killer might be a woman. But, as I was saying, at least we know our killer has lost some hairs, and might well be walking about with a small bald spot."

The Sergeant made no reply. She was now quite used to her boss's bizarre logic, and thought that the best chance the serial killer had for evading capture was to have Chief Inspector Edgar Briggs in charge of the case.

Chapter Ten

Ronald Perkins had returned home to Bumstead on the Wold. His mother and Angela Cobblers thought he had been away on a short business trip. News of the curate's death from a heart attack was village gossip within twenty-four hours. It was not known to be murder until police got back their forensic tests a week later. Angela Cobblers was heart-broken, but she put a brave face on in front of Ronald Perkins and his mother, but secretly wept in her bedroom when she was alone. She did not suspect Ronald Perkins of being implicated. Because she had read in the newspapers that Peter Catchpole had died in a convent bed, and Ronald Perkins, who did not believe in God, would not have been found within half-a-mile of a convent, and anyway was away on business at the time of the murder.

"Buy yourself something," said Ronald Perkins at the breakfast table, as he handed Angela Cobblers a thick wad of banknotes. "Go up to London and treat yourself to something nice."

Hetty Rose Perkins scowled and bashed in the top of her egg with a teaspoon. She did not like Angela Cobblers, and felt her son gave her too much money. They were not married after all, and being only his partner it was like being paid expenses for being a mistress.

Angela Cobblers gratefully took the money. "Thanks, Ronnie," she said.

"Think nothing of it, Angie. Nothing's too good for my girl."

"How much is it?" asked Angela Cobblers.

"More than you deserve," snapped Hetty Rose Perkins.

"Enough to buy something really nice, Angie," said Ronald Perkins. "It's five thousand pounds."

"Ooooh, Ronnie, you spoil me," cooed Angela Cobblers.

"Only because I love you, Angie."

Angela Cobblers looked Ronald Perkins steadily in the eyes for several seconds before replying as if trying to read his innermost thoughts. "I know you do, Ronnie."

Ronald Perkins reached across the breakfast table and placed his hand gently on Angela Cobblers' hand. "I know it isn't the time or place, Angie, and a woman wants to hear what I'm about to ask you in a more romantic setting."

"Ask me?"

"Will you marry me?"

"Yes, Ronnie, I'll marry you."

"And all his money," scowled Hetty Rose Perkins, who hated the idea of having Angela Cobblers as her daughter-in-law. When she was only a mistress she could have been turned out of the house without a penny, but as a wife she would have the legal right to half of everything her son possessed.

"When would you like us to wed?" asked Ronald Perkins.

"Whenever you say, Ronnie."

"Registry or Church?"

"I'd like a church wedding please, Ronnie, with all the trimmings, a white dress and bridesmaids."

"You shall have it, Angie."

"When?"

"Well, I've got a little business trip coming up in the near future. Let's say when I get back. How's that sound, Angie?" The business trip Ronald Perkins was referring to was to go and murder the Prime Minister. The murder contract was with fish and chip tycoon Sidney Frogmorton, who wanted the Prime Minister dead for not including his name for a knighthood on the Queen's honours list. For years Sidney Frogmorton had been donating vast sums of money to well-placed politicians and to party funds, also making the odd bribe here and there, and all to be knighted by the Queen. Promises had been made and his name had been submitted four times in four years, but each time the Prime Minister had crossed it out with a blue pencil. He reasoned that another Prime Minister might not be so handy with a blue pencil, and he would get his knighthood.

"Oooh, Ronnie," cooed Angela Cobblers, "shouldn't I have a diamond engagement ring?"

"We'll go shopping for one this afternoon."

"Ooooh, Ronnie, with a really big diamond?"

"But of course, Angie, nothing's too good for my future wife."

"And I'll be Mrs Angela Perkins."

Hetty Rose Perkins said nothing but scowled. She had made up her mind to do all she could to stop the marriage from going ahead. There must be something she could do to stop her son from making his wedding plans. If he married Angela Cobblers it would be disastrous for her, no longer would she be in command of the house, but marriage would put Angela in a most formidable position. In law a wife has equal rights to that of her husband over estate and money, but a mother-in-law is just a mother-in-law with no legal rights on her son's estate.

Allan Hawes and Doctor Windrush had returned to London before the discovery of the curate's body in the convent bedroom. The newspapers had first reported it as a heart attack on page three, and after the police got back the forensic report and declared it to be a murder, the newspapers thought it was stale news and only gave it a small paragraph on page twelve under the agony aunt column. The murder report had gone unread by both Allan Hawes and Doctor Windrush, who had no interest in either writing to an agony aunt, or reading letters of those who had done so. Allan Hawes was pacing up and down on the carpet, his mind working overtime as he planned how to help his client Mabel Frogmorton, and stop her husband from having the Prime Minister killed. He knew the person; a woman calling herself Marion Pringle had been overheard by Mrs Mabel Frogmorton discussing the murder on the telephone with her husband Sidney Frogmorton. Doctor Windrush sat on the sofa reading a motoring magazine. He was thinking of buying himself a new car and wanted to see what was having a good review by motoring critics. He wanted something big and gleaming, which would impress his patients, but most importantly it had to be cheap. He was not fitting so many penile correctors as he had been, and the cash flow from his medical work had been falling off alarmingly.

"Old banger on page three, Hawes," he said. "Looks like a

140

right goer to me."

"Please, Windrush, don't talk about women like that. You know I don't like it."

"But it's not a woman – it's an old banger."

"No woman is refereed to as an old banger, Windrush, unless she's a mother-in-law; then it's quite acceptable."

"I'm taking about a car, Hawes."

Allan Hawes scowled. "I've more important things on my mind than discussing cars with you, Windrush. I'm trying to plan our next move to stop the Prime Minister being murdered."

"Shouldn't we inform the police, Hawes?"

"Not for the moment. Mrs Frogmorton wants confidentiality at all costs and doesn't want her family name dragged into a media circus."

"But surely if there's going to be a murder, and even more so if the victim is going to be the Prime Minister of Britain, the police should be informed."

"There won't be a victim, because we'll have prevented it."

"Oh, and if we don't, Hawes?"

"Then we learn from our mistakes and notify the police."

"That won't be of much help to the Prime Minister, will it?"

"Perhaps not, but we must first honour the confidentiality of the client who employed us, Windrush. Who would want to employ a private detective who could not keep secrets, and who rushed off to the police at the first opportunity to get them to finish the job? No, my dear Windrush, we are employed by a client to carry out instructions to the letter, and do nothing without her consent."

"I feel sorry for the Prime Minister, Hawes."

"But we're on the case."

"I know – and that's why I feel sorry for him."

The door opened and Mrs Howard came bustling in. She held a tray on which stood two cups of tea and a plate of shortbread biscuits.

"I thought you might like a cup of tea. Mister Hawes," she said brightly as she placed the tray on the table.

"Ah, yes, Mrs Howard, thank you," replied the detective.

"That convent you visited the other week, Mister Hawes, was it the Sisters of Mercy convent?" asked Mrs Howard,

"Because there's a bit in the newspaper this morning about that poor young curate who died there. It seems it wasn't a natural death. The police are saying their forensics tests have concluded it to be definitely murder."

"Murder, by God," gasped Doctor Windrush his face turning ashen, "and to think I was sitting next to the chap at the meal table."

"Murder's not infectious, Windrush," exclaimed Allan Hawes hotly. "It's impossible to catch it off anybody else, otherwise the world would be full of murdered people just lying about waiting to be buried."

"I didn't mean that, Hawes. I know perfectly well as a medical consultant that murder isn't infectious. I was merely pointing out how bizarre it was that for two days I sat next to a murder victim sharing the salt and pepper."

"Life is full of bizarre coincidences, Windrush."

"Did I ever tell you," began Mrs Howard, who was about to tell another of her jolly quips, "that..."

"I'm sure you have," interrupted Allan Hawes, who, knowing his housekeeper and her determination, realised she was about to give utterance to one of her awful cockney quips. "Shall we save it for another time?"

The smile faded from Mrs Howard's face, to be replaced with a disappointed look. "I was going to say..."

"Please, Mrs Howard," retorted the detective as he tried to assert some authority over his housekeeper.

"I was only going to ask, Mister Hawes, what's the maximum penalty for bigamy?"

"All right, Mrs Howard. I give in," replied the detective with a shrug of his shoulders. The housekeeper's persistence had paid off. "What is the penalty?"

"Two mothers-in-law," Mrs Howard chuckled, who enjoyed the quip immensely. It was the way she said them.

Allan Hawes looked at Doctor Windrush, who looked at Allan Hawes. Both men were straight-faced with a stricken look. Allan Hawes shook his head. "I just knew I would regret letting Mrs Howard finish the joke."

"Would you like lunch at the usual time, Mister Hawes?" asked Mrs Howard.

"What is it?" asked Doctor Windrush, "Anything special?"

"Fish and chips," declared Mrs Howard brightly, "with mushy peas and three pickled onions each."

"Fish and chips," cried Allan Hawes, "that reminds me of our case in hand, stopping the fish and chip empire magnate, Sidney Frogmorton, from carrying out his evil plan."

"Well, gentleman?" asked Mrs Howard impatiently.

"Well, what, Mrs Howard?" asked Doctor Windrush.

"Do you want your lunch at the usual time or not?"

"Fish and chips," said Doctor Windrush with a look of utter disdain. "The later the better I should think. What about you, Hawes?"

"Don't bother me now, Windrush, there's a good chap. I'm just formulating a plan to trace Marion Pringle, the woman hired to do Sidney Frogmorton's dirty work."

"Onions," cried Mrs Howard indignantly as she made for the door.

"Pardon?" gasped the detective.

"I said onions, Mister Hawes," replied Mrs Howard as she paused at the door. "Three enough, or would you like more?"

"Three would be more than sufficient," replied Doctor Windrush bleakly. "Pickled onions always make me fart uproariously."

"No onions, Mrs Howard," called Allan Hawes, "The Doctor's right they do bring on the wind something awful."

"Very good, Mister Hawes," replied Mrs Howard. She left the room and closed the door behind her.

"Now, Hawes, what's your plan for tracing Marion Pringle?" asked the Doctor. "She's only made contact by telephone, hasn't she?"

"We bug Sidney Frogmorton's study phone."

"Isn't that illegal, Hawes?"

"So is murdering the Prime Minister. I think a wire tap to save a life is definitely the lesser of two evils, don't you?"

"I don't want to end up in prison, Hawes. I hear it's a dreadful place."

"You won't, I promise you. The Prime Minister will be far too pleased to let the police prosecute us for bugging a phone. We might even end up with a knighthood; you never know."

"Sir Albert Windrush," repeated the Doctor slowly. "Yes, Hawes, it does have a nice ring about it."

Ronald Perkins drove three miles out from Bumstead on the Wold and stopped the car outside a red public telephone box. He had arranged to call Sidney Frogmorton at 3.30 p.m. on the dot. He was casually dressed in a tweed jacket and grey trousers. He dialled Sidney Frogmorton's number from memory. The phone rang three times as arranged, then it was picked up.

"Hello, Sidney Frogmorton speaking."

"It's me," replied Ronald Perkins in the high pitched squeaky voice he used for playing the part of Marion Pringle, "Miss Marion Pringle."

"Can you confirm who you are by telling me the prearranged code word?" asked Sidney Frogmorton. "I don't want to be talking to the wrong person in error."

"Tory."

"Correct."

"We need to meet face to face, Mister Frogmorton. It's always dangerous to discuss our sort of business over the telephone. You never know who might be listening."

"I agree, Miss Pringle, we certainly don't want people knowing about the little removal job you're arranging for me. The item of furniture to be removed is delicate and must be treated with care."

"I suggest we meet next Monday evening at nine, at the Saucy Gander tavern in Lower Bingley, in East Sussex. Can you make it?"

"I see in my diary that I've an important meeting with all my fish and chip shop owners that night."

"Couldn't you cancel it?"

"No, I'm afraid I can't. The meeting was planned weeks ago and all the managers have gone to a great deal of trouble to make sure they'll be there."

"Can you make any date next week?"

"I seem to be fully booked – can you phone me back after I've checked about moving some of my appointments around?"

"All right."

"What about 10 a.m. next Wednesday?"

144

"That's ideal, Mister Frogmorton; I'll call you then."

"And what is the new code word?"

"Pussy."

"Goodbye, Miss Pringle."

"Goodbye."

Three days later a white van drove up the long gravel driveway towards the Frogmorton manor house. Driving the van was Doctor Albert Windrush, and sitting next to him in the front passenger seat was Allan Hawes. Both men were dressed in working men's overalls, flat caps, and to add to the illusion they had not shaved that morning. The van had "TELEPHONE REPAIRS" painted on both sides. The van stopped outside the front door of the manor house, and both men got out. Allan Hawes was carrying a canvas tool bag. He put an unlit cigarette in his mouth to look more like a British workman. He knocked boldly on the door. The door was opened by the butler; a tall pale-faced individual wearing black tails and bow tie. He stared at the two men with a shocked look on his face, as if he could not believe his eyes.

"Workmen round the back," he said in a haughty voice.

"But Mrs Frogmorton is expecting us," said Allan Hawes.

"Round the back," replied the butler.

"Can't you go and tell Mrs Frogmorton that the two telephone repairmen are here. She's is expecting us I can assure you."

"Round the back," insisted the butler, his eyes becoming two slits of menace.

Allan Hawes turned to Doctor Windrush. "Round the back," he said.

"Right," replied the Doctor, "round the back."

The butler closed the door.

Allan Hawes led the way round to the back of the manor house. Doctor Windrush was muttering angrily all the way under his breath. "Damn idiot butler, who does he think he is, the toffee nosed twit."

Allan Hawes knocked on the back door, which was promptly opened by the butler. "Cook says will you wipe your feet before entering the kitchen. She likes to keep it spick and span."

They wiped their feet on a coconut mat inside the door.

"Madam is expecting, you," said the butler. "She is waiting in the master's study. If you would both like to follow me, please."

They followed the butler down a long hallway with expensive looking oil paintings on the walls. He stopped outside an oak door with a gold door handle and knocked politely.

"Enter," cried Mrs Mabel Frogmorton from the other side of the door.

The butler opened the door and entered the room followed by Allan Hawes and Doctor Windrush. "The gentleman you were expecting, Madam," he said with a slight bow of the head.

"Thank you, Weatherspoon," replied Mabel Frogmorton curtly. "You may go now."

"Very good, Madam." The butler turned and left the room closing the door behind him.

"Mister Hawes," cried Mrs Frogmorton, "You've come. I was beginning to think you had changed your mind about helping me."

"No, dear lady, the van broke down three times on the way here, and the last time we had to call out the AA. The patrolman said we had dirty plugs."

"Sounds frightful," said Mrs Frogmorton. "But at least you're here now."

"Your husband is still out?" asked Allan Hawes.

"Playing golf, I told you – he won't be back for hours. He always visits the nineteenth hole after completing a round, to celebrate finishing eighteen holes."

"Good, then if you can keep watch outside in the corridor to make certain none of the servants come wandering in, Doctor Windrush and I will insert a bug into the handset of your husband's study telephone."

Mrs Frogmorton left the room. For the next fifteen minutes she paced slowly up and down the long corridor, stopping every now again to study one of the oil paintings on the wall.

Meanwhile, back in the study, Allan Hawes and Doctor Windrush set to work. The bottom of the telephone cradle was unscrewed and removed, and working from a sheet of paper giving step-by-step instructions on how to bug a phone, Allan Hawes inserted the small bugging receiver and transmitter, which was no bigger than a one penny coin. Two wires, red and a black, were soldered into place by the Doctor, who was more than adequate at soldering wires with all his experiences of putting penile correctors on patients in the operating room.

"There," he said when he had finished. "All done."

"And the distance for our receiver and recorder?" asked Allan Hawes.

"We need to be within two hundred yards of the house."

"Which means..."

"That we go camping for the next few days in the back garden," interrupted the Doctor, who was appalled by the idea. He was a gentleman who enjoyed the finer things of life, and camping was most definitely not one of them, sleeping on hard ground and being bitten black and blue by hordes of midges. He preferred a nice warm bed with a flushing toilet nearby.

Two hours later, after concealing the van in a copse of pine trees, Allan Hawes and Doctor Windrush, now dressed in camping gear of shorts, short sleeved shirts and heavy walking boots, with socks rolled down over the ankles sat beside a smoking wood fire. Allan Hawes was trying to cook some sausages in a frying pan for their tea. But the handle of the frying pan had become too hot, and he had to hold it with his flat cap wrapped round the handle. Doctor Windrush sat looking utterly miserable. He was now experiencing what he considered to be hell on earth, sleeping under canvas with a bellyful of food cooked by Allan Hawes. The one thing the detective was not was a cook in any shape or form. He could not even boil an egg successfully. And yet he had insisted on cooking their tea, putting eight beef sausages into a frying pan and holding it above the flames. When he decided they were ready, they were burnt cinder black on the outside, and found to be raw inside. Both men ate the sausages with slices of bread. There was nothing else but bacon and eggs and they were for breakfast.

"All right, Windrush?" asked Allan Hawes when he saw the Doctor chewing on a piece of sausage.

"I've tasted worse," lied the Doctor who did not want to

offend his friend.

"Have another sausage, I can't eat all of mine."

"No, thank you, Hawes, I don't want to make a glutton of myself."

Later that evening, Sidney Frogmorton returned home from the nineteenth hole. He was driven in a gleaming Rolls Royce by a smart-looking peaked-cap chauffeur wearing a grey uniform with polished black boots. He was far too merry on booze to drive himself home. Allan Hawes watched through a powerful pair of binoculars. The chauffeur helped his master into the house, half-carrying and half-pulling him. Moments later the chauffeur reappeared to collect a set of golf clubs from the car. Allan Hawes and Doctor Windrush crawled into the low two-man pup tent and switched on the black box receiver and recorder. The box buzzed ominously and a few sparks flew out as Allan Hawes plugged in the earphones. Doctor Windrush with a startled look sprang backwards away from the black box, knocking it with his right elbow. The box fell over onto Allan Hawes's right foot. He screamed. The Doctor screamed. Then there was a long silence. Both men looked at each other.

"He'll be too drunk to get a call," he said.

"You don't think Marion Pringle will call tonight, Hawes?"

"Sidney Frogmorton would have a prearranged time for her to call – and that wouldn't be while he's drunk. I reckon we'll get something tomorrow."

"Well, if you say so, Hawes."

Allan Hawes switched off the black box. "Let's have an early night, Windrush, so we can wake up in the morning full of beans and raring to go."

"Full of your under-done sausages more like," muttered the Doctor under his breath.

"What did you say, Windrush?"

"I said goodnight, Hawes."

"Goodnight, Windrush."

Chief Inspector Edgar Briggs stood in the mortuary with Sergeant Jenny Hopper and police pathologist Professor Arthur Dean. They were looking down at the naked dead body of curate

148

Peter Catchpole lying on the mortuary slab with mouth and eyes open. There was a long line of stitches down from his throat to his belly button, where he had been cut open for his heart to be examined, then sewn up again.

"Poor devil," exclaimed the Chief Inspector. "Well, at least he was in bed when his time came."

"I've never seen anything like it before, sir," gasped Sergeant Jenny Hopper.

"I'm sorry," apologised Professor Dean, "But he is a big strapping lad. Would you like me to put some trousers on him, Sergeant, so your modesty won't be offended any more. It'll save your blushes."

"But I wasn't talking about his endowment, Professor," replied the Sergeant coldly. "I've seen better and worse, although not on a corpse. No, I was talking about his murder – I've never seen anything like it before in my life, to kill with a syringe and an injected air bubble."

"Well, I have, Sergeant," said the Professor. "I had just started my studies under Professor Raymond Bertie Brown at the London School of Pathology, and a body of a young Russian, said to be a spy, was bought in by MI6. He had been dispatched in the same syringe and air bubble method of murder. MI6 had done the murder themselves, as the Russian, who they said was a double agent, sat on a park bench eating a pork pie. We found the tiny needle mark, like an ant bite in the crook of his left arm, and when we opened him up on the mortuary table, we found his heart had virtually exploded. The curate's heart was exactly the same as the young Russian's"

"Are you saying MI6 killed Peter Catchpole?" asked the Chief Inspector in a surprised tone of voice.

"No, Chief Inspector, I'm not saying that," replied the Professor. "But the person who killed Peter Catchpole is a cold calculating professional who knows his business."

Allan Hawes lay in the darkness in a sleeping bag. His mind was focused on the archdeacon, Jonathan Needham, whom he had met while on retreat with the Sisters of Mercy. There was something very familiar about his facial bone structure, and the large nose, which dwarfed the rest of his face. He knew that he had met the man before, but could not remember where or when. He had been tossing and turning in his sleeping bag for half the night, unable to sleep or think of anything else but where had he seen the Archdeacon before. Then he remembered. It was like a flash of lightning zapping through his brain. He had seen him at the Braddock Towers Hotel some twenty years earlier, when he was a desk clerk there. The man, with the same facial bone structure and big nose was the mysterious man who claimed to be American tourist Roger Shepherd. No trace of Roger Shepherd was ever found. The FBI searched America, and Interpol the rest of the world.

"Are you awake, Windrush?" asked Allan Hawes, giving his friend a hard nudge in the ribs with his elbow.

"What's happening?" gasped the Doctor sitting bolt upright. "Is the tent on fire?"

"Get dressed, Windrush. We must drive to the nearest police station without delay. I've some vital information to give them. The Archdeacon is the man they've been hunting for the last twenty years; the very same man they suspect is the Barnes Railway Bridge murderer."

Doctor Windrush picked up a torch. He switched it on and directed its slender beam down at his wristwatch. "But, Hawes," he sighed unhappily "It's only just gone midnight."

"That's all right, Windrush, but police stations stay open all night, didn't you know, old chap. Now get your trousers on."

Chapter Eleven

The statement made by Allan Hawes was passed on to Chief Inspector Edgar Briggs, who sat at his desk eating a jam doughnut as he read it. Sergeant Jenny Hopper sat at her desk, half the size of the Chief Inspector's desk, at the opposite side of the room. She was whispering into her phone hoping the Chief Inspector would not overhear what she was saying. She was talking to her lover, Professor Arthur Dean.

"I can't say it, Arthur," she whispered with a giggle. "He'll hear me."

"What's he doing?"

"He's eating a jam doughnut and reading a statement."

"Go on, please say it."

"All right then, Arthur... I love you."

"And Cuddly Bear loves his Pussy Amore."

"Oh, Arthur, that makes me go weak at the knees."

"Oh, Jenny."

"Who's on the phone?" called out the Chief Inspector.

"It's a wrong number, sir," replied the Sergeant as she put the phone down.

"Funny wrong number – you've been on the phone for at least half an hour."

"Sorry, sir. The person thought they knew me."

"And did they?"

"No, sir, it was a wrong number."

"I want you to order up a car right away for us to go to the Convent of the Sisters of Mercy. I think we might be hot on the trail of our serial killer. It appears he stayed there on retreat with the murdered curate Peter Catchpole. He's an Archdeacon called Jonathan Needham."

"Shall I get Detective Constable Robins to contact Church House and get a fix on the Archdeacon's present whereabouts?

151

He could have come from any diocese in the Church of England. The records at Church House will show where he resides."

"Good thinking, Sergeant, you do that and I'll call up a panda car."

It was precisely at ten a.m. on Wednesday morning when Sidney Frogmorton received his telephone call from Marion Pringle. He did not know that the conversation was being bugged, and that Allan Hawes, some one hundred and fifty yards away in a small tent, was recording it as evidence on his black box receiver recorder. The telephone rang three times before it was nervously picked up.

"Hello, Sidney Frogmorton."

"It's me," said Ronald Perkins in the high-pitched voice he used as Miss Marion Pringle.

"Code word if you please, Miss Pringle."

"Pussy."

"Good morning Miss Pringle. Let's keep this short and sweet. I can meet you tomorrow at 8 pm on the dot, in the Saucy Gander Tavern in Lower Bingley, East Sussex. I know how to find it. I've marked the route on my road map."

"How will I know you?"

"I'll be wearing a red carnation in my button hole and a rolled up copy of the Times carried under my right arm. And how will I know you, Miss Pringle?"

"I shall be wearing green tweeds and carrying a black leather handbag."

"See you tomorrow, Miss Pringle."

"Goodbye, Mister Frogmorton."

Mother Superior Sister Rosebud was deeply shocked. "But are you sure, Chief Inspector?" she asked. "There can be no mistake?" She was standing in her office in the convent talking to Chief Inspector Edgar Briggs and Sergeant Jenny Hopper.

"I'm afraid not, Sister, there's evidence and an eye-witness account, which all points to it being the Archdeacon."

"How dreadful, an Archdeacon being a serial killer, Chief Inspector," said Sister Rosebud. "Whatever is the Church coming to these days? It'll be some batty old Bishop going

152

berserk with his shepherd's crook next. You mentioned there was an eyewitness to the murder? I didn't know there was one. It's not Sister Buttercup, is it? She does tend to make things up."

"Not to the actual murder, Sister, but he did recognise the Archdeacon as being the same man police wanted to question some twenty years ago."

"What an amazing memory, Chief Inspector," replied the impressed nun. "I sometimes find it difficult to remember what I did last week."

"Have you the address for the Archdeacon?" asked the Sergeant.

Sister Rosebud went over to her desk and opened a large red book. She ran her finger down a page, then looked up at the Sergeant. "The Archdeacon hasn't put an address. He's just written 'between parishes'."

Sergeant Jenny Hopper turned to her boss. "Let's hope Detective Constable Robins had better luck at Church House tracing the Archdeacon," she said hopefully.

"Come on, Sergeant," called the Chief Inspector as he made for the door, "Let's return to London and see if Robins has found our man."

"Thank you, Sister," said the Sergeant before hurrying after her boss. "You've been most helpful."

"Goodbye," called Sister Rosebud waving her hand.

Allan Hawes and Doctor Windrush arrived an hour early at the Saucy Gander Tavern in Lower Bingley. They sat in a corner drinking Guinness, talking in Irish accents. They were pretending to be Irish tourists. On the table in front of Allan Hawes was a small canvas bag, in which was a powerful directional microphone plugged into a miniature tape recorder. Allan Hawes as usual was wearing his deerstalker hat.

"Well, Paddy," said Allan Hawes to Doctor Windrush who was sipping his glass of Guinness, "and how are we doing this fine evening?"

"As bright as a Belfast shilling, Sean," replied the Doctor with a sly wink of an eye. "Must be heaven to be standing in Galway Bay this night watching the sun go down."

"Don't wink at me," whispered Allan Hawes, "It scares the

life out me when you do it, Windrush."

"Sorry, Hawes, old chap," replied the Doctor in his normal voice.

"Irish accents," whispered Allan Hawes, "if you please."

"Top of the morning to you, Sean."

"And the top of the morning to you, Paddy."

The two conspirators did not know that a thickset man standing at the bar was watching them. He wore a navy blue suit and white spats. The man was working undercover for MI5, and was looking for a three-man IRA sabotage strike team, who were known to be in the area. He watched Allan Hawes and Doctor Windrush for another ten minutes, before asking the barmaid if he could use the telephone. He dialled MI5 headquarters in London.

"Put me through to Major Golightly," he told the operator. "Tell him it's Larry Parks."

"Major Golightly here," said a voice with an educated public school accent.

"Larry Parks reporting in, Major. I think I've spotted two of the IRA sabotage team. They're sitting in the public bar of the Saucy Gander Tavern in Lower Bingley, East Sussex."

"And what makes you think it's them, Parks?"

"They look very shifty, Major, and speak with Irish accents. And the smaller one is wearing a deerstalker hat. He seems to be the one in charge."

"Yes, they certainly sound like our chummies, Parks. Have you a gun with you?

"Yes Major I have."

"Keep an eye on them, but don't do anything unless they try to leave the tavern. I hope you're a good shot with the gun, Parks. We don't want innocent people being shot now do we?"

"No, Major, that's the last thing we want. I think you should know there's a large canvas bag on the table between the two men."

"My God, Parks, and you think it's a bomb?"

"Why else should they have a canvas bag on the table, Major?"

"That's right, I'll get the nearest rapid response team over to you as quick as possible, and an army bomb squad too."

"Thanks, Major."

"Remember Parks, that England expects you to keep a stiff upper lip."

"I know, Major."

"Good man, Parks, now you hang on in there until help arrives."

"Yes, Major, I will." Parks put down the phone and felt in his right trouser pocket for the six-shot revolver. He held the butt of the gun cupped in the palm of his hand with a finger on the trigger, ready in an instant to pull it out and open fire.

Five minutes later Sidney Frogmorton, wearing a red carnation in his buttonhole, with a rolled up copy of 'The Times' under his right arm, strolled casually into the public bar. He glanced around looking for a woman wearing green tweeds with a black handbag. Miss Marion Pringle had not yet arrived. He went over to the bar and ordered lemonade with a packet of ready salted crisps. Larry Parks watched him intently, thinking he was the third IRA man here to meet the two sitting in the corner. Miss Marion Pringle, dressed in green tweeds and carrying a black handbag, entered the tavern. The disguise of the middle-aged woman, with bulky padding and wearing the 'lucky' ginger theatrical wig, made Ronald Perkins look every inch a spinster lady with attitude. He paused momentarily as he spotted Sidney Frogmorton standing at the bar, then walked over to a table in the corner and sat down, placing the black handbag on the table in front of him where it could clearly be seen from the bar. Sidney Frogmorton spotted Miss Pringle and strolled over.

"Miss Pringle?" he asked.

Ronald Perkins nodded.

Sidney Frogmorton sat down. "Would you like a drink?" he asked.

"I'd rather get down to business. Do you still want me to make the hit?"

"But of course."

"And you accept my price for the removal?"

"It's a great deal of money, much more than I had expected to pay."

"I don't give discounts."

155

"All right, I agree to the sum requested, Miss Pringle, although it's more than I make from my fish and chip empire over a two-year period."

"This will be my biggest hit ever. I'll have to retire after doing it, because the item to be removed is so high profile. The removal will cause a national crisis and might even bring the government down. The British people voted for the personality and not the politics."

"I understand. And how do I settle your account, Miss Pringle?"

"I want half paid within four days into a Swiss bank. I'll give you the account number. And the rest when you hear on the radio that the hit has been made."

"Agreed, Miss Pringle."

Allan Hawes, sitting at a table across the other side of the bar, had switched on the miniature tape recorder and directional microphone in the canvas bag, and was recording Miss Pringle's conversation with Sidney Frogmorton. He was listening to the recording through an earpiece. The microphone was picking up the conversation loud and clear. Doctor Windrush was looking glum because there was only one earpiece and Allan Hawes had that. He sat sipping a glass of Guinness.

Larry Parks was seated at the bar with a double whisky on the rocks. He nervously held the revolver in his pocket. He was wondering if Miss Pringle was connected with the IRA. Sidney Frogmorton did not seem the least bit interested in the two Irishmen. He sat with his back towards them. Could it be that he and the bulky woman in green tweeds were romantically involved, perhaps on a blind date? They did not look at ease with each other, and acted as if they were strangers. Larry Parks took a sip of the whisky to focus his thoughts. He glanced at his wristwatch. Neither the rapid response team sent by Major Golightly had arrived nor the army bomb squad. He looked at the canvas bag on the table in front of Allan Hawes and at Doctor Windrush, thinking it definitely was a bomb. He wondered if the Irish men were armed. He knew IRA men were crack shots trained to handle their weapons in tight corners.

They would not surrender without a fight, and the bar was slowly filling up with customers. To take the Irishmen down he would need the promised MI5 back-up, but where was the rapid response team? Most probably they were caught up in a traffic jam somewhere. The situation was becoming tenser by the second, and Larry Parks decided that he would wait for five more minutes, then act on his own and try to arrest the Irishmen. He hoped his first assumption about Sidney Frogmorton had not been correct and he was not a member of the IRA. To try and take three IRA men by surprise, when they were sitting at opposite sides of the bar, was impossible. And what if they pulled their guns and a gunfight ensured? The bar would become a slaughterhouse in seconds, with innocent people being shot. The situation needed caution and the most careful handling. Larry Parks glanced at his wristwatch. Only another two minutes before he would take action if the rapid response team still had not arrived. Nervously he bit his lip, and gazed at the canvas bag on the table between the two Irishmen. Was the IRA going to bomb the tavern, or were they taking it somewhere else, to a city centre perhaps? The second hand on Larry Parks' wristwatch was ticking the remaining minutes away. Beads of sweat formed on his forehead and trickled down his face. He began to ease his gun out of his trouser pocket.

Meanwhile, Miss Pringle had almost completed her business with Sidney Frogmorton.

"You leave first and I'll follow five minutes later," she said.

Sidney Frogmorton stood up. "When will I hear from you again, Miss Pringle?"

"You won't, not unless you're late making a payment. I really hate bad payers, Mister Frogmorton. I hope you understand my meaning."

Sidney Frogmorton's face went a deathly pale. "The payments will be made as agreed, Miss Pringle, right on time."

"I do hope so, otherwise I'll be making a removal that isn't scheduled."

"There'll be no need for that, Miss Pringle. I'm a man of my word. Once I've made it I never go back on it."

"There's still time to cancel the removal, Mister Frogmorton."

"No, I want the item removed."

"Very well, Mister Frogmorton, then you'll not be hearing from me again unless you fail to keep your side of the bargain."

"Goodbye, Miss Pringle."

"Goodbye, Mister Frogmorton." Sidney Frogmorton turned and walked rapidly from the tavern. He felt a cold shiver go up and down his spine, and he knew instinctively that Miss Pringle would kill him if he failed to make the two payments as agreed. Miss Pringle had scribbled the Swiss bank account details for the payments on the back of a beer mat, which he carried in his pocket. First thing in the morning he would arrange for his accountant to dispatch the first payment. He did not want Miss Pringle thinking he was a bad payer. Indeed, that was the last thing he wanted. He got into his car and was driving out of the car park, when three saloon cars followed by an army lorry came sweeping past him. The vehicles pulled up with a squeal of tyres and men leapt out and ran towards the tavern. Sidney Frogmorton was watching in his rear view mirror as he motored away. "Good heavens, they must be really thirsty," he thought as he applied his foot to the accelerator and sped away.

Allan Hawes and Doctor Windrush sat watching Miss Pringle. They planned to make a citizen's arrest.

"Wait until she stands up, Windrush," said Allan Hawes, "Then we'll go over and make our arrest. We've got the proof we need to prove she's the serial killer."

"And what if she won't come quietly?"

"Did you bring your trusty old revolver?"

"No, Hawes, I forgot."

"Well, now isn't that priceless, Windrush. How can you forget the revolver when you knew we were dealing with a serial killer?"

"Sorry, Hawes, I won't forget it the next time, I promise you. It's just that guns make me terribly nervous, especially when pointed at me."

"We'll have to use karate then. I'll take her from the front and you take her from behind."

"Behind what?"

"Her back of course."

"Hawes?"

"Yes, Windrush?"

"I don't really know karate sufficiently to subdue somebody."

"What? But I thought you had taken lessons?"

"I did – but only the first one."

"The first one?"

"On how to relax sitting on a mat."

"I don't believe I'm hearing this, Windrush."

"I meant to finish the course, Hawes, but there always seemed to be more important things to do."

"All right, Windrush, then you leap on Miss Pringle from behind and hold her arms pinned to her side. Can you do that?"

Doctor Windrush nodded. "I think so, Hawes."

Miss Pringle stood up and began to walk towards the door. Ronald Perkins was well satisfied with the bargain he had made with Sidney Frogmorton. He now planned to retire with the money for the hit and buy a villa in sunny southern Spain, and live there happily ever after. He would marry the lovely Angela, and they would set up house together with his mother Hetty Rose Perkins.

Allan Hawes and Doctor Windrush stood up and moved towards Miss Pringle. The canvas bag was still on the table. Larry Parks, seeing the two Irish men walking away from the table leaving behind the canvas bag, concluded they must have primed the bomb inside the bag and were making their getaway. The bar was full of people.

"Cold-blooded IRA swines," he thought as he sprang to his feet and pulled the revolver free from his pocket. Allan Hawes had almost reached Miss Pringle, and was about to step in front of her, and Doctor Windrush, wishing he were miles away, nervously stepped up behind Miss Pringle.

"Don't move," shouted Larry Parks pointing his revolver at Allan Hawes.

Allan Hawes turned and saw the gun, and, thinking Larry Parks was Miss Pringle's accomplice, raised his hands. Doctor Windrush fainted.

"You're under arrest," said Larry Parks.

Miss Pringle hurried on towards the door. Ronald Perkins

had no idea what was happening but wanted nothing to do with it. Through the door burst half-a-dozen men wearing black suits. They were the MI5 rapid response team. Ronald Perkins hurried out to the car park, got in his car and drove away at full speed.

Captain Derek Fanshawe, tall and blue-eyed, an officer and gentleman, was in command of the MI5 rapid response team. Pulling a pair of handcuffs from his jacket pocket he ran over to Larry Parks, who stood with his gun pointing at a very nervous-looking Allan Hawes.

"Good man, Parks," said the captain. "I see you've bagged both the bastards."

"What's happening?" cried Allan Hawes.

"Keep your mouth shut," snarled the captain. "Bloody IRA swine." He clicked the handcuffs onto Allan Hawes's wrists.

"But I'm not in the IRA," pleaded Allan Hawes. "There's been a mistake."

"And you've made it, Paddy. Now shut up," said the captain grimly. "I won't tell you again." He turned to Larry Parks and pointed to the canvas bag on the table.

"Is that the bomb?"

"Yes, Captain," replied Larry Parks.

"But it's not a bomb," cried Allan Hawes, "it's evidence."

"I warned you to keep your mouth shut," said the captain pulling a gun from its holster, and levelling it at Allan Hawes. "Anything more to say, Paddy?"

Allan Hawes shook his head. "Only I'm no Paddy," he muttered meekly.

"What shall we do about the bag, Captain?" asked a fat MI5 man. "The bomb might go off at any moment. We're packed like sardines in here. There'd be one bloody great mess if it does go off."

"Clear the tavern," cried the captain, "and leave the bag to the bomb squad."

"Yes, Captain," replied the fat MI5 man as he turned and ran for the door. He had decided that fresh air outside the tavern was definitely the order of the day.

The tavern was cleared in less than thirty seconds when somebody shouted, "Get out, there's a bomb." Allan Hawes was marched out at gunpoint by Captain Fanshawe and put into the back of a car, and two burly MI5 men carried out the unconscious Doctor Windrush, who had knocked his head on a table when he fainted. He was handcuffed and laid on a grass verge under armed guard. The landlord of the Saucy Gander Tavern, Clive Heely, a roly-poly bald man with slobbering lips, gathered his customers around him and led them in a lively sing-song to keep their spirits up. Six times they sang "There'll always be an England", because it was the landlord's favourite song, and the only one to which he knew all the words. Second-lieutenant David Sackville was officer commanding the army bomb squad, and at fifty-three was the longest serving second-lieutenant in the British Army. He had joined as a Second-lieutenant serving in the cookhouse, supervising the boiling, roasting, mashing and chipping of potatoes. And after twenty-five years in the cookhouse, and by then hopelessly bored out of his mind with potatoes, he requested a posting to the bomb squad. This was immediately granted because his superior officer, who did not like him, saw it as a way of getting him out of the army with a big bang.

"Sergeant Baker," called the Second-lieutenant briskly in his best parade-ground voice, "to me at the double."

A tough-looking army Sergeant came running and jumped smartly to attention in front of the Second-lieutenant. He saluted smartly.

"Sir," he shouted at the top of his voice.

Second-lieutenant Fanshawe returned the salute by touching the peak of his hat with his swagger stick. "Now about this damn bomb, Sergeant."

"Yes, sir."

"Nasty thing a bomb, Sergeant, what, what."

"I had heard, sir."

"There's a bomb in the bar on a table in a canvas bag, Sergeant. I want you to be a very brave chap and go and bring it here to me."

"Might it explode, sir?"

"Not if you're careful, what, what."

"Wouldn't you like to help me carry it, sir? I'm a bit of a butterfingers and we don't want to blow me up now do we?"

161

"What do you suggest we do with the bomb, Sergeant?"

"I say leave it where it is, sir."

"Don't be silly, man, we can't do that. It's our job to deal with the damn thing. We're the bomb squad. It's our job to sort the blithering thing out."

"You out-rank me, Sir."

"What does that mean?"

"That you're in charge, Sir, and a bleeding sight more responsible for the bomb than me."

"Sergeant, bring me the bomb."

"Do I have to, Sir? Couldn't it wait until the next bomb squad comes on duty tomorrow morning?

"Are you a coward, Sergeant?"

"No, Sir, a Methodist and proud of it."

"Well, Sergeant, I can see a yellow line a foot wide running down your back."

"Down my what, Sir?"

"Back, man, back."

"Yes, Sir, thank you." The Sergeant saluted, turned on his heel, and started marching smartly away as if on the parade ground, down the road and away from the Saucy Gander Tavern.

"Where are you going, Sergeant?" shouted Second-lieutenant Sackville. "Come back immediately; I haven't dismissed you."

The Sergeant looking miserable, reluctantly returned to the officer and stood to attention. "But I thought you had dismissed me, Sir."

"Where the hell were you going?"

"Back to barracks, Sir."

"I didn't say you could return to barracks, Sergeant. For God's sake, man, you're the only one who can drive the truck. How would the rest of us return to barracks?"

"But you did order me back, Sir. I distinctly heard you say 'back, man, back'."

"I meant your back, man, between your head and arse. Not for you to go back to barracks. Tell me, Sergeant, do you think I'm a fool?"

The Sergeant made no reply but looked very thoughtful indeed.

"Well," demanded the second-lieutenant, "Do you think I'm a fool?"

"Can I have a few moments to think about it, Sir?"

"Sergeant, get me the damn bomb or you'll be up on charges."

"I certainly will if it explodes, Sir, bleeding great charges from several sticks of dynamite, I shouldn't wonder."

"Sergeant, I'm waiting."

"So am I, Sir, as far away from the bomb as possible."

"The bomb, Sergeant, now. Go and get it."

"If you insist, Sir."

"I bloody well do, Sergeant."

The Sergeant saluted, turned on his heel, and marched away into the tavern. He returned a few minutes later carrying the canvas bag with outstretched hands as far away from his body as possible.

"Where shall I put it, Sir?" he called out in a trembly, nervous voice.

"I could tell him," muttered a ginger-haired soldier as he stepped smartly behind the army truck for cover.

Second-lieutenant Sackville, who was also hiding behind the truck, put his head round and shouted, "Put the bomb down in the middle of the car park, Sergeant."

"That's my car park!" exclaimed landlord, Clive Heely.

"That's where they'll explode the bomb," replied an MI5 man ominously.

"Oh, bloody hell," cried the landlord in a panic. "The army's going to blow up my car park."

Meanwhile, the Sergeant had reached the middle of the car park. He gently lowered the canvas bag to the ground, then raced away as fast as his legs would carry him.

"Mission accomplished, sir," he called as he ran to hide behind the truck. The Second-lieutenant slowly advanced towards the canvas bag, carrying a small detonator in his right hand. He set the timer for two minutes and placed it gently on top of the canvas bag. The Second-lieutenant then ran the fastest one hundred yards in the history of running. He dived head-first into a ditch and lay on his stomach with his hands pressed over his ears. Seconds later, there was a small explosion, and the canvas bag blew up with a great tongue of flame followed by black billowing smoke. The receiver and tape-recorder with its 'evidence tape' of Marion Pringle talking to Sidney Frogmorton about the removal deal were blown to smithereens. Now there was no evidence that Marion Pringle existed, because the bomb squad had blown up the wrong thing, which was a regular habit with them since Second-lieutenant Sackville had joined the unit. On his first outing with the squad he blew up a public toilet, thinking the IRA had stuffed a small bomb down one of the toilet's S-bends. Then he blew-up a pig farmer's sty, insisting the powerful aroma coming from the pigpen was from a leaking IRA bomb. "Semtex has that peculiar smell," he explained to the shocked farmer afterwards. "And smells just like pig shit, don't you think?"

The farmer had to agree, but only because both he and the lieutenant were splattered from head to toe in pig shit.

Allan Hawes and Doctor Windrush were taken to the nearest police station to be questioned as IRA suspects. The handcuffs were removed, and they were taken before the Custody Sergeant who made out a charge sheet. All personal items such as wallets, money and credit cards were put into a prisoner's property bag. One telephone call was allowed for each prisoner. Allan Hawes phoned his solicitor. Doctor Windrush phoned his dentist for an appointment. They were taken to a cell by a muscular-looking policewoman, protesting their innocence all the way and saying they were most definitely not Irishmen. The large policewoman only grunted in reply. Outside the cell door they were asked to remove their shoes and trouser belt, then told to enter the cell. The door clanged shut behind them, and they found themselves alone in the confines of a small tile-covered cell. It was like being in a very small public toilet. There was a bunk with a blue mattress and a flushing toilet in the corner. Both men sat down on the bunk.

"What do we do now, Hawes?" asked Doctor Windrush unhappily.

"Sit and wait, my old friend. That's all we can do unless you've got a key to the cell door?"

"They didn't give me one, Hawes. Should they have done?"

Ronald Perkins, arm-in-arm with Angela Cobblers, walked up to the Vicarage front door and rang the bell. They had come to make arrangements for their wedding. Howard Peel the hump-back Vicar opened the door.

"Not collecting money are we?" he jokingly asked. "If so, then perhaps you've got some to spare." He always liked to greet people visiting the Vicarage with a cheery amusing comment. It always helped he thought, especially with grieving relatives who had come to book a funeral for a loved one, to see somebody still cheerful.

Angela Cobblers smiled. "We've come to see you about a wedding, Vicar."

"And whose wedding might that be, I wonder?"

"Ours, of course," replied Angela Cobblers with a girlish giggle.

"Well, step inside to my little study and we'll talk about it."

A few minutes later, in the study, Ronald Perkins and Angela Cobblers sat together on an old brown leather sofa, facing the Vicar, who sat in a matching armchair.

"Now," beamed the Vicar, "and what denomination are you?"

"Well, my father came from Catford and my mother from the Isle of Man," replied Angela Cobblers proudly, "so I suppose that must make me English? Doesn't it?"

"No, Angela, I meant what religion are you?" asked the Vicar gently as if talking to a small child. He now realised Angela Cobblers was not the sharpest pin in the pincushion.

"Does it matter, Vicar?"

"Well it does if you want to marry in the Church of England, my dear."

"But why?"

"Because we only marry Church of England folk, that's why."

"Oh, well, I was christened in a Church of England church, if that's any help, Vicar. I know, because my mother loved to tell a story to embarrass me, how I did a piddle down the front of a Vicar as he was holding me over the font. I was only three years old."

"Very good, Angela, then you're a member of the Church of

England. Tell me, have you been confirmed?"

"Confirmed as what, Vicar?"

"Oh dear, I see that you haven't been, but, never mind, it's not important for getting married in church." The Vicar turned to Ronald Perkins. "And what about you, Ronald?"

"What about me, Vicar?"

"What denomination are you?"

"Church of England. It says so in my Army pay book."

"Confirmed?"

"Yes, as a matter-of-fact it is, Vicar. It's written down in black and white and the Army never lies."

"I see – and is there any reason why you shouldn't be married in church?"

"Only if you say we can't, Vicar."

"No, Ronald, you misunderstand me. I was asking if you're already married to somebody else!"

"He'd better not be," snapped Angela Cobblers angrily.

"I've never been married, Vicar," said Ronald Perkins quickly.

"And you, Angela? Have you been joined in holy matrimony?"

"Certainly not, Vicar, I'd want to be married first, unless I knew him very well and could trust him not to tell anyone else he'd had a leg over."

"I meant have you been married before, Angela," persisted the Vicar.

"Before what?"

"You don't have a husband now, Angela, do you?" asked the Vicar with a roll of his eyes. This was proving to be the most difficult interview of a couple wanting to getting married that he had ever conducted.

"No, Vicar, that's why we're here. I want to get a husband before it's too late."

The grill on the cell door slid back, and the muscular policewoman peered through at Allan Hawes and Doctor Windrush. The Doctor lay stretched out on his back on the bunk bed snoring steadily and sounding like a rasping saw. Allan Hawes was pacing up and down, contemplating what he should do to track down the elusive Miss Marion Pringle.

"Your solicitor's here to see you," called the muscular

policewoman. There was the sound of a rattling chain and a key being turned in the lock. The door opened. The muscular policewoman stood massively astride the threshold, blocking most of the light, she beckoned with a shovel of a hand for Allan Hawes to follow her. Allan Hawes made for the door. "What about him?" she asked pointing to the sleeping Doctor Windrush.

"Oh, let him sleep," replied Allan Hawes. "I phoned for a solicitor. He phoned for a dentist. Let the dentist come and set him free."

Chapter Twelve

Time was running out for Ronald Perkins if he was to murder the British Prime Minister before going on honeymoon with Angela Cobblers. He had tried to talk her into having her wedding at a registry office, but she insisted on a church wedding with all the trimmings. Howard Peel, the hunch-back vicar, specially wanted a peal of bells before services, so he could swing on the bell rope. He was becoming strangely addicted to the habit, and his wife had reported it to the village Doctor, who prescribed a strong purgative both night and morning, and thrice on Sundays when the vicar was most at risk. Hetty Rose Perkins had become very strange and moody since learning of her son's wedding plans. She would give Angela Cobblers the most frightening looks whenever they met in the house; spine-chilling looks, which made the younger woman feel she was in the presence of madness. The wedding plans had indeed affected Hetty Rose Perkins's mind, replacing reason with insanity, and she harboured deep, dark, sinister thoughts about Angela Cobblers's untimely demise. Angela Cobblers became more and more afraid of her future mother-in-law, and did her best to keep out of her way.

Ronald Perkins, dressed in green tweeds with a black bag as Miss Marion Pringle, stepped onto the tube train to go to Westminster. Miss Pringle was going to the House of Commons to watch Prime Minister's Questions. Ronald Perkins wanted to see the great man, cigar-smoking Sir Antony Dingle, overtly fat with huge flabby jowls, looking a bit like a boxer dog, head set with hardly any neck on huge shoulders, close up and in the flesh. Being a professional killer, he wanted to size up his victim before making the hit. He wanted the great man dead within the next two weeks, because Angela Cobblers had booked the church in Bumstead on the Wold for the third week. They would marry, and retire to the sunshine of southern Spain. Hetty Rose Perkins would come as well. The tube train was packed with people like sardines in a tin, as it thundered through the dark underground tunnels. Ronald Perkins was standing at the sliding doors, face pressed up against the glass. He was worried that his wig might come off as the train rattled and rolled along. Suddenly, between two stations, he felt a hand on his left buttock. With difficulty, he managed to turn to see who was groping him. It was a ferret-faced man wearing a bowler hat and pin-striped trousers. The man gazed up adoringly into Marion Pringle's eyes. The fingers clutched tighter onto the buttock. The man smiled happily. Marion Pringle slapped him a stinging blow across the face. The hand was instantly removed from the buttock. The man politely raised his bowler hat saying meekly, "Thank you, madam, you're most kind," Then he turned and pushed his way through the throng, moving as far away from Marion Pringle as possible. He was frightened she was going to call the police.

Marion Pringle sat in the stranger's gallery in the House of Commons. The Tory Prime Minister, Sir Antony Dingle, was already on his feet, amidst a furious barrage of howls and catcalls from the Opposition benches.

"Sit down, fatty," called a thin woman dressed entirely in red. She was Miss Judy Upstarter-Brown, renowned for her home-made fish cakes and sweet pickle. She was the Labour Shadow Cabinet Minister on Embroidery and Wicker Bottom Chair Repairs.

"I would if I had a face like yours," retorted the Prime Minister.

Everybody on the Tory benches laughed and waved their order papers. There was a deathly silence from the Labour benches with stony glares at the Prime Minister.

"What about the workers?" called a voice from the back row of the Liberal Party benches.

"There aren't any workers here in this House," declared the Prime Minister, wagging his finger at the Opposition, "unless you mean here on the Tory benches."

There was a flood of booing from the Opposition benches.

"What about the workers?" cried the voice from the back row of the Liberal Party benches.

"Oh, the loony's back," declared the Prime Minister with a broad smile. He was greatly enjoying himself. Centre stage and working the hecklers well.

"Oh, no I'm not," shouted back the voice from the Liberal Party benches. "I'm not a loony. I've my Army demob papers to prove it."

"Oh, but you are back, loony," responded the Prime Minister gleefully. "I can hear you can't I?"

"Yes," replied the voice plaintively.

"Then you're back, loony, agreed?"

"Agreed. But I'm not a loony, Prime Minister. I'm Donald Day, the Labour MP for Upper Moulding."

"Which day is that?" asked a sleepy voice from the Tory benches.

"Certainly not this one," responded the Prime Minister. "He's a loony!"

"No, I'm not."

"Who's that speaking?" asked the Prime Minister, cupping a hand to his ear.

"It's me, the loony…"

The Tory benches broke into thunderous applause and wild cheering. The Prime Minister bowed from the waist to his adoring fans.

Ronald Perkins was studying the great man through a pair of opera glasses, contemplating some suitable perfect murder for him but so far had not come up with an idea to pass muster. Suddenly a melodious feminine voice called from behind him,

"Ice cream, choc ices or ice drinks on a stick." He turned to see a very shapely blonde ice cream seller wearing a tight white mini-skirted uniform with 'Daisy Ices' written across her ample bosom. The girl moved slowly down the aisle showing off her extraordinary long legs, as she sold her frozen wares to the visitors.

"Choc ice for one please," called Ronald Perkins as the girl reached him.

"I've run out of choc ices, sorry."

"What about an ice cream cornet?"

"Sold out, sorry."
"Ice lolly?"
"Sold out."
"All right, then, so what have you got left?"
"Nothing, I'm all sold out."

Angela Cobblers lay in the big double bed sleeping. She was alone. Ronald Perkins was away on one of his trips visiting London. It had just gone midnight, and an owl could be heard hooting ominously in the distance. There was a light breeze fluttering the curtains of the half-opened window. Outside it was a full moon, which cast its silvery light through the window and onto the sleeping Angela. There was no sound in the room but the faint tick tock of the bedside alarm clock. The door knob slowly turned and a deranged-looking figure, bare-footed, wearing a long pale blue nightie, with long white hair hanging down to the narrow shoulders, slowly advanced on tiptoe into the room. It was Hetty Rose Perkins come to pay her future daughter-in-law a visit. She held a bread knife in her right hand. Her eyes were wide open and ablaze with madness. Angela sighed in her sleep, dreaming of her dead lover Peter Catchpole.

"All right, if you're quick," she muttered to her dream lover. "Just one more time, you naughty boy, then we must be going home."

Hetty paused, hardly daring to breathe, worried that Angela was now awake. She knew the younger woman was much stronger and fitter than she was, she was old and feeble, and knew Angela could only be overpowered while she slept. Hetty raised the knife, the moonlight gleaming on the long blade, and advanced very slowly towards the bed. When Angela was found dead in the morning, people would think a burglar had broken in and stabbed her as she slept. Nobody would suspect the grieving Hetty Rose Perkins, who would put on the performance of her life. In the distance the owl hooted, and a tiny field mouse paused in the grass making itself an easy target for the winged terror above in the tree.

"Oh, yes, yes," gasped Angela, twisting and turning in passion, as the curate in her dream finished giving her a thrill which curled her toes. Hetty fearing Angela was now awake, turned and fled from the room. She closed the bedroom door behind her. The noise of the door closing woke Angela from her sweet slumbers. She had an overwhelming feeling that something was wrong, very wrong indeed. Feeling deadly afraid, and not knowing why, she sat up and switched on the bedroom light. With a sigh of relief at seeing nothing wrong in the room, she switched off the light and returned to the arms of the young rampant curate lover of her dreams.

The Prime Minister put up his hand for silence in the House of Commons and gave his famous two-fingered gesture to the Opposition benches.

"The voters, and I especially love those voters who voted for me at the last election, should count their blessings since the Conservative Party came to power. We've given them a far better lifestyle than they've ever known before, more money in their pockets, and cut taxes and..."

"Go on fatty, let's hear the same old story," interrupted Miss Judy Upstarter-Brown as she leapt to her feet.

There were loud boos and howls of derision from the Conservative benches, and cries for Miss Judy Upstarter-Brown to sit down.

"I would tell the Honourable member of Bexley Wood," Miss Upstarter-Brown," said the Prime Minister, fixing her with a steely eye, "that her Party made a right pig's ear out of running this country during their last term of office. It was chaos and mayhem everywhere when I took over. There were strikes and protest marches, people waving banners demanding a better life. And that's what the Conservative Party provided for them."

"What about the workers?" cried a voice.

"For God's sake don't ask the Honourable member of Bexley Wood," chuckled the Prime Minister. "She mistakenly thinks she is one."

"You're drunk, Mister Prime Minister," cried Miss Judy Upstarter-Brown indignantly. "I can tell by your extremely rude behaviour."

"No other female politician in this house has filled so large a space and left it so empty," replied the Prime Minister.

Ronald Perkins, watching from the stranger's gallery

disguised as Miss Marion Pringle, smiled, enjoying the humour. This was his second visit to the House of Commons in three days to study his murder assignment, the demise of the Prime Minster Sir Antony Dingle. He got up and made his way down the stairway towards the great hallway. Ronald Perkins knew it was going to be impossible to kill the Prime Minister in the Houses of Parliament. The man was too well guarded. There were security men, MI5 and SAS everywhere you looked, all trying to look as inconspicuous as possible, standing with their backs pressed up against the walls pretending they were not really there. Ronald Perkins's experienced eye could easily pick out the SAS men guarding the Prime Minister. They wore army camouflage jackets, and stood behind columns peering out. He had to come up with a plan to kill the Prime Minister while he was away from his guards. But how? The Prime Minister was always closely guarded. It was a puzzle that had to be quickly solved. Time was running out. The day of his marriage to Angela Cobblers was looming ever closer, and he had already put a down payment on a villa in sunny southern Spain. Ronald Perkins was just leaving the House of Commons down some stone steps, when a man wearing a bowler hat and pin-striped trousers came prancing up towards 'her'. The man was engaged in conversation with a tall man wearing a barrister's wig and gown. It was the same man who had groped Miss Marion Pringle on the tube train three days earlier.

"But that's a real howler, Judge," laughed the tall man. "I really must tell it to the chaps down at the club. They'll be splitting their sides when they hear it."

The judge smiled, enjoying the praise for his funny story. "Yes, but you have to laugh, Smethers, don't you," he said happily.

"Oh, yes," thought Smethers, "I jolly well do, especially if I want to remain on your good side, and keep your patronage for advancement in the law firm you run as Head of Chambers."

"Here's another good one," continued the judge with a knowing chuckle.

"There was this naked man who walks into a psychiatrist's office wearing nothing but cling film for shorts. The psychiatrist calls out 'I can clearly see you're nuts'."

Ronald Perkins watched as the judge and his companion continued up the steps. He was tempted to say something to the judge about the grope on the tube train, but decided against it.

Chief Inspector Edgar Briggs was sitting in the back of an unmarked police car with Sergeant Jenny Hopper. Police Constable Douglas Higgins, a broad-shouldered officer with long legs, who had been in the police force for just under a year, was driving the car. He had previously been, before joining the police force, a tank driver in the Army and filling out his application form to join the police force, no senior police officer thought to question what sort of vehicle he was a driver of. And on leaving Hendon he was assigned as a police driver. Constable Douglas Higgins drove the unmarked police car like it was a tank, grinding gears at every turn, and travelling at less than 20mph.

"Can't we go any faster?" asked the Chief Inspector impatiently. "It's already taken us an hour to travel eight miles."

"Sorry, it's the traffic, Sir, never known it so busy," replied the constable with a grinding of gears. "And I'm just not used to driving with a lot of other vehicles bumper to bumper. When I was in the Army and stationed out in the desert driving a tank, Sir, there wasn't any other vehicles to be seen but a few tanks, and camels with their Arab riders."

"What? You drive a tank as well as a car?" asked the Chief Inspector, now understanding the young constable's appalling driving abilities. He felt a sudden overwhelming impulse to leap from the car. "You do have a driving licence for a car, Constable, don't you?"

"Oh, yes, sir, of course I do," replied the constable with a chuckle. "I got it the same time I got my licence to drive a tank."

"And what was the vehicle in which you took your driving test, Constable?" asked the Chief Inspector, who was thinking it might be safer to get out of the car and walk to Scotland Yard.

"It was a tank, Sir."

"You took your driving test for a car in a tank?"

"That's right, sir, the officer in charge of transport, Captain Gates, who was giving the driving test, said as there wasn't a car available right then, I could use a tank."

174

"And did you get your driving licence on the first attempt?"

"Oh, no, Sir, I think it was the third or fourth attempt. But I blamed the camel for being too slow getting out of the way for failing the first time. And the second time I panicked and slammed my foot down on the accelerator instead of the brake and smashed the guard house down. It was a mistake anybody could have made."

The Chief Inspector made no reply but his face turned a deathly pale.

"Perhaps you'd like me to drive, Sir?" asked Sergeant Jenny Hopper.

"Oh, God yes, Sergeant, please do get behind the wheel, otherwise we won't get back to Scotland Yard until after the canteen has closed. And I'm dying for a steak and kidney pie with chips and a cup of extra sweet tea for the shock of being driven by a licensed tank driver."

"Shock?" asked Constable Higgins.

The Chief Inspector nodded. "Promise you'll never drive me again, Constable?"

Constable Douglas Higgins nodded his head.

"Pull over, Constable," cried the Sergeant, "I'll drive from here."

Constable Higgins spun the steering wheel hard over, and took the vehicle over to the kerbside. But too late he saw a plump middle-aged woman dressed in green tweeds, carrying a black bag, stepping briskly off the pavement to cross the road. The front bumper caught the woman and spun her up into the air feet first. She did a perfect somersault.

"Oops," cried the horrified young constable. "The same thing happened in Cairo, El Bardenna and South Watford. I always press my foot down on the wrong pedal in an emergency. In a tank the accelerator pedal is where the brake pedal is on a car. It's a simple enough mistake to make, now isn't it?"

"Yes, for a tank driver," snapped the Chief Inspector angrily as he opened the door and got out the car.

"Do you think he's annoyed with me?" asked the constable looking at Jenny Hopper.

The Sergeant nodded. "Very, Constable, and so am I, Constable, very annoyed indeed."

The woman dressed in green tweeds with a black bag lay stunned and sprawled like a rag doll across the pavement. It was Ronald Perkins, disguised as Marion Pringle. And it was only his training in the Parachute Regiment while doing national service twenty-three earlier in Cyprus, which saved him from landing badly and seriously hurting himself. He opened his eyes and saw the Chief Inspector bending over him with a worried look on his face.

"Madam," asked the Chief Inspector gently, "are you hurt?"

"No, but thank you for asking," replied Ronald Perkins in the high-pitched squeaky feminine voice he used while pretending to be Marion Pringle. "I'll be all right in a moment or two." He put his hand up to feel if the ginger wig was still in place, and breathed a sigh of relief that it was. The wig was such a tight-fitting hair-piece that it had been advertised as taking a force-nine gale to blow it away.

"Are you sure, Madam, you're not hurt? You came down very hard. Let me call for an ambulance."

"No, thank you. I mustn't be late getting home to cook my husband's tea. It's smoked haddock with brown bread tonight."

"Don't worry about that. I'm sure your husband can cook his own tea. I'll ask over the car radio for him to be notified about what's happened to you."

"But I can notify him myself when I get home, thank you."

"What's your name?"

"Marion... Marion Pringle. I'm a Miss."

"Well, Miss Pringle, I think you should go to hospital and be checked over by a Doctor. It's best not to take risks with one's health, you know."

"Please, I'm perfectly all right now." Ronald Perkins got to his feet. He felt dazed and bruised, especially bruised where he had landed on his buttocks after somersaulting from off the car's front bumper. It was then he noticed that his ginger wig, worn for his Marion Pringle disguise, had slipped very slightly over to one side. Quickly he brushed it back with a sweep of his right hand. Chief Inspector Edgar Briggs had not noticed. He had gone back to the police car to ask Constable Higgins to get out and assist him with getting Miss Pringle onto the back seat. Ronald Perkins gasped when shock when he saw the uniformed young police constable getting out of the car.

"Oh my God," he thought in a desperate panic, "they're police officers."

"I'm terribly sorry about this," said Constable Higgins as he took Ronald Perkins gently by the left arm, "But it's not the same as driving a tank, you see. Now I know where everything is on a tank. And I like driving a tank."

"Oh, look, over there," cried Ronald Perkins pointing across the road at a red double-decker bus which had just pulled up at a bus stop, "There's my bus. I must go or I'll miss it."

The constable shook his head. "Sorry, Miss Pringle, but you must let us take you to hospital. You might well be concussed, and that could be serious. And what about any possible internal injuries? No, you really must let a Doctor take a look at you."

"But I've only laddered my stockings. I tell you, Constable. I'm as right as rain now. I must go home to sort out the smoked haddock."

The constable took a firmer grip on Ronald Perkins's elbow and led him protesting towards the car. He dared not struggle too violently for fear he might reveal by his strength that he really was a man and not a woman. Sergeant Jenny Hopper opened the rear passenger door from inside the vehicle, and reached up to help Ronald Perkins onto the back seat.

"There, there, my dear," she said sympathetically. "You just lay back and relax. You've had a very nasty shock."

Ronald Perkins was now desperate. Here he was, disguised as a woman, sitting in the back of a police car, and being taken for a hospital for a medical check-up. The Doctors in the Casualty Department were in for a really big surprise when the nurses removed Miss Pringle's clothes. Constable Higgins got in and sat down. Ronald Perkins was now wedged firmly and trapped between two police officers on the back seat. There was no means of escape. Things were becoming worse by the second. He lay back and closed his eyes, desperately trying to think up some way of stopping the police officers from taking him to hospital. Chief Inspector Edgar Briggs, who was driving, because he no longer trusted Constable Higgins, glanced in the rear view mirror and was startled to see Miss Pringle lying back with eyes closed.

"She's not dead is she?" he asked, wondering what the Superintendent would say if a woman had died in the back of a police car. Constable Higgins bent over Ronald Perkins, his face a few inches from his face, looking for signs of life. Suddenly Ronald Perkins opened his eyes, and stared up into the constable's worried face. The constable, caught unaware, and thinking she had died, but then had had miraculously come back to life, screamed in terror. He claimed not to believe in ghosts but would never spend the night in a haunted house. Ronald Perkins screamed because the constable screamed. Chief Inspector screamed because they both screamed. But Sergeant Jenny Hopper, determined to keep her womanly cool, managed to stifle her scream. She did not want her male colleagues to think she was a weak frail female who was prone to screaming at the slightest thing. It was only men who did that.

"She's not dead, sir," cried the constable after he had regained his composure.

"Thank God for that," replied the Chief Inspector, "we'd better get her to hospital as fast as we can." He slipped into first gear, pressed his foot down on the accelerator pedal, and the car sped away into the rush-hour traffic. "It's a pity this is an unmarked police car."

"Why, Sir?" asked the Sergeant.

"Because we could use the siren to get through the traffic."

"I could lean out the window and blow my whistle," offered Constable Higgins.

Casualty Doctor Percy Mackey was tired. It had been a long hard shift and he was almost asleep on his feet. There had been a whole series of emergencies for him to cope with, ranging from a marble stuffed up a man's nose, to a woman with extra tight jeans which had to be removed under a general anaesthetic. Doctor Percy Mackey was of average height with delicate hands with long slim fingers. His mother had said that with hands like those he would have made a brilliant concert pianist. She had been disappointed when he entered medicine. He glanced at his wristwatch. There was less than half an hour to go before he could go off duty and slip into his nice soft bed. He sat down on a chair, yawned and closed his eyes.

"Coffee, Doctor?" asked a familiar soft female voice.

He opened his eyes and saw Staff Nurse Caroline Baker standing with two mugs of steaming coffee in her hands. She was a Yorkshire lass, an efficient dedicated nurse, caring with an outgoing personality.

"Thank you, Staff," he said, "that's very thoughtful of you." He took the mug and sipped the hot coffee.

"Not long, Doctor, is it?" she asked with a smile.

"I beg your pardon?" he gasped almost choking on his coffee. He mistakenly thought Nurse Jane Adams, with whom he had recently made love, and who was Staff Nurse Baker's best friend, told her about the diminutive size of his penis. Sadly it was the size of a cigarette, and was only brought out for rampant use after the bedroom lights had been switched off.

"It's not long," repeated Staff Nurse Adams, who was talking about the time when the shift ended and she could go off duty.

"Please don't tell anyone else," he pleaded in a whisper. "It's bad enough you and Jill knowing about it. But she did promise to keep it a secret."

"But everybody on the shift knows it."

"What? Not everybody surely?"

"But of course, Doctor, even the hospital porters know."

"They do?"

She nodded and smiled. "Sister Morgan was even talking about it in her office just now!"

Doctor Percy Mackey closed his eyes, his face flushed with embarrassment.

Oh dear God, he thought miserably, the size of my penis is now the talk of the entire hospital.

Chief Inspector Edgar Briggs drove through the hospital gates, and up towards the sign-posted Casualty Department. Constable Higgins was leaning out of a rear passenger window blowing his police whistle. The car sped up and stopped in front of the glass doors of Casualty with a scream of tyres. Ronald Perkins sat in the back wedged between the Sergeant and constable. He was desperate to do anything to delay going through the hospital swing doors.

"I feel sick," he said as a delaying tactic.

"Quick she's going to be sick," cried the Sergeant, grabbing the constable's peaked hat and thrusting it under Ronald Perkins's chin. "Here, use this," she said.

Ronald Perkins leant forward and made some suitable being sick noises.

"But that's my best hat," cried the constable with a look of disdain, as he wondered who was going to pay for a new one.

Sergeant Jenny Hopper opened the rear passenger door and stepped out. Seeing his chance, Ronald Perkins leapt out and legged it off down the driveway towards the hospital gates.

"Quickly," shouted the Chief Inspector, "After her. She's badly concussed and doesn't know what's she's doing."

Constable Higgins, who had the longest legs, overtook Ronald Perkins just as he reached the hospital gates. Puffing and blowing with the effort of the run, he reached out and grabbed Ronald Perkins in a tight bear hug from behind. "It's all right, Miss Pringle," he said gently in her ear. "You've been concussed and don't know what you're doing."

Ronald Perkins bought his knee hard up into the constable's groin.

"Aaaah," gasped the constable in agony, as he dropped to his knees like a sack of potatoes.

Ronald Perkins was about to run out through the hospital gates and lose himself among the milling crowds when Sergeant Hopper and the Chief Inspector arrived on the scene. They grabbed him in a restraining double arm lock and frog-marched him back to the hospital.

"We had no choice but to use reasonable force to subdue her," said the Chief Inspector, who was thinking of his report to the Superintendent on the police car accident. "We can't have a seriously concussed woman running amok, Sergeant. God's knows what she might do."

"No, sir, that wouldn't be right," replied the Sergeant balefully.

"But I'm not concussed," pleaded Ronald Perkins, "I just want to go home."

There were a number of miserable-looking people sitting around on chairs waiting to be seen by a Doctor, with forlorn expressions on their faces. Most of them had been waiting a considerably long time. At the reception desk, a big black woman dressed in a white overall was talking on the telephone.

"Oh, yes and she said the father was the Brigade of Guards." she confided with a giggle. She glanced up to see the Chief Inspector and the Sergeant, both holding tightly onto the struggling Ronald Perkins by the elbows, come bustling towards the receptionist desk. "Can I call you back in a bit, Jean," she said hurriedly into the telephone, "There's something come up which needs my urgent attention."

"This woman, is I believe, seriously concussed," declared the Chief Inspector.

"I'm not, I'm really not," responded Ronald Perkins desperately, "I just want to go home to cook my husband's smoked haddock."

"Can we see a Doctor quickly?" asked the Chief Inspector. "She's just run amok down the hospital driveway."

"I did not run amok," cried Ronald Perkins indignantly, knowing he was now only minutes away from being undressed and examined by a casualty Doctor.

"Poor old soul," said the receptionist sympathetically looking at Ronald Perkins, "Doesn't she look simply awful. What was it, drugs?"

"Road accident," replied Sergeant Hopper.

"Oh, dear," said the receptionist. "And she hit her face did she? What was it a bus?"

"No, I wasn't hit by a bus," spluttered Ronald Perkins, "This is my normal face."

The receptionist looked at Ronald Perkins's manly face with its square set jaw, and thinking that he was really a woman, dressed in green tweeds with lipstick and face powder, thought what a terrible face it was for any woman to have.

"How sad. You poor old thing," she said with a shake of her head. "But a bus might have improved it."

"She needs a Doctor fast," said the Chief Inspector. "Not a discussion on what her face looks like."

"You're right, of course," replied the receptionist stepping out from behind her desk. "If you'll follow me I'll find you a nurse."

"But I need a Doctor," insisted the Chief Inspector.

"Sorry, Sir," replied the receptionist, "but first you must see an experienced staff nurse. She'll determine just how life-threatening the patient's medical problem might be. The Doctor's far too busy to see anyone at the moment. He can only look at the really serious cases. It's staff levels you see, hospital management can't get the staff these days, not for love or money." She led the way through some swing doors and into the treatment area with curtained cubicles on either side of a large well-lit room. Staff Nurse Caroline Baker stepped forward with a look of concern on her lovely face.

"What's happened?" she asked in a professional tone of voice, running her eye expertly over the ginger-haired woman in green tweeds, who was still being held tightly by the elbows by the Chief Inspector and his Sergeant.

"Road accident," said the receptionist knowingly.

"Well, bring her straight into this cubicle and I'll fetch the Doctor," said the staff nurse as she pulled aside the curtain. "She certainly looks like an emergency case to me."

"Please, you don't understand, Nurse," implored Ronald Perkins. "I just want to go home and sort out my husband's smoked haddock and slices of brown bread."

"Sounds concussed to me," said the staff nurse. "Help her up on the trolley please. I'll just pop out and get the Doctor. You'll like him," she said to Ronald Perkins. "He has such nice warm hands." She turned and left the cubicle drawing the curtain behind her.

The Chief Inspector and Sergeant Jenny Hopper struggled to lift the heavy Ronald Perkins up onto the trolley. "My, but aren't you a heavy girl, Miss Pringle," puffed the Chief Inspector, face red with exertion, and now wishing he had done some weightlifting to harden up his muscles to keep himself in shape.

"Shouldn't we hold her down on the trolley until the Doctor comes, sir?" asked the Sergeant, a worried look on her face. "She might fall off."

"I won't try to get off the trolley," cried Ronald Perkins, who was still desperately looking for any chance to escape. He stopped struggling and lay quiet. "I promise you. You're quite right. I should see a Doctor." He hoped the police officer would relax for a moment so he could make a run for it.

"Now that's being sensible, Miss Pringle," said the Chief Inspector.

The curtain was pulled aside and Doctor Percy Mackey strode in followed by Staff Nurse Caroline Baker. The Doctor went straight over to the trolley and put his stethoscope in his ears. He turned to Chief Inspector Edgar Briggs and Sergeant Jenny Hopper. "Can you wait outside. I need some privacy to conduct my examination. There's a coffee vending machine down the corridor."

"Your constable's already there," said the staff nurse.

"Thank you," replied the Chief Inspector, "we'll do just that."

"I want to go home," wailed Ronald Perkins. "What will happen to the smoked haddock?"

"Now don't you go worrying about that, Miss Pringle, you're in very good hands. I'll come back later for you to write out your statement on the accident," said the Chief Inspector. "It was a police car that caused it, and so you can sue Scotland Yard if you want!"

"But I don't want to sue Scotland Yard," cried Ronald Perkins, "I just want to go home."

"Please go," said Doctor Mackey to the Chief Inspector, "This lady looks as if she's in need of urgent medical treatment. She must be examined without delay."

"But of course, Doctor," replied the Chief Inspector, "we'll go and get ourselves a coffee." He left the cubicle followed by the Sergeant. The staff nurse closed the curtain after them.

"Now let's have a look at you," said the Doctor as he blew on the end of his stethoscope to warm it. "Can you tell me what happened?"

"It was nothing really, Doctor, there's no need to waste your valuable time," replied Ronald Perkins. "I'll take a couple of aspirin when I get home." He sat up and made to swing his legs over the side of the trolley but the Doctor gently pushed him back. "You must let me be the best judge of that... Mrs eh..."

"Miss Pringle," said the staff nurse. "The constable said she was bounced off the bonnet of a police car. He was the driver."

"Now that does sound serious," replied the Doctor with a grave look.

"It was nothing really," responded Ronald Perkins. "I'll go straight home and have a hot cup of cocoa, then pop into bed. I'll be right as rain in the morning."

"Not until I check that everything's all right first, Miss Pringle." He put a stethoscope in his ears, turned to Staff Nurse Caroline Baker and said, "Loosen Miss Pringle's clothes, Nurse, I would like to listen to her heart."

Ronald Perkins lay on the trolley gripped with indecision. What should he do? The fact that he was really a man was about to be starkly revealed, and the police were just down the hallway at a coffee vending machine. The police would surely be suspicious as to why he was walking around London dressed as a woman in green tweeds.

The staff nurse bent over Ronald Perkins and unbuttoned the top button of the green tweed jacket. She glanced back over her shoulder. "Shall I remove the skirt as well, Doctor?"

"Yes, best to get them all off, Nurse, so I can see what I'm doing."

Staff Nurse Caroline Baker returned to her task of unbuttoning the green tweed jacket. Button number two and three were opened. The jacket fell open revealing a huge bosom. The staff nurse began to unbutton the white shirt. As each button was unbuttoned Ronald Perkins gave a nervous little squeak.

"Must have bruised her chest," said the Doctor, poised with his stethoscope and ready to go into action. "Careful, she might have a cracked rib or two."

The nurse opened the shirt to reveal a large bra. From the top of the right cup dangled a piece of cotton wool. The nurse took hold of the cotton wool and started to pull it out of the cup. She watched in open-mouthed astonishment as a long line of cotton wool was pulled forth, and the well-padded breast deflated before her very eyes.

"Doctor," she gasped in a shocked voice, "I think you should see this – all is not as it seems."

The Doctor stepped forward and looked down at the deflated bra cup, then he looked at Miss Pringle. "Have you had a breast removed, Miss Pringle?" he asked.

184

Ronald Pringle's ginger wig slipped slightly down his forehead. Staff Nurse Caroline Baker reached up to brush back the hair. To her amazement it slipped right off Ronald Pringle's head. The nurse could hardly believe her eyes. Miss Pringle was wearing a wig.

Ronald Pringle decided that it was now or never. He sat up and pushed the Doctor and nurse aside and leapt down from the trolley.

"I'm off. Goodbye, and thank you," he cried as he scurried from the cubicle. Down the corridor to his left he could see the three police officers grouped around a vending machine, drinking coffee from plastic cups. He turned and fled down the right corridor running as fast as his legs would carry him.

The 'lucky' ginger wig was given to Chief Inspector Edgar Briggs who wanted to hand it in to the London Transport Lost Property Office. But Sergeant Jenny Hopper, deeply suspicious of the wig, and the deflated right bra cup, convinced her boss that the wig should go to Forensics for tests. Police Constable Douglas Higgins, with his preference for driving tanks and not police cars, resigned from the Metropolitan Police Force a week later, and returned to the Army to drive tanks. Ronald Perkins had made good his escape. He had hailed a taxi outside the hospital. The cabbie had given him a most peculiar look as he climbed into the back of the cab, with his short back and sides male haircut, wearing a green tweed skirt, lipstick and eye makeup. But the driver decided that there were a lot of strange-looking women wandering about London these days, and why should he care as long as they paid their fare. The taxi took Ronald Perkins back to his London hotel, where he crept unseen up the back fire escape to his room on the sixth floor. He stripped out of the green tweeds and bundled Miss Marion Pringle's clothes into a suitcase, took a shower, had a shave, got dressed in his own male clothes, and within the hour he was on a train pulling into the railway station at Bumstead on the Wold. It had been the second time in twenty years that he had been forced to flee from London wanted by the police.

Chapter Thirteen

Chief Inspector Edgar Briggs was horrified. He could not believe what he was hearing from his Sergeant. She had just read him the forensic report on the tests carried out on the ginger wig of Miss Marion Pringle. The tests taken from traces of sweat left on the wig gave the DNA of the person who had worn it. The DNA found on the wig had checked exactly with that of other DNA samples taken from murder cases being investigated by the police. There was found to be a perfect match with the DNA from two murder cases – Police Constable Robert MacDougal and Jamaican railway employee Barry Coles in the Barnes Railway Bridge Murder, and the murder of Wing Commander Hughie Lampton in the Cigar Butt Murder. The Chief Inspector paced up and down the room in front of his desk in great agitation.

"I just don't believe it, Sergeant," he exclaimed angrily. "The woman we took to hospital was the serial killer we've been hunting? The serial killer who murdered my colleague, Police Constable Robert MacDougal, twenty years ago at the controls of a police launch, by dropping a weighted holdall from off Barnes Railway Bridge? Are you telling me that she sat on the back seat of our police car, wedged in between you, Sergeant, and Police Constable Douglas Higgins?"

Sergeant Jenny Hopper nodded her head.

"But that's going to make us the laughing stock of Scotland Yard for years to come," continued the Chief Inspector, who was beside himself with rage. "And to think we helped her into the Casualty Department for a check-up by a Doctor."

"But it was a he, Sir."

"He what?"

"The serial killer is male, Sir. He's not a woman. DNA has established it as being one hundred percent certain that it's a man."

"I know that, Sergeant, I know that. I'm not a fool you know."

"If you say so, Sir," muttered the Sergeant under her breath.

"Pardon? What did you say?"

"I said you're no fool, Sir."

"That's quite right, I'm not – but now the Superintendent will think I'm a fool. And that doesn't help my chances of promotion, Sergeant, does it?"

"I wouldn't worry too much about promotion if I were you, Sir."

"I even helped the killer up onto a trolley in the hospital cubicle. It's just so embarrassing. What will the Chief Constable think?"

"Probably the same as me, Sir."

"And what do you think?"

"Not very much, Sir."

"Well, there you are, Sergeant, I do. It's the detective in me – the experienced copper's nose, which can sniff out crime half a mile away."

"But the killer was restrained by you, Sir, I saw you holding his elbow."

"So did you. I saw you, Sergeant."

"Yes, Sir, but I'm not the superior officer here, you are."

"Meaning what?"

"That the buck stops right here, Sir, at your office desk."

Angela Cobblers lay in a hot bubble bath relaxing in the soothing warm water. She wriggled her toes, and gently pushed along with her right hand a little yellow plastic duck bobbing between her knees, which she had named Pete, after her dead lover Peter Catchpole. She had not grieved openly for him, grieving only in the quiet privacy of solitude, sobbing into a pillow in the seclusion of her bedroom, not wanting Ronald Perkins to see how much she missed her young curate lover Peter Catchpole. There was gentle knock on the bathroom door.

"Are you decent, Angie?" called Ronald Perkins through the keyhole.

"Never when you're around," she called back. "You always bring out the animal in me, you naughty boy, Ronnie."

"Can I come in Angie?"

"Only if you're going to be good."

"But how can I be good when you're naked in the bath?"

"Come in, Ronnie, but no patty fingers, I'm warning you."

The door opened and Ronald Perkins strolled in smoking a large Havana cigar. He was wearing a black evening jacket and bow tie. He walked over to the bath and gazed down at Angela Cobblers.

"My, my," he said in an awed tone of voice, "but aren't you simply gorgeous. Just like a little pink mermaid." He took a puff of his cigar. "I've got to go away next week for a few days. I hope you don't mind, Angie."

She gazed up at him and forced herself to smile. "But you know I'll miss you terribly."

"And I'll miss you too, Angie."

"Will you be taking your mother with you?"

"Not this time."

"Oh."

"What's the matter?"

"Well, I don't like being left alone with her."

"But why ever not?"

"She gives me the creeps, that's why – it's the way she stares at me with those cold eyes of hers. I'm afraid of her, Ronnie."

"Don't be silly, Angie. Mother would never harm you?"

"Well, I get this terrible shiver running up and down my spine whenever she's in a room with me. Why, only the other day out in the back garden, she startled me almost witless, by dropping a flowerpot from off her bedroom balcony, just as I was walking underneath. I think she meant to hit me with it."

"Come now, Angie, I think you're getting a little hysterical about Mother. She's not that bad, now is she?"

"Well, you don't have to stay here alone with her like me. When I'm in the sitting room watching TV, she comes in and sits down…"

"Well, that's not too bad, now is it, Angie?" interrupted Ronald Perkins. "The two of you watching TV together?"

"She doesn't watch TV – she just sits and watches me."

"Oh."

"You won't be away for too long, Ronnie, will you? Don't forget our wedding day is only seventeen days away."

"How could I, Angie? But I really must go away for a few days. I've been hired as a consultant to organise a very important removal. It'll mean lots of money for us."

"Oh, you and your removals, Ronnie, you're antiques mad. Would you like to come and join me in my bubble bath?"

"I thought you'd never ask."

Allan Hawes and Doctor Windrush were taking an evening stroll over London Bridge. The stars twinkled brightly in a cloudless sky, and there was the sound of gentle lapping water of the river against the bridge.

"It's a real problem," said Allan Hawes thoughtfully. "What can we do about the killer hired by Sidney Frogmorton? We had our chance and blew it."

"But that's not strictly true, Hawes, it was the Army bomb squad who blew it in the car park of the Saucy Gander Tavern."

"Yes," agreed Hawes, "When they thought your canvas bag, with transmitter and receiver inside, was an IRA bomb."

"Made quite a bang, didn't it?"

"And blew up the tape we'd made of Sidney Frogmorton talking to Miss Marion Pringle, or as I like to think of her, the lady in green tweeds. We needed that tape for evidence for the police."

"What are we going to do, Hawes? Shouldn't we go to the police and warn them that an attempt is to be made on the Prime Minister's life? After all, you did vote for the man at the last election, and should be doing your best to keep him in office."

"But there's client confidentiality to consider, Windrush."

"Well, that won't help the Prime Minister or his widow, Hawes."

"But what about Mrs Mabel Frogmorton? She's our client isn't she? We should respect her wishes. And she wants the police kept out of it."

"I think we should go to the police."

"Well, I don't know, Windrush, I still think we should wait a few more days."

"The Prime Minister might be dead by then, Hawes."

"All right, I agree, Windrush, we can't allow that to happen. But I still think that given a few more days we might have run the serial murderer to ground."

"Well, I think the Prime Minister will be jolly pleased that the police are involved, Hawes. I know I would be if I were him."

Ronald Perkins, dressed as a rambler in grey shorts, open-neck white shirt, heavy-duty walking shoes with grey socks rolled down to the ankles, strode in a leisurely fashion down a twisting country lane. He had a theatrical grey goatee beard glued to his chin, and wore a pair of black horn-rimmed spectacles. On his head was a blue sun hat. It was a hot sunny day and on his back he carried a haversack. He was within seven miles directly across country in a straight line from the Prime Minister, country house, Chequers. Ronald Perkins purpose was to ascertain just how well guarded the Prime Minister would be when staying at Chequers. He was considering making the 'removal' at Chequers at a later date. Ronald Perkins whistled softly as he strode along. It was such a nice day. Birds were singing in the hedgerows, cows and sheep idly munched grass in fields and meadows. It was a bright cloudless day with the sun relentlessly blazing down. Ronald Perkins stopped near a farm gate and took a small, round, black metal box compass from his pocket. It was the same army compass he had used and carried in Cyprus while serving with the Parachute Regiment. After taking a reading with the compass, he returned it to his pocket. The way he had to go now was directly across country to the south-west, and that according to his compass bearing would bring him directly onto Chequers. Ronald Perkins climbed over the farm gate into a large rising meadow with a wood at the top. At the far end of the meadow to his right he could see some horses grouped together in a corner. He began to climb the meadow towards the wood. And as he walked he pondered on different ideas for killing the Prime Minister and making it look like a perfect murder. But it was proving somewhat difficult. The great man was never left unguarded, with dozens of security men always in attendance, mostly hidden away out of sight. Ronald Perkins only carried out a killing when he and the victim were alone together somewhere quiet, and the victim was unguarded. To try and kill a man surrounded by security was going to be a huge problem. But every problem had its answer. The serial killer had three fairly good ideas for killing the Prime Minister, written down in his secret notebooks back at home in Bumstead on the Wold. He had decided a week earlier, to find out how well guarded Chequers was, with MI5 and the SAS guarding the place. These were the top-notch security men, exceptionally well trained and highly professional and knew their job inside out. They would leave nothing to chance while guarding the Prime Minister. Chequers was the Prime Minister's weekend country retreat, and so the security would appear to be less tight on the ground, than it was when he was high profile in the House of Commons. The MI5 and SAS would want the Prime Minister to feel that he had more privacy to relax with his family.

Ronald Perkins had been walking for about half an hour, when he clambered over a style into a field, which had two long wooden fenced pigpens with metal roofs. There was the sound of squealing and grunting pigs and piglets coming from the pigpens, but no pig was in sight. Unfortunately for Ronald Perkins, he was down wind, and the powerful, almost overwhelming aroma of pig dung became ever stronger with every step he took towards the pigpens. He intended to pass the pigpens and continue towards a distance copse of elm trees. Ronald Perkins had no knowledge of pigs except as ham, bacon, and sausages. Would a pig attack a man? And if one did so, should he stand perfectly still as one did for a dog, or run like hell for the nearest gate? As he drew closer to the pigpens, he noticed a tall middle-aged man with dark hair leaning on a pigpen wall watching him. The man was dressed in old dirty jeans and a shirt that might have been white when it was originally purchased many years before. The shirt looked as if it had never been washed. Ronald Perkins took the man to be the pig farmer. The man opened a gate in the pigpen and stepped out to confront Ronald Perkins. He had a long piece of straw dangling from the corner of his mouth and was constantly chewing upon it.

"Morning, sir," he said, eyeing Ronald Perkins slowly up and down.

"Good morning, to you," replied the serial killer, putting on a false Welsh accent. "Lovely day, isn't it?"

"We don't see many people hereabouts. Going far?"

"I'm walking to the next town. How far is that?"

"About three mile, I reckon, as the crow flies."

"Thank you."

"May I ask your name, Sir?"

"Robert Peters."

"Which way did you come, Sir?"

"Over the hill back there and through the woods. I parked my car a mile from Kempton Bottom." This was not true, Ronald Perkins had not travelled there by car. He had not wanted his car to be traced. Police often jotted down the numbers of cars they found parked in the countryside. The registration number might have police knocking on his door back in Bumstead on the Wold doing a vehicle check. He had travelled by train to Kempton Bottom railway station to cover his tracks. He wanted to be as invisible as possible while surveying the layout of Chequers.

"I thought you might be lost when I first saw you, Sir."

"Oh, no, I've been taking regular compass bearings."

"Have you now, Sir. And do you know where you are?"

"I've no idea."

"That accent of yours – sounds Welsh to me. Are you Welsh?"

Ronald Perkins nodded. "I come from smoky old Cardiff with all its factory chimneys. That's why I always take a country walking holiday each year."

"Then you're alone?"

The serial killer nodded.

"Well, enjoy your walk, Mr Peters," smiled the man, chewing on his blade of straw.

Ronald Perkins nodded and strode off across the field. The man watched him until he had disappeared from sight among the trees. He then took a mobile radio from his pocket and switched it on.

"Nothing to worry about here, Captain," he said into the phone. "Only some rambler out for a walk. Said he was walking to the next town."

"Very good, Sergeant Jeeves."

The Sergeant switched off the radio. He walked into the pigpen and on into the hut behind it. There were no pigs to be seen, only a tape-recorder standing on a bench table with wires running to loudspeakers, from which could heard the squealing and grunting of pigs. There was a burly man in camouflage jacket and trousers sitting at a table drinking tea from a mug. He glanced up as the Sergeant entered.

"Like some tea, Sarge?" he asked. They were both SAS on surveillance protecting Chequers.

Ronald Perkins clambered over a small stone wall and entered what seemed to be a large meadow, with scattered clumps of yellow primroses, which sloped gently away to a small winding river. He looked for any animal inhabitants, especially pigs, before entering, but saw none. Feeling somewhat reassured, he proceeded to walk down towards the river, planning to rest there for a few minutes, and take a compass bearing, eat a cheese sandwich and drink tea from his flask. He had gone over halfway to the river when he heard a thundering of hooves coming up behind him. Glancing over his shoulder, he saw to his horror a massive bull with steam coming from its nostrils, bearing down on him like an express train.

"Oh, dear God," he cried as he broke into a desperate run towards the river. He threw off his haversack, which was slowing him down. The bull was fast closing the distance between them with every stride. Ronald Perkins saw the looming riverbank and the gleaming sun-speckled water ahead of him, felt the hot breath of the bull on his neck, and made one frantic dive into the river. He felt the cold water envelope him. He surfaced a minute later and saw the bull, standing on the riverbank, angrily pawing at the ground with its front hooves. The bull remained at the riverbank for some twenty minutes before it trotted over to the haversack, which it tossed several times into the air and trampled on it. Ronald Perkins decided not to leave the safety of the river. He could wait just as long as a bull.

Six hours later he was still waiting. The bull would saunter over to the riverbank to watch him for a few minutes, then go off nearby to chew grass. The bull finally walked away up the meadow and out of sight as the sun was beginning to set. Ronald Perkins still did not risk getting out of the river. He was now very cold and his skin had wrinkled up with being in the water for so long. He waited another twenty minutes, measured on his waterproof wristwatch, then clambered miserably up the riverbank. He retrieved the haversack and its scattered contents. There was a change of clothes, underwear, trousers, jacket, pullover, socks, and a plastic box of cheese sandwiches; some with pickle and some without pickle, but no sign of the flask of tea. The bull must have kicked it rolling down into the river. There was a box of matches in the haversack, and Ronald Perkins soon had a small fire crackling away in a nearby wood, which he used to warm himself and dry his soaking clothes. He would wait for daylight before venturing on towards Chequers.

Angela Cobblers sat opposite Hetty Rose Perkins at the supper table. They were having shepherd's pie and green peas, followed by hot chocolate sauce poured over ice cream straight from the freezer. It was Angela Cobblers's favourite pudding. The two women sat in silence. They had not spoken all evening, nor in fact for days and even weeks to each other. There was something spine-chilling about the way Hetty Rose Perkins fixed Angela Cobblers with her eyes, like a snake which is about to strike. Angela Cobblers felt very uneasy, and was tempted to leave the table before the butler served the pudding. Was it just her imagination or was Ronald's mother glaring hatred at her down the table? The women had almost finished their shepherd's pie, when Hetty Rose Perkins stood up and shook an angry finger at Angela Cobblers.

"Sow the wind and reap the storm," she called out.

"What's wrong?" asked Angela fearfully, "Don't you like ice cream?"

"It's you," cried Hetty Rose Perkins. "You're what's wrong."

"Me? But surely not."

"Why don't you leave my son alone?"

Flynn the butler entered the room carrying a silver tray on which stood two tall glasses full of vanilla ice cream. There was a glass jug full of hot chocolate sauce. Hetty Rose Perkins sat down and glared at Angela Cobblers. Flynn placed a glass of ice cream in front of each woman and poured chocolate sauce over it.

"Would there be anything else, Madam?" he asked in the haughty voice which butlers love to use.

"No, that's all, Flynn," replied Hetty Rose Perkins, still fixing her crazy eyes steadily on Angela Cobblers. "You may go now."

"Very good, Madam." Flynn turned, and went out of the door and closed it behind him.

Angela Cobblers felt a desperate urge to call him back but stifled the impulse. How could she explain why she wanted him to stay in the room? She could not say she was terrified of Hetty Rose Perkins. Now the two women were alone and facing each other across the length of the dinning room table. Hetty Rose Perkins, who had not touched her ice cream, stood up and took a step towards Angela Cobblers, holding a long stem ice cream spoon in her hand.

"You can't marry my Ronnie," she hissed her face twisted with hate. "I won't allow it. You're only after his money."

"More ice cream?" gasped Angela Cobblers who was deeply shocked, and desperate to change the subject, hoping it would pacify Hetty Rose Perkins. She would have to have a serious talk with Ronald when he got home. It had become intolerable living under the same roof as his mother; and one of them would have to go. Angela Cobblers stood up and backed away down the table, followed by Hetty Rose Perkins.

"It's not too late," cried Hetty Rose Perkins through gritted teeth, as she stabbed the air in front of her with the ice cream spoon.

"What? For more chocolate sauce?" replied Angela Cobblers, face ashen and knees knocking like castanets, as she backed away with ever-quicker steps. "We can always send out for more. I'm sure cook won't mind."

"But I mind," stormed Hetty Rose Perkins. "I mind very much."

"Can't we sit down and talk it over?" asked Angela Cobblers. "I'm sure we can sort it all out between us without doing anything silly."

"You're not marrying my Ronnie," screamed Hetty Rose

Perkins, as she broke into a fast run. Angela Cobblers fled for her life, desperate to keep the table length between them. She was the younger fitter woman, but Hetty Rose Perkins was more agile and determined. The door opened and Flynn the butler appeared carrying a silver tray with two coffee cups. He seemed oblivious to what was happening between the women. It was not for him to be judgmental of employers' behaviour. Indeed, in his career spanning thirty-three years, rising from boot boy to butler, working for some of the best known families in the land, he had seen it all before. Nothing shocked or surprised him about rich people. They had money and he did not, and money gave them the right to be as eccentric as they wanted. And anyway, he thought the two women were playing some childish game, without any real risk to the two players being hurt. Hetty Rose Perkins continued to run after Angela Cobblers, threatening her with the ice cream spoon.

"Will there be anything else, Madam?" asked Flynn.

"Yes," cried Angela Cobblers. "Open the door and stand back."

"Yes, Madam, at once." Flynn obediently opened the door wide and Angela Cobblers flew past him like a bat out of hell. She did not stop running until she reached her bedroom. She slammed the door behind her and turned the key in the lock. Gasping for breath, she sat down on the bed, put her head in her hands, and broke into pitiful sobs. Her future husband's mother was trying to kill her. But what should she do about it? Hetty Rose Perkins must be having a mental breakdown. There could be no other explanation. If only Ronald Perkins was home to deal with it.

There was a rapid knocking on the door.

"Angela," called Hetty Rose Perkins from the other side of the door, "Can I come in? I've something for you."

In a wild panic, fearing for her life, Angela Cobblers reached over and grabbed the telephone on the bedside table. Picking up the phone she hurriedly dialled 999. Hetty Rose Perkins, now babbling incoherently, pounded the door with her ice cream spoon.

The police were there within ten minutes, racing with sirens blaring and lights flashing. Hetty Rose Perkins was subdued by two police officers, who held her down in an armchair, while a third officer spoke to his station on the car radio. The local GP was summoned, and Doctor George Pegs, after giving Hetty Rose Perkins a sedative, arranged for her to be taken away in an ambulance. She was diagnosed as having a mental breakdown.

Ronald Perkins had slept under a tree using the haversack as a pillow, and to keep warm had covered himself with leaves. The loud chirping of birds twittering on overhead branches woke him. He sat up and saw the welcoming first rays of sunlight spreading like fingers across the landscape. Every muscle in body ached and his feet felt like blocks of ice. It was not good for a man of his age to spend the night sleeping rough, without tent or sleeping bag. He did a few minutes of running on the spot to warm himself up and to get the blood moving through his veins. Then, with the haversack on his back and the last cheese sandwich eaten, he moved off at a steady walking pace in the direction of Chequers.

Allan Hawes and Doctor Windrush were shown into Chief Inspector Edgar Briggs's office. He was sitting at his desk and stood up to greet the two men. Sergeant Jenny Hopper was sitting at her desk typing up a report, her fingers clicking away on the keys. She glanced up and nodded to them.

"Thank you for coming over so quickly, gentlemen," said the Chief Inspector, holding out his hand for them both to shake in turn. "I'm told by Inspector Gatwood from London Bridge Police Station that you've reported to him that there's going to be an attempt on the Prime Minister's, life."

"Precisely," said Allan Hawes, who was still wearing his deerstalker hat.

"Do you know when, sir?"

"Soon," said Doctor Windrush ominously. "Very soon."

"But how soon?"

"I'd hazard a guess, Chief Inspector," replied Allan Hawes, "and I'd say within the next few days."

"And who do you think is going to make the attempt? The IRA?"

Allan Hawes looked at Doctor Windrush, unsure if he

should mention Sidney Frogmorton and the mysterious Miss Marion Pringle. Doctor Windrush nodded his head for him to tell the Chief Inspector. The great detective did not want to break a client's confidentiality, but as Windrush had earlier pointed out as they talked on London Bridge, there was no choice in the matter. It was either that or the Prime Minister being killed. "I think it's a serial killer hired by Sidney Frogmorton," said the detective gravely.

"What? Not the fish and chip empire magnate, Sir?"

"The very same, Chief Inspector," agreed Doctor Windrush.

"Have you proof of this?"

"We did, Chief Inspector," replied Allan Hawes.

"You did?"

"But it got blown up," said Doctor Windrush.

"How?"

"An Army bomb squad thought it was an IRA bomb, Chief Inspector," said Allan Hawes, remembering the incident with a feeling of dread and disaster.

"Ah, so the IRA are involved?"

"No, it was a canvas bag, Chief Inspector," said Doctor Windrush.

"Then who did the canvas bag belong to?"

"It was ours, Chief Inspector," declared Allan Hawes.

"Yours?"

The Chief Inspector slumped down in his chair, his head spinning. This was all too confusing for him to take in all at once. He took a deep breath to steady himself.

Sergeant Jenny Hopper, looking worried, stood up and hurried over to her boss. "Would you like a glass of water, Sir?"

"No thank you, Sergeant. It's all rather confusing, that's all."

"We had a tape recorder and directional microphone hidden inside the bag," explained Allan Hawes. "We had learnt of a meeting between Sidney Frogmorton and a mysterious woman, the serial killer. And went to the Saucy Gander Tavern to try and record the conversation between serial killer and client. We sat at a nearby table with our canvas bag."

"Then you saw the serial killer?" asked Sergeant Jenny Hopper.

"We most certainly did," agreed Doctor Windrush.

"Can you give us a description of the serial killer?" asked the sergeant.

"Well, yes, she was a big buxom woman with ginger hair, dressed in green tweeds with matching hat and black bag."

"What?" cried the Chief Inspector, jumping excitedly to his feet. He had recognised the description instantly. It was the woman he had taken to hospital after Constable Higgins had bounced her off the front bumper. "Was her name Pringle?"

"Yes, it was, Chief Inspector, Marion Pringle."

"Then I've got news for you. She's not a woman."

"She's not?" gasped Allan Hawes, who was deeply shocked by the revelation.

"No, she's definitely a man."

Allan Hawes and Doctor Windrush looked incredulously at each other.

"Yes, a man," continued the Chief Inspector. "We did a DNA forensic test on the ginger wig he left behind at the hospital, and the result matched exactly with other DNA evidence we've got for two other murder cases."

"Do you know his name, Chief Inspector?" asked Allan Hawes.

"No, but that's the only missing piece of the jigsaw. We do know he has murdered over a twenty-year period. The number of his victims we don't know, but a professional serial killer works on contract. And as we know, there are many people who would willingly hire a killer to do a job for them. We can trace his handiwork to three murder victims so far."

"How dreadful," gasped Doctor Windrush, who was feeling rather queasy.

"I shall contact Inspector Lionel Harper of Special Branch," said the Chief Inspector, "and put him in the picture. He is the man responsible for the Prime Minister's protection. Then I think we should pay Sidney Frogmorton a visit, and find out if a date and time has been fixed with the serial killer for the murder of Sir Antony Dingle."

"Good show!" exclaimed Doctor Windrush. "Jolly good show."

Prime Minister Sir Antony Dingle sat in the back of a Silver Fox

Rolls Royce, drinking a large whisky he had poured himself from the drinks cabinet. He was on his way to Chequers to join his wife and daughters for the weekend. There were two black saloon cars in front and two behind the Rolls Royce, each packed with armed security men. And leading the convoy up front were two motorcycle policemen. The convoy had left behind the teeming streets of London and entered the plush green landscape of the rolling hills of Buckinghamshire. Sitting in the front of the Rolls Royce next to the MI5 trained driver was an SAS corporal, wearing bowler hat and pinstripe trousers. On his lap covered by a raincoat, he held a machine gun. The car was specially reinforced with armour plating and bullet-proof windows. In the back of the car sitting with the Prime Minister, was his personal secretary Miss Constance Goodbody, who put career before having a husband and children. She was totally dedicated to the Prime Minister, and was more loyal to him than a lap dog. She had been with Sir Antony for over ten years, before he first took political office as Minister of Fish and Veg. The great man was dictating a speech to her, which she quickly scribbled down in shorthand in her notebook. He always spoke rapidly when speech making, and she found it difficult to keep up with him, although she could muster over 150 words a minute. Sir Antony Dingle was planning to make the speech on the following Tuesday afternoon in the House of Commons, when the topic to be debated was going to be 'More Taxes'. The Minister paused for breath and took a sip of whisky.

"Tell me, Miss Goodbody, what do you think of income tax? Do you think you pay too much or too little?"

"I'd rather not say, Prime Minister."

"Please Miss Goodbody, I'd like to know."

"I can't."

"Please, Miss Goodbody – I value your opinion, you know that."

"All right then, Prime Minister, but you won't like it. I think that I most definitely pay too much tax. My father always said he paid too much tax as well, as did his father before him, and his father before him. The working man and woman in this country pay far too much tax. We're the most heavily taxed nation in the world. And it's your Party which is always raising income tax."

The Prime Minister took a puff of his cigar and frowned. He was sorry now that he asked Miss Goodbody the question. People without much money always hated paying tax, he knew that. But being fabulously rich it had never bothered him to pay it himself.

"After breakfast tomorrow at Chequers, Miss Goodbody, I would like you to help me continue writing my memoirs. As you know, I'm already up to chapter five of volume twenty-seven, and I do want it completed before I die. The great British nation deserves to have a complete record of my life and thoughts as seen from my own perspective, don't you think so?"

"But who else could undertake such a bountiful work, Prime Minister, and give it the full credit which you truly think it deserves."

The Prime Minister sipped his whisky and smiled. "You're right of course, Miss Goodbody," he said puffing his cigar. "Nobody knows me like I know myself."

"Have you decided on a title for your memoirs, Prime Minister?"

The Prime Minister nodded. "I thought 'Greatness Was Upon Him'."

"You don't think the title is a little too blatant, Prime Minister?"

"But how?"

"Well, it does give away the plot, don't you think? It's rather like buying a murder mystery and being told on page one who the killer is."

Chapter Fourteen

The IRA had a three-man strike team in southern England with the purpose of killing the Prime Minister. They were a crack team from Belfast, and this was their first trip to the mainland. Commander Sean O'Gully was in charge, Patrick Dobbs and Roy McCluster were his right and left hand men, depending on which side of him they were standing at the time. They had all grown up together in the same slum back streets of dirty red brick semi-detached houses, played football using dustbins as goal posts, and had even been altar boys together.

Sean O'Gully was a big powerful man with hands like shovels, and a singing voice like an angel. He was dedicated to the cause and the wearing of the green, and had a wife and four children waiting for him at home.

Patrick Dobbs, the silent thoughtful one of the team, had learnt his explosive skills from off the back of cornflake packets. Patrick, known as Pat by friends or Paddy by those who could not care less, had a wife and five children waiting for him back in Belfast. He had been a plumber's assistant, a pizza delivery boy and twice, when out of work over the Christmas period, a department store's fairy grotto Father Christmas. But he was forced to give it up on medical advice after hurting himself when he sat down accidentally on a fairy's wand, which scarred him for life. And now he walked with a slight limp to the right. Roy McCluster was the youngest of the three, and the joker in the pack. He prided himself on his joke telling, and felt if life had only treated him differently then he would have ended up as a top paid comedian working television and the end of the pier panto. He was the only unmarried man in the strike team, and was seriously dating Mary MacCuddy, the cousin of Patrick Dobbs. They planned to marry in the New Year.

The strike team had gone operational when Commander

Sean O'Gully received a phone call from Jean Neely, his cousin three times removed, who was working under cover near the House of Commons as a traffic warden. She had been writing out a ticket when the Prime Minister's convoy drove past on its way to Chequers. Jean Neely did not finish writing out the ticket, which was lucky for the motorist concerned, but unlucky for the Prime Minister's convoy. She had raced away to the nearest telephone box to make an urgent call to the strike team leader.

"It's him all right," she said into the phone. "There was no mistaking the car with the police outriders. I'd reckon he'd be with you in about an hour's time."

"Thanks, Jean," said Sean O'Gully at the other end of the line. "We'll be ready for him. Ireland forever."

"Ireland forever," cried the traffic warden. She replaced the phone and went back to finish writing out the ticket, but the car had gone.

The strike team had chosen to detonate the bomb, built by Patrick Dobbs from a sweet tin packed with a small torch battery powering a tiny receiver, and one pound of Semtex, on a sharp bend in the road four miles from Chequers. In the middle of the road the night before, close to the midnight hour, while two of the team kept watch, the third man worked, digging a hole eight inches deep and a eight inches square. The bomb was placed in the hole and covered with stones and a layer of tarmac. A remote control device made by Patrick Dobbs would explode it.

The three Irishmen waited, concealed behind some bushes several yards from the road. The spot under which the bomb was hidden had been marked with a small chalk cross, and Commander Sean O'Gully was watching it intently through a pair of binoculars. His mouth was dry with the nervous fear he felt churning away inside him.

"Right, lads," he said in a quiet, determined voice which he hoped would convey to his companions both his authority and resolve to have the bomb exploded. It was the first time the strike team had been in action. None of the men had killed nor fired a shot in anger. And for the IRA this was the really big one – the assassination of a British Prime Minister, which would show that no British politician was safe from them.

"Will he be late?" asked Patrick Dobbs who held the remote

control in his right hand with his finger pressed gently on the red firing button.

"Not for his own funeral," chuckled Roy McCluster.

The other two men laughed.

"Remember, lads," said Commander Sean O'Gully, "This is a great historical moment for Ireland. I think we should bow our heads and say a little prayer, don't you."

"No," replied Roy McCluster, "I bloody well do not."

"Well, I do," persisted Sean O'Gully. "We should pray for the man's soul."

"I will not," replied Roy McCluster. "He'd never have prayed for me."

"Now that's a very hard attitude to be taking and no mistake," said Patrick Dobbs. "And here was me thinking that some Christian charity had rubbed off on you, when you were an altar boy back at St Mary's with Father Barry."

"Be quiet now lads," called Sean O'Gully. "I can hear motorbikes. That'll be the police outriders."

"Is it himself, then?" asked Roy McCluster nervously, his mouth dry with fear, and the palms of his hands sticky with sweat. The first time in action effected each man differently. Some wanted to run away, some to wet their pants, but most wished they were safely at home. Only idiots wanted to stand and die.

"Who else but he would have a motorbike escort?" replied Patrick Dobbs, "out on a country road so close to Chequers. It's him, I'd bet my life on it."

"I wouldn't give anything for his life," smiled Roy McCluster.

"Nor would I, Roy."

They all laughed.

"Ready with the button, Pat?" asked Commander Sean O'Gully nervously.

Patrick Dobbs nodded his head. "I'm ready for him to come round the bend, Sean, and drive over the spot marked with a chalk cross. Then bang. Goodbye Prime Minister."

"Don't press the button until the chalk mark is right under the car," warned Sean O'Gully. "Then let him have it."

"You can be sure of that," replied Patrick Dobbs. "He'll be

sky high before he knows it."

The sound of the motorbikes drew louder and the two police outriders came roaring round the bend. They were closely followed by two black saloon cars. "Get ready, now, Pat, don't miss the bastard," shouted Sean O'Gully excitedly.

The Rolls Royce Silver Fox swept almost silently into view.

"The Brits make bloody good cars, I'll give them that," said Roy McCluster, who was greatly impressed by the silent engine of the Rolls Royce. "If I had the money I'd treat myself to one."

"Ready... ready... ready," chanted Patrick Dobbs quietly under his breath, his thumb poised to press hard down on the red button. His fingers visibly shook at the thought that he was about to send anyone travelling in a Rolls Royce with the British Prime Minister to Kingdom Come. Killing was hard for a Catholic man who was also a vegetarian. The Rolls Royce moved effortlessly with hardly any sound coming from its powerful engine. Sean O'Gully was looking at the Rolls Royce through binoculars, hoping to see if he could see through the darkened bullet-proof glass to the Prime Minister sitting on the back seat. But the window was too dark.

"Now," cried Patrick Dobbs excitedly as his thumb pressed fully down on the red button of the remote control. The three Irishmen threw themselves flat on their stomachs expecting to be a blinding explosion, billowing black smoke, and chunks of Rolls Royce and British Prime Minister flying everywhere. But there was a deathly silence. The convoy continued on its way to Chequers, blissfully unaware that the hand of death had momentarily hovered over it ready to come crashing down with a fearful oblivion. The three Irishmen slowly got to their feet and dusted themselves down. What had happened to the bomb? Why had it not exploded? "Well, that's blown it," stormed Sean O'Gully, clenching his fists in frustration. He was thinking what the IRA high command would say at their next general meeting; about his failure do the 'Big One' for Ireland. His name would surely be mud down the drinking men's club in South Belfast for years to come.

"No, you haven't blown it," said Roy McCluster trying to comfort him, who was somewhat alarmed by his leader's fury.

He had never seen him so angry before, and they had known each other for over thirty years.

"Oh, yes, I have," insisted Sean O'Gully. "I've blown it really big time."

"But you haven't," persisted Roy McCluster. "How could you blow it, Sean, when the bomb didn't even go off?"

Sean O'Gully turned furiously on Patrick Dobbs and stabbed him viciously in the chest with a forefinger. "It was you wasn't it, you bastard?"

"What?" gasped Patrick Dobbs taking a hasty step backwards from his leader with a frightened look on his face. "I don't know what you're talking about!"

"Steady there, Sean," cried Roy McCluster stepping between the two men and holding them apart with his hands. "We don't want any arguing among ourselves. The bomb was a dude and that's all there is to and nobody's to blame. These things happen in war. It's unfortunate but there's nothing we can do about it."

"This didn't just happen," fumed Sean O'Gully, glaring at Patrick Dobbs.

"What do you mean?" asked Patrick Dobbs, taking another step backwards, making sure he was beyond the fists of his leader.

"I think you forgot to put in the battery – just like you did during a training session back in Ireland."

"I'd never do that, Sean. I wouldn't make such a silly mistake again."

"Look in your trouser pocket!"

Patrick Dobbs reached into his right trouser pocket. "Oops," he gasped, his face turning the colour of a beetroot, as he pulled his hand out. Grasped in his fingers was an Ever Ready battery.

"You bastard," screamed Sean O'Gully, throwing a wild punch at him.

Patrick Dodd turned and raced away as fast as his legs would carry him, hotly pursued by his leader, who was screaming abuse at him and trying to hit him with his fists. The two men ran down the road in the opposite direction to Chequers until they were out of sight. Roy McCluster stood watching them shaking his head.

"Oh, lads," he muttered sadly to himself, "And didn't I say we shouldn't be arguing among ourselves."

The Prime Minister, Sir Antony Dingle, sat in the back of the Rolls Royce, blissfully unaware that heaven had just smiled upon him with an IRA bomb without a battery.

"It's been a long tiring day, Miss Goodbody," he said taking a puff of his cigar.

"It most certainly has, Prime Minister."

"How much longer before we reach Chequers?"

Constance Goodbody glanced at her wristwatch. "About eight minutes, Prime Minister."

"Good, I could certainly do with stretching my legs. Can you type up my speech before dinner? It's only a draft but I'd like to work on it this evening."

Constance Goodbody nodded wearily. "Certainly Prime Minister." She closed her notepad, which was full of her shorthand scribbles made from the great man's dictation. She would have liked to put her feet up for an hour before dinner, like she knew the Prime Minister was going to do. But she was the personal secretary and he was the Prime Minister. "Will you do any painting over the weekend, Prime Minister?" she asked, knowing full well that he would be doing exactly that, because oil painting was his favourite way to relax. And he would sit out in the gardens somewhere, with brushes and canvas, painting landscape views mostly woodlands. He never painted portraits, finding it too difficult to do eyes and hands. But then he could not do trees either.

"I thought it might be an ideal way to spend Sunday afternoon, Miss Goodbody, a paint brush in hand. Have you a hobby?" He smiled broadly to encourage her. "I've known you for over ten years, but I don't think I've ever asked you about your hobbies before now have I?"

"I like stamp collecting, Prime Minster."

"You do?"

"And train spotting."

The smile faded on the great man's face. "You will finish typing up my speech before dinner, Miss Goodbody, won't you. I can correct it in bed tonight, so it will be ready for you to retype in the morning."

"Yes, Prime Minister," replied Constance Goodbody with a forced smile. She had been looking forward to sitting out in a deck chair on Saturday morning to soak in the sunshine, not typing up another draft of the speech. She knew it would have been her only break from the tiresome task. But Sir Antony Dingle was a perfectionist with his speeches, making endless corrections right up to the very last moment. Miss Goodbody knew how she was going to spend this weekend... typing drafts of speeches. The convoy turned off the road and passed through open iron gates guarded by armed police in bullet-proof vests, and up a long winding gravel driveway. They had arrived at Chequers.

Sidney Frogmorton had taken his wife Mabel up to London to see Oscar Wilde's play 'The Importance of Being Ernest', which they both enjoyed immensely. Sidney Frogmorton was planning go on to a restaurant afterwards, and tell his wife that they were going on a sea cruise, setting sail within two days from Southampton. They would be at sea for one month. He would say the cruise was a delayed birthday present for Mabel. She had her birthday some five months earlier. But really, he wanted to be far away and out of the country when the Prime Minister was murdered. Sidney Frogmorton took Mabel for dinner to Alfonso's, considered the best Italian gourmet restaurant in town. Marcus Alfonso, a fat jolly man with a bald spot on top of his head which made him look like a monk, served them himself at table, and insisted they accept with his compliments a bottle of champagne.

"It's always nice to see you here, Mr and Mrs Frogmorton," he said with a beaming smile as he poured champagne into their glasses. "Would you like to order now?"

"Later, thank you," replied Sidney Frogmorton.

Marcus Alfonso bowed. "But of course. Whenever you are ready." He turned and walked away leaving the couple alone together.

Sidney Frogmorton told his wife about the planned sea cruise. She listened quietly with a serious look on her face, then shook her head slowly.

"Sorry," she told him, "but I don't think that's very good idea."

Sidney was astonished. He had expected his wife to leap at the chance of a month away at sea. Mabel had good sea legs. In fact she also had a good seat for horse riding too, broad and very plump. Both talents came quite naturally to the children of titled people.

"But why ever not, Mabel?" he asked. "I know you'll just love it."

Mabel Frogmorton reached across the table and put her hand gently on top of her husband's hand.

"Sidney," she said in a low whisper so she would not be overheard from nearby tables, "there's something I've been meaning to ask you."

"Yes, my dear, and what's that?"

"Is   there...?"   Her   voice   faltered   momentarily, "...something deeply troubling you? Something it would help for you to share with me?"

"Like what, dear? I don't understand."

"Well, I was hoping that you might tell me that, Sidney."

"I'm sorry, old thing, but I haven't the faintest idea of what you're talking about."

"Oh, please, Sidney, do remember that I'm your wife and you can trust me. Please do trust me. Things are never so bad that they can't be sorted. I want you to be open and honest with me now."

"But I'm always that with you dear, you know that."

Mabel looked at her husband and gave no reply. She wanted to tell him that she knew he had hired a professional killer to murder the Prime Minister, and that she herself had hired a private detective to stop the killing. But she just could not bring herself to do it. There had been a steadily growing gap in their relationship over the years, and sometimes when they talked, it was as if they were strangers to each other. There was no bonding. The fish and chip magnate wanted a knighthood and she wanted a title. That was quite true, and that was why she married him, believing money can buy anything, even a title for herself. Three times, Sidney Frogmorton had been refused a knighthood by the Prime Minister, and in Sidney Frogmorton's book three times was three times too many, and that was why the Prime Minister had to die. Mabel Frogmorton hoped that Allan Hawes and Doctor Windrush would save her family honour and prevent the police becoming involved. She did not know that Allan Hawes had already contacted the police and they were already on their way to his house to arrest him.

Ronald Perkins was close to Chequers. He could see grey smoke wafting up above the treetops. Moving towards the smoke he heard distant voices, and dived into the nearest thicket and lay face down. Two armed policemen with sten guns and bullet proof-vests sauntered by, discussing the forthcoming football match to be played between Liverpool and Manchester United on Saturday afternoon.

"Won't see it now, of course," complained the shorter of the two policemen, "Not with the Prime Minister down for the whole weekend."

"Yeah, and to think I voted for him," grinned the other police officer. "We won't see two teams like Liverpool and Manchester United playing a Cup Final again for a very long time, Joe."

"Not in my lifetime, Steve."

"Yeah, I agree Joe."

The two policemen walked away into the distant elm trees.

Ronald Perkins felt the hairs rise up on the nape of his neck at the mention of the Prime Minister. He had only been planning to reconnoitre Chequers to get the lay of the land, and had not expected his prime target Sir Antony Dingle would be down for the weekend. It was known the Prime Minister liked to visit Chequers every other week during the summer and monthly throughout the winter. It had been reported widely in the press that the great man had visited Chequers only the previous weekend. And so Ronald Perkins had not expected him to be there this weekend. The serial killer smiled to himself. Now his plan to reconnoitre Chequers had turned to one of accomplishing his mission. The Prime Minister would now be leaving to drive back to London, lying in a coffin in the back of a hearse. Ronald Perkins chuckled, thinking that if it had not been for that bull yesterday, making him spend hours up to his neck freezing in a river, then he would have come yesterday, sketched his map of Chequers with, hopefully, security weak points marked in, and have returned home. This was going to be his lucky day; he could feel it in his bones. And the murder of the British Prime Minister, made to look accidental, would be the final accolade to his dazzling career as a serial killer. This was the real big one – the one which would be recorded forever by the world's historians. This would be his page in history. His fame would be like that of Jack the Ripper... with people trying to establish for generation after generation all down the annals of history, what was the true identity of the mysterious killer of Sir Antony Dingle. Who was Miss Marion Pringle?

The three members of the IRA strike team were sitting at a corner table in O'Leary's Bar in Staines, Surrey. It was early evening on the Friday. Roy McCluster, the youngest of the team, was trying hard to patch up the differences between his two companions, Sean O'Gully, the petulant leader, and Patrick Dobbs, the dubious explosive expert who forgot to put a battery in the home-made IRA bomb. Patrick Dobbs had a black eye and a fat lip. He had not managed to outrun his leader as he was being chased down the road, shortly after the bomb failed to explode under the British Prime Minister's Rolls Royce.

"Now, lads," said Roy Cluster, as he tried to be the peace maker, "we've still got a chance here to put things right. And that doesn't happen every day I can tell you. We know where Sir Antony Dingle is now don't we? Didn't we see him drive on to Chequers?"

The other two Irishmen nodded glumly.

"Well, lads, why don't we go to Chequers and finish the job?"

The IRA had an insider working at 10 Downing Street, a personal private secretary with impeccable references and no traceable Irish connections. It was this female mole who had notified the strike team through traffic warden Jean Neely that the British Prime Minister was driving down to Chequers for the weekend to meet and have talks with the American President Robert R Rooker. President Rooker had started, since coming to office three months earlier, a crack-down by the FBI and CIA on the IRA buying guns in America. The President wanted help from the British government, with his plans to invade a small three-wide-mile island off the south tip of Cuba, and build an air base there.

"What about the bomb?" demanded Sean O'Gully, glaring at Patrick Dobbs who nervously sipped a glass of foaming Guinness. "We'll need one that won't need a battery to make go off."

"There he goes again," grumbled Patrick Dobbs. "Going on about that damn battery again. I really do wish it hadn't happened but I can't turn back the clock, now can I?"

"Well, I'd like to turn you back, Paddy," snapped Sean O'Gully furiously.

"Look, lads," said Roy McCluster, "can't we forget about the bomb, for God's sake? I'm fed up hearing about the bloody thing."

"Forget it?" exclaimed Sean O'Gully furiously. "I'll never forget it as long as I live. This stupid bastard sitting opposite me forgot to put in the battery. What a laugh the lads will have when they hear back home on the Falls Road."

"I've said I was sorry," mumbled Patrick Dobbs unhappily. "What more can I say?"

"Well, try goodbye – that'll be about right for my ears to hear."

Patrick Dobbs stood up. "I'll not stay where I'm not wanted."

"Sit down, Pat," said Roy McCluster, "and finish your Guinness."

"Let him go," insisted Sean O'Gully, "we're better off without him."

"That's not so, Sean. We're a team," declared Roy McCluster. "The best in the IRA. We're handpicked to a man and trained to do our job. We can't have come so far together to let a tiny little battery beat us. Can't we forget our differences, shake hands, and make another strike for Ireland to bring Sir Antony Dingle down?"

"Do you really think there's a chance?" asked Sean O'Gully.

Roy McCluster nodded. He turned to Patrick Dobbs. "Can you put another bomb together, Pat? Is there enough Semtex to blow-up a house? We won't have time to return to Liverpool for more from the safe house. We must hit with what we've got here and now. And if we can't have a bomb then it'll have to be with the gun."

"I've enough Semtex for a small bomb," replied Patrick Dobbs.

"Good man," cried Roy McCluster, "Then is it a go?"

Sean O'Gully and Patrick Dobbs looked at each other, shook hands and smiled, and nodded their heads. The three men stood up and raised their Guinness glasses. "One for all and all for Ireland," they cried excitedly. There conversation had been loud and it was lucky for them that the only other person in O'Leary's bar so early in the evening was O'Leary himself, who already was too drunk to hear or see what was being planned in his bar. He lay stretched out on his back behind the bar counter, with a silly grin on his face, humming quietly to himself lost in his own drunken stupor. He would be up on his feet within the passing of an hour, up and ready to drunkenly greet his regulars and pay homage to the whisky bottle.

It was late evening when Sidney Frogmorton drove slowly up the driveway to his house and caught, in the full glare of the headlights, a dozen or so uniformed police officers. They stood waiting, faces grim, beside their parked police cars outside the front door. Sidney Frogmorton was mortified to see the police. He was returning with his wife from their night out in London to see Oscar Wilde's play.

"What the hell is..." he gasped, deeply shocked. "Why are the police here?"

"Oh, no," cried Mabel Frogmorton, bursting into floods of tears and burying her face in her hands. She thought of the terrible scandal when the press found out that her husband had been arrested. It was more than she could bear. She had known instantly on seeing them why the police were there. But how did they know? Who had told them about her husband hiring a serial killer? Then, she saw in the headlight beams, standing slightly to the left of the uniformed police officers, with a man and woman in plain clothes, obviously CID detectives, super-sleuth Allan Hawes and his trusted companion Doctor Windrush. Mabel

Frogmorton was horror-stricken. The very same man she had hired to protect her family name had betrayed her honour. Sidney Frogmorton got out the car and was confronted by two plain clothed CID officers.

"Mister Sidney Frogmorton? asked Chief Inspector Edgar Briggs sternly.

"Yes. What's wrong?"

"I want you to accompany me back to Scotland Yard, Sir, to answer some questions."

"Am I under arrest?"

"No, Sir, but I do have that option if I so choose."

"Will I need a solicitor?"

Prime Minister Sir Antony Dingle sat in a bath smoking a large cigar. He had just finished dictating some official letters to his personal secretary Constance Goodbody. She had sat on the other side of a pale blue plastic shower curtain so that she would not have to see the blubbery naked Sir Antony, who had splashed throughout the dictation like a stranded whale as he soaped himself down and then washed away the lather.

"Now get those letters off by motor bike courier," he called from the bath, "the moment you've finished typing them up, Miss Goodbody. They're important and I want my cabinet ministers to have them by teatime."

"Yes, Prime Minister." She stood up to leave the bathroom.

"When does the American President arrive, Miss Goodbody?"

"President Rooker will arrive in Airforce One at Stansted Airport at eleven o'clock tomorrow morning, Prime Minister. He will then travel here secretly in a five-car convoy and should arrive at about lunch time."

"Good, Miss Goodbody, the President's visit must at all costs be kept secret. I don't want the media circus getting hold of it. We must step carefully with Castro. He's nobody's fool and his country produces the best cigars in the world which I myself greatly enjoy."

"So I've noticed, Prime Minister."

"I hope to bargain with President Rooker. He wants Britain's help, and of course I shall give it, but at a price. Perhaps

214

he'll be prepared to be a little more helpful with cracking down on IRA fund raisers in America, and those loathsome gun runners."

"Yes, Prime Minister."

"Do you know if the First Lady will be accompanying President Rooker, Miss Goodbody?"

"She is coming with him, Prime Minister."

"Oh, good, then perhaps I can sell her one of my oil-paintings."

"I'm sure she'll know the right place to hang it, Prime Minister," replied Constance Goodbody with a grimace, as she remembered how bad the Prime Minister's paintings were. It was extremely difficult to tell what they were supposed to be. He called them 'landscapes', but they looked more like somebody with bad taste had squirted tubes of bright paint all over the canvas. The Prime Minister had once insisted that she accepted a painting as a Christmas present. She knew exactly where to hang it, on the toilet room wall, to inspire visitors to be quick about their business and leave. Caroline Rooker, America's First Lady, tall and slim with dark hair, was a generous woman who could be easily sweet-talked into anything. Which was how she got herself pregnant at the age of twenty-one at a university campus dance by the future President. She was the only known collector of the British Prime Minister, Sir Antony Dingle's oil paintings who actually paid for them.

"And where will the First Lady hang my painting, Miss Goodbody? In the Oval Office?"

"I had thought the smallest room in the White House, Prime Minister."

There was a momentary pause while Sir Antony Dingle digested the reply and its meaning. He did not appreciate humour directed at himself. "It's good to see you haven't lost your sense of fun, Miss Goodbody," replied the great man icily. "But don't you think it's better to lose that than lose one's job?"

"I'm sorry, Prime Minister, but I was not meaning to offend."

"And no offence taken, Miss Goodbody, at least not this time."

"Thank you, Prime Minister."

"When you've finished the letters, Miss Goodbody, will you type up the new draft of my speech, the one for the Tuesday afternoon debate in the House of Commons? You'll see where

I've marked the corrections in red pen as usual."

Sidney Frogmorton had been questioned for three hours in the presence of his legal representative, Sir Hilary Harker QC. The interview, conducted at Scotland Yard by Chief Inspector Edgar Briggs and Sergeant Jenny Hopper, was taped, and copies of the tapes given to Sidney Frogmorton's legal adviser. He was charged with conspiracy to murder, and remanded in custody. He had confessed to the police to hiring a professional killer to murder the British Prime Minister Sir Antony Dingle. And hoping the courts would take a lenient view of a man who owned up to his crime, he identified the hired killer as being a Miss Marion Pringle. He was unable to provide police with any helpful clues to help track the murderer down. However, he did confirm the murder attempt on the life of Sir Antony Dingle was to happen soon, but had not been given a date nor time. Marion Pringle had told him to book up without delay on a long sea cruise, and so provide himself with an alibi when the murder took place. The murder victim was such a high profile political figure, that all those people known by the Secret Service to have spoken out against him would be questioned. And Sidney Frogmorton, without his knighthood, was high on the list.

Chief Inspector Edgar Briggs sat in his office drinking tea with Sergeant Jenny Hopper, Allan Hawes and Doctor Windrush. They were discussing the taped interview with Sidney Frogmorton, which had been forwarded to Inspector Lionel Harper of Special Branch. He would now lead the investigation because the Prime Minister was the intended victim.

"Sadly," said the Chief Inspector, "we're still no closer to finding the killer's identity than we were yesterday morning. Let's consider the facts shall we? We know the hired killer is a man who dresses as a woman to meet clients and possibly to commit murder."

"Miss Marion Pringle," exclaimed super sleuth Allan Hawes.

"Precisely," agreed the Chief Inspector. "Marion Pringle. The man we hunt is a most devious and clever killer. And we have no idea if he uses other disguises."

"But couldn't he be a transvestite?" asked Doctor Windrush, who had said nothing for the last five minutes and thought it time his voice was heard again, "I've read about them in medical books. They're not gay, you'll understand, but just love to put on lipstick and high heels and prance about in a dress. They like the feel of smooth cool silk of ladies' undies next to their skin. And it feels so..." The Doctor's voice trailed off when he noticed the others were looking at him with peculiar expressions on their faces, as if they were wondering what sort of underwear he was wearing at the moment.

"We don't think our man is a transvestite, Doctor," said Sergeant Jenny Hopper. "We think it's merely a clever disguise meant to throw us off the scent. If the killer was spotted near the scene of a crime, then he would only be identified by any eyewitnesses as being a female. Then the police would be looking for a woman and not a man. Simple but very effective don't you think?"

"Well, bless my soul," exclaimed Doctor Windrush. "What a tricky blighter he is and no mistake. Good thing Hawes is here on the case."

Chief Inspector Edgar Briggs scowled but made no comment. As far as he was concerned, the most brilliant detective in the room was himself, and he was going to be the man who tracked down and arrested the elusive serial killer, not a private detective wearing a deerstalker hat.

"Yes, the killer is tricky, Doctor," agreed Allan Hawes. "And it demonstrates that we're dealing with a very cunning individual. This man isn't your ordinary run-of-the-mill serial killer."

"He's not?" asked Doctor Windrush with a look of surprise.

"No," said the Chief Inspector, "He's the true professional..."

"But a professional who makes mistakes," interrupted Sergeant Jenny Hopper. "We mustn't forget that. And that's how we'll catch him."

"Mistakes?" asked Doctor Windrush, his interest further aroused. "What sort of mistakes?" He wondered what mistakes the serial killer could have possibly made that would give his true identity away.

Well, like the ginger wig, for example," continued the Sergeant, "which I pulled from off the killer's head in a hospital casualty treatment cubicle. The wig provided Forensics with

217

DNA which matched with DNA taken from two other clues found at murder scenes. We can link Marion Pringle to four murders, including that of curate Peter Catchpole."

"The curate?" asked the Doctor.

"From the few hairs found clutched in the curate's dead fingers," said the sergeant.

"Horse hair in fact," declared the Chief Inspector.

"Well, there's a vital clue," said Allan Hawes, wanting to show off his brilliance. "The killer must surely associate with horses. Perhaps he's a jockey?"

"There was some theatrical glue found on the hair," explained Sergeant Jenny Hopper. "Plus traces of human sweat. And we got a very good trace of DNA from it all. Which means the killer was wearing a false beard when he murdered curate Peter Catchpole. We've checked with make-up artists working in show business, and they have told us that most artificial hairpieces, such as wigs, beards and moustaches, are made from the best horsehair available. Real human hair is rarely used."

"Then he wasn't a jockey?" asked Doctor Windrush.

"Have another cup of tea, Doctor," said Sergeant Jenny Hopper kindly.

Chapter Fifteen

Ronald Perkins had spent hours sitting up a tree overlooking the distant rear gardens of Chequers. The tree, a spreading oak with large branches, was in a thickly-wooded area on a hillside some thousand yards from the ten-foot-high red brick wall which surrounded the gardens. From his position near the top of the tree, he had a clear view right up to the french windows of the house. It was an ideal position for a sniper, but Ronald Perkins was not armed, and anyway the death of Sir Anthony Dingle was to be a perfect murder, untraceable back to the person who had executed it. It was now late on the Saturday afternoon. Ronald Perkins was surprised there were so few security people to be seen guarding the house and grounds. He did not know that he had passed by sheer chance through the SAS unimpregnable outer ring of surveillance when he met the "pig farmer," who, satisfied he was a rambler, had let him carry on towards the next village. But once out of sight of the pig farmer, Ronald Perkins had turned off into thick woodland heading towards Chequers. The outer perimeter of surveillance was closed and sealed drum-tight, with SAS, MI5 and armed police patrolling beyond the half-mile-wide diameter. The inner area of the circle with Chequers right in the centre was only loosely guarded to give the Prime Minister and his family a feeling they were not at the busy centre of a swarming beehive of security activity. It was so they could relax in the house and gardens feeling as if they were really alone without being watched by dozens of security people hiding among nearby flower beds. There should have been security cameras and infra red beams set up at vantage points in the grounds at Chequers, but the Prime Minister's wife, Lady Jane Dingle, had prevailed on her husband to have them all switched off during their visits, because she could not bear to live inside a goldfish bowl on open display to the television screens of security men. She was a very private person. Security bosses had reluctantly agreed, but insisted that the wooded areas outside the ten-foot high brick wall surrounding the garden must be patrolled by armed police patrols. And the occasional police helicopter flew high over head. But only those with the highest level of authority could pass through the highly guarded outer perimeter of surveillance controlled by the SAS and MI5. Ronald Perkins had managed to pacify his hunger pangs by eating mushrooms and some blackberries. He returned once to the river where he had encountered the bull for water. And now, up near the top of the oak tree, he was waiting for an opportunity to become a footnote on the history page of his time.

The IRA strike team had entered the supposedly unimpregnable, outer ring of surveillance surrounding Chequers, by hiding in the back of an old council dustcart. The dustcart was on its way to empty the dustbins at Chequers, and made a routine stop at a police checkpoint to be searched. The dustcart was searched by a highly trained six-man squad using sniffer dogs. The dustcart was pronounced 'all clear'. And it was while the four dustmen and police were standing grouped together talking at the front of the vehicle that three shadowy figures crept quickly out from some nearby trees, and clambered up into the back of the dustcart. They knew that a dustcart which had just been searched thoroughly would not be searched again until it arrived back from Chequers. The dustmen climbed up into the front of the dustcart, and the driver started the engine.

"Well, lads," whispered Sean O'Gully triumphantly on hearing the motor burst into life, "it looks like if we're on our way."

"Ireland forever," whispered Roy McCluster.

"Ireland forever," replied his two friends, grinning broadly.

The dustcart drove off towards Chequers.

"Pat," whispered Sean O'Gully, "you did remember to bring a battery?"

"Of course, Sean, I'll not be bitten twice by the same dog."

"We'll succeed this time, lads," chuckled Roy McCluster. "I can feel it in my bones, can't you?"

"I've been thinking, Sean," said Patrick Dobbs thoughtfully.

"After the bomb has gone off taking Sir Antony Dingle away for a nice long rest, just how are we going to make it back to dear old Ireland? I haven't heard you mention any escape plan yet. There is an escape plan, isn't there?"

Sean O'Gully did not answer. There was no escape plan. It was now do and die for the cause of a united Ireland. The British Prime Minister had to be killed by the IRA whatever the cost involved for the strike team. They had blown their first attempt when they tried to explode a bomb under Sir Antony Dingle's Rolls Royce as it drove to Chequers. This time the bomb would go off... even if it took them along with it. But it was a decision the IRA strike team commander thought was best kept to himself for the moment. Only after the bomb had killed the British Prime Minister would Commander Sean O'Gully give thought to their escape from the mainland back to Ireland. But in truth, he expected both him and his companions to become martyrs for the cause. And in his mind he proudly thought "Ireland forever".

"Well, is there an escape route?" demanded Patrick Dobbs. "Do we get home to our loved ones?"

"We're all in God's hands lads," replied Sean O'Gully quietly.

Roy McCluster and Patrick Dobbs looked uneasily at each other but said nothing.

Prime Minister Sir Anthony Dingle, dressed in a white boiler suit, smoking a huge cigar, took a stroll in the garden before tea. He strolled thoughtfully down a well-manicured lawn to some red rose bushes, and plucked himself a flaming red rose, which he put carefully in his buttonhole.

"Ah, England's fair rose," he thought with pride. "It's a symbol of a truly great people." He turned and sauntered slowly back towards the house. The great man was pondering on what he would say to the American President Robert R Rooker the following day. And he knew it would for both of them be like a titanic game of chess between two masters, each one searching for the other's weakness, and ready in an instant to win the game with a brilliant verbal checkmate. Sir Antony Dingle was never a man to belittle his own genius, nor that of other world leaders whom he considered had an intellect which almost equalled his own. There was a strong bond between Britain and the United

States of America. Both nations relied on support from each other in moments of world crisis. But this did not stop the two leaders from having many disagreements over world politics. President R Rooker was ever mindful of the number of Irish Americans with a vote, when bargaining with Sir Antony Dingle on any possible White House measure against the IRA.

From his vantage point up the oak tree, Ronald Perkins watched the distant rotund figure of the British Prime Minister. Sir Antony Dingle was alone in the garden, unaware that his every move was being watched by the serial killer who had been hired to kill him. If Ronald Perkins had been a sniper with a powerful telescopic rifle in his hands, then the red rose on the great man's chest would have made an ideal target. The Prime Minister moved slowly back up the lawn and entered the house and closed the door. Ronald Perkins settled himself down for the night, legs astride a branch, back resting against the trunk of the tree, left wrist strapped by his trouser belt to a branch above his head in case he fell during the night. In the morning he would put into operation his plan for killing Sir Antony Dingle.

Inspector Lionel Harper of Special Branch stood in his office in front of a large wall map of Buckinghamshire. He was a robust middle aged man, of average height with piercing dark eyes and thoughtful expression. Married with three grown-up daughters, all still at home, with a wife and grim-faced mother-in-law, he was never known to laugh. Sitting on hard-backed chairs facing the wall map were Chief Inspector Edgar Briggs, Sergeant Jenny Hopper, Allan Hawes and Doctor Albert Windrush. Inspector Lionel Harper pointed at Chequers on the map with a twelve-inch ruler.

"There's Chequers," he cried triumphantly, stabbing at the name with the end of the ruler.

"Well done!" called Doctor Windrush, clapping his hands enthusiastically.

Inspector Lionel Harper scowled.

Looking somewhat embarrassed the Doctor stopped clapping and sat quietly with his arms folded.

"Sorry," he mumbled.

"The Prime Minister Sir Antony Dingle is at Chequers for

the weekend," continued the Inspector. He peered closely at his audience as if expecting some reaction to his disclosure, then whispered, "This is of course classified information that I'm telling you now. You could be jailed if you reveal it to anyone else outside this room. Do you understand?"

Everybody nodded their head in agreement.

The Inspector hurried over to the door, opened it and peered out. Satisfied there was nobody lurking outside in the corridor that might have been listening to what he had been saying, he closed the door and returned to stand in front of the wall map.

"Can't take any chances these days with security," he explained. "Eyes and ears everywhere, don't you know."

"Do you think our serial killer is going to try for the Prime Minister at Chequers, Inspector?" asked Chief Inspector Edgar Briggs.

Inspector Lionel Harper shook his head.

"No, Chief Inspector, I do not. He can't possibly know that the Prime Minister is there this weekend," he replied confidently. "It's a top government secret. All under lock and key stuff. Because not only is the British Prime Minister down at Chequers, but tomorrow for one day only, and for very important talks, Robert R Rooker the President of the United States of America will also be there."

There were gasps of surprise from his audience.

"The Prime Minister is thought by the general public to be visiting Chequers next weekend," continued the Inspector. "It has been published widely in the press that he will be doing so. But of course he won't be setting foot outside of London next weekend. MI5 will see to that. He'll be with his family in a safe house in Shepherd's Bush."

"And you think our serial killer will visit Chequers next weekend?" asked Sergeant Jenny Hopper. "Hoping to get to the Prime Minister?"

"Yes, I most certainly do," replied the Inspector. "Chequers will be the cheese in the trap to snare our cunning mouse."

"But I thought Chequers was well guarded by the SAS and MI5," said Allan Hawes. "They're the best in the world aren't they? So why would one man stupidly risk going up against them? It doesn't make sense."

"Because like all serial killers over a long period of time," explained the Inspector, "he comes to think that he's the best there is at what he does. And he can outwit the best crimebusters going. We had our criminal psychologist Doctor Joan Poppywell do a profile on what we know of our man. She says that he is highly intelligent, ruthless, determined, and cannot resist a difficult challenge, and in fact the more difficult the challenge then the more he'll rise to the occasion – and that's his great weakness. He has accepted a contract to kill Sir Antony Dingle and must, according to his own cold-blooded code of practice, achieve that targeted murder at whatever cost it takes for him to do it. Our serial killer is a master of disguise, hence how easily he fooled Chief Inspector Briggs and Sergeant Hopper, when they thought they were helping a woman road accident victim to hospital, and it was none other than the serial killer himself, portraying himself as Miss Marion Pringle."

"Good God," gasped Doctor Windrush, "but isn't that truly amazing? I've never heard anything like it before. Master of disguise? And there was I thinking the man was a transvestite."

"But what makes you think our man will try his hand next weekend at Chequers?" asked Allan Hawes. "Sidney Frogmorton said in his statement that the second and final payment for the murder was to be paid into a Swiss bank account four days after he had learnt of Sir Antony Dingle's death. Perhaps our serial killer is working to a much slower timetable than you think, and will not try for the Prime Minister until much later in the year."

"Doctor Poppywell is convinced that our man will want an early strike," replied Inspector Lionel Harper, "and that he doesn't like a murder contract to last too long. She believes him to be married or in a close partnership, and that he will not want to be too long away from home."

"If our serial killer is as good as you say, Inspector Harper," said Sergeant Jenny Hopper thoughtfully, "then might he not be clever enough to be unpredictable as well? Doing the opposite to what the police would expect him to do?"

"Meaning?"

"Well, we're expecting him to visit Chequers next weekend," replied the Sergeant. "Couldn't he have decided to visit Chequers this weekend instead?"

Inspector Lionel Harper shook his head. "You're forgetting, Sergeant, that nobody knows outside those in the know, and of course we know, but most do not know, that the Prime Minister is down at Chequers this weekend. No, our serial killer will try his hand next week and we'll be ready for him."

"But what if you're wrong?" asked the Sergeant.

"Well, I suppose it's best not to take chances," replied the Inspector. "But I'm as certain in my own mind as I can be that our serial killer has no idea whatsoever of the present whereabouts of the Prime Minister. Chequers this weekend would be the last place he would think of looking."

"Best to cover all possibilities, Inspector," said Allan Hawes. "The one thing I've learnt over the years of the master criminal mind is that it is unpredictable."

The old council dustcart drove slowly up the long tarmac driveway towards the big country house of Chequers. Hiding in the grimy back of the dustcart was the IRA strike team, Sean O'Gully, Patrick Dobbs and Roy McCluster, who were preparing to abandon ship.

"Right, now, lads," whispered Sean O'Gully. "Get ready to make a jump for it when the dustcart stops. Keep your heads down and make a dash for the nearest bit of cover you can find. We'll all meet up as quickly as we can afterwards. Now remember this is the big one for Ireland."

"But won't we be spotted the moment we jump, Sean?" asked Roy McCluster nervously. "There's got to be security men everywhere you look out there."

"I shouldn't think that the SAS and MI5 men will be too bothered with a dustcart that has already been searched, Roy. They're be far too busy with other things on their minds, I can assure you."

"I hope you're right, Sean."

The dustcart reached the house, drove slowly round the back and stopped beside a dozen dustbins grouped near the kitchen door. Instantly the IRA strike team, pistols in hand, were clambering over the dustcart tailgate. They dropped to the ground and sprinted for the nearest cover... and in their panic to conceal themselves, they hid behind the dustbins, which was not a good place to hide because the dustmen were just about to empty the dustbins into the back of the dustcart. The Irishmen would be certain to be seen and armed security called. They crouched as low as they could behind the dustbins, and with sinking hearts realised their big mistake.

"Quick lads, for God's sake," whispered Sean O'Gully frantically, "let's get out of here." But it was too late. Three of the dustmen had come round from the front of the dustcart and were walking towards the dustbins. "Follow my lead," whispered Sean O'Gully, before leaping to his feet to confront the startled dustmen, with his pistol pointed at them.

The dustmen, looking terrified, raised their hands above their heads.

"Please don't shoot, mate," said a fat dustmen nervously. "We're only here to empty the bins. We don't want any trouble."

The other two Irishmen sprang up, pistols in hand, like jack-in-the-boxes and stood behind their leader, guns pointing at the dustmen.

"We're SAS," said Sean O'Gully in a terrible rendering of an English accent, "checking out that the dustbins are safe to be emptied."

The three dustmen nodded.

"We have checked the dustbins for any explosive devices," continued Sean O'Gully. "They can be hidden anywhere, you know. We can't take chances with security. One mistake and all can be lost in one big bang. I had a friend in Germany who was blown up because he didn't search a discarded baked bean tin."

The three dustmen nodded.

"Right, now chaps," said Sean O'Gully quietly, trying to sound as much as possible like a British Army officer. "We'll let you get on with your job and empty the bins. But don't say a word to anyone about seeing us here. We're working under cover. Do you understand?"

The three dustmen nodded.

"Jolly good show, chaps, then keep up the good work," cried Sean O'Gully as he darted swiftly away and through the nearest open door... and fell tumbling head over heels twelve feet into the darkness below. He was closely followed by the other two Irishmen who suffered the same fate. The wooden stairs that should have been there had been removed because of woodworm, and were to be replaced. The last Irishman through the door had slammed it shut behind him cutting off the only source of light. The Irishmen had fallen down into a pitch-black coal cellar. The startled dustmen heard muffled grunts and groans intermingled with swearing as the Irishmen landed in an agonising heap. Then there was a deathly silence.

"Bloody amazing these SAS blokes, ain't they," said the fat dustman in an awed tone of voice. "They appear and disappear as if by magic."

"Highly trained, that's why, mate," replied the taller of his two companions knowingly. "Best in the world, they reckon."

The dustmen, feeling privileged at having witnessed the SAS in action, quickly emptied the bins into the back of the dustcart and joined their work mates in the front of the vehicle. The dustcart drove away back down the driveway, where it was stopped at the police check point at the main gate and searched.

Meanwhile in the darkness down in the coal cellar, Sean O'Gully whispered urgently to his strike team. "Are you all right, lads?"

There was no response.

"Lads!" whispered the leader slightly louder than before, "Are you there? Please speak to me if you can!"

"But of course we're bloody well here," retorted Roy McCluster angrily, as he began to untangle himself from his two compatriots, who lay twisted under him like discarded rag dolls. "And where else do you think we'd be?"

"When we took an oath to follow our commander before coming on this mission in Belfast," said Patrick Dobbs, "I had no idea it meant tumbling down into a coal cellar behind him."

"But how do you know it's a coal cellar, Pat?" asked Sean O'Gully. "It's so dark down here that I can't see a thing."

"Because I landed with my mouth open and almost swallowed a mouthful of coal."

"What'll we do now, Sean?" asked Roy McCluster miserably.

"Carry on regardless for Ireland."

There was an ominous silence which lasted for almost a minute.

"Are you there, lads?" asked Sean O'Gully.

Still no response from the other two Irishmen.

"Come on now, lads," whispered the commander. "I damn well know you're there. Now speak up... that's an order."

"Yes, Sean," said the other two Irishmen in unison.

"Try and look on the bright side, lads," said the commander, trying to sweet talk his men, "At least we're alive..."

"And down a coal cellar, Sean," interrupted Patrick Dobbs angrily.

"We can regroup down here, lads," replied the commander. "Stay quietly down here until we're ready to enter the house and place the bomb. There's no rush. I doubt that the SAS and MI5 have any idea whatsoever that the IRA's finest strike team are hiding down in the coal cellar in Chequers. Just think for a moment of what we've achieved... we're actually under the same roof as the British Prime Minister Sir Antony Dingle, and can strike him down for Ireland whenever we choose."

"But aren't you forgetting about the SAS and MI5, Sean?" asked Patrick Dobbs. "They're be buzzing about up in the house like flies on a slice of bread and jam. It seems to me that we're stuck down here in the cellar with nowhere to go."

"Why must you always look at the worst things that can happen in life, Pat?" asked the commander. "You were always doing it as a kid back on the Falls Road, I remember."

"Because then I'm prepared for the worst when it comes, Sean."

"Have you got your bomb with you?"

"I have, Sean. It's in my jacket pocket."

"Good man – and is it operational?"

"No, Sean, it isn't."

"No?"

"No, it still needs the wires to be fixed to the live, neutral and earth connections on both the detonator and timer. There's enough Semtex to blow up a fair-sized room and kill anyone who's in it."

"Then make it operational, Pat."

"I can't do that, Sean."

"But why not?"

"It's too dark down here to see, Sean."

"Too dark, Pat, but surely you've got a torch with you?"

"No. I didn't think we'd end up down a coal, cellar now did I?"

"Matches then?

"No."

"Lighter?"

"I don't smoke, Sean, you know that."

"So we're down a coal cellar with a bomb which we can't make operational, and the British Prime Minister is up in the house above us and we can't touch him? I suppose, Paddy, just out for my own personal interest... you did remember to bring the battery for the bomb?"

"It's in the bomb, Sean, already to set off the detonator..."

"But only if the detonator is attached to the wires," interrupted the commander, who was seething with anger.

"That's about it, Sean."

There was the sound of fisticuffs in the darkness as the commander struck out with failing fists at Patrick Dobbs. Unfortunately for Roy McCluster, who was standing next to Patrick Dobbs, he took a couple of direct blows to the face before shouting out "Stop it, Sean, that's me you've been hitting, for God's sake."

"Where's the bastard?" cried the commander furiously, "I'll get him this time for sure."

Ronald Perkins timed the two-man armed police patrol that passed near the oak tree in which he was hiding. The sten gun-carrying officers in their bullet-proof vests were as regular as clockwork, appearing on the dot every thirty-three minutes precisely. This meant they were patrolling the whole length of the outside of the brick wall that encircled Chequers, and that it took them thirty-three minutes to do one circuit around the wall. The serial killer knew there must be other police patrols outside the wall, most definitely SAS patrols as well, but he never saw them. And from his vantage point up near the top of the oak tree, from where he could get a clear view of most of the back garden of Chequers, he never saw any armed security men. But he did not know that Lady Jane Dingle, the Prime Minister's wife, had an aversion to having security measures too open and visible inside the high walls of Chequers because she did not want to live in constant view on security monitors or being watched by concealed security men. The area up to the brick wall was patrolled but the grounds inside hardly ever. It was thought that any attacker would have to first break through the half-mile circle line that surrounded Chequers, and that was controlled by the SAS and MI5, and judged as being invincible.

"Not even a bird could enter without us knowing," proclaimed Colonel Derek Slatterhouse proudly, officer commanding the SAS forces committed to guarding the British Prime Minister and the American President Robert R Rooker.

Ronald Perkins decided it was now time for him to risk a visit over the wall and into the gardens of Chequers. He wanted to make his murderous move on Sir Antony Dingle, possibly within the next twelve hours, but needed to know more precisely the layout of the gardens. He had climbed down from the oak tree, and was lying on his stomach several yards from the brick wall, watching the two-man police patrol disappearing from sight. Then he was up and running towards the brick wall. It proved difficult to climb but he managed it. Fortunately for him, that stretch of the wall, some sixty yards, had been built by the great man himself, Sir Antony Dingle, as a publicity gimmick. He had wanted to show voters that he was a stout-hearted man of the people and a really good bricklayer to boot. But the wall was shabbily built. Indeed, the pointing between the bricks was so badly done, with a bad cement mix, that in places it had crumpled away giving a firm grip for fingers and toes. Ronald Perkins sat astride the top of the wall and peered down into the gardens of Chequers. There was no sign of life. He dropped effortlessly like a cat into the garden and sprinted for the near cover of an apple tree. He swung himself up into the lower branches where he was hidden by the foliage, and helped himself to a couple of apples. Food was proving a problem for the serial killer. He was hungry and had run out of mushrooms and wild berries. The apples would keep him going until he returned to Bumstead on the Wold.

The big coal truck backed slowly up towards the open manhole at Chequers which led to the coal cellar below. There were three

SAS men in battle fatigues, armed with light machine guns, standing outside the kitchen door drinking mugs of steaming tea and eating a cake each, as they watched the manoeuvring of the coal truck. They should have been low profile and out of sight, but the offer of a cup of tea and one of chef's fairy cakes had proved too tempting. The driver's mate, a tall, broad-shouldered man covered in coal dust, his face smudged black, looking like a Black and White Minstrel, was standing next to the open manhole shouting and waving directions at the driver.

"Keep coming back, Charlie," he shouted. "That's it, mate, a bit slower... right, stop."

The coal truck crunched to a stop.

The driver's mate pulled the metal chute on the back of the coal truck over the open manhole and positioned it. "Right, Charlie," he cried. "Let it go."

The driver pulled a lever in his cab and three tons of best Yorkshire coal poured down the chute into the cellar. The rumpling and roaring of the coal muffled the frantic cries of the IRA strike team down in the cellar, as it poured down upon them. The driver got out the cab and helped his assistant to lift back the heavy manhole cover with metal lifting tongs. Just as they were about to lower the manhole cover back into place, there was a short squeaky sound which came eerily up from the depths of the coal cellar. "What's that?" asked the driver nervously.

The short squeaky sound was a very muffled and faint "Ireland forever," gasped out by IRA commander Sean O'Gully, as he struggled to keep his nose and mouth free from the great pile of coal that had almost buried him.

"It's a rat, I shouldn't wonder," said the driver's mate.

"Sure to be," agreed the driver.

The men lowered the manhole cover into place.

Ronald Perkins climbed down from the apple tree and began to explore the garden, memorising any places which would provide future concealment, and offer avenues for a speedy retreat to the brick wall after the killing was done. There was a well-kept orchard which led down to a large pond with water lillies and reeds. Goldfish swam through the crystal-clear water. Ronald

Perkins knelt and, using both hands as a cup, drank some of the water. It tasted foul but to a thirsty man it was refreshing. He continued round the edge of the pond keeping to the reeds as cover. There was large greenhouse which he entered hoping to find something edible. But the greenhouse was full of flowers at various stages of growth in flower-pots on benches. He left the greenhouse and came to the big lawn. The serial killer turned to retrace his steps thinking it was too dangerous to approach the house directly.

"New here aren't you?" asked a familiar voice from behind him.

Ronald Perkins turned in the direction of the voice. It was the great man himself, the British Prime Minister Sir Antony Dingle. He was dressed in an artist's white smock, smudged down the front with various colours of oil paint, grey baggy shorts, and was wearing open toe sandals. On his head was a large white straw sun hat. Ronald Perkins thought quickly of a cover story. He knew that Chequers with such big lavish gardens must employ at least a dozen gardeners.

"I'm the new gardener, sir," he said hesitantly, hoping his face would not betray the lie. "I started at the beginning of the month."

The Prime Minister smiled warmly. Everyone he met was a potential voter as far as he was concerned, and it never did any harm to do a little canvassing. Elections were always just round the corner. "What's your name?"

"Harry Quemby, Sir."

"I hope that I can rely on your vote, Harry." The Prime Minister knew that by calling a person whom he had only just met by their Christian name made them feel they had established a bond of friendship with him. This was nonsense of course, because Sir Antony Dingle was only interested in getting their vote.

"But of course, sir. I've voted Conservative all my adult life, so did my father before me."

"Good man. And how are you finding the work?"

"Hard but satisfying, thank you, sir."

"What are you working on now, Harry?"

"Rhubarb, sir."

"Ah, yes, rhubarb – nothing like rhubarb crumble and

custard, I say. Couldn't have enough of it when I was a boy. Nanny said it was a wonderful purgative and kept a body regular. Far better than stewed prunes, I understand."

"So I've heard, sir."

The Prime Minister held out his hand for Ronald Perkins to shake. "It was nice talking to you, Harry," he said.

Ronald Perkins took the hand and shook it.

"And I suppose," continued the great man, "that talking to me must be one of the high moments of your life? Something to tell the grandchildren, I shouldn't wonder."

Ronald Perkins forced a smiled and nodded. "Yes, sir," he replied, but he was really thinking what a prize egoist the Prime Minister really was. Why do politicians always think they are more important than anyone else?

"Well, I must get back to my painting," said the Prime Minister as he began to walk away. "I want to get the rose bushes down on canvas before the light begins to fade. Goodbye, Harry."

"Goodbye, sir."

Ronald Perkins watched the portly figure walking away from him, and being ever the opportunist, decided this was the best chance he might ever have to effect the murder of Sir Antony Dingle. The Prime Minister was alone and there might never be such a moment again. It would have to be rough and ready with no thought-out plan. Perhaps a crude bash on the head with rock, then making it look as if the Prime Minister had slipped beside the pond, hit his head on falling and had drowned. Crude but acceptable and most certainly a perfect murder. Ronald Perkins picked up a rock the size of a house brick and followed the great man. The Prime Minister sat down at his easel on a little stool and picked up his pallet of paints. He dabbed with a brush at the pallet and began to paint on the canvas. Ronald Perkins crept silently up behind him, the rock held in both hands at forehead level, ready to bring it crashing down on Sir Antony Dingle's head. The Prime Minister whistled a bright breezy little tune as he painted. He was relaxed and happy. Ronald Perkins raised the rock, then paused when he saw the painting. And for a moment could not believe his eyes. It was a great mass of assorted colours, and was unrecognisable as a landscape or indeed anything else. The great man was painting the south view of the house from the end of the great lawn, across to the maze, with the pond positioned slightly to the left side. And yet none of those things seemed to feature anywhere in the Prime Minister's awful painting, which looked like the handiwork of a child of three who had just discovered the joys of a paintbox. But it was Ronald Perkins pausing which saved Sir Antony Dingle's life, because before the serial killer could bring the rock smashing down, a voice with an American accent called out, "Hi, there, Sir Antony."

Ronald Perkins dropped the rock as if it were red hot, and glanced in the direction of the American voice. President Robert R Rooker, with two Secret Service agents in attendance, both wearing black suits and dark glasses, came striding down the lawn with a big smile on his face. The British Prime Minister turned in the direction of the American President and waved a paint brush at him.

"Mr President!" he called back." What a delight and a pleasure."

The two men shook hands.

"Still painting I see, Sir Antony," chuckled the President. The two Secret Service agents quickly moved up to stand either side of the President, their right hands inside their jackets gripping the butt of their revolvers, ready in an instant to draw and fire. The motto of the Secret Service agents who guarded the President was "I'll take one for the Man." This meant they would take a bullet meant for the President.

"Perhaps you would like it for the Oval Office when it's finished, Mr President?" said the Prime Minister. "I'll include gift wrapping in the price."

For a brief moment the President looked horrified; the idea of seeing that painting every day in the Oval office was a sight he would not have wished on his worst enemy. The President smiled weakly. "We must talk about it sometime, Sir Antony."

"As you wish, Mr President, but my paintings are an investment for the future and I urge you to invest while you can." It was then the Prime Minister spotted Ronald Perkins standing nearby. "Ah, Harry the gardener – another great moment for you to tell the grandchildren," he called out brightly, "seeing me and the American President together. History in the making, wouldn't you say?"

"Yes, sir," replied the serial killer, thinking it was time to make himself scarce. The Secret Service agents were making him feel uneasy. It was difficult to know what they were thinking behind their black sunglasses. They stood motionless, ready to take one for the Man.

"What is it, Harry?" asked the Prime Minister.

"What is what, Sir?"

"Well, why did you follow me? What do you want, Harry?"

Ronald Perkins thought quickly. "It's the rhubarb, sir," he said. "I was wondering if you wanted me to pick a few sticks for a rhubarb crumble?"

"Oh, what a jolly good idea, Harry. Yes, see to it for me, there's a good chap. Give the rhubarb to the chef and say it's for my rhubarb crumble for dinner tonight."

"Yes, sir, I'll see to it straight away." Ronald Perkins nodded and turned and walked away at a slightly faster pace than a normal walking step.

"Salt of the earth, the Conservative gardener and voter," said the Prime Minister proudly to the American President. "I wonder how many of your voters would have offered to pick rhubarb to make you a rhubarb crumble?"

"None, I guess," replied the President. "I don't like rhubarb."

Chapter Sixteen

Inspector Lionel Harper of Special Branch sat packed in a police car like sardines, with Chief Inspector Edgar Briggs, Sergeant Jenny Hopper, and super-sleuth Allan Hawes and his trusted companion Doctor Windrush. They were speeding with siren blaring and lights flashing to Chequers. There was no need for the siren and lights, but they had all voted for them to be switched on.

"Makes a more exciting trip," explained the Chief Inspector before the vote was taken. Inspector Lionel Harper, who had arranged the trip, did not think the serial killer would be at Chequers, but had thought it best to take no chances.

"Do you think he'll be in disguise?" asked Doctor Windrush.

"Most certainly," replied Allan Hawes.

"What? Not as Miss Marion Pringle?" exclaimed the Chief Inspector.

"He's a master of disguise," said Allan Hawes. "He could be anybody at all at Chequers, male or female. But I doubt he'll ever be Miss Pringle again. He knows she's been seen by the police and that they're hunting her. You must remember that we're not dealing with a fool but with a highly intelligent master criminal. The sort of man who is good at chess and doing 'The Times' crossword in under ten minutes."

"And he doesn't know we're closing the net on him," said the Chief Inspector confidently. "Master of disguise or not, I'll know him when I see him at Chequers. It's the experienced copper's nose you see. It never lets me down."

"If he's there," responded Inspector Harper, "which I very much doubt."

"We can't take the chance, Inspector," said Allan Hawes. "Think of the fuss there'd be if the Prime Minister was murdered by our serial killer, and the press found out we had done nothing because we thought he wouldn't know the Prime Minister's whereabouts?"

"But how could he know the Prime Minster is at Chequers? No, it's just too improbable for me to accept. But still in this case I bow to the majority decision."

"You know it makes sense," said Allan Hawes with a smile.

"How long before we reach Chequers?" asked Sergeant Jenny Hopper.

"About forty-five minutes," replied Inspector Lionel Harper.

The IRA strike team had managed in the pitch-darkness of the coal cellar, to struggle free from the great heap of best Yorkshire coal which had dropped through the manhole. Battered, bruised, choking from the billowing dust, covered in coal dust, faces and hands blacker than the ace of spades, they had frantically dug to free themselves. "Are we all here?" asked Sean O'Gully nervously.

"We are," replied a frightened voice.

"That's right," agreed a third voice. "We are."

"Give your names, for God's sake," said the commander angrily. "I need to know if one of us is still buried under the coal or not."

"Patrick Dobbs."

"Roy McCluster."

"And I'm Sean O'Gully," replied the commander, greatly relieved to hear his two companions speak their names. "Do you know what this means, lads? The strike team is operational again."

The other two Irishmen made no reply but sighed miserably. Would the commander never give in and let them return home to Ireland?

"We can still complete our mission to take out the British Prime Minister," continued the commander confidently, who was thinking of how famous it would make him back on the Falls Road in Belfast. There might even be songs written about him. "All we've got to do is come up with a good plan, lads. Now what do you say?"

"How about a plan for getting out of here?" suggested Patrick Dobbs.

"Have you still got the bomb, Pat?" asked the commander.

Patrick Dobbs felt in his jacket pocket. "I have, Sean."

"And all it needs is for the wires to be connected to the detonator and timer, Pat?"

"That's the size of it, Sean."

"Right, then, lads," said the commander thoughtfully, "let's find a way out of here and connect those wires. Now are you with me?"

"Yes," replied the two Irishmen sheepishly. They were very unhappy with the situation, and wanted to be on their way home to Belfast and not preparing to bomb the British Prime Minister. The mission so far had proved to be a colossal disaster with one mishap after another, and they could not understand why the commander would not call off the mission and take them back to Ireland.

"Then let's hear it, lads?"

"Ireland forever," they chorused unhappily.

"Ireland forever," echoed the commander triumphantly.

Ronald Perkins searched the gardens for rhubarb. He had decided to enter the house by way of the kitchen with a few sticks of rhubarb which the Prime Minister had asked him to pick for his rhubarb crumble. The serial killer reasoned that if he was stopped and questioned with a few sticks of rhubarb in his hand, then his story of the rhubarb crumble would be confirmed by the Prime Minister. There could be no better cover story than to have one vouched for by Sir Antony Dingle himself. Who would doubt the British Prime Minister? Ronald Perkins found the rhubarb and picked half a dozen sticks, then proceeded directly to the house. There was a small courtyard on the far left of the house leading to the kitchen area, from which wafted the most delicious smell of freshly-baked bread. The serial killer had forgotten just how hungry he was. Next to the kitchen door, which was wide open to let the cool breeze flow inside was a smaller door near some dustbins. What was behind the smaller door? It might be useful to know if he wanted a quick way in or out of the house. Ronald Perkins went over to the door, opened it a few inches and peered inside... it was the pitch-black coal cellar.

"Hello," called a timid voice from the darkness in the cellar below.

"Hello," replied Ronald Perkins nervously, ready in an instant to flee.

"Who are you?" asked Commander Sean O'Gully, using an English upper class accent.

"Harry Quemby," replied Ronald Perkins.

"SAS or MI5?" asked the commander, who was preparing to die for Ireland, thinking the SAS and MI5 had arrived in force outside the cellar door. He eased back the safety catch on his revolver and aimed it directly up at the shaft of sunlight beaming through the doorway. He could not distinguish a figure in the bright light, but would fire in the direction of the voice.

"No, I'm just a gardener," replied Ronald Perkins.

"A gardener?"

"Yes. I've got some sticks of rhubarb here for the chef. Can I ask who you are?" asked Ronald Perkins as he peered down into the cellar. He could just make out three shadowy shapes caught in the shaft of light from the doorway.

There was a momentarily hesitation before the commander replied. "We're SAS checking out the coal down here for any concealed explosive devices. I'm Lieutenant James Bryant."

The word "SAS" sent chills up and down Ronald Perkins's spine. "Well, I must be going," said the serial killer quickly, "Chef is waiting for my sticks of rhubarb for the Prime Minister's crumble." Ronald Perkins wanted to distance himself from these SAS men. They might not be so easily fooled as ordinary household staff.

"Before you go, Harry," called the commander, "I suppose you haven't a ladder handy have you? We forgot to bring one ourselves and now we're trapped down here."

"I'll see what I can do, Lieutenant."

"Oh, and Harry," called the commander, "Can you leave the door open while you're gone? My Sergeant here is afraid of the dark, isn't that so, Sergeant?"

Both Patrick Dobbs and Roy McCluster mumbled a hasty "Yes."

"I won't be long," lied Ronald Perkins, who had no intention of looking for a ladder. Indeed, the longer he could keep the SAS men down the cellar the better it was for him. He hurried away and entered the kitchen door. The serial killer was now inside Chequers. Ronald Perkins carried the sticks of rhubarb into the kitchen where various pots and pans were steaming and bubbling away on the cookers. There were half a dozen people, men and women, dressed in white, preparing and cooking food. The serial killer put the rhubarb sticks down on a table next to some cauliflowers and cabbages.

"What are you doing?" demanded a man's angry voice with a strong French accent.

Ronald Perkins turned to look in the direction of the voice, and saw a small wiry man, no more than five foot tall, with a small black-trimmed moustache, wearing white jacket and trousers, with a tall chef's hat on his head. The man was red-faced and his eyes were blazing with anger. Ronald Perkins just stared at the man.

"What are you doing?" demanded the man again.

"I've brought the rhubarb," replied Ronald Perkins.

"Why are you so late?" demanded the little man.

"I didn't know I was."

"And look at the state of you! Filthy clothes, and in need of a shave. I will not have a vegetable cook working in my kitchen who's so lax in his personal appearance. I am the great Claude Dupier, gourmet chef, a genius of taste, and I expect only the very best from people fortunate enough to work in my kitchen."

"Work in your kitchen?"

"You are Monsieur John Vale? The vegetable cook sent down by the London agency?"

"No, I'm Harry Quemby the gardener," replied Ronald Perkins.

"What?" screamed the little chef furiously, waving his arms about wildly above his head. "You are a gardener with dirty hands. How dare you enter my kitchen in such a filthy state, with mud all over your boots and clothes. This is where food is prepared, not some garden shed. I shall report you to the head gardener. Now please leave my kitchen at once."

Ronald Perkins turned and walked slowly away, retracing

his steps towards the kitchen door. He could feel the angry little chef's eyes boring into his back. When he reached the kitchen door he paused, and glanced back over his shoulder. The little chef was no longer standing at the table with the sticks of rhubarb, but had moved on elsewhere in his busy kitchen. The serial killer turned and hurried back the way he had come through the kitchen and out through a swing door. He found himself in a long corridor with doors on either side. Following the corridor he came to a big domed hallway with a huge glass chandelier, and a wide red-carpeted staircase with marble banisters. Ronald Perkins wanted to find a bathroom where he could clean himself up and change his appearance. He would also need a change of clothes. He knew that no mud-covered gardener would be allowed into the house, and that it would be difficult if not impossible to explain his presence if confronted. He heard voices coming from the corridor behind him. Ronald Perkins pressed himself back against the wall. Two maids busily talking to each other came walking towards him. They were so wrapped up in their conversation that they did not see him.

The serial killer dashed up the stairway and onto the first landing and through the first door he came to. It was a large bedroom with a double bed. There was a pale blue-tiled bathroom suit attached, with toilet, shower and bath. In the bathroom cabinet he found a man's shaving gear, safety razor, shaving brush and soap. Locking the bathroom door, he stripped out of his filthy rambler's clothes and put them in a linen basket. He filled the bath with hot water, poured in some bubble bath and bath salts, and climbed in. After five minutes in the bath and washing himself all over, he stepped out, dried himself on a large white bath towel. Ronald Perkins used the small mirror on the bathroom cabinet to shave. When he had finished shaving he combed his hair.

"Now all I need is some clothes," he thought as he wrapped the towel around his waist. He went into to the bedroom and searched for items of clothing to wear. In a drawer he found underwear, a white shirt and black socks. And in the bedroom wardrobe a choice of eight expensive tailor-made suits, a dozen pairs of shoes, and an abundance of ties for all occasions. He chose a charcoal three-piece suit and matching tie. The man to whom the clothing belonged was shorter and thinner than the serial killer, but they did fit him well enough to pass muster at a glance. But a close inspection would reveal they had not been made for the person who was wearing them. Ronald Perkins studied himself in the full-length mirror on the bedroom wardrobe. He felt satisfied with what he saw. Opening the door he stepped briskly out onto the landing and proceeded at a leisurely pace up the stairway. He was the hunter looking for his prey.

President Robert R Rooker was in his bedroom with his wife, America's First Lady, Caroline Rooker. They were changing for dinner.

"He didn't try to sell you one of his paintings again, did he dear?" asked the President as he stood behind his wife doing up his black bow-tie. Caroline Rooker nodded and smiled. She was gazing at herself and her husband in the dressing table mirror. "Well, it's not going up on a White House wall. That's the third painting he's sold you, Caroline. Can't you just say no like I do?"

"Sir Antony is such a good persuader, Robert, exactly the same as you. He could charm the birds off the trees."

"Yeah, I guess so."

"They're not so bad really – I've seen worse but I can't remember where."

They both laughed.

"You know, Caroline, that every time Sir Antony comes on a visit to the White House those damn pictures will have to be hung on a prominent wall somewhere... until he goes that is."

"Never mind, Robert, that's not too much to pay for his friendship and support."

"I'm having that talk with Sir Antony after dinner, Caroline, the one about the island off the tip of Cuba. I'd really like to extend American's foothold in the world if I can before my term of office ends, even if only by one small island less than six miles long."

"I'm sure Sir Antony will understand, Robert, and help you if he can."

"Yeah, I like the guy – he's like me, a crafty sly old dog."

"What necklace shall I wear, Robert? Pearls or diamonds?"

"Diamonds, Caroline. Pearls make you look cheap."

"I think you're right. Diamonds are a girl's best friend."

The President went over to the bedroom wardrobe and opened the door. Inside stood a Secret Service agent, black suit and sunglasses. The President reached in and lifted out a dinner jacket on a coat hook.

"We've got the best damn security men in the world," he said proudly, and closed the door on the Secret Service agent.

The Prime Minister Sir Antony Dingle sat at his desk in his study. He had just finished draft number six of his speech for Tuesday in the House of Commons debate on taxes. He was smoking a fat Havana cigar and was holding a glass of whisky. A very tired Constance Goodbody was walking wearily towards the door carrying the corrected speech in a folder.

"How long for you to type up a new draft, Miss Goodbody?" called the Prime Minister, "I'd like to do some more work on my memoirs after I'd had my talk with President Rooker."

Miss Goodbody, who had spent most of the weekend typing for the Prime Minister, either correcting drafts for the speech, government letters or work on his memoirs, turned to face the great man. "Well, if I went without my dinner," she began, never thinking for a moment that he would accept her proposal, "and typed up your speech straight away, then I could work on the memoirs immediately afterwards, Prime Minister."

"That's splendid, Miss Goodbody, really splendid. It must be hard sometimes for you to keep up with such an old work-horse like me. I thrive on work as you and my voters well know. Hardly any time to relax and always with my shoulder to the wheel. But that's me, a man of destiny."

"Yes, Prime Minister," replied Miss Goodbody wearily, "very hard indeed." She knew that most of the Prime Minister's work was done by people such as herself, and that he always seemed to be relaxing or about to relax. And as for being a man of destiny, that seemed to be all in his own mind.

"Can you tell Jackson to run my bath, Miss Goodbody. I'll have a bath before dinner. It'll help to relax me after all this work I've been doing."

"It's nice to be able to relax, Prime Minister, when you get the chance."

"Yes, Miss Goodbody, and I deserve it don't you think?"

"Yes, Prime Minister, you certainly deserve something."

The IRA strike team trapped down in the coal cellar had waited impatiently for gardener Harry Quemby to return with a ladder. But when he failed to return after half an hour, they decided they must try to get out of the coal cellar by themselves. They knew it would not be long before some security check would be made of the coal cellar and the strike team discovered. It was decided, after some fierce debate, that one of them should stand on another man's shoulders and form a human ladder. Commander Sean O'Gully would be the man at the bottom because he had the sturdiest legs, and Patrick Dobbs would stand on his shoulders. Roy McCluster the youngest and most agile of the team, would then clamber up his two companions like a monkey up a tree and pull himself out at the top. Then he would pull up Patrick Dobbs, and together they would haul the commander out. It sounded a straight forward plan until they put it into practice. It took nine attempts to get Patrick Dobbs balanced on the commander's shoulders, and a further fifteen attempts before the agile Roy McCluster finally pulled himself clear of the coal cellar. It was not too difficult then to pull Patrick Dobbs up and out. But the commander proved a difficult problem. He could not reach up far enough to grab a helping hand, and they could not reach down far enough to offer a helping hand. Finally Patrick Dobbs and Roy McCluster removed their trousers, jackets, shirts, and belts, and made a rope of sorts by tying them together end to end. The commander was finally freed from the coal cellar. "Well, done, lads," said the commander, "I'm proud of you."

Patrick Dobbs and Roy McCluster untied the home-made rope and put their clothes on. "Are we going home now, Sean?" asked Patrick Dobbs hopefully.

"Home?" gasped the commander, shocked at hearing such a request.

"Don't you think we've done our best now, Sean?" asked Roy McCluster.

"Not until we're done the big one for Ireland," replied the

commander. "Then we can return home in triumph, feted by the boys as heroes."

"Oh dear God, no," muttered Roy McCluster under his breath. He had already decided that he would never again volunteer for another IRA mission to the mainland. He might well end up with Sean O'Gully being the commander again. All he wanted now was to go home to his girlfriend and to support his local football team from the terraces on a Saturday afternoon.

"What was that, Roy?" asked the commander.

"I said," replied Roy McCluster with a forced smile, "Ireland forever."

"Good man, Roy, that's what I like to hear, a patriotic Irishman."

"What are we going to do now?" asked Patrick Dobbs.

"Have you got the bomb, Pat?" asked the commander.

"I have, Sean."

"And all it needs is for the wires to be connected?"

"It does, Sean."

"Then we're in business, lads."

Jonathan Jackson, the personal valet of Sir Antony Dingle, had run the great man's bath. He poured in a bottle of foaming bubble bath and two jars of bath salts. There was a little yellow plastic duck floating in the bath. Jackson a bland grey-faced Scotsman, who had been the Prime Minister's personal valet for over thirty years, removed his jacket, rolled up his right shirt sleeve and tested the water temperature with his elbow. Sir Antony Dingle was very fussy about his bath time and everything had to be exactly as he wanted it. The water was just a little too hot. Jackson turned on the cold water tap for a few seconds, then retested the water with his elbow. Satisfied, he rolled down his sleeve and put on his jacket.

"The bath is ready, sir," he called.

Prime Minister Sir Antony Dingle, naked as the day he was born, came strutting into the bathroom. He was smoking an Havana cigar.

"Thank you, Jackson," he said as he stepped into the bath and sat down. "Can you put the decanter of whisky on the stool so I can help myself as needs be?"

"But of course, sir," replied the valet as he put a silver tray with a decanter three quarters full of whisky and an empty glass on the stool. There was no jug of water because Sir Antony liked to drink his whisky neat. "Will there be anything else?"

"Yes, Jackson, there's a fifteen minute talk by the Opposition Leader Clive Clanker on the Home Service directly after the concert. Can you bring a radio so I can hear what old blabbermouth has to say for himself? I'd like to know what the old devil has to say to the voters."

"Very good, sir." Jackson bowed his head then turned and left the bathroom. He returned moments later carrying a small white plastic radio, which he positioned on a shelf some two feet above the hot and cold taps of the Prime Minister's bath. There was a black power cable with a three pin plug. "Where shall I plug it in, sir?"

"Over by the bathroom cabinet, Jackson, where I plug in my electric razor."

Jackson plugged in the radio and tuned it to the Home Service. There was classical music being played. The concert had not yet finished. "Ah, sweet ecstasy to my ears," sighed the Prime Minister, closing his eyes in rapture.

"Shall I pour you a whisky, Sir?"

"What a great idea, Jackson. Make it a double."

Jackson poured a good measure of whisky from the decanter into the glass. "Is there anything else, Sir?"

"Come back in half an hour and switch off the radio."

"Yes, Sir."

"Thank you, Jackson."

Jackson quietly left the bathroom and closed the door behind him.

Meanwhile, down in the kitchen of Chequers, Claude Dupier, the little French gourmet chef, was rushing about excitedly urging on his team of cooks. Dupier was a chef of world renown and every single taste he created in his kitchen had to be perfection. Food to him was a work of art, and each meal had to be a masterpiece. The little chef hurried from cook to cook, to taste from pots and saucepans, to scold and encourage. "Good, good," he would cry, "But just a touch more seasoning," or "This is foul, throw it away and start again." The minutes were ticking away and this particular masterpiece had to be ready to be served to the Prime Minister and his dinner guests in less than an hour. Claude Dupier had worked extra hard creating a special new dish, roasted pheasant stuffed with eight different sorts of nuts, onions, berries and sultanas, for the American President. Which he had called 'Nuts To The President'. The little French chef was inspecting the roast beef by peering through the glass panel on the door of the cooker, when the IRA strike team, clothes caked in coal dust and faces and hands as black as night, came bursting into the kitchen. They held revolvers in their hands.

"Hands up," cried Roy McCluster nervously.

The kitchen staff, with the exception of the chef, raised their hands, and stood looking terrified facing the gunmen.

"What's the meaning of this?" demanded the little chef angrily, his eyes almost bulging from their sockets.

"We're the IRA," proclaimed Sean O'Gully, as he advanced towards the chef.

"I don't care if you are the RAC," stormed the chef. "This is my kitchen and nobody enters without my permission. I have a dinner to prepare."

Patrick Dobbs waved his gun. "This gives us permission," he said grimly.

The little French chef was unabashed. "I order you to leave my kitchen immediately."

"Be quiet, little man," said Sean O'Gully. "You're giving me a headache."

"We must be quick here, Sean," cried Roy McCluster, who was worried that the SAS or MI5 might suddenly come bursting through the door firing a hail of bullets. He knew the SAS were hard men who never took prisoners in a hostage situation.

"There's time enough, Roy," replied the commander. "Now gather up the prisoners and take them to the far end of the kitchen."

The cooks with their irate chef were gathered together at gunpoint at the far end of kitchen, and made to turn and face the wall.

"Have you made the bomb operational Pat?" asked the commander.

"I have, Sean."

"And is the timer set, Pat?"

"It is, Sean, set to explode in twenty minutes time exactly."

"Then hide it somewhere in the kitchen where it'll be difficult for any British search squad to find."

Patrick Dobbs nodded and walked slowly down the line of cookers looking for somewhere suitable to put the bomb. He was tempted to drop it into a large saucepan of tomato soup simmering on a cooker, but remembered just in time that liquid would ruin the electrical connections of the timer and detonator. He needed somewhere that was not too moist. Then he spotted a huge turkey, half-stuffed. Within seconds the bomb was inside the massive bird, and several handfuls of stuffing plugged in behind it. The IRA had planted its bomb and the British Prime Minister was going to get the bird.

Patrick Dobbs returned to Sean O'Gully and whispered in his ear, telling him where he had hidden the bomb. The commander chuckled and said, "What? Right under the Parson's nose."

"What about my beautiful dinner being ruined?" demanded the little French chef as he turned to confront Roy McCluster.

"That should be the least of your worries," replied the Irishman.

"But I spent hours preparing it," persisted the chef. "Could you not put your bomb somewhere else where it will not ruin my beautiful dinner?"

"Sorry," replied Roy McCluster. "But war's a terrible thing. It's better a dinner be lost than your life don't you think?"

The chef made no reply but meekly turned and faced the wall. Tears were trickling down his cheeks.

"Right, lads," called the commander, "It's time for us to go."

"What about us?" called a woman cook.

"Well, I'd leave as well if I were you," replied the commander, "Unless you want to be here when the bomb goes off."

"You mean we can go?"

"Yes, go. Hurry before it's too late."

The cooks in a wild desperate panic, followed by the little French chef whose legs were much shorter than theirs, raced from the kitchen as if their very lives depended upon it, which of course they did. The three Irishmen ran close behind them hoping in the melee outside in the courtyard to find an opportunity to escape.

Chapter Seventeen

Ronald Perkins was checking bedroom after bedroom seeking his quarry, Sir Antony Dingle. He knew it was only a matter of time before he tracked him down. Several times he encountered people when he knocked at a bedroom door. And, speaking with an American accent, he would tell them he was an American Secret Service agent looking for the Prime Minister with an urgent message from the President. But nobody seemed to know where the great man was. Ronald Perkins was on the second floor after covering all the rooms on the third and fourth floor, when he encountered Jonathan Jackson, the Prime Minister's Scottish valet coming out of a room.

"I say there," he called out brightly, "I'm looking for Sir Antony Dingle. Have you seen him?"

"Indeed, I have," replied Jackson. "And may I ask why you wish to see the Prime Minister?"

"President Rooker has sent me with an important message for him."

"May I pass the message on for you, sir?"

"Sorry, but it's top secret. I've been told to give the message directly to Sir Antony Dingle and nobody else. It's a verbal message and not written down. Orders of the President."

"And you are?"

"Secret Service Agent Eric Gatwood, Sir."

Jonathan Jackson should have asked to see some identification but the thought did not enter his mind. Chequers was so well protected with security forces, that the valet never thought for a moment that the man standing in front of him was anything else than what he claimed to be, an American Secret Service agent.

"You will find the Prime Minister in the bath in the bedroom behind me."

"Thank you, sir."

Jonathan Jackson stepped aside and opened the door for Ronald Perkins to enter.

"Try not to be too long, Agent Gatwood, the Prime Minister is trying to relax before dinner. He needs all the peace and quiet he can get."

"I won't disturb him more than I have to, you can rest assured on that. Once my business is accomplished with the Prime Minister then I'll be on my way as quickly as possible."

"Thank you, Agent Gatwood."

Smiling like a cat who had just got all the cream, Ronald Perkins entered the bedroom and Jackson quietly closed the door behind him. There was the sound of a radio coming from the bathroom. The serial killer moved silently towards the bathroom, heart pounding, his thoughts focused on his mission of death.

The cooks closely followed by little gourmet French chef Claude Dupier rushed through the kitchen door and out into the courtyard.

"There's a bomb," was the universal cry, as they milled about in utter confusion. The three Irishmen, covered in coal dust and looking like three black men, strode quickly around the house to the front lawn, and then away down the driveway towards the main gates. "What about my beautiful dinner?" sobbed the chef who was becoming more hysterical by the minute. "My lovely roast pheasant for the President of America?"

"What's this about a bomb?" asked an SAS man in army fatigues holding a sten gun, who had suddenly appeared from behind the dustbins.

"There's a bomb in the kitchen," cried a tall ashen-faced cook pointing with trembling hand at the kitchen door.

"Are you sure?" asked the SAS man.

The cook nodded. "They said they're IRA."

"Blimey," gasped the SAS man. "It's the real thing at last." He pulled a whistle from his pocket and blew on it three times.

Dozens of SAS and MI5 agents suddenly appeared in the courtyard milling about with the cooks and adding to the general confusion. The little French gourmet chef Claude Dupier had to be restrained by his staff when he tried to go back into the kitchen, shouting he was going to rescue his roast pheasant for the American President.

"Clear the area," ordered a senior SAS officer. And with whistles blowing security men ushered the crowd away down the back garden to safety.

Sir Antony Dingle heard the whistles but did not pay them much heed. If something was wrong then he would be notified. He settled back in his bath listening to the talk given by his arch rival Clive Clanker, Leader of the Opposition. In the talk he touched on all his usual points, blaming the Conservatives for all the bad things in British politics and his own Party for the good things. He promised, as he always did except when in government himself, to reduce taxes and put more money into the NHS and education. The Prime Minister took a puff on his Havana cigar. Jackson would be returning shortly to switch off the radio. He closed his eyes and sank back into the water, the little yellow plastic duck bobbing between his knees. Once he had got his big toe stuck up the spout of the cold tap and an emergency plumber, who had to sign the Official Secrets Act, had to come and cut him free with a hacksaw. It was then he heard a faint rustling sound coming from the other side of the pink bath curtain which was half drawn.

"Anybody there?" called the Prime Minister.

There was no reply.

The rustling sounded again.

"Jackson? Is that you?"

Ronald Perkins pulled aside the bath curtain and looked down at Sir Antony Dingle. "Good evening, Prime Minister."

Sir Antony Dingle took a puff of his cigar. "Where's Jackson?"

"He's had some bad news I'm afraid, Prime Minister. And I've been asked to look after you in his place."

"Not serious I hope?"

"What, Prime Minister?"

"Jackson's bad news."

"I wasn't told, Prime Minister. But I believe it's to do with a sick old auntie in Watford."

"I didn't know Jackson had an aunt in Watford and I've known him over thirty years."

"That's a long time, Prime Minister."

"There's something about your face," said the Prime Minister thoughtfully as he stared closely up at Ronald Perkins's face. "I know I've seen it before but I can't place where or when. We have met before haven't we? I never forget a face."

"Yes, Prime Minister, we have met before."

"There, I knew I was right. When was it?"

"This afternoon, Prime Minister, out in the back garden while you were painting. Don't you remember we discussed rhubarb?"

"Rhubarb?"

"For your rhubarb crumble, Prime Minister."

"Good God, you're Harry the gardener."

"Correct, sir."

"Didn't I say I had a memory for faces?"

"You most certainly did, Prime Minister. Now any last words?"

"Last words?"

"Your last words spoken before departing this vale of tears."

Sir Antony Dingle sat bolt upright in the bath, a frightened look on his face. "What are you talking about?" he gasped. "Is this a sick joke?"

"I'm afraid not, Prime Minister. I'm deadly serious. Have you some last words? Something you want people to remember after you've gone."

"Help," screamed the Prime Minister.

Ronald Perkins reached over and knocked the radio from off the shelf above the taps into the bath. "Oops," he said. "Butterfingers!"

The electrocution of Sir Antony Dingle was over very quickly. The water bubbled for a few moments after the radio entered the bath. The Prime Minister, still smoking his cigar, went into convulsions. He was dead in under thirty seconds. Ronald Perkins timed it with his wristwatch. This was a perfect murder. It would be thought that the Prime Minister had himself been the cause of his own demise. Foolishly listening to a radio while sitting in the bath, he had accidentally knocked the radio into the water and had passed 250,000 volts through his body.

"Well," thought Ronald Perkins as he looked down at the body of the late Sir Antony Dingle, "at least you were a bright spark at the end." The serial killer was well satisfied. But he still had a huge problem. How to escape from Chequers. He went into the bedroom and took a cigar from a box on the bedside table, sat on the bed and took a few puffs. Suddenly there was an almighty explosion which rocked the house. Ronald Perkins hurriedly stubbed out the cigar and left it in an ashtray on the bedside table. He ran out onto the landing and down the stairway. People in great distress and confusion, were running about shouting and screaming. Smoke was billowing up the hallway from the direction of the kitchen. The serial killer joined a throng of people, household staff and guests, all struggling to get out of the front door of Chequers and onto the lawn. "Don't panic," shouted a police officer who was brushed aside in the stampede to get out of the house.

Ronald Perkins hurried round to the back of the house and was confronted with the kitchen which was ablaze and black smoke billowing out of shattered windows. There was a small crowd of onlookers, mostly the cooks, who stood looking forlornly at the fire. One little man in a chef's hat was sobbing uncontrollably and exclaiming in a French accent

"Oh, my beautiful dinner. Why could they not have waited until after it had been eaten by the Prime Minister and his guests? Such a terrible waste of my cooking genius."

The Irishmen from the IRA strike team, covered with coal dust, hands and faces black as a raven's wing, had got less than a hundred yards from the house when the bomb exploded. They threw themselves flat on their stomachs on the gravel driveway. Armed police at the main gates run up the driveway towards the house. The first policeman to reach the Irishmen knelt beside Patrick Dobbs, who had the good sense to close his eyes and keep perfectly still, and felt for a pulse on the Irishman's neck. The policeman thought Patrick Dobbs was a black man because of the coal dust, thinking there were no black men serving with the IRA, and so the three black men lying on the driveway must be from the Prime Minister's household staff. The officer checked the pulses of Sean O'Gully and Roy McCluster.

"They're alive, thank God," he called out, "Quick, get an ambulance."

Inspector Lionel Harper of Special Branch packed in a police car with Chief Inspector Edgar Briggs, Sergeant Jenny Hopper, super-sleuth Allan Hawes and his trusted companion Doctor Windrush was less than half-a-mile from Chequers when the bomb went off. They heard a dull explosion in the distance coming from the direction of Chequers.

"My God," gasped Allan Hawes, "we're too late."

Inspector Lionel Harper leant forward to speak to the driver. "Put your foot down, this is an emergency."

Ronald Perkins stood with the cooks watching the burning kitchen. An ambulance drew up and two ambulance men leapt out. They seemed confused and not sure what to do. "Anyone hurt here?" asked a fat ambulance man with glasses.

Ronald Perkins stepped forward. "I'm a Doctor," he said.

"Anyone injured here, Doctor?" asked the fat ambulance man.

Ronald Perkins pointed at the little French chef who was still sobbing uncontrollably. The chef was on his knees wringing his hands in anguish facing the burning kitchen, calling out desperately, "Oh, my beautiful dinner, my beautiful dinner."

"What's wrong with him, Doctor?"

"Badly shocked. He's needs urgent hospital treatment."

The fat ambulance man turned to his colleague a tall bland faced man. "Doctor says this bloke needs urgent hospital treatment, Ernie."

"Well, he's the only one in need of treatment here, Bert, so let's bundle him in the back and get him off to hospital pronto."

The two ambulance men gently helped the sobbing little French chef to his feet and guided him into the back of the ambulance. Ronald Perkins followed.

"I'd better come with you," he said, "in case there are any complications on the way."

"That's very good of you, Doctor," said the fat ambulance man who was somewhat relieved because he was not experienced in dealing with severe shock cases. Indeed, the worst shock case he had ever encountered was the man who answered a knock on his front door one morning, to find his mother-in-law with her suitcases saying she had come for an indefinite stay.

"Put the siren on," ordered Ronald Perkins. He was hoping that an ambulance leaving with siren going full blast from Chequers might not be stopped at the check point at the main gates, but waved on through as an emergency by the armed police. "I'm worried about the man's condition. He seems to be getting worse."

The ambulance sped off down the gravel driveway towards the main gates and Ronald Perkins could hardly believe his luck. Freedom was so close. Then the ambulance stopped with a squeal of tyres. A police officer had waved it down. He walked to the back of the ambulance and knocked on the rear door. The fat ambulance man opened the door. The young policeman, holding a sten gun, stared up at the faces of the fat ambulance man and Ronald Perkins, and then at the little French chef who lay on the trolley still sobbing for his ruined dinner.

"Got room for three more?" he asked. "They're household staff who got knocked over in the blast."

"We'll squeeze them in, won't we, Doctor?" cried the fat ambulance man.

"But of course," replied Ronald Perkins who was desperate to be on his way. "Get them on board, officer."

The policeman stepped aside, and the three Irishmen from the IRA strike team, Commander Sean O'Gully, Patrick Dobbs and Roy McCluster, climbed up into the ambulance. Black faces and coal dust covered clothes, they sat silently on a trolley opposite to the little French chef. "God speed," called the policeman as he closed the ambulance door, "and a fast safe journey."

The ambulance sped away down the driveway with siren at full blast. There was a police car coming through the main gates, and the ambulance driver had to stop to allow it to pass. Sitting in the car was Inspector Lionel Harper of Special Branch, Chief

Inspector Edgar Briggs, Sergeant Jenny Hopper, Allan Hawes and his trusted colleague Doctor Windrush. An armed woman police officer hurriedly waved the ambulance through the gates and it drove away down the road at top speed.

When the ambulance arrived at the hospital Casualty Department, the two ambulance men quickly wheeled the little French chef away on a trolley as the priority emergency, saying they would return for the three black men. The 'doctor' volunteered to wait with the black men. When the ambulance men returned a few minutes later they found the back of the ambulance empty. The three black men and the Doctor had disappeared.